The Tribe of Iodine Wine

The Tribe of Iodine Wine

A NOVEL

• • •

Decades, Book One

Brian Pacini

ISBN-13: **9780692865828**
ISBN-10: **0692865829**
Library of Congress Control Number: **2017905011**
HuffPuffPress, Denver, CO

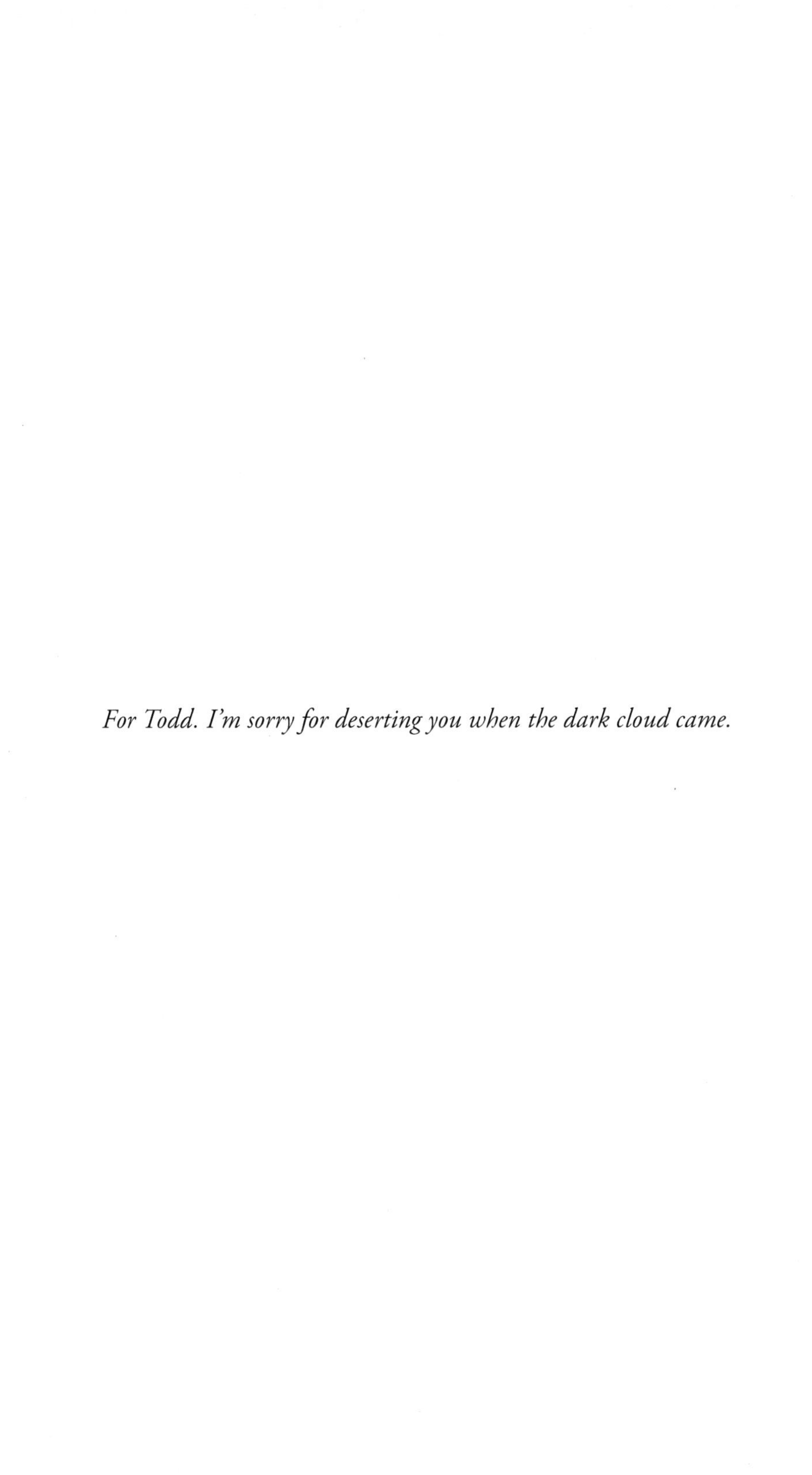

For Todd. I'm sorry for deserting you when the dark cloud came.

Let this grisly beginning be none other to you than is to wayfarers a rugged and steep mountain.

—Boccaccio, *Decameron*

First Story: Counting Coup

CHAPTER 1

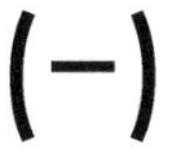

● ● ●

"How much are Bad Boys worth?" Jaden asked as he rambled the old baby-blue Monte Carlo down Colorado Boulevard. We headed onto the I-25 entrance and veered southeast, away from the mountains and into the southern suburbs of Denver.

From my view in the back seat, Jaden's smallish frame and tall, Afro high-top hair looked funny in such a big car. Michael sat next to him, no seat belt on, leaning against the car door so he could look at Jaden in the front and Kevin and me in the back.

The beaten and battered car merged into the late-night highway traffic. Jaden had picked up the car online, with money we all pooled together. The old car was an ironic purchase, an imitation of wannabe gangsters imitating gangsters.

An empty slot gaped in the dash where the car radio had departed with the help of the local neighborhood thieves. The old vinyl seats were breaking apart in thin, hard shards. Strips of duct tape tried to patch the seats together, but months of sunlight and use had turned the tape sticky and abrasive. If I wore shorts, I typically had to put a towel or jacket between my legs and the bench seat to keep from scratching the underside of my legs. But on that night, we wore dark jeans and dark hoodies.

A replacement for the missing radio, Kevin's portable speaker box sat on the shelf near the back window. The postpunk or post-postpunk music Kevin favored drummed through the car with its deep bass lines and depressing industrial lyrics.

"Say again, Jaden?" I asked, unsure if I had heard right over the droning music. Jaden didn't hear me.

"Hey, Kevin, turn it down, man," I said.

Kevin was staring out the window, daydreaming as usual. He turned to me. "What's that, Pax?"

"Can you turn it down?"

He played with his phone and lowered the volume on the speaker box.

"Jaden, what did you ask?" I repeated.

"How much are Bad Boys worth again? Sports stickers are worth one, right? Republicans are two, but these Bad Boy bumper stickers, they're five?" Jaden asked.

"No, man, Bad Boys are ten; No Fear is five," Kevin corrected in his lethargic but lethal voice.

"Ten points," Michael repeated. He kept bobbing his head with the heavy bass line as he widened his ever-present smile. The mix of his mischievous smile and the dark music seemed jokerish, surreal. A nicked-up wooden baseball bat balanced on his right thigh, with the barrel on the floor mat. He turned the knob and spun the bat. Michael didn't play baseball; he got the bat to go with a Halloween costume, some character from an old gang movie that he and Kevin watched obsessively. On Halloween, Michael wore pinstripes and a painted mime face and went around scaring people with his large body and the menacing bat hanging over his shoulder.

I felt alive but out of place. Michael was intimidating as hell. He was a big, crazy-smart kid who scared the shit out of the white kids, and not even the big black football players at East High would mess with him or tease him like they did the other biracial kids—like they did Jaden.

Kevin was smaller and reserved, and he usually stared off into the distance through the dark-circled eyes set on his pale face. But he was even more dangerous than Michael. His mind just worked in different ways. He seemed soft and sensitive but was just a natural-born destroyer. His mom had died a few years earlier, and he had spun out of control shortly after, jumping from oxycodone to heroin to a suicide path. His dad, an avid adventurer, got him into an outdoor expedition for grieving teens. This and bikepacking the Colorado Trail with his dad last summer got him completely off drugs. The outdoors cleaned him up and saved him, but he'd found his true purpose through juvenile delinquency—not ideal, but hey, it was still a purpose.

The baseball-bat game was his idea—earn points for smashing side-view mirrors on vehicles with the offending bumper stickers. The point system was his idea too—a way to give structure to the chaos of life, as Kevin liked to put it.

I went along with the game because it seemed cool, almost a connection to the past, to the stories of rebellion my once-punk dad and once-hippie grandpa would tell about causing trouble in their youths.

And Kevin was right. "Kids are too obedient now." With their gadgets and their feelings and their fear of being labeled as a terrorist or school shooter or whatever, they were not disrupting the system.

Jaden went along because it was a chance to wreak havoc on rich punks from the suburbs. But in truth, I think we all just went along with Kevin's mayhem because it made us feel alive in a desensitized world.

The old Monte Carlo slid down the suburban street in a crawl, looking for offending bumper stickers. The car's big engine purred loudly even at an idle. Michael moved both feet to the floorboards and perched forward, the handle of the bat gripped between both hands like some kind of prayer.

"You know, this would be easier in Denver," Michael said. "There are way more cars parked on the street."

Jaden corrected him. "Yeah, but so many more Republicans in the suburbs.".

"Oh, that reminds me," I said. "Did I ever thank you and your brethren for scaring all the small-minded Republicans out of the city?"

"Don't mention it," Michael replied flatly.

"True. And hey, winner, winner, chicken dinner," Jaden said. He pointed to a minivan parked on the street with a faded bumper sticker. Jaden directed the Monte Carlo toward it, a deadly blue shark gliding toward its kill. Michael leaned his big body out of the car window, the baseball bat perched on his shoulder. The Monte Carlo came up to the minivan, and Michael swung, a hard axman swing that sent the minivan's side mirror bouncing down the street.

"So strong—he's so strong," Jaden said in a goofy, fake-scared voice.

"Whoo! Two points!" Michael yelled, too loud for the quiet neighborhood. He slid back into the car. Jaden floored the Monte Carlo. I looked out the window to see the mirror tumble and come to a stop on the street.

"Your turn, Pax," Michael said. He turned around, flashed his best devilish smile, and slowly slid the bat, handle first, to me. I gripped it hard. Michael gripped the other side and then launched his big body into the back seat. I squeezed against the wall of the car as Michael landed between Kevin and me after somehow turning in midair.

Although a big brute of a car, the Monte Carlo only had two long doors. To switch seats or even get out from the back, we became skilled at jumping and sliding over the front bench seat instead of pushing it forward.

I was tall like Michael, but I wasn't nearly as ripped. I dove into the front seat as gracefully as I could without kicking anyone in the face, but I ended up with my hands on the floorboards and my ass in the air. I quickly sat up, swept my crazy Jewfro hair out of my eyes, and brought the bat to my chest.

Jaden took a fast route out of the neighborhood and into the next—an even fancier one adorned with three-car garages and their huge attached houses. "Big three-car garages hold their cars safe from the street," I thought and started to feel good about the lack of visible cars. The idea of bashing a side-view mirror seemed scarier than I had initially imagined. I could miss. I could fall out of the car. I could swing as a middle-aged man with a revolver sat in the front seat wondering if he should just end it all.

We kept cruising. Jaden picked up speed to cover more ground.

"Stop the car," Kevin said. He didn't talk much, but when he did, he commanded attention. The car came to a halt.

"Look." He pointed to a large corner house on a hill with a long, wrapping driveway. At the top of the driveway stood a huge black pickup truck. The truck had two exhaust stacks sticking up behind the cab. It looked like the kind of truck seen on YouTube videos pulling up next to cyclists or pedestrians to purposely "roll coal" and kick out a cloud of black diesel smoke in their faces.

"That's not on the street," I said, turning around to look at Michael and Kevin. "How am I supposed to get the mirror?"

Kevin gave me a soft, sad look. He held my gaze for a second and then smiled. He leaned forward and grabbed the bat from my hands. He glided it into the back seat across the seat back. He sneaked his other hand up the side of the car and pulled on the door handle; then he slid his lean body out of the car from the back seat without having to move Jaden forward. We all turned to watch Kevin run past the back window and across the lawn up toward the truck. The music stopped playing when Kevin ran his phone's Bluetooth transmission out of range. We all jumped as the silence rang out.

"Shit. This is whacked," Jaden said. I nodded as we watched Kevin climb into the bed of the truck. Kevin walked up to one of the smokestacks. He took a couple of practice swings like a batter on deck. Michael chuckled as Kevin stepped his front foot forward and swung hard at the stack. The sound of the hard ash wood on metal rang out over the neighborhood like an old church bell. The stack leaned to the left but stayed attached. Kevin swung again and again—fast, rapid church-bell clangs forewarning some kind of imminent danger. Finally, the stack broke apart from the truck and hit the ground with dancing dings before it started to roll down the driveway toward us.

Kevin moved on to the other smokestack.

"What the hell is he doing?" Jaden yelled. Lights started to turn on in the neighborhood. Michael and I watched in fascination. "Should I go? Should I go?" Jaden asked as more church-bell clangs rang out from the other smokestack.

"No," Michael said.

"Todd's listening to the police scanner from home and tracking our movement via my phone. If he hears anything, he'll buzz us," I said.

Jaden shot me a fierce look. "That shit won't work!"

Just then, the door of the big house opened, and a short, stocky teenage kid in his underwear came out. We watched him, stunned.

"What the fuck?" he mouthed over the loud clangs.

Kevin stopped banging on the remaining smokestack and looked at the teenager. They didn't move for a second. The kid started to take a step forward but then stopped as Kevin lunged and took one last swing at the standing smokestack. It flew off the truck toward the kid.

"Dad!" he yelled as loud as he could.

"I'm going to go. This is crazy," Jaden said.

Michael pushed my half of the seat back forward, smashing me against the dashboard. He opened the door and jumped out of the car. I watched him jog toward Kevin.

"Don't leave, Jaden," I said. I pulled a few strips of old duct tape off the front seat and followed Michael's exit from the Monte Carlo. Somehow, despite my earlier fear and the nerve-racking clangs of the bat, I felt calm. I ran around to the back of the car with the strips of duct tape trailing from my fingers.

"Hey!" Michael yelled in his booming voice. "Let's go now!"

Kevin turned back toward us, an odd smile on his face.

On the other side of the truck, a large, potbellied man came running out, wearing only tighty-whities. He too was carrying a bat, a shiny aluminum one, and he was running straight at Kevin.

"Look out!" I yelled. Kevin turned around. The beer-gut man swung at Kevin, who jumped back out of range and then gracefully jumped off the other side of the truck just as Michael reached him. The dad ran around the truck toward them. Kevin tossed the baseball bat to Michael. He caught it midair and turned toward the charging dad. The dad stopped, taking in Michael, now armed. He tried to circle him, but Michael just moved to face him. Kevin took off around the dad and down the driveway but not toward our car. The dad seemed to try to cut Michael off from our car but didn't move forward to attack.

"Dillon, go get my gun from the basement!" the dad yelled.

The son hesitated and then ran into the house.

I put the strips of duct tape over the license plate, covering the numbers and letters. I watched Kevin jog down the driveway.

"Where are you going?" I yelled. He ignored me as he reached the bottom of the driveway. He picked up the smokestack and headed back toward Michael and the dad, still circling each other in some weird dance.

As Kevin sauntered up the driveway, he let the broken end of the metal smokestack drag on the cement. The smokestack on concrete made an eerie scratching sound.

The dad glanced back slowly, watching Michael while trying to see what brought the approaching noise. He saw Kevin out of the corner of his eye just as Michael took a dab step forward. He stepped back and then scooted toward the house, giving Michael an open route to the car. The dad looked frightened.

"Someone call the cops!" he yelled to the neighborhood. His voice trembled and cracked.

"Let's go!" I yelled out. My voice sounded different, adultlike.

Michael looked down toward me and smiled his crooked smile. He started off in a jog to the car.

But Kevin kept walking toward the dad with the smokestack dragging.

"Now!" I yelled.

Kevin stopped. Even from behind, I could sense Kevin staring the dad down. His head moved to glance at the numbered address above the garage door and then back at the dad. The dad's face turned even paler. He swallowed.

Kevin turned around and walked back toward the car without looking back toward the dad, still standing shivering in his underwear by the stackless truck.

I got back in the car about the same time as Michael. I followed him into the back seat.

As Kevin approached, the music started playing, causing us to all jump with fright again. I usually ignored Kevin's music, but I distinctly remember the lyrics, firing over and over. "Dance! Dance! Dance!" a desperate voice called out.

Kevin calmly reached the car. He slid into the front seat with the smokestack cradled in his arms.

No one said anything as Jaden sped the car down the street and into the darkness.

CHAPTER 1

(+)

• • •

KEVIN ISN'T AT SCHOOL WHEN the Transmission comes. A weird alarm simultaneously rings out on everyone's cell phone like an Amber Alert. The whole class jumps collectively. Many of the kids in the class are sneaking views of a video on their cell phones when the alarm goes off. They are all watching the same video, a video I don't want to see again, especially in public. They instinctively move their thumbs to get rid of the interrupting message, but they stop when they read it and almost all gasp in unison.

I slide my phone out of my back pocket.

"Possible nuclear event. Seek shelter immediately!" it says.

Those who were not watching the video are now looking at their phones too. We are just staring, each thinking, somehow, that this is a message sent only to us.

"Hey, hey," I say to the kid to my left. "What does your phone say?"

He looks at me with a blank stare and shows me the phone. It says the same thing. Other kids start showing their phones to each other now.

"Is this some kind of joke?" someone asks. "Maybe somebody hacked the cell towers?"

"The towers of all providers, at the same time?"

"Yeah, it could happen," another kid says. His voice sounds nervous. But then again no one is brave enough to look out the window either. We still stare helplessly at our phones.

"Do you think the cops just want to put schools on lockdown—you know, because of what happened last weekend?" someone says.

A loud siren blasts across the school. We all jump. It sounds far away, like on the roof of the school, but it is very loud. A couple of whimpers respond to the siren. We all know this isn't a joke.

Everyone looks deathly scared, even our teacher. Collectively, we all turn to look out the window. Our timid gaze is ready to draw back into hiding like a scared kid watching a horror movie. I hear a sigh of relief come over the class as the window shows no mushroom cloud, no darkness overcoming the light sky.

Most of us look back to the teacher for guidance on what to do next, but her lips are trembling. She glances back to her phone and presses it. She lifts the phone to her ear. "John, where are the kids? Are you with the kids right now? John, John, are you there?" She looks at her phone with a panic-stricken face.

We feel alone. Our teacher's concerns are somewhere else. Some kids start to cry. I feel a strong need to help, to take the lead. I remember my dad telling me about the drills he had to do during the Cold War while he was in school. I want to tell the other students to hide under their desks, but this seems too ridiculous.

Just then, the principal's voice comes over the intercom. "All students and faculty, go to the main gym immediately," he orders and repeats.

This snaps the teacher out of her stupor, and she looks up. I can see tears streaking down her face. She takes a deep breath and says, "OK, kids, you heard him; let's head to the gym."

Out in the hallway, lines of shell-shocked kids are walking toward the gym. It looks like a scene from a movie with robotic soldiers. All the kids are walking in line, doing what they're told.

I am looking for our squad—Michael, Jaden, Todd, Charlotte, and Lupina, especially Lupina—but I do not see her or anyone else.

I am also hoping to see Kevin in the crowd but know I won't. This is disheartening. Kevin would know what to do—whether we should walk in line or ditch the school and go outside.

I feel a strong hand on my shoulder and turn around to see Michael. For once, he isn't smiling, but he doesn't look shell shocked either. I am relieved to see him.

"What should we do?" I ask.

"I don't know, man. I wish Kevin was here," he says.

"Me too." I scan the halls as Jaden runs up to us. He looks scared.

"Should we ditch this place?" he asks nervously.

Just then, we see the principal marching down the hall, herding kids to the gym. He sees us just standing there and comes running up to us. He has short crew-cut hair and a military presence.

"What are you doing?" he barks. "Get to the gym!"

We stand there with blank looks on our faces.

He walks up to Michael and gets in his face. They are of equal height and size, but Michael looks like he is starting to crack at the face-off. Michael's gaze goes down. He is staring at the principal's waist. I follow his stare.

On the principal's hip is a pistol.

"Now!" he says. He grabs Michael's shoulders and turns him around. We start walking toward the gym.

We crowd into the gymnasium. The principal marches past us and toward the front of the gym underneath a basketball hoop. There are kids on the bleachers and on the floor. Many of them are holding and hugging each other.

I spot Lupina and Charlotte on the other side of the gym. I want to walk over to them, but I would have to cross in front of the open space between the principal and the crowd.

Michael nudges us. "Let's stay toward the back, near a door."

I agree. I figure I could go outside and around the back of the gym to reach Lupina if needed. Jaden, Michael, and I let all the other kids come in. We wait by the door.

The principal is handed a bullhorn. "All," he starts. His voice on the bullhorn is even sharper and more abrasive. "I am going to be blunt, because we don't have much time," he says.

"When is he not blunt?" Jaden mutters under his breath.

"Some kind of massive bomb went off in Wyoming."

"Wyoming? Who bombs Wyoming?" Michael says. "It's the least-populated state."

"The bomb may have been nuclear in nature and was…" The principal takes a breath. "And was used to trigger the supervolcano in Yellowstone National Park. A huge eruption has occurred. Within several hours, much of the western United States will be covered in ash, possibly radioactive ash."

Whimpers and cries cascade across the gym. Even the principal seems moved. He looks down and rubs his fingers across his forehead. He looks back up to the students with resolve.

"An order for evacuation has been issued for the state. The government has decided those between fourteen and eighteen years of age will be part of the first evacuation. There are buses out front to take everyone to the airport. We only have a few hours before the ash reaches Denver, so there will be no delay. You will not have time to go home; you will not have time to say good-bye to your parents, but trust me on this…" The principal's voice starts to crack. I remember that he has three kids of his own. "They will—they will all want you to be safe."

* * *

After the doomsday speech from the principal, I give Lupina a signal to exit out her nearest door. Jaden, Michael, and I take off outside and come around the other side of the building.

Outside, cops are waiting for us. They see kids running and stop them from running away. This seems odd, but we just stick near the wall and circumvent the building to where Lupina and Charlotte are waiting on the other side.

We don't say anything to each other—just share a firm hug to get rid of the fear and tension. Our embrace breaks when the cops herd us onto buses. I hold Lupina's hand and right my backpack. Our only possessions are what we were carrying to class. Luckily, I carry my backpack to class to avoid going to my locker, but an inventory in my mind produces nothing useful: books, some snacks, a hoodie, a water bottle. I wish again that Kevin were here.

I look around for him hopelessly while we start to load the buses. I look for my sister, Vivi, too, but she is at the elementary school near our home. Sadness starts to overcome me. I hate not knowing if she will make the cut. I miss Vivi. I miss my parents. I don't want to get on the bus, but now there are too many cops around. They have cordoned off the school. I see other parents trying to get in. I see some kids trying to get out, but the police hold them back.

I reach the bus. I feel that I am at a crux in my life. I can try to make a run for it. If I succeed, I may not survive. I wonder about wanting to survive if my sister can't. I also don't want to leave Lupina and my friends. I pause on the steps of the bus. I feel Michael's big hand on my shoulder.

"Let's go, Pax," he says. "We'll take care of each other."

I look back. He has one arm over Jaden's shoulder, and he is patting my pack with his other hand. A warm smile adorns his face. I step up into the bus and grab a window seat near the front. Lupina sits next to me. Jaden and Charlotte are in front of us, and Michael goes one row behind us.

The buses finally start to move. There are more police here now. Adults are lining the exit out of the school. They look panicked and griefstricken. A few kids on my bus lower their windows and yell out to their parents, a sad exchange of words and cries. I check my phone. There is still no service. I know my parents work too far away to make it to the school. Instead of looking for them, I shut my eyes tight. I don't want to think of my sister either, but I can't help it. I want to grab control of the bus and take it to her school, but I know this is futile. Maybe they will make a second pass at evacuation. Maybe cars will get out in time.

On the way to the airport, no one is talking. Our bus joins a caravan of buses heading to I-70. When we get close to the highway, I see a traffic jam clogging the eastbound side. "Crap," I think, "not only was I just split off from seeing my family, but now I am going to die in traffic."

The line of buses crosses the road and heads onto the westbound entrance ramp.

"This can't be right," I tell Lupina. "We are going the wrong way."

Panic again starts to spread across the bus. I watch the buses pull up the entrance ramp and slow down. Instead of heading west toward the mountains, they turn east toward the plains, going the wrong way to the airport—eastbound in the westbound lane. Well-armed cops and flares mark the way down the opposite side of the highway.

We turn onto Peña Boulevard and join the long line of buses heading to the airport. Most of the cars are still stuck in traffic on the other side of the highway, trying to head due east.

We reach the airport to meet more police who rush off the buses. I look down the departure line of buses, and I recognize that the kids getting off the near buses are from East High School. In the long line of buses, there is a short bus, with a handicap access lift. The short bus looks out of place in the endless line of long buses. I watch the kids get off the short bus. I look for my friend Todd, but there are no kids in wheelchairs. They herd us toward the airport door with abrupt yells and commands. Our buses take off behind us. I look back to the short bus. I don't see Todd or any kids from special ed get off the bus or any of the buses, and this puts a strange, heavy lump in my stomach.

CHAPTER 2

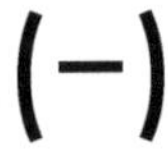

● ● ●

Jaden played the fool. He even started styling his high-top hair to look like a jester hat. Lupina and Charlotte ran the costume team and were sizing Jaden's outfit and trying to tame his clown hair so he could actually wear a real jester hat. I was watching from backstage while getting out the cordless drill from the stagecraft toolbox. I grabbed the battery and jammed it into the drill like an action hero shoving a magazine into a gun.

We were putting on *King Lear*. Lupina and Charlotte were most excited about making Jaden's costume. There were many old Shakespearean costumes around the theater department to choose from, even some fool costumes, but Lupina and Charlotte were creating all their own new costumes. The advent of the nerd culture and Comic-Con was turning out a whole generation of creative kids who could sew and make crazy costumes from scratch.

Charlotte, the main costume designer, was working long nights on Jaden's costume—a mix of Shakespeare, the Joker, and Harley Quinn. Jaden reveled in the attention. In many ways, the fool was stealing the show.

"Here, you hold down his hair while I put the hat on," Charlotte suggested to Lupina.

Jaden bounced back and forth as if he were dancing in some hip-hop video.

"Hold still," she said. Charlotte was always serious. She carried a natural beauty that was hidden behind glasses, nerd quotes, and an F-the-world disposition. Her penetrating eyes glared through her rectangle glasses framed by bangs and a short square hairstyle.

"No, wait, wait." Jaden jump-stepped back. "How about I don't wear a hat and keep growing my hair out? We can dye it red and blue and even put some bells in it."

"I spent ten hours hand sewing this damn hat!" Charlotte exclaimed. Her tough exterior made her seem frustrated, but a crack of a smile escaped.

Lupina turned to me and said, "Pax, can you come hold him down?"

Like Charlotte, Lupina was sleeper beautiful. Tall and long legged, she could easily have become a model if she had cared about such things. Her long dark hair and thick eyelashes contrasted with the most amazing green eyes.

I felt myself blushing as I jumped down off the scaffolding with the drill in hand. I grabbed a two-by-four and said, "Here, let's pin him down." I punctuated my words with two quick zaps from the drill.

Jaden took another jump back. A big, foolish smile was on his face.

"I got it—no, listen. Listen! How 'bout at some point in the play, I give a bow, take off the hat, and then stand up with my hair still looking like a jester hat?"

"That's actually a pretty good idea," Lupina said to Charlotte.

"If we let you do that, can you hold still so we can put on this hat?" Charlotte said.

"Sure." Jaden gracefully crossed his legs and lowered himself to the ground in a seated position. He held perfectly still with eyes closed, looking like a meditating Buddha—forearms resting on his knees, fingers pinched together, contemplating qi.

The girls stepped forward and fastened the hat to Jaden's head.

"So…no two-by-four or drill needed?" I asked jokingly, holding them up like a kid wanting to play catch.

"Why don't you go screw something in the back, Pax?" Jaden said while maintaining his perfect meditative posture and closed eyes.

I was trying to think of a good reply when Lupina turned to me and gave me a wink, and that pretty much stopped my brain from working.

"Ah, dude, dude, she totally winked at me when you said I should screw something," I told Jaden as we walked—hell, more like skipped—toward the cafeteria. He still had the jester hat. The bells bounced with our fast and jumpy cadence.

"Right on, Pax. You have been in love with her since, like, forever."

"What, no, what?"

Jaden gave me a stern sideways glance that was hard to take seriously with a jester bell dangling in his face.

"You should ask her to prom," he added.

"You should ask Charlotte," I countered, but it was true; I had been thinking about asking Lupina for weeks—well, years, actually.

Charlotte was totally not Jaden's type, but he just smiled and nodded. "All right, all right." Then he stopped in his tracks. "Come with me." He turned around and headed back toward the theater department.

"Wait, wait! What are you doing? We aren't going to ask them now, are we?" I asked. I wanted this more than anything, but we were moving too fast. I was the type who needed to plan things out and then worry about them.

"Relax, Pax. I am not going to ask your crush to prom for you," Jaden said. "I'm just going to give you an in."

I wanted to protest, but then I realized I couldn't think of an in; that was more Jaden's thing.

He opened the door to the theater department and barged back in. Lupina and Charlotte were back by the sewing machines, making adjustments to the costumes.

"Hey, ladies," Jaden announced.

"Oh great, the clown is back." Charlotte smirked.

Unfazed, Jaden said, "You two going to Maker tonight?"

"Of course. We need to work on Comic-Con costumes—you know, shit that really matters," Charlotte said.

"OK, we'll buy you some smoothies and help with the costumes."

"Ah, OK," Charlotte responded.

I could feel myself blush as Lupina smiled.

"It's a date then. Meet you at Maker," Jaden said.

"Meet you at Maker," they replied in unison.

We walked back out of the theater department. I had to concentrate really hard to keep myself from bouncing up and down.

We reached the cafeteria, feeling like conquering knights.

Michael, Todd, and Kevin sat at our regular table. Todd was at the end in his big electric wheelchair. As usual, Kevin was feeding Todd in between his own bites.

We plopped down on our seats and took out our lunches. Everyone looked at Jaden's hat but didn't say anything. It fit his personality that well.

Todd looked like a king at the end of the table with his wheelchair a throne. His right hand rested on his wheelchair's joystick, and his left hand lay across his lap. As always, his left hand held his rosary beads. He habitually ran the beads through his thumb and forefingers. His hands still worked pretty well; he used the rosary beads as a form of physical and spiritual therapy.

A big smile adorned his face. It was Thursday, and we had promised him we had to wait a few days before we told him the details of the "Tale of the Smokestack Escapade."

We had been scared all weekend and most of the week, especially Jaden, expecting the cops to show up with a description of his unique car, a warrant for his arrest, and some questions about his friends. We didn't want Todd to be called as some kind of witness.

Kevin said tighty-whitey dad would never call the cops. And they never showed up, never questioned us. We now felt free to regale Todd with the story.

Underneath his Google Glass, his eyes widened when we described the part about Kevin scraping the smokestack on his way back up the driveway toward the caveman dad. He broke out in a weak, almost painful laugh when we told how the music suddenly came back on and scared the daylights out of us when Kevin reached the car.

Todd had been diagnosed with muscular dystrophy a few years back. We all watched him slowly change from a kid running around the neighborhood to a kid stuck in a wheelchair while his muscles stopped working. Though MD had ruined his mobility, he wore specially modified glasses and a Bluetooth earpiece to connect and communicate well online and while hacking code with Kevin.

Todd and Kevin were especially good friends, and Kevin had taken it hard. Kevin had already lost his mom, and the fragility of life seemed to make him crazy. Todd, with his strong Catholic faith, took it a lot better than Kevin. Todd was the nicest, calmest person I ever met. He wasn't openly bitter about the cards he had been dealt. He would listen to our stories of mischief or Michael's sexual exploits with no envy but just wonder and love.

"So, if Michael got one point for the side-view mirror…" Todd said. His voice was soft and slight. We could hear the clicks of his rosary beads between his words. "How many points are smokestacks worth?" He was fascinated with Kevin's point system and was working on an app to track it all.

"Ten points. Each," Kevin said.

"What?" Michael shook his head. "You just can't make the rules up as you go."

"Why not? Adaptability is the key to survival," Kevin replied.

"Yeah, but why are smokestacks worth ten points?"

"I climbed into the truck bed. I fought off two underwear-clad cavemen."

"I helped," Michael added.

Jaden and I watched the cheerful exchange of the two close friends—the always smiling Michael and the always somber Kevin—but even Kevin was smiling, slightly.

"So, I guess you should get points for an assist?" Kevin asked. Jaden and I looked at each other with skepticism.

"Yeah, assist points." Michael smiled and nodded in agreement.

"But I drove," added Jaden.

"And I covered the license plate," I said.

"That was a smart move," Todd said. "Only smart move of the night apparently." He looked at me, and I gave him a wink. Todd replied with his signature eyebrow raise.

We all broke out in a big laugh. The tables around us seemed to be watching us in wonder, as if we had some big secret, and they wanted in. Even the jock-cheerleader table was watching us with smiles.

We basked in our reigning delinquency, silent, happy, glowing in the conquest of the weekend. We were stuck on the value of smokestack points but content. We looked at each other, trying to gauge a solution. Michael took a big bite of his hamburger. Jaden spun a ketchup bottle on the table.

"You know…" Kevin broke the silence. "It doesn't have to be a zero-sum game."

"What the hell does that mean?" Jaden stopped spinning the ketchup.

"There's no winner or loser," Michael garbled through a mouthful of hamburger.

"What?" Jaden blurted. "Then it's not a game."

"Do you guys know what gamification is?" Kevin asked us. He was talking to us, but he had that staring-into-the-distance look on his face.

"It's like in a video game when there's a leaderboard, and you get points for unlocking achievements, and those get compared to other players'," Todd said.

"Yeah, Todd, that's a good example."

Kevin changed his focus. You could tell we were going to get another criminal-genius lecture.

"Another example is when an airline grants frequent-flyer miles. You fly; you get points. You track these points and spend them on more flights. Airlines call it a loyalty program. But whether it's a video game or a miles program, it's just a ploy to get you to spend more money. You think you are winning, but in truth, it's just the company that wins."

I thought about my parents. They both traveled a lot for work and earned a bunch of miles that resulted in a trip to Hawaii last summer. It didn't seem like we had been gamed. I was going to interject this, but Kevin had that intensity in his eyes. Everyone was transfixed.

"So, what I suggest is the opposite: a disloyalty program. We destroy shit and get points for it. We can keep collecting points for each task, each achievement. But we earn points as a group, and they all tally together."

"Until when? How do we win?" I asked.

"It's not a zero-sum game," Jaden added.

"Well, I guess we win when we destroy society," Kevin said.

Jaden and Michael chuckled. Todd and I looked at each other. They seemed to think Kevin was joking. We'd known him long enough to know that he was not.

"Or until we get caught," I said.

Kevin just shrugged.

The bell rang, and I jumped. Kevin smiled his sly smile and then turned to Todd. Todd looked up at him while Kevin scanned behind him.

A year before, doctors had fused a rod to Todd's spine so he could still sit up straight, but it prevented him from being able to turn his neck and glance backward.

Kevin stood up and held one hand up to stop people from walking behind Todd's wheelchair. "Back it up, buddy. Back it up," Kevin said.

Todd backed up, and we heard multiple pops from underneath his back tires. Someone had put a line of mayonnaise packets in the path of his wheelchair, which resulted in exploding white jizz all over Kevin's pants.

A loud wave of laughter burst out from the jock table—a mix of boys and girls—and in the middle sat the Oreo Sisters. Eva and Fetien were wearing their cheerleading uniforms and jeer-leading the laughter. Annie was between them in her typical jock-goth clothes. Already tattooed, she looked like a punk CrossFitter. The Oreo Sisters were a force of nature. The favorite way at East High to explain them was two rich black girls trying to act white and a poor white girl trying to act black. As much as I disliked the Oreo Sisters, I never agreed with these stupid stereotypes—created mainly because Annie, the poor white girl, was athletic and muscular as hell, while Fetien and Eva, the rich black girls, were feminine cheerleaders.

Annie was pure fire and brimstone. She wore her hair short and manly and was hypersexual and hypercompetitive. She was the school's fastest cross-country runner—quite an accomplishment in a school that was 40 percent black and full of Ethiopians.

Fetien, one of the many Ethiopians, wasn't an athlete but a tall, gorgeous cheerleader with delicate East African features and dark-honey skin. She was quiet but elegantly comfortable with the attention. I would often spot her wearing all white and covered in a shroud on the way to her Orthodox church on my block. She looked like a model in an exotic photoshoot.

Like Jaden and Michael, Eva had a white mom and a black father. And like mine, her mom was Jewish. Where Fetien was reserved, Eva never hesitated to speak her mind. She was tall and voluptuous, but her voice was even more outspoken than her curves.

But no doubt the mayonnaise trick was Annie's idea. It was her modus operandi. And she was laughing the hardest.

Annie pointed at Kevin and started laughing. "Circle jerk! Circle jerk!" she chanted over and over. The jock boys surrounding the Oreo Sisters mimicked the chant.

Todd maneuvered his joystick to turn his wheelchair around and check out the commotion. He made multiple small turns and adjustments. I wanted to help, but I watched Kevin closely to see his reaction. He stood there and slowly, calmly wiped the mayonnaise off his black pants and black boots, knowing it would leave a stain like yogurt—or like jizz. He shook his head and glanced over at Michael.

Michael got up, and the jock boys followed suit. Danny, the biggest one, East's fearless linebacker, got in Michael's face. Despite their ironic name combination, Danny was hooking up with Annie. He needed to act chivalrous.

"You gonna fight for your boyfriend, snowflake?" he said to Michael.

They lined up, equal in size. There was a tension in the room. Everyone focused on the two heavyweights bumping chests.

Out of the corner of my eye, I saw Jaden sneaking around the jocks and coming up behind the Oreo Sisters. He was holding the ketchup bottle behind his back. He sneaked up behind them and started spraying their asses with the ketchup.

They screamed and turned around. Annie lunged for Jaden, but he moved to spray her again. She backed off.

Jaden ran backward and taunted them with a big smile. His jester hat and bells bounced up and down. "Aw, you're on your periods? Well, at least you can't get pregnant."

Everyone watched the girls and Jaden, but I kept watching Kevin. He lunged forward and jumped toward Danny. He planted his boot into Danny's knee from the side with a hard stomp. Danny's leg folded, and he crashed to the ground with a cry of pain. He curled into a ball on the ground while clutching his knee. Kevin bent down and whispered in Danny's ear, "I fight my own battles. Too bad you can't lead yours."

Kevin stood up straight and marched out the door with Michael, Jaden, Todd, and me following. The jocks and cheerleaders brushed past us, going back to help Danny.

As we exited the cafeteria, I heard Todd mumble, "How much are linebackers worth?"

CHAPTER 2

● ● ●

I LOOK OVER MY SHOULDER and see a massive gray mass hanging above the mountains. In the distance, at a quick glimpse, it looks only like a cloud on the horizon. But the gray mass is too tall, too dark to be a cloud.

Everyone turns around and looks at it. An eerie quiet comes over the crowd outside the airport. Even the cops herding the kids inside are mesmerized as they look toward the ash. We stare for what seems like an eternity.

The silence breaks as the automatic doors into the airport open. A rush of yelling from inside rolls out. I hear gunshots and screams. We all instinctively huddle closer to each other. I want to comfort Lupina, to tell her everything is going to be OK. But I am worried that I might break down and cry if I do. If I give words to what we are going through, I could lose control.

All of a sudden, a cop yells, "Get inside! Now!"

We take sheepish steps inside. I cross the threshold into the airport and see the cause of the chaos. Adults, business travelers, are sequestered away from the security lines, gathered in a great big, angry mass. Between them and us are cops with machine guns. Maybe they are soldiers, because they are in full battle gear. I am not sure of the difference. Lucky for us, the machine guns are aimed at the adults.

I feel hate emanating from the adults. They are yelling at the cops, yelling at us. It is apparent they have been pulled from flights, pulled from the lines, and told they cannot travel—their seats given up to make room for teenagers being evacuated out of Colorado.

The adults look angry. I can sense their hatred but more than that their fear. They can look out the airport windows and see what is coming. They think they will probably die here, away from their homes, away from their families.

I see a plastic bottle fly from the crowd at a helmeted soldier—a move angrier in its futility. The bottle misses the soldier and skids along the marble floor toward us. It bounces off a foot and pinballs between the kids in front of us. The bottle comes to a spinning stop. I focus on it as we march past. I keep my head down. I don't want to look at the angry crowd. We keep marching forward. I glance over to Michael without looking up. His fists are clenched, and he is slightly turned to the crowd defensively. This makes me feel safer somehow than the line of soldiers holding the crowd back.

I hear whimpers from kids ahead of me as they walk past something horrific. I raise my gaze and instantly regret it. Between the angry adults and the cops, three dead bodies are sprawled out on the floor in unnatural positions. Circles of blood darken their blue suits and gather in red pools on the white marble.

"This can't be happening," I think. "This can't be happening. I am a people pleaser—a peaceful person. My name is Pax, for Chrissake." I can feel the hate from the adult business travelers. They are screaming at us. Used to getting their way, these leaders of men have been usurped by a bunch of teenagers and are powerless to do anything about it. Their rage poisons the air.

We rush through the security lines. The guards are not checking us for weapons. They are hurrying us straight to the trains that will take us out to the concourses. We crowd onto the trains, and I can't help but think of the images from World War II of Jews being crowded onto trains, on to a holocaust.

But in this case, maybe the trains are saving us from a holocaust.

On the concourse, we gather by an empty gate. A case of hurry up and wait. Jaden, Michael, and I are together by the window, keeping a nervous watch on the gray cloud. It looks bigger than when we stared at it outside. Lupina and Charlotte are nearby. I reach out and hold Lupina's hand, and she squeezes mine in response.

I glance around at the kids they put at the gate. I see a lot of kids from East. The Oreo Sisters are here. I see Danny still with crutches, and I am glad that Kevin's kick didn't keep him from making it; somehow being disabled kept Todd off the buses.

There are other kids from other schools. I can tell many of them are from the suburbs by their lily whiteness, by their uniformity.

East Denver High School is unique in its diversity. It's an urban school mainly fed by the Park Hill and Capitol Hill neighborhoods, which never experienced the white flight of so many other neighborhoods over the last century. East Denver prides itself on having a great mix of people from all backgrounds. A typical block can contain a huge mansion and a subsidized apartment building. Even our squad, not only were we diverse in ethnicity but in backgrounds as well: two biracial kids—one rich, one poor; a kid in a wheelchair; an only child raised by a single dad; and a kid of two well-off secular Jews. And that pretty much sums up East. This contrast to uniform suburban kids by the gate is noticeable. They keep shooting sideways glances at Michael, Jaden, Danny, and many of our black students.

This sizing up ends when a plane finally arrives. A rush of relief runs over the teenagers. Even some of the kids from the suburban schools start cheering, but I shake my head and stomp my feet. Tears are starting to form in my eyes. I don't want to cry in front of all these kids, in front of Lupina.

But she notices. "What's wrong, Pax? This is great. We are going to get out of here. We're saved."

I feel Michael and Jaden shift their gaze to me. I shut my eyes and take a breath. "Planes don't fly empty," I say.

"So?"

"So the people on the plane now are going to die to save us."

Almost on cue, I see a line of soldiers jogging in two lines toward our gate. They look haggard and dazed. They are heading toward the plane to clear passengers. A couple of soldiers have blood on their uniforms. I assume this isn't their first plane to clear.

The door opens up. The soldiers run down the ramp. We hear yelling of orders and screams of protest. A single shot rings out from the ramp. The yelling subsides.

I look around the gate area. The joy of being rescued is gone as everyone realizes what I realized when the plane pulled up.

I don't want to see the passengers pulled from the plane and marched down the ramp toward us. I don't want to feel their animosity like the businesspeople in the main terminal.

A chorus of cries breaks out by the students near the window. They are watching the plane. Michael gets up on the chair and tries to see what they are seeing.

"What's going on?" I ask.

He shakes his head and steps back down.

"What?"

"They just threw a body off the plane. The rest of the passengers are heading down the stairs to the cement," he says and sits on the chair. He looks defeated.

Part of me feels relief that I don't have to be confronted by the passengers exiting the plane. I bury my secret relief and go to comfort Michael. I put my hand on his shoulder.

He looks up and then past me. His eyes grow huge. "What the..." he mutters. A look of utter surprise covers his face. Lupina and I slowly turn around to see.

I am really, really not ready for any more surprises. I was looking forward to taking Lupina to prom, to Comic-Con, and to the upcoming summer break. Now I am part of an evacuation, escaping nuclear ash, and separated from my family. I need no more surprises, but what I see is impossible.

Standing near a clique of suburban kids, sweaty and covered in dirt, is Kevin. And by his side is my sister, Vivi.

CHAPTER 3

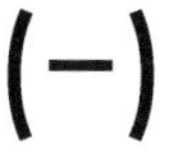

• • •

TODD AND I WERE WAITING on the blacktop for Kevin to get out of refocus—or as my dad liked to call it, detention. Kevin's punishment for hobbling Danny was a month of refocus and no prom. It was a light sentence. Kevin expertly argued that they were threatening Todd, and he acted out of defense of someone in a wheelchair. Anyway, Kevin wasn't planning on going to prom, and during refocus, he worked on the code for the app he and Todd were creating. The football season was over anyway, so Danny's injury wasn't that big of a deal.

Michael and Jaden strutted their way across the blacktop, bouncing a basketball back and forth.

"Oh, look, two black kids in East Denver with a basketball," I joked.

Todd rolled his eyes, while Michael threw me a look. The joke was a little too touchy with Michael. Despite being very athletic, Michael's white mom wanted him to focus on other things besides sports. He only competed in academic competitions like chess club, and the middle school geography bee which he won. Michael's dad, a former Division I football player with a battered body, was cool with that. Michael's mom was always on some crusade to "raise him right." Look what happened. He was hanging out and playing basketball with a squad who tracked points for destruction and delinquency.

"How much longer does he have?" Michael asked.

I shrugged. "I don't know. Twenty to thirty minutes."

Jaden knocked the ball out of Michael's hand. "Come on—quick game of twenty-one."

Todd and I turned to watch them play. Unlike Michael, Jaden's parents pushed him hard in sports, especially basketball, and despite his small size, he was good. He matched up well against the bigger Michael.

"Come on, Pax; let's play cutthroat," Michael taunted me.

I glanced at Todd. "Go ahead. I'll keep score," he said.

"You can't bet on us, Jew boy, 'cause I know Jaden's nappy ass will throw the match for a couple of bucks," Michael said.

"Daaamn! And the racist jokes keep coming," Jaden added.

Although I was tall, my basketball pedigree was limited to rec leagues, a fine collection of Kobe and LeBron sneakers, and pickup games after school. "But what the hell?" I thought.

I answered them by jogging toward the court and putting my longish hair into a ponytail. "Nothing like a little race baiting between friends," I said.

"Nice man bun," Michael said.

Todd followed me to the court but stayed near the edge.

The outside court was in the shadow of one of East's big redbrick walls. The backboard was made of metal with a chain net. Someone had spray-painted a stencil of Tupac's head, and above it, "Bob was here!!!" was written with a Sharpie.

Jaden drained a three-pointer and turned to Michael. "I get to start."

Michael lined up on Jaden, close to take away the three-pointer, so I played behind Michael—a good position to get rebounds and stop a take if Jaden could get by Michael.

Jaden shot out a jab step to the right and then crossed to the left. I moved up to help cover, but Michael was too fast. Jaden couldn't get around, so he jumped back with a sloppy fadeaway that Michael nicked. I grabbed the ball out of the air. It had never hit the rim, so I didn't have to take it back. I quickly made a lay-up to score two points.

"Yes, I can do this," I thought as I lined up on the free-throw line. My only chance was to pick up scraps and make my free throws. Sometimes the weaker opponent gained the advantage by being ignored.

"Hey, Todd, do I get assist points for that?" Michael called out as he lined up for my free throws.

Todd said, "No."

I took a deep breath. I drained the first and second.

"Four to zero to zero," I heard Todd trying to yell. We all noticed that Todd's diaphragm muscles had been weakening lately, and he was having trouble raising his voice, not that he was ever much of a yeller.

I shot my third and final free throw. The ball bounced off the rim and into Michael's hands. Michael took the ball back behind the three-point line and came barreling toward me. I got in front of him to direct him toward Jaden for the trap, but Michael just lowered his shoulder and knocked me down. He then banked in an easy lay-up.

"Hey, man, that's a charge," I yelled from the ground.

"Nah, Pax, you were moving," he responded.

Todd gave a weak shrug.

I hopped up and realized that maybe taunting Michael wasn't a good idea.

He missed his free throw, and I snagged the rebound. I put my hip into Jaden as I grabbed it. "This is how we are going to play," I thought.

"Oh, so that's how we gonna play, Pax?" Jaden quipped. "That's how we gonna play!" He yelled in my face as he followed me close all the way to the three-point line.

"Great," I thought, "now I have pissed them both off. So much for being ignored."

Jaden was covering me close to the point where I was posting up on the three-point line to keep him from stealing the ball. I turned around and tried a long jump shot, but it didn't even make the rim. Michael alley-ooped it for another easy two points.

"Nice pass, Pax," Jaden said.

"Hey, man, don't guard me so close."

Again, Michael missed his free throws. Jaden quickly grabbed the ball and darted to the three-point line. He turned around and drained it.

"Pax, you gotta play him like he played you," Michael ordered.

"Naw, man, you pick him up," I said.

Jaden nailed all three free throws and took the ball to the top of the key.

"What's the score, Todd?" he asked.

"Six to four to four," Todd said.

"You hear that, big boys? Six to four to four," Jaden said as he checked the ball to Michael. Michael played him close now.

"Good," I thought. "I am being ignored again."

The game was tight when Kevin walked out of refocus. Michael and Jaden were tied at nineteen, and I was at sixteen. They were playing each other very hard. Jaden was too quick and too good an outside shooter, but Michael's size was hard to stop on his drives and rebounding.

When we saw Kevin walk up, everyone stopped. Michael bent over and tried to catch his breath. I noticed that Jaden and Michael were tiring each other out while I was hanging back, trying to shag rebounds.

"No, come on. Let's keep going," I said, not wanting to give them any rest. I ran cross-country, and stamina was my one advantage.

Kevin stood by Todd. "We all ready for tonight?" he asked him.

Todd smiled a devilish smile and pointed his eyes down to the phone in his front shirt pocket. Kevin slid it out and punched in the passcode.

"Let's go! Let's go! Jaden's ball," I said.

Jaden took the ball at the top of the key and checked it to me. Michael and I both covered him close. He tried to split us, but Michael blocked him off. He bounced backward and dribbled the ball back and forth through his legs.

"Nigga, please," Michael taunted. "You ain't getting that schoolyard shit past me."

"Only 'cause you double-teaming, Bucky," Jaden said.

We took a step closer.

He shook his head, getting frustrated at the defense. He bolted to my side and tried to get around me but couldn't. He then stepped back before Michael or I could get to him and shot a fadeaway.

I turned and ran full speed to the net while Michael watched to see if Jaden would make the game-winning shot. The ball bounced off the rim to the backboard, hit the rim again, and fell off to the right. I grabbed the ball and dribbled to the three-point line. I touched the line and ran back toward the net full speed as Michael and Jaden headed toward me. Before they could get to me, I stopped, popped, and sank a ten-footer.

Yes, eighteen to nineteen to nineteen.

I lined up at the free-throw line with everyone watching. Even Kevin looked up from Todd's phone to watch.

"You can't sink three in a row, Pax," Jaden said.

"Just make the first one," Todd suggested.

I bounced the ball on the line a few times. In the game of twenty-one, if you didn't land on twenty-one exactly, you went back to thirteen. The smart play for me was to make the first free throw and then purposely miss the second and try to get the rebound, but I figured if we were all at nineteen, I wouldn't be ignored anymore and would have the least chance of making the final basket.

I looked up at Kevin and wondered what he would do in this situation. I smiled. I stepped my right foot back and threw the ball hard at the backboard. The ball hit the backboard and bounced back to me before Michael could grab it. I caught it and ran back to the three-point line, turned around, and threw up a prayer. The ball flew through the air and banked off the backboard and into the net.

I jumped up with my arms in a V and yelled, "Jew-boy power!"

I did a little dance toward Kevin and Todd. Todd had a big smile on his face. Michael and Jaden were shaking their heads.

"We'll finish this another time," Michael told Jaden as they walked toward Kevin and Todd.

"You guys done playing your games and such?" Kevin asked.

"Ah, Mr. I'm-too-cool-to-play-sports," Jaden said. "I'm just going to listen to my sad music, paint dark pictures, and plan the destruction of the world."

Kevin looked at Jaden with an absent expression. He cocked his head to the side and said, "Sports are gay."

We all scoffed.

"What the hell?" Jaden said.

Kevin cut Jaden off. "I don't mean gay in any sexist way. I mean gay like two guys wanting to suck each other's dick gay."

"Yep, that's gay," I said.

"Think about it: if all you do is watch sports and talk about sports, all the fucking time, then you are pretty much worshiping masculinity, worshiping men, and that's pretty fucking gay."

"No wonder my mom loves you," Michael added.

"Yeah, well, anyway, Todd has something to show you," Kevin said.

Kevin handed the phone to Michael. Jaden and I got on either side of him. We looked around to check for anyone watching, like this was some kind of drug deal.

The setting sun was moving west toward the mountains. A shadow cast from East High sliced across the basketball court, cutting us in half—Todd and Kevin on one side and Michael, Jaden, and me on the other.

We looked at the phone. The glare from the sun in our eyes made it hard to see. Michael took a step forward into the shadows, toward Todd and Kevin. Jaden and I followed.

We peered down at the screen.

"Press the app with the anarchy A," Todd said.

"What's an anarchy A?" Michael asked.

"The red A with the circle around it," Kevin snapped.

Michael pushed the button, and an "anarchy A" in spray-paint red came up. On the screen below it were the words:

App-It-Tight
4 Destruction

CHAPTER 3

• • •

VIVI LOOKS SHELL SHOCKED. I let go of Lupina's hand, run to her, and sweep her up in my arms.

"Oh, thank God, thank God," I say.

Out of the corner of my eye, I see Kevin cock his head at this. I continue to hold Vivi tight against me. She starts to cry.

"How—how did you get her? How did you get out?" I ask him.

"Where are Mom and Dad?" Vivi asks me.

I am struggling to find an answer when a voice comes over the intercom at our gate.

"We are now boarding flight number..." The gate agent's voice trembles. She stops when she realizes there is no flight number, and she doesn't know the destination.

The suburban kids start rushing toward the gate.

I want to stay and hold Vivi, comfort her, and hear Kevin's explanation, but I realize why the kids are hurrying. They don't want to miss the flight and be stuck here when the ash arrives.

We head toward the gate. Kevin is wearing a camping backpack and clutching Vivi's schoolbag in his hand.

A bunch of East kids form a V to wedge into the crowd. Jaden and Michael are at the tip, followed by Kevin. I am still carrying Vivi and walking behind Kevin. Her head is buried in my shoulder. I look around and see more East kids join our V. Danny hurries to get behind Michael, next to Kevin. The Oreo Sisters and many others are close by.

I see Jaden duck under some people ahead while Michael opens the wedge behind him. This works. We are making our way to the front when two tall blond kids grab Jaden by the shoulders and throw him back into Michael.

"Watch it, nigger!" one of them says.

They turn around and take us in. They are sizing up Michael and glance at Danny and his crutches. A smirk comes over their collective faces.

I can see from behind that Michael, Danny, and Jaden are just utterly shocked. Everyone stops except Kevin, who walks up next to Jaden.

Despite going to a diverse school and hearing the word *nigga* all the time, you can tell the East kids are stunned. They've never heard it said like that before. We knew it could be said like that. We just never heard it.

Other suburban kids are lining up to face us. "Cutting in line—could expect as much from a nigger," another kid adds. He is portly and hiding behind his athletic friends.

I see Jaden shake his head as if waking up from a daze. He turns to the tall kid and starts to lunge, but Kevin steps in front of him. Kevin juts out his left arm to block Jaden's path with Vivi's pink backpack dangling in front of him.

Kevin holding the pink backpack as a shield looks comical, and some of the kids start to snicker, but Kevin's right hand quickly slips into his pocket. He pulls out his SOG camping knife. He straightens his right arm and points it diagonally at the ground. His thumb moves the knob on the knife, and the blade springs open with a sharp click. With the knife and the pink backpack jutting out like a big pink shield, it looks like a cartoonish sword and shield prepped for battle.

"Back the fuck off!" he says. This is not cartoonish. His words are not petty name-calling or an idle threat but a command. Everyone freezes.

Kevin takes a bold lunge forward, and the suburban kids jump back.

He starts walking forward, and they part for him. We follow Kevin and his sword and shield through the crowd.

The tall racist kid watches Kevin pass. I glance over at him. He looks like he is going to say something, to yell an insult at Kevin walking away, but Jaden jumps up and punches him in the jaw. The kid staggers back and drops while his friends try to catch his fall.

"Expect that from a nigga," Jaden tells the crowd as he joins the rest of the East students walking toward the gate.

The gate agent is frazzled. She doesn't notice the quarrel. She is staring at the ground, shaking her head. Her reddish curly hair is shaking and dancing in her face. It too looks worn.

Still staring at the ground, she points to the gate, and in a dazed stupor, she says over and over, "This is the way. This is the way. Step inside."

I look back over my shoulder at the gate attendant as we approach the open doors of the gate. She is still shaking her head and mumbling the words repeatedly. We step inside and start to walk down the gangway to the airplane.

In the gangway, we pass by travel posters of fun destinations like Miami and Cabo San Lucas. The posters show many smiling and scantily clad tourists on sun-drenched beaches, but this is not where we are going.

Toward the end of the gangway, the soldier-cops are lined up against the wall. They have cleared the plane and are waiting for us to board. They are holding their guns, and this is intimidating.

I start to worry that they will see Vivi in my arms and stop us. They'll know there should only be high school kids on this flight. I think about putting Vivi down and having her walk to be less visible.

"Vivi, Vivi, sweetie, you need to walk," I say.

I feel her shake her head no on my shoulder.

"Come on, Vivi. Let's walk."

She doesn't budge. I look at the guards. We are getting closer to them. I don't want to stop and cause attention. I wish my mom and dad were with us. I think about what they would do.

"Security, security," I whisper to Vivi. Her head moves to attention. *Security* is the secret word my parents say to alert us to any danger or really to get us to knock off any bullshit when things are chaotic in a dangerous situation.

Vivi slides down to the floor, turns around, and starts walking with us toward the plane. I take her hand. Lupina takes her other. I try to block the view of the guards just in case they notice how young she looks.

We start walking by the guards lining the gateway. My heart is drumming in my chest. I feel at any second they are going to step forward, stop us, and take Vivi from me.

I watch their faces to look for any sign of suspicion. I see the one guard with dark blood on his uniform. His face is young and handsome, but he has small splats of blood on his cheeks. He is too young to have blood on his face. I stare at him, and he looks at me. I realize staring at him is stupid, as I am calling attention to myself. We lock gazes. I cannot turn away. But there is no animosity in his eyes or suspicion. He looks scared and lonely, and his eyes seem to be saying, "I still exist."

CHAPTER 4

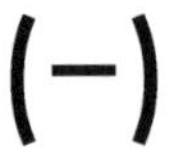

• • •

MAKER COFFEE AND SMOOTHIES SERVED as a home away from home for the geeks of East High School. The old Victorian house was nestled into the grittier part of Colfax Avenue, between the school and local music venues like the Bluebird, Ogden, and Fillmore. Once known for prostitution and drug deals, the area was cleaned up some but was still nowhere near the gentrified SoDoSoPa areas of town.

The Maker house had a commercial storefront where people could buy coffee and food and make their own smoothies at the smoothie bar. Although awesome, it wasn't the smoothie bar that attracted the Comic-Con crowd—it was a maker's paradise. Spread across multiple floors and the garage out back were tools and stations to build and create. On the second floor, there were stacks of fabric and tables with industrial sewing machines where kids could make their costumes. A decked-out computer lab synced to beefed-up servers for gaming and design. They had even crowdsourced a state-of-the-art 3-D printer. The art garage in the back was filled with easels, metalworking equipment, and sculpting stations.

Maker sublet the former residential rooms on the third floor out to various small businesses, from massage therapists to psychics to tattoo artists. The open loft on the fourth floor could host anything from yoga classes to poetry readings to small music shows.

The equipment and unlimited smoothie access were available for rental or via membership. Todd and Kevin had helped set up and administer the stations and received discounted memberships in return. The owner was really cool and had even installed a lift in the back so Todd could get to the second floor.

On most days, Todd and Kevin hacked away at the computer stations. They had an eerie way of hacking together where Todd would control the cursor of the mouse via his modified glasses and keypad while Kevin ferociously typed code. Using one operating-system interface on multiple monitors, Todd would manipulate objects while Kevin typed coding instructions. They even spoke to each other in this weird mumbling language. But they could rip out code faster than any hack around.

I didn't see Todd and Kevin when Jaden and I walked up the stairs to meet Lupina and Charlotte. I felt relief. I got nervous enough without a peer audience. In my head, I played out different scenarios and approaches to ask Lupina to prom. I finally settled on improvising while following Jaden's lead—feeling reassured that I could surf his coattails.

Jaden bounced into the room, and I tried hard to keep up. Lupina and Charlotte were in the sewing area. They stood at the large standing table, measuring out fabric.

"Madame Charlotte and Madame Lupina, your faithful servants kindly await your smoothie orders," Jaden said with a twirl of the arm and a formal bow. I quickly copied his bow. After a second or two of silence, I glanced up nervously. Charlotte was giving us an incredulous look. I felt a ball in my gut. I looked at Lupina, and she smiled her sweet smile.

"Surprise us," she said.

Jaden and I stood up straight, clicked our heels together, and turned around to march toward the stairs.

"I wasn't expecting a 'Surprise us,'" Jaden said.

We held the mixing glasses in our hands while staring down at the massive number of ingredients to choose from. A similar concept to Froyo, Maker's smoothie bar allowed customers to throw a bunch of ingredients, like fruit, yogurt, juice, and powders, into big mixing glasses for the barista to blend.

"Yeah, I know. I think we just got set up for a test to fail," I said. "Should we go healthy green or fruity fun?"

"I don't even know what she likes," Jaden added.

I tried to remember any special foods that Lupina liked, and all I could think of was Hawaiian pizza.

"Well…we know they like to be creative, so let's get creative."

Jaden shot me a look.

I went with the Hawaiian theme and threw pineapple, banana, coconut milk, honey, and yogurt into the mixing cup. I topped it off with ginseng powder.

I held the cup in both hands like a divine offering.

"I shall call it Lupina colada."

"Nice, Pax. Nice," Jaden said.

Then he got a sly smile. He shimmied back and forth along the smoothie bar, shaking his butt in excitement like a puppy. He threw frozen pitted cherries, a banana, coconut milk, yogurt, and a bunch of vanilla protein powder into his cup.

He turned around and showed me the cup with a mischievous look on his face. "She's my vanilla-cherry-cream dream."

"Why you smiling like that?" I asked. "What? Oh, yeah, you better not say that to Charlotte with that big smile on your face."

We handed the large cups to the barista, who blended them and placed them back on the counter. Jaden grabbed four big straws and stuck two in each cup.

"Cute, Jaden." I shook my head as we headed to the stairs. I remembered when my family was by the pool in Hawaii, my dad kept singing some dorky song about piña coladas. Every time he ordered one or took a drink from one or finished one, he would sing that damned song. I didn't have confidence in remembering the exact words, but for some reason, I decided to hum the tune when we reached the top of the stairs. I even started to dance a dorky saunter over to Lupina and Charlotte as I hummed. I expected Jaden to play along, but when I looked up to see the girls smiling and watching us, I realized they were just watching me.

"No, Pax. Just no," Jaden said from the top of the stairs.

I decided to just go full dork and kept up the humming and dork saunter until I reached them at the table.

I stopped and said in my best Latino accent, "Do chou like Lupina colada?" I handed the smoothie to Lupina.

My dorkiness and my embarrassment were worth it, because Lupina smiled the cutest, coyest smile and then lowered her long dark eyelashes as she looked into the cup and took a sip.

"It's wonderful, Pax," she said.

"OK, so, I don't know what to follow Pax's dance with." Jaden shook his head while holding the smoothie in his hands. "Oh wait. I know…"

Lupina and I were staring at each other when Jaden just blurted out, "Do you two want to go to prom with us?"

Our eyes went wide in shock. We turned to watch Charlotte's reaction.

"We aren't going to prom."

"Char!" Lupina exclaimed.

"What? We are too busy making *King Lear* costumes and our Comic-Con costumes. I am not making prom dresses on top of it."

"Just buy a dress," Jaden said.

Charlotte shot him a vicious look that actually made him flinch backward.

"Well, what are you making for Comic-Com?" I asked.

"We're dragon queens," Charlotte said and fluffed up the velvety fabric she had spread on the table.

"So why don't you just wear that to prom?" I suggested, grasping at straws.

Charlotte looked at me like I was a drooling toddler.

"Yeah, yeah. And how can dragon queens have no dragon?" Jaden added.

I threw him a perplexed look.

"We'll make you a dragon," he said.

"We will?"

"Yeah, and we'll be, like, your, ah, dragon handlers."

"You're going to make us a dragon for Comic-Con if we go to prom with you?"

"Sure."

"It can't suck. This is Comic-Con, after all," she added.

Jaden and I looked at each other. We could tell we were both thinking the same thing: Kevin.

"Ah, no problem. Hey, where's Kevin and Todd?" he asked.

"They're in the art garage with Michael," Lupina answered.

"What are they doing down there?" I asked.

"All I know is I don't want to know," Charlotte said.

"OK then. We're going to get on that dragon making," Jaden said.

We started walking to the back stairs when Jaden realized he was still holding Charlotte's smoothie.

"Oh, Dragon Queen, your chalice," he said.

"Just put it on the table. And don't spill it," she said. After a moment, she added, "And thanks, Jaden."

"Sure."

* * *

We opened the door to the art garage, and Kevin quickly threw a tarp over whatever he was working on.

"We need to make a dragon!" Jaden exclaimed.

Michael turned to us and seemed to be relieved it was just us.

"Ha, they got you to make a dragon," he said. His big smile stretched even bigger.

"It's like a dowry." Kevin smirked.

Behind him, his e-bike, Bucephalus, was in pieces on the floor. The frame was drying from what looked like a recent repainting to matte black.

"No, no," I said. "They are just too busy to make dresses for prom, and we suggested that they wear their Comic-Con costumes to prom. What are you working on?"

"So, they also got you to commit to going to Comic-Con?" Michael said.

"No, man, it's not like that," Jaden argued.

I was replaying the conversation over in my mind when Todd maneuvered his wheelchair around to face us and said, "Michael told them that you two were going to ask them to prom. They were excited to go…even Charlotte."

I started to protest, but I couldn't shake the smile from my face. Lupina was excited to go to prom with me.

"Look at him smirk," Michael said. "Don't ever play poker, man. You can't hide shit."

I shrugged. "Speaking of hiding things, what's under the tarp?"

Michael looked to Kevin, and they nodded. Michael pulled back the tarp. I was expecting to see a weapon or elaborate contraption, but instead, there were a bunch of small green plastic tubs.

"What the hell are those?" I asked.

"What are *thoooose*?" Jaden mimicked.

Michael started to explain, but Kevin interrupted.

"First, what's this about a dragon?" he asked.

"Lupina and Charlotte want us to make a dragon to go with their Comic-Con costumes. Numb nuts over there volunteered the idea," I said.

"Do you have an idea how to make a dragon?" Jaden asked.

"Sure, easy." He sat back down on the stool and started to explain. "I would fasten the frame to a cart or, better yet, a bike that they could ride. Once you build the frame with PVC and wire, papier-mâché and paint the body and buy fabric for the wings. The face would be hard to make well, so I recommend buying a dragon costume mask from Wizard's Chest."

Jaden and I looked at each other with WTF looks on our faces.

"Now," Kevin said as he leaned forward. "I can help you make the dragon, but we need your help tonight."

CHAPTER 4

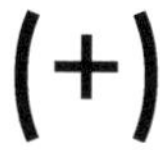

● ● ●

WE TAKE SEATS AT THE back of the plane. The aircraft is a large international one and can accommodate many people, but I realize that not all East students are on the flight. We must have split up via the buses and security lines.

I recognize about fifty or sixty East students boarding before I see the suburban kids getting on. I am in the left window row with Lupina and Vivi next to me. Vivi's head is lying in my lap. Lupina is resting her head on my shoulder while running her fingers through Vivi's hair. I feel Lupina's tears wet my shirt. I realize Lupina is probably thinking about her younger sisters and her mom.

"Don't worry. I am sure they will be OK," I say unconvincingly.

Lupina nods her head against me.

In the larger middle aisle are Michael, Kevin, Jaden, Charlotte, and Danny. In front of them are the Oreo Sisters and a couple of other jocks. Kevin and Annie are sitting on the aisle seats across from Lupina, Vivi, and me.

There is no sign of Todd. I feel deep down that I won't see him again. I look at Kevin, and he looks at me. I can tell he is having the same thought.

The students on the plane are fairly quiet during takeoff. A few cries ripple through the cabin, peppered with incessant attempts to use cell phones, but most kids are trying to process what is going on. This morning, we were happy high school students, and now we are refugees—ripped away from our families to escape some kind of catastrophe.

Kevin breaks the silence when he gets up and takes his backpack down from the overhead bin.

He gets out a large Nalgene bottle full of water and drops a couple of pills in it. I think for a second that it might be his epilepsy medicine. It starts to stain the water red. I figure it is probably iodine. He shakes the bottle. Annie turns around to see what he is doing. Kevin looks at the bottle and opens the lid to drop in more pills.

"Strange time to do drugs, I guess," Annie says to Kevin.

Kevin is still shaking the bottle. It turns a darker red. "Like water into wine," I think to myself and then snicker at the irony of me thinking that thought.

"It's iodine. It will help counter radiation sickness," Kevin replies. He keeps shaking the bottle vigorously for a minute. It's almost comical, like he is playing the maracas.

Finally, Kevin opens the bottle and takes two big gulps. He looks at Annie and then passes her the bottle.

"Thank you," she says and takes a drink. The big bottle gets passed around to our group in the back corner. I get Vivi to sit up and take a drink, which she does without protest. I take a drink and realize how thirsty I am, but the taste kind of shocks me—it tastes more like blood and iron than wine.

"So," Annie says to Kevin, "you're kind of a badass."

Kevin smirks. "I burn bright," he replies. He pauses for a second and then gives her a sincere look. "As do you."

They look at each other. It doesn't need to be said. The passing of the iodine wine consummated it; we are of the same tribe.

As if on cue, three hot girls are standing in the aisle in front of us. The leading one is tall and conventionally attractive but with too much fakeness and makeup.

"I like badasses," she says with a creepy-sexy smile. This receives no response. She inches closer to Kevin.

"Pretty bold move sneaking a knife on an airplane."

Kevin looks up and shows a rare look of confusion. He is not used to being hit on.

One of the other girls behind the lead girl turns my way and looks me over. She sees Lupina nestled into my shoulder. They lock gazes.

"Oh my God, you could be soooo pretty. You should totally let me do your makeup," she says to Lupina.

"Piss off!" Lupina responds.

With this, Vivi sits up.

The girl takes a step back, but their leader takes a step forward, closer to Kevin, standing in the aisle.

Her big, pointy tits are nearly touching Kevin, but he is staring at her face with his tired, dark-circled eyes. Michael and Jaden, not so much.

"Can I have some wine?" she asks with a honey voice.

"No," Kevin says. "Now fuck off."

The girl is taken aback. You can tell she rarely hears no, especially from teenage boys.

"You should know, I am really popular, and I can get guys—well, ah, straight guys—to do whatever I want."

With that, Annie stands up behind the leader girl and grabs ahold of her hair. She pulls her head down to the seat back and says, "Can they stop me from breaking your nose?"

The girl lets out a squeal. Annie pulls her hair back and throws her toward her friends. There are tears in her eyes. The third friend puts her arms around her.

"You know, we were just trying to be nice," says the girl who asked to put makeup on Lupina.

"No, you weren't!" Eva replies. "You insulted my friend, and you asked for something that wasn't yours, and when you didn't get it, you threatened us. You are anything but nice."

The leader pulls away from her friend and gives us a raging scold.

"Yeah, well, you better watch it. Wait until the authorities find out about your knife," she says.

Annie takes a step forward. The leader flinches back.

But Kevin just says in his tired, lethargic voice, "If you tell anyone, I'll kill you first."

An eerie chill comes over the back of the plane. The girls turn around and retreat back to the front. As they sulk down the aisle, I hear one of them say, "Fucking psycho."

A few of us laugh at the encounter, but Kevin puts his backpack away and slips back into his seat.

"Thanks, Annie," he finally says to the seat in front of him.

"No worries," she throws back.

Kevin doesn't smile. He closes his eyes and starts to fall asleep. I look at his face for a minute. He looks drained from the previous weekend, from the shadowplay, as Lupina called it, and all the drama that came with it. His face is hollowed and even paler than usual with dark whirlpool circles around his eyes.

But more than that, it's been years of adversity. His mom was always a hateful figure in his life. I remember going out to dinner with his family once when we were in elementary school. Kevin had a seizure in the restaurant. There was a huge commotion when he hit the table and then fell to the ground. Many staff and patrons gathered around to watch, *to help*. Mark, his dad, pragmatically hushed them away and made sure Kevin was safe and not going to choke or hurt himself, but his mom just stood there with a furious look on her face.

Her high cheekbones turned red with anger as she pinched her eyes and lips. I was just a kid, but I swear I had never seen anything so menacing up to that point.

Kevin once told me that his mom belonged to a sorority in college. He said that they once voted to keep a girl out because she had an eating disorder. They felt she would have trouble interacting with all the *normal* girls. But in truth, he told me, they only accepted perfection.

As talented as Kevin is, he isn't perfect, and his epilepsy was a fatal flaw in his mom's eyes. He could never do anything to please her, and he stopped trying. And then she died. I'm sure he wished for a different mom over the years, so the guilt of having her disappear from his life must have been as hard to handle as the grief. His dad too disappeared in a way after the death. He had his own shit to deal with. When he was around, he was engaging and full of life, but he often took off into the wilderness to deal with the loss of his wife while leaving Kevin with his grandma or just alone. He even stayed with my family for a bit. He and Vivi struck up a special friendship. She too was unwanted. A weak Band-Aid applied to an already failed marriage.

No wonder Kevin couldn't understand when that girl was hitting on him; no wonder he's self-destructive. For all his talents, it seems apparent that he thinks little of himself.

I realize, in many ways, we are the only family Kevin has. I feel bad that I was hard on him, that I gave up on him so quickly. Lupina was right; if one of us was in Kevin's situation, he would have done anything to help us, but it's hard to love and care for a person who hates himself.

The flight is long. Everyone around me seems to be sleeping. I could never sleep on flights. Despite the long and stressful weekend and the catastrophic shock this morning, I remain wide awake. On the flight to Hawaii, I was awake the whole time and arrived totally wiped out.

I figure we have traveled about four hours when we start our descent. No message comes from the pilot, only the ding of the "fasten your seatbelt" sign.

I look out the window, curious about where we are going. I know the plane is heading east, but I have no idea where we will land. I wake Lupina and Vivi and tell them we are landing soon. I sit up in my seat to get a better view out of Vivi's window. I instantly recognize the city. I can see an island full of skyscrapers coming up. We are going to New York City. I see the Statue of Liberty and point it out to Vivi. I feel a moment of pride. But as we pass the city, I see pillars of smoke rise up to the sky. I start to feel queasy.

"Kevin, hey, man, check this out," I say to Kevin. He is awake but groggy.

A mumble of chatter breaks across the plane as others see the smoke. Kevin comes to full attention. He unbuckles his seat belt and jumps up. He looks out the window and sees the smoke. Everyone turns to watch Kevin as he gets his backpack down again and pulls out his binoculars.

Kevin stands up on Lupina's seat arm and looks through the window. I don't want to take the seat belt off Vivi while we descend, so I get up and hop over Lupina. Kevin steps over me and into my seat. He is squatting on my seat, fixing the binoculars on a point and then moving on to the next point like a bird of prey. He does this for a minute and then turns to us all.

"Mosques," he says. "They're burning mosques."

CHAPTER 5

(–)

• • •

KEVIN PULLED THE LEVER ON the hydraulic lift. Todd slowly rose up and gave us one of his funny eyebrow winks. Kevin guided the wheelchair's joystick and moved Todd into the van. He jumped up on the lift and continued to move Todd back and then ducked and disappeared into the van to adjust Todd's wheelchair seat back—leaning Todd backward so he wouldn't fall forward when the van was moving.

"You need help?" Jaden asked.

"I've got it," Kevin replied. "You OK, buddy?" Kevin asked Todd.

It was weird to see Kevin take care of Todd. Not because friends shouldn't help friends or teenage guys shouldn't be so caring, so empathetic—it was that Kevin projected such a dark presence, always brooding, looking straight through you with his intense stare. Even before his mom had died, he was dark and dreary.

I remember in elementary school, our teacher had contests around long division. Two students would go up to the front of the class and race to solve a long-division problem projected onto the front board. Each student had his or her own problem, but whoever finished first and finished correct stayed and faced a new opponent.

The teacher and Kevin had despised each other. The teacher had her favorites whom she treated totally differently from the rest of the class, which drove Kevin to act up. In return, she treated him and his friends, like Todd and me, even worse. Once, we even heard her mumble his dreaded nickname, "Shakes," under her breath when he acted up. The insult happened a couple of days after he had an epileptic fit in her class. We despised her even more for the low blow.

Before the start of the contest, the teacher announced that whoever won the most division battles would get to lead the upcoming field trip to the Denver Art Museum—her "little slice of joy in this cow town."

She asked for two volunteers to start, and Kevin blurted out, "I'll go."

Everyone was shocked. Kevin never raised his hand in class, never volunteered for anything. Kevin walked toward the front of the class, turned around, and just stared the teacher down.

The teacher returned Kevin's hard stare. "Wendy, would you like to join Kevin at the front of the class?"

A collective "whoa" came over the class. Wendy was her favorite favorite—a typical brainy, overachieving Little Miss Perfect. Kevin continued to stare at the teacher.

She snapped on the projector. The light blasted Kevin in the face. I distinctly remember Kevin quickly shutting his eyes and keeping them shut as he took a couple of steps to the side, out of the shine. He opened his eyes again and glanced at the board and back at the teacher. He took a big breath in through his nose and gave her a cold, hard stare.

"Well…go!" the teacher commanded and pointed at the two division problems projected on the board. Wendy quickly snapped to and started working on the problem, but Kevin continued to give the teacher the stink-eye.

Everyone laughed and thought Kevin was just being a smartass. Wendy was busily working out the division while Kevin just stared at the teacher.

But when Wendy was about to finish, Kevin took a couple steps forward into the light and wrote his answer on the board. Nobody laughed. Everyone, including Wendy, just looked to the teacher.

After a deathly long wait, the teacher said, "That's correct."

"This is fuuuun! Let's do it again," Kevin said sarcastically.

A few more kids went, and Kevin did the same thing: writing down the correct answer after staring down the teacher and then saying, "Do it again! Do it again!" when he finished.

Finally, she went to the board and wrote a division problem by hand—she assumed Kevin had cheated, that he had seen the problems ahead of time and calculated and then memorized the answers. She even wrote down a division problem with more digits, but he still just stared off into the distance for a few seconds more and then wrote down the answer.

We didn't finish the division game. And the teacher called in sick on the day of the field trip. Classic Kevin—never a good student, never one to achieve, but he could do long division in his head to show up our jerky teacher.

So, to see this genius devil who stole the joy from the teacher in a division contest take care of Todd with such authentic warmth was a bit unnerving.

Even Michael and Jaden seemed a bit thrown off by it. But our parents, especially Todd's, thought it was "wonderful" how Kevin went out of his way to help Todd, to learn how to use the van so he could take Todd places, to feed Todd at lunchtime so he could eat with us in the cafeteria. Some teachers were so taken aback by Kevin's caretaking of Todd that they cut Kevin some slack when he got especially self-destructive.

We all left Todd's house in the big handicap van, driving around Denver, casing our targets. Todd was OK with me driving while

Kevin was in the open slot next to him changing into his "bum" costume. Michael and Jaden were sitting in the back-row seats, decked out in their red East Angels hoodies. Kevin called them "red herring" outfits, but nobody knew what that meant.

You could feel the tension in the car. We were about to do something highly illegal. I looked at Michael and Jaden in the rearview mirror. They looked kind of hilarious, like two scared gangbangers. It seemed like we each wanted to say something, to question this escapade, but nobody wanted to speak up, especially since Kevin would be the one taking all the risks.

Even Todd, who was excited to go out with us, also looked nervous. He was still lying back in his wheelchair, his rosary beads frantically passing between the fingers of his left hand. Looking up at the ceiling of the van, he cast a sideways glance toward Kevin. He asked, "You sure you want to do this? This is really serious if you get caught."

Kevin had finished putting on his grungy army fatigues and now was applying mud to his face.

He stopped and stood up straight.

"Do you know what today is?" he asked.

"One month until prom," I replied from the driver's seat. "I'd really like to go to prom...instead of, you know, jail."

"Funny," he said. "Today is the anniversary of when Snowden first leaked information about government spying."

"Oh, OK then. Never mind," I said.

"We are in a turnkey surveillance state."

"Turnkey surveillance state," Jaden repeated.

"With hacked smartphones, cameras everywhere, huge data centers tracking it all. The government just needs to flip a switch, and it's 1984."

"Nineteen eighty-four, Pax! Wait. They have time travel too?" Jaden joked.

"Big Brother. A surveillance state that can easily watch and repress the population. We are one flip of a switch away."

"I don't think so," I said.

"That's 'cause you entitled, Pax," Jaden said in his fake gang-banger voice.

"Yeah, you entitled, Pax," Michael agreed.

They knew how much that bugged me.

"Screw you, Michael. Your family is a lot richer than mine. Your dad drives a freaking Bentley."

"Sure, Pax, you got me there," Michael replied.

"It doesn't matter if you're rich; doesn't matter if you're white. You're the state's bitch," Kevin concluded.

"But not tonight," Jaden quipped from the back of the van. "Not tonight!"

"Whatever, Kevin. Get hurt—or, better yet, get caught and go to prison—we'll see whose bitch you are."

Kevin shot up front next to me. I turned and looked up at his face. His makeup made him look scruffy and dirty. He looked older, like the pictures of his dad, Mark, posted on social from one of his expeditions.

"It's not your problem, Pax."

His words were a command. I felt humiliated. I wanted to end the escapade—to not follow his orders—just stop the van and walk away. But my role was to serve as a lookout with Todd, and I didn't want Todd going out on the streets by himself. Plus, Kevin had tied this escapade to helping us with the dragon and thus to me taking Lupina to prom. I was stuck.

"Whatever, man," I said. And besides, deep down, part of me wanted to see if Kevin would get busted.

We parked on a dark residential backstreet. I sat sulking in the driver's seat as Kevin in his homeless-person costume guided Todd out of the van. In the side mirror, I saw Kevin pick up Todd's right hand and gently place it on the joystick. Todd maneuvered himself down the street alone. I took a breath and opened the door. I hopped out of the van and jogged down the street after him. I caught up and didn't say anything. I just looked back over my shoulder at the van. Kevin had raised the lift back up. Michael and Jaden walked out with small backpacks slung over their shoulders. They reached the end of the lift and jumped off like pirates walking the plank. They hit the ground, put their red hoods over their heads, and walked off in the other direction without saying anything to Kevin.

Todd and I took up our positions in a fast-food restaurant on Sixth Avenue. I sat in a booth with Todd at the end of the table. Every couple of minutes, Todd would raise his eyebrows as his way of asking for a sip of pop without having to ask.

The restaurant was fairly busy for the late hour. The typical late-night crowd sat around, keeping the appropriate distance from other late-night dwellers. A couple of munchie-seeking party groups ate their food with a quiet intensity out of whack for people so whacked out. In the corner, a real homeless person sat by himself—not eating or drinking anything—just looking for shelter for a part of the night. Ignored by others, he proved Kevin's theory about using a homeless-person costume for invisibility.

Part of me felt vulnerable to be there with Todd, like we were targets, but nobody paid us any attention.

I looked down at Todd's tablet. The screen was divided in half with two different images on the screen. Jaden and Michael had launched two drones and piloted them with their phones. The drones streamed images through a Bluetooth relay back to Todd and me. Todd connected to Kevin through his earpiece to tip him off on any danger.

The plan was for the drones to follow Kevin and send images to the tablet so we could serve as a lookout. All the communication happened through Bluetooth on the app Todd and Kevin had built, so it was untraceable by the phone companies. This was the App-It-Tight 4 Destruction code they were working on at Maker all the time. It just wasn't to track a score; it was encrypted and extended communication protocols via Bluetooth.

"We're online," I said to Todd.

I nudged closer toward him and angled the tablet so Todd could see. On screen, two bird's-eye views of Speer Boulevard and Sixth Avenue showed very little movement. Between and below Speer Boulevard, Cherry Creek split the boulevard in half with a popular bike path meandering alongside the large creek.

We stared at the screens, watching for Kevin to come down the bike path on the e-bike he had stashed earlier.

The tension was surreal. Waiting, watching for a crime to happen live on a screen, viewing the familiar city streets from a new, unnatural angle via the drones, I felt like some kind of angel from above, waiting for my keep to make a decision, a choice between right and wrong.

We waited longer than I expected. The wait and silence were deafening. The only sounds were the buzz of the fluorescent lights and Todd's clicking of the rosary beads in his left hand.

I was beginning to think Kevin was going to back out. That he got scared and changed his mind.

"Here he comes," Todd said softly.

"Where?"

I scanned the screens looking for Kevin when I saw what looked like a shadow come down the Cheery Creek bike path at an eerily smooth speed. Kevin rode his newly upgraded e-bike. Todd said that Kevin had added more engines to Bucephalus, and it moved spooky fast.

"What the…is he wearing a cape?" I asked.

"Yeah, he wanted two different disguises."

"But a cape, though? Like a superhero?"

"Or supervillain," Todd corrected.

The Kevin Shadow disappeared underneath the Sixth Avenue overpass, and a few seconds later, what looked like a homeless person emerged. The Homeless Kevin climbed the retaining wall while carrying a green rucksack. From the high, two-dimensional angle of the drone, it looked like was doing some kind of goofy exercise. I looked up from the screen to see Kevin in the distance, now on the ground level of the corner of Sixth and Speer. He was holding a cardboard sign, so if anyone drove by, he just looked like another homeless man asking for money.

Todd was watching the screen and said into his mouthpiece, "The coast is clear." Even in the distance, I could see a slight nod from Kevin. I changed my gaze from Kevin in real life back to Kevin via a drone from above on the tablet.

Kevin slid his rucksack off and looked around. He bent down and reached into the large sack. Kevin's movements mesmerized me. With the tension of wondering whether or not he would execute the plan, I didn't see the headlights show up on the tablet screen.

"Car approaching down Speer," Todd quickly said into his earpiece.

Kevin stopped digging in the sack and stood up. He held the cardboard sign back up and tried to look forlorn.

I looked up from the screen and watched Kevin in the distance holding the sign. The car stopped at the stoplight, full of late-night partiers. One of them rolled down the window and tossed Kevin a beer. Then he raised his arms in a V. It looked like he yelled in triumph for his buddies. I could see both on the screen and live that Kevin was tempted to throw the beer back at the dude.

"What's his sign say?" I asked.

"Fuck the man," Todd replied.

"Of course it does."

Kevin watched the car drive off and tossed the unopened beer into the grass. He pulled out a small wooden stepladder from his rucksack. He set up the ladder next to the traffic-camera pole and then reached back into the backpack and carefully pulled out a flat green tub—about six inches wide and long and three inches thick. Kevin walked over to the ladder and walked up the steps while holding the small tub like an offering to the gods.

Balancing on the ladder, he placed the tub on top of the large metal camera. The tub perfectly matched the color and shape of the camera.

Kevin reached behind the camera and slid a panel out from the tub. Then he reached up with his other hand and pressed down on the tub, fixing it to the camera.

The tub was filled with an acid solution that would slowly eat through the metal box of the camera and then everything inside. Kevin said the solution would take about two weeks to eat through the paint and metal to disable the camera. The delay should put the crime outside the save date of video footage from other cameras in the area. Even better, it would allow us take out multiple cameras in one night without alerting authorities.

They had made ten tubs at Maker. Todd, Michael, and Kevin had created them with the 3-D printer, using a plastic insoluble to the acid.

There were two different traffic cameras at Speer and Sixth. Kevin topped the other one with a tub and then put the stepladder in the rucksack and started walking toward Santa Fe Boulevard.

The images from the drones started to move as Michael and Jaden shadowed them after Kevin. I looked up from the screen and watched Kevin get smaller in the distance. The scene seemed sad—Kevin, dressed as a homeless person, walking off to chase some destructive fantasy. I remember wondering at the time what Kevin would be like in the future when we were all grown up. He was the smartest, most talented person I knew but also the most self-destructive. I had a strong feeling as I watched Kevin walk, carrying a heavy bag full of acid, that he wouldn't make it to grown up, but in many ways, he was already there.

I knew Todd was still watching the screen intensely, so I kept staring outside for a long time, just feeling sad, almost missing Kevin, or at least missing our childhood together. Out of the corner of my eye, I saw flashing sirens coming up Speer. I jumped up in my seat.

"Shit, Todd, cops, cops!" I said to Todd.

He squinted and looked closer at the tablet.

"No, no, there!" I pointed out the window as three cop cars flew by us and turned toward Santa Fe.

"Kevin, you have three police cars closing in fast with lights on but sirens off," Todd calmly said into his earpiece.

Todd's coolness under pressure surprised me. My heart was racing, and Todd was like mission control.

We both stared at the tablet, waiting for the cops to close in on Kevin, but they never did. Instead, I flinched back as if bracing for a crash. The drones fell to the ground. The image of the ground grew and closed in on the screen. And then the tablet screen went black.

CHAPTER 5

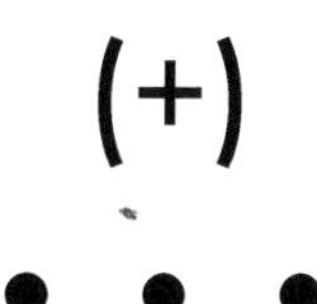

We deplane on the tarmac. Emergency slides are unfolded at the front and back doors, and we get to slide down to the ground, but it is not fun. We are scared. Soldiers are waiting for us. They tell us to walk toward a large group of teenagers standing by the water.

Deafening wails from jet engines surround us as planes land and taxi nearby. The wind is blowing cold and wet in our faces. We instinctively cluster in groups, shoulder to shoulder, to protect ourselves from the elements and the unknown. Our group moves in a solid mass as we shuffle forward toward the water.

We get to the waterfront and join a larger group of teenagers. From first glance, they look to be from other western states. I spot the words *Salt Lake City* on some clothing and see some letter jackets from New Mexico and Colorado schools too.

On the cement, near the water, we wait. It is starting to get colder. The sun is beginning to set and cast weird fallen flames of orange streaks through all the grayness of the sky, the water, and the dreary buildings. The ash hasn't reached New York, but a sullen gray shroud still covers the city.

Real flames from the mosque fires also crawl up the grayness in the distance. They look like tribal campfires spread out over a darkened horizon.

Finally, ferryboats show up in the distance and head our way. We walk through a run-down section of the tarmac to some shoddy old docks. We step off the cement and onto rough dirt paths. Random industrial junk is strewn about, leaving rusty stains bleeding deep into the ground.

We are instructed to climb rope ladders to board the ferry ships, and this takes a long time. I take my hoodie out of my backpack and put it on Vivi. Lupina and I sandwich her between us.

I look to Kevin for direction, but he looks zoned out. He stares off into the distance, at the multiple fires burning in the city. He wears his camping backpack while still clutching Vivi's pink backpack.

"Hey, man, let me take that," I tell him.

"No, I've got it. Why don't you just help Vivi with the ladder?"

We finally get to the ladders, and Vivi climbs without instruction or problem. I watched earlier as a couple of other kids freaked out toward the top and needed coaching to get over the rail. The portly racist kid got so nervous near the top that all the other kids below him climbed down so they could pull him and the rope ladder up from above. I take no satisfaction in this, and even Jaden doesn't say anything. We get on the ship and finally get some food—stale hot dogs and weak hot chocolate—but aside from the iodine wine, it is the first thing we've consumed since escaping East. I take a couple of bites and give the rest to Vivi.

After eating, we all join Kevin on the top deck. He is still watching the city mosques burn. Large buildings surround us on both sides as we head downriver. On our right, I recognize Manhattan. I try to remember where the World Trade Center buildings once stood, but I am not sure. In the distance, we can hear what sounds like gunfire and sirens.

"Out of the frying pan and into the fire, huh?" I joke.

Kevin actually laughs.

"Yeah, we're not going into that fire," he says.

He puts his foot on the lower bar of the railing and steps up to get a better view. He looks downstream. Everyone in our group and even in other groups on the deck is watching him. They too want to know his insights.

He points downriver and says, "That's where we're going."

"The Statue of Liberty?" someone asks.

Kevin looks back at the crowd and sees everyone staring up at him. A slight look of shock slides across his face.

"Ah, no. We're going to Ellis Island."

Kevin is right. We are interned at Ellis Island. There is no Internet and no cell-phone service. Rumor around camp is that the government shut down both because of the chaos breaking out around the country. Vigilantes are going after Muslims, and Muslims are defending themselves, but most of all, people are starting to freak out about food supplies, so there is a lot of looting and random violence, and the government is cracking down and cutting communications. There is even talk of both left-wing liberals and right-wing libertarians taking up arms to fight the government crackdown. It is apparent that part of the reason we are on Ellis Island is to keep us protected from the chaos.

Our group has taken a corner of a big, open part of a museum on the island. We are lucky, as we get to sleep inside on cots with blankets. There are tents set up outside as well. They handed out rucksacks, like the army one Kevin put the acid tubs in, which contain sleeping bags and some army clothes that don't fit many of us.

We are in the corner when a stocky young man in a suit comes up to us. Two soldiers with guns flank him.

He pulls out a clipboard and reads off Kevin, Michael, Jaden, and my name.

"Grab your stuff, and place it on this cot," he orders.

We grab our school backpacks and the rucksacks they gave us and place them on the cot. Kevin brings over his camping backpack and lays it on top. The suit nods at the soldiers, and they start going through the packs, with Kevin's first. They pull out and inspect each item and then place it on an empty cot next to them.

We are all interested in what Kevin has packed. Our tribe gathers around in a circle. I look up and see Lupina and Vivi. Lupina is holding her close. Vivi looks scared, concerned about the soldiers with guns.

Out of Kevin's pack, they pull a tarp, a cord, a gravity filter, a small camp stove, cooking utensils, dehydrated food, and plenty of cold- and wet-weather clothing. Funny enough, he also has his speaker box and a small bag full of hardware. The soldiers open the bag of electronics, peek inside, close it back up, and throw it to the suit, who catches it and places it in a small bag. When they reach the bottom of the pack, they pull out two intact packages of the cannabis chocolates.

One of the soldiers laughs and throws the chocolate to the suit. "Fucking Colorado," he says.

The suit catches the chocolate and grips it to his clipboard.

I look at Kevin. I expect him to protest, to tell them, "It's medicine." But he is quiet and cold, just staring down the suit.

The soldiers move on to the small sections of Kevin's backpack. They pull out a Leatherman and throw it to the suit. They pull out a medical kit, nightlights, binoculars, a GPS device, and a solar-panel charger. They find the bottle of iodine pills and look at it, perplexed.

"What's that?" asks the suit.

"It's iodine," Kevin replies.

The suit gives him a "So what?" look.

"It purifies water!" Kevin snaps. "Don't get out much?"

One of the soldiers smirks.

"Do you normally bring all this stuff to school?"

"I wasn't at school."

"Yeah, where were you?"

"I was sick."

"Oh. I see. And you had all this stuff packed, and you went to school when the alarms went off?"

"My dad and I are avid backcountry campers. We have go-packs ready at all times. When the alarms sounded, I grabbed the packs and went to join my friends."

The suit nods in a sarcastic New York way. I glance at the soldiers, and they look at Kevin with what seems like respect.

"Why? Why did you join your friends?" the suit asks.

Kevin's eyes scan the circle that has formed around him, from our squad to Annie and her friends to other East students and some kids others schools who joined us.

"To help them."

"To help them?"

"Yeah. To protect them," Kevin says.

The suit smirks. "Protect them? From who?"

"From people like you." Kevin stares down the suit.

The soldiers let out a laugh. The suit's face turns red. A vein engorges on his temple.

"Search him," he orders the soldiers.

The soldiers step forward and grab Kevin. They spin him around and throw him onto the cot. Kevin is bent over as they kick his legs apart. One soldier holds Kevin by the back of the neck while the other pats him down.

They find Kevin's epilepsy medicine and throw it to the suit. Kevin shakes his head in defeat.

I take a step to the suit and say, "What the hell is this about?" I place my hand on his shoulder.

He swats my hand away with his left hand and then jabs me with it hard in the chest. I stagger back a couple of steps. I feel the energy drain out of me when the fist hits my heart. I look at the suit. He has dropped Kevin's bag of contraband and the clipboard. His other hand grips the handle of his holstered pistol.

"Sit down!" he yells. "Sit down now!"

I plop down on a cot and look over at Lupina with embarrassment. Her eyes are wide, full of concern. Vivi is hugging her tight. She is crying.

"Here it is," one of the soldiers says. He holds Kevin's camping knife up.

The suit keeps staring me down and then finally looks to the soldier. The knife flies through the air, and the suit snags it. He puts it in his pocket and then picks up the bag and clipboard.

"Search the rest of their stuff," he orders.

They start going through our stuff. The suit throws me another mean look. I look at Kevin. He has gone over and started comforting Vivi. She puts her arms around him. He picks her up.

I start to think this is out of character, but then I remember how nurturing Kevin can be with Todd. Kevin carries her over to her cot, and they get out her backpack. He pulls out one of her books and reads to her as the soldiers finish searching our stuff.

They find no contraband in Jaden's, Michael's, or my stuff. I think we are done, but the suit says, "You four, come with us."

They escort us through the museum. Everyone is staring. We climb up some steps and are led to a conference room.

Leaning against the wall on the other side of the conference table is a middle-aged man. He too is wearing a suit, but a hardened look is chiseled into his face. A long scar stretches across his balding head and crosses the weathered wrinkles lining his forehead.

The soldiers come in, give him a crisp salute, and then exit the room and close the door. The suit tells us to sit down and then joins the man on the other side of the room. The suit takes the middle seat across from us. He lays out Kevin's confiscated stuff in front of him.

The man stays standing against the wall.

Kevin and the suit are sitting across from each other. The suit is smirking like a glutton ready to enjoy a feast. He takes out Kevin's knife and places it on the table. He spins Kevin's knife and then looks up.

"So, do you know why you're in this room?" he starts.

"Because you ordered us to come in here," Kevin replies.

"Do you know why I ordered you in here?"

"'Cause you're a dick."

The suit clenches his teeth.

"Get on with it," the man orders from the wall.

"You're in the room because of terrorist acts."

"Yeah, no shit. Someone blew up Yellowstone."

"No, not *that* terrorist act. I'm talking about the rampage last weekend, the destruction of traffic cameras before that, the terrorizing of suburban neighborhoods. We know about all of it. And you know what? You're going to jail, you freaking sociopath." He points his finger at Kevin and then strafes the rest of us with it, moving his hand back and forth like it's a machine gun. "All four of you are going to jail. All of your pussyfooted friends out there are going to be safe in refugee camps, but not you four. You four are going to rot in jail until the day you die."

I tense up and feel Jaden tense up next to me. Jaden starts to protest, but Kevin barks, "Quiet!"

He stares down the suit. "We're not going to jail."

"Oh, you're not? New orders: terrorists go straight to jail, no trial, no jury, permanent internment, you smug little fuck."

Kevin just laughs. "You keep using that word, *terrorist*. 'I do not think it means what you think it means,'" he quotes. "But I get it. You're also the type of idiot that thinks the Patriot Act was patriotic and that Citizens United united citizens."

The suit slams his hands on the table. Kevin's contraband bounces up. The flying contraband distracts us, and Kevin springs up.

By the time I look up from the table, I see Kevin has a gun pointed right at the forehead of the suit.

Jaden and I pull close to each other. We are in shock. I look at Kevin. He is pointing at the man against the wall with his free hand.

"Don't move," he commands.

The man is still leaning against the wall with folded arms. He looks perfectly calm, maybe even a bit amused. The suit is staring at the barrel of the gun—eyes crossed—and a stupid, petrified look covers his face. On the other side of Kevin, I see Michael out of his chair, crouched, ready to pounce on the man standing against the wall.

"You stupid little shit," the suit says. "You're going down for—"

"I'm stupid?" Kevin interrupts. "You're the one who brought a knife to a gunfight.

"So now," Kevin continues. "If I am going down, if I am going to rot to death in jail, then that means I really have nothing to lose. And if I have nothing to lose, well then, you have a lot to lose."

The suit looks like he wants to say something but doesn't. His face is in utter shock. If they know about all of our crimes, then they probably know about Kevin's history. And if they know that, they know Kevin isn't bluffing.

"Let me ask you something. Not you, you little shit stain. You, the man against the wall."

"Yeah?"

"You know what's coming, right? I don't mean today in this room; I mean out there. You know what's coming?"

"Yep."

"And do you really think these—what was the word, *pussyfooted*—do you think these pussyfooted kids can handle it?"

"Nope."

"So, do you think we should all die today, in this room, or do you think we should all die out there, fighting the fight?"

"Out there."

"Do I have your word on that?"

"Yep."

The suit twitches and turns his head slightly but doesn't take his eyes off of Kevin's gun.

"Good. Now, shit stain," Kevin says to the suit. "Give me back my stuff."

CHAPTER 6

(–)

• • •

I CRUISED THROUGH A RED stoplight on my bike without looking. A driver hit his brakes and honked at me. I heard muffled yelling through the car windows but couldn't make out the words. I gave a weak wave and continued to pedal down Sixteenth Avenue toward Lupina's house in Capitol Hill.

The events from the night before still garbled my mind. The three cop cars we had seen barrel past us were not going after Kevin. They were going after Jaden and Michael.

Jaden retold the story afterward. They had just been staring at their phones, tracking the drones, when three cop cars had come to a screeching halt in some weird triangle pattern that blocked off their exits. Jaden and Michael had looked up from their phones, and the cops were already out of their cars with guns drawn.

Jaden and Michael had put their hands above their heads and powered down their smartphones as Kevin had drilled them to do in the preplanning. That was when the drones crashed and Todd's screen went black.

The cops had kept yelling at Jaden and Michael to drop to the ground, but they just stood there, frozen. They finally went to the ground and waited for the cops, who then kicked their dead phones away and pinned them down.

Michael had started yelling that his dad was a lawyer, but the cops didn't care. They kept them on the ground until they had searched the backpacks and patted them for weapons or drugs. They found neither, so the police drove off without an apology.

Later, almost through tears, Jaden confessed to me that he thought the cops were going to shoot him like all those other black kids in the news.

Kevin was pissed when he found out. He was pissed that he couldn't go after the cops, he said. He was pissed that they had interrupted his master plan. He said he was pissed that the cops had targeted two young black students. But really, I knew what pissed him off most was not being in control.

We all decided it was OK to talk about the incident with others. Hell, we even broadcast it all over social media. We told a story that Jaden and Michael were just walking by themselves when the cops accosted them. We said that Kevin, Todd, and I weren't around. They even joked that if we were around, the police wouldn't have swarmed them.

On top of worrying about the police, I was also excited to finally have a date with Lupina. But I felt like crap that I couldn't tell Lupina the whole story. I didn't like starting our relationship off with a lie of omission, but Kevin said others could be wrapped up in our trouble if they knew the whole truth. We were concerned the cops would tie Jaden and Michael to Kevin planting four acid tubs on the cameras. Still, we decided to keep the tubs there, come what may, as payback to the cops for messing with Jaden and Michael.

This was all on my mind when I wheeled my bike up onto Lupina's lawn. She waited for me on their big porch swing. She had a warm smile on her face that seemed to sweep away my dark clouds.

"Hey, MatchPax," she said.

"Hey, Tinderella321," I replied while climbing the stairs of the porch.

"You ready for our big date?" she asked.

I smiled and nodded. "Yep."

The week before, we had joked about going on a date like adults, so we set up online dating profiles. We found each other's profiles and then sent cheesy pickup lines and lurid date suggestions. We had to lie about our real ages to use the apps, but then Lupina kept getting messages from creepy older men. The messages were funny until they weren't, so we deleted the profiles.

We settled on a bike date through the sights of Denver. In our fake dating-app conversations, Lupina was playing the role of a flight attendant coming in from Germany. My role was to show her around Denver.

"So, Fraulein, are you ready to see the Mile High City?" I said with a wave of my hand toward downtown.

Lupina stood up, grabbed the corners of her sundress, and did a curtsy. "Danke schoen," she replied.

I tried to come up with a witty reply, but my mind went blank. I could only stare at Lupina. The morning sun seeped through her dress, silhouetting her long legs and body. She saw me staring wide eyed and lowered her gaze. I remember her long dark hair falling into her eyes, highlighted by the sun and her blushing cheeks. She brushed her hair away and looked up at me. Her green eyes radiated shades of color in the sunlight that I had never seen before.

"Come on, cowboy," she said and reached out her hand. I took her hand and instantly felt heat like a lightning bolt go through my body.

We walked down the steps and around the side of her house to her bike. All of a sudden, I didn't want to go biking. I didn't want to have to let go of her hand and that heat. She was starting to slip her hand from mine to reach for her bike when I lightly squeezed. She stopped and turned my way. I didn't know what to do. I just knew I didn't want to lose her touch. Without thinking, I pulled her close to me and kissed her.

I felt and heard a gasp come from her breath as my lips touched hers. I started to worry that I was being too brazen, too forward, but she reached around to the small of my back, pulled me in closer, and kissed me harder. The heat between our bodies touching that way for the first time eclipsed the heat of our hands. I ran my fingers up her bare back and into her hair and moved my mouth and tongue to explore.

We were heating up even more, and I wanted more but knew we should stop. Her mom was home, and this was not the way I wanted to pursue the relationship. I think Lupina felt the same way, because we stopped kissing. We just stared at each other through heavy breaths.

She lowered her eyes and demurely said, "That was pretty bold for a first date."

"I'm sorry. I just—" I started to stutter, but she stopped me.

"Oh, Pax, no need to apologize. I've been waiting years for you to kiss me like that."

That did it. I was gone. Was it really possible that the girl I had been crushing on for the longest time felt the same way about me?

"Me too," I managed to whisper.

She smiled at me. "Can I get my bike now?"

I nodded and watched her as she turned, dress twirling in the air. I adjusted myself and went to the sidewalk to grab my bike. Lupina walked her bike down the small hill and joined me on the sidewalk.

"Vell, tour guide, I am veddy to see this city of yours," she said in a terrible German accent.

"Ha. Yeah. Let's go."

We hopped on our bikes. Lupina was riding a cute city cruiser with a basket in the front, which held her purse and sweater. I was on a mountain bike—the only bike I owned. It was not cute or convenient, but I figured I could impress Lupina by going down stairs and jumping curbs.

I jumped off the curb into the street and looked back. Lupina was still cruising down the sidewalk and did not look impressed. At the end of the block, she joined me in the street, and we headed toward Sixteenth Avenue.

“So, first sight on our tour is the Civic Center Park. Home of the Parade of Lights, Capitol Building, and 420 Festival—crucial in getting support for the legalization of marijuana in Colorado,” I said.

“Ah yes, I have heard of this news in Germany.”

We turned onto Sixteenth and met the wind in our faces. I noticed but tried not to stare as Lupina’s dress flapped up in the strong breeze. She patted it down and blushed.

We kept cruising down Sixteenth and picked up speed on the descent to downtown. Her dress frantically danced in the wind. I could tell Lupina was frustrated. The avenue was crowded with pedestrians and bikers, and she was embarrassed about showing too much.

I was frustrated too. I worried the bike date was a bad idea. I thought about other options. We could stop somewhere, walk our bikes, but I knew this would make Lupina feel bad.

“I shouldn’t have worn this dress,” she said.

“Oh no, I love that dress,” I admitted and realized that this could come out wrong, like I loved the fact that it was flapping up. “When I saw you on the porch, it was, it was the most beautiful sight I’ve ever seen.”

“Thanks,” she said. “But it’s not very practical for riding a bike.”

I nodded. We kept biking in silence until I got an idea.

“Hey, do you have any change?” I asked.

“Ah, yeah, probably, do you need to make a phone call? Do they still have those things?”

“Pay phones? I’m not sure.” I guided my bike out of the bike path and into a shaded spot in the parking lane. Lupina followed.

I put my bike on the grass and turned to Lupina. She was digging in her small purse. "How much do you need?" she asked.

"Just a couple of coins," I replied.

Lupina handed me two quarters. I knelt down while she stayed on her bike.

"Here, put your leg up," I said. Lupina put her right foot on the lower bar.

I slipped off the hair tie from my ponytail—or man bun, as my friends liked to call it—and shook my head. I could feel my kinky hair explode out.

I took the corner of her dress that she had used to curtsy and folded a quarter into it. Then I bound the quarter and fabric in the hair tie. This, I figured, would weigh the dress down and keep it from flapping.

"Do you have another hair tie?" I asked. I wanted to weigh down the other side, but Lupina didn't answer. I looked up to see what was wrong. She was just staring at me with a look of wonder on her face.

I suddenly realized that I was on one knee, looking up at her as if giving a proposal, *the proposal*. And in my mind, I decided right then it was a sort of proposal. That even though I was only seventeen, I knew this was the person I was going to marry.

I kept staring into Lupina's wondrous green eyes when I felt her thigh press against my hand. I looked down. She slightly opened her legs. I could see her long, tan thigh stretched out in front of me, and at the end of the view…wow. I felt my heart race as I traced my fingers around her knee. I slipped my hand to the inside of her thigh and slowly and lightly brushed my fingers up and down her leg, across her soft skin and taut muscles. I saw goose bumps raise and a felt a slight shudder against my fingers.

"Oh, Pax," she moaned.

I continued to trace light figure eights on her thigh, taking it all in—her skin, the light shining through her dress, the way her eyes looked at me.

"Say yes! For Chrissake, say yes!" a disheveled man with crazy hair yelled. He was cruising by on a goofy cargo bike loaded with groceries. He looked like a refined bum, intelligent and recalcitrant at the same time.

I was embarrassed. I had forgotten we were in public. I stood up and instinctively pulled myself closer to Lupina. I nuzzled into her and kissed her cheek when I heard the softest whisper, "Yes."

We traced our way through the Greek columns and fountains of Civic Center Park on our bikes. Lupina's dress barely flapped. We didn't talk much. Our hearts were racing and our souls swimming in *the proposal.*

Every so often, I would look to Lupina and smile. Smile returned, we continued biking through the park. True to form, homeless denizens were scattered around the park, and the smell of weed feathered into the morning air.

We biked toward the courthouse. "So my dress fix seemed to work?"

"Perfectly. You should move from stagecraft to costuming."

"I would like that very much," I said with a blushing smile.

We stopped on Bannock Street in front of the courthouse and turned around to take in the view. The capitol building with its large gold dome reigned high on the other side of the park. To the right, we could see the Denver Art Museum and Denver Central Library with their unique architecture. On the left stood the skyscrapers of downtown Denver, bristling with new construction.

"Not bad, for America," Lupina said in an even weaker German accent.

"Yeah, not bad," I agreed.

"Where to now?"

I thought about it for a minute and then stood up on my bike. "Here, follow me," I said. "I've got something to show you." I started pedaling toward Speer Boulevard and the Cherry Creek bike path.

"Look across the street. What do you see?" I asked Lupina while staring down at the water in the creek. I didn't want to stare too, and I definitely didn't want to point. "You see the traffic camera?"

"Um, yeah."

"Notice anything different?"

"No. What's going on, Pax? You look really troubled."

"Well, it's good you can't see it, I guess."

With this, Lupina took another look across the street. She shook her head.

"You see that little tub on top of the camera?"

"Yeah. Does this have anything to do with Jaden and Michael getting harassed by the police last night?"

"You know about that?" I asked.

"Everyone knows about that. It was all over social. Some people want to organize a protest."

"Oh shit. Don't do that."

"Pax! What is going on?" Lupina put her hand on my shoulder.

I felt a weight lift. She rubbed my back in small circles as I watched bikers pass on the crowded path below. They looked oblivious, happy.

I didn't realize how the stress bore down on me—from the night before, from the other nights out causing destruction. I felt tears start to form, but I didn't want to cry in front of Lupina. I looked into the thin, wide creek and took a deep breath.

"We've been doing things at night that we shouldn't be doing," I finally said.

I told her about the smokestacks, the App-It-Tight 4 Destruction, and the acid tubs. I relayed the full story Jaden had told about how the cops pounced on him and Michael and how he thought he was going to get shot.

Lupina took it all in. I was expecting to get admonished or at least lectured.

"Wow. That's crazy. How is everyone else holding up?" she asked.

It was an insightful question, one I hadn't really considered.

"Well, let's see; Kevin wants to go on some kind of vendetta against the police. Jaden was really shaken up about, you know, having guns pointed at his face. He called me crying this morning. Michael was superpissed. When he got back to the van, he attacked me. He pushed me up against the van and kept yelling at me, 'You still think I'm entitled, Pax! You still think I'm entitled!' Ha. Well, at least Todd is chill, but Todd is always chill."

"Wow. What did Kevin do when Michael attacked you?"

"Nothing. He wasn't there. He was still out planting the acid tubs. I mean, I guess Michael has a point. He has everything going for him. He's the son of a well-known CU football player. He's rich, good looking, and college bound, and he still gets harassed by the police for wearing the wrong clothes in the wrong part of town."

"Yeah, maybe you guys should just take it easy on the shadowplay for a while. You know, work on college prep and prom and dragons."

"Yeah, I agree, but tell Kevin that. Oh, speaking of Kevin, don't tell him or anyone what I told you. He thinks the more people who know, the better chance we have of getting busted."

"I won't tell anyone, Pax, and besides, we're kind of engaged now. I can't be forced to testify," she said with a sly smile.

I leaned in and started to kiss her again. I couldn't resist. Despite the story and the stress, I was just too enamored and excited about finally being able to kiss Lupina Alvarez!

We kissed above the heavy bike traffic on the bike path. I pulled back from her mouth and planted light kisses on her cheek, her ears, and her neck.

"Oh, Pax. This isn't fair."

"What?"

"There are all these people around, and I just want to throw you on the ground," she said.

"Oh." I didn't know what else to say. My mind started thinking about whose parents were home, but Lupina cut in.

"Music and ice cream," she said.

"What's that?"

"Always a good distraction—for whatever ails you—sexual desire or nightly destructions."

She reached into her basket and pulled out a small speaker box. She screwed it into a bracket on her handlebars and then synced up her phone. She started playing some weird music that I had never heard before—I'd never heard any music like it before.

"CocoRosie," she said.

"They're…they're interesting."

"Come on, big man; let's go to Little Man. I'll let you buy me an ice cream cone."

Lupina smiled at me, and we saddled up and started heading toward the ramp of the bike path.

CHAPTER 6

(+)

• • •

A FEW DAYS LATER, WE are on another plane. The plane is not a commercial airliner but a huge military plane. The plane is loud and cold and full of equipment. An hour or so after takeoff, we leave the seats lined along the wall of the cabin and huddle in groups on the floor. We nest with blankets and sleeping bags. Vivi and Lupina fall asleep intertwined. It's adorable. I think for a split second that I should take a picture and post it. Ha.

Kevin has his back against a big pallet of supplies. He looks to be in one of his isolation moods. He isn't sulking. I can just see the engines running in his mind at full speed.

Eva is next to Kevin, reading one of the books he got from the camp. She is quiet and doesn't interact with Kevin.

Charlotte and Fetien are mending clothes and blankets while Annie exercises.

Jaden, Michael, Danny, and I are playing poker. Some soldiers gave us a deck on Ellis Island. We are betting snacks.

The plane is stocked full of teenagers, soldiers, and equipment. We are grouped together with many of the same people as on the flight out of Denver. The three hot girls—Kelly, Becky, and their leader, Lily—are all flirty with the National Guard troops on our flight. Lily keeps looking over at Kevin with an angry-scared look on her face. She knows we know she snitched about the knife. The

National Guard troops are eating up the attention. They seem like twentysomething ex-athletes who never got over the glory of high school, but early success atrophied like their muscles and drive.

In contrast, a group of professional soldiers sits toward the back of the plane. They stay seated for most of the flight, sleeping or quietly talking but mainly just staring at the floor. They don't interact with anyone else on the flight. They remind me of the man from the conference room—the one who saved us from the suit—hardened and polished.

After losing too many calories playing poker, I get off my ass. They're right; my poker face sucks. I start stretching. I look over at Annie. She is still doing some kind of CrossFit routine. It looks exhausting. After she starts feeling her oats, she saunters over to Kevin.

"Hey, do you know where we're going?"

Kevin nods.

"You fucking cunt!" Annie barks at Kevin. "You knew, and you didn't say a fucking thing." She sounds aggressive, but it's just her joking style.

Kevin shrugs. "No one but Eva asked."

Jaden, Danny, and Michael get up and join others going over to Annie, Eva, and Kevin.

"Well? Where the hell are we going?" Annie says.

Kevin looks tired, burdened.

"Tajikistan," Eva intercedes.

"Ta-sheek-a-what?" Jaden asks.

"Tajikistan," she repeats and holds up a book. It has English and Russian words on it, like some kind of bilingual dictionary.

"Where the hell is that?"

"It's in Central Asia," Michael says. "They're sending us to a refugee camp in a Muslim country?"

"Ah, yeah, it's not a refugee camp," Kevin replies.

I'm afraid to ask. "What is it?"

"A colony."

There is a long silence as everyone grasps what this means. A massive terrorist attack, mosques being burned in the city, and now we are being shipped off to form a colony in a Muslim country.

I start to feel terrible, worse than I have since being whisked away from our school. It becomes deadly apparent: they aren't trying to save us; they're just using us.

"So. What's your plan?" Jaden asks.

"My plan?"

"Yeah, man, I saw you over here all Rain Man for the past two hours. What's going through that big brain of yours?"

"Oh, I was just calculating."

"Calculating what?"

"How much time we have until it all goes to shit."

Awesome. Even better news. I don't know if this is coming from Kevin's high intellect or his pessimistic view of everything. I look back over at Lupina and Vivi still sleeping on the floor. They look warm and comforting. I am in need of both, so I join their nest.

I spoon next to Lupina on the floor. I put my arm around her and place my body close to hers. With my free hand, I gently pat Vivi's head. She is still sleeping, facing Lupina and me with her arms wrapped in Lupina's. I feel Lupina instinctively nestle her body in closer to me like we're an old married couple.

I decide right then and there: it doesn't matter if we are going to a refugee camp or a colony or back to an ash-covered West. My one and only goal is to protect Lupina and Vivi. Kevin's right; the world is going to shit. The only thing we have is each other—my loves and even the Tribe of Iodine Wine. They are my family now.

* * *

Many hours later, we arrive in Tajikistan. We land on a barren airstrip next to an army base. We expect to be herded to the next destination, but we are put to work.

When the ramp of the big cargo plane lowers to the ground, an officer is waiting for us. Her long hair spills out from under her hat and frames parentheses around her glasses.

"OK. Let's get to work!" she yells.

I think she is yelling at the stoic soldiers, but they just walk past her with a quick salute.

"You, cherries, off your asses now, and start hauling out gear! Put your shitty belongings down on the tarmac, out of the way, and then start helping with the shit that you actually need. Move!" she yells.

We are shocked out of our stupor. We have been waiting around for a long time, not doing anything, and now we are told to work.

The National Guard troops are gathering their stuff and packing it into their rucksacks. We follow suit. While we pack our stuff, the NGs start throwing their rucksacks at our feet.

"Start with these first," their leader barks. He is older, with thinning hair and a paunchy face. The rest of the troops throw their rucksacks near us and go back to readying the pallets and equipment.

We look outside to the officer, but she is gone. I shrug and start to pick up one of their bags.

"No, don't," Kevin says.

I look up at him, and he is shaking his head.

"Don't start that precedent."

"Yeah, man," Michael jumps in. "They have nothing over us. If we leave their stuff on the plane, they will get in trouble with the major."

"Sure. I was just being helpful." I put the pack back down.

Kevin slides on his camping backpack and grabs his rucksack. He and Michael carry Danny's rucksack down the ramp. Danny is getting better on his crutches. But he waits on the tarmac and watches our stuff as we keep unloading.

I grab my backpack and rucksack and carry them outside. I place them on the tarmac. I see Vivi and Lupina coming down. Vivi is wearing her pink backpack. It looks out of place, but I think, "At least it doesn't have Kevin's gun anymore." I figure Kevin is still carrying the gun. The man in the conference room let him keep all his contraband. They even met a few times and talked while we were in camp. That's probably how Kevin knew we were headed to Tajikistan.

We are taking in the scenery from the tarmac. An arid wind strips the sweat off us. We look at the base. It looks more like a prison—surrounded by high wire fences interspersed with watchtowers. Functional concrete buildings are stacked up in the center, far from the first line of fences.

"Looks like Colorado," Danny says, looking the other way toward the mountains.

"Yeah, but the mountains are east, and the plains are west," Michael says.

"Good to know."

I look to the east, to the foothills and the mountains climbing in the distance. Denver always offered a steady reference point because of the mountains to the west. "Funny," I think, "we flipped to the other side of the world, and the reference point flipped too."

"At least there are mountains," Kevin says.

"Hey, dickheads!" The older National Guard leader interrupts our sightseeing. "You forgot our bags."

He is standing at the top of the ramp with a couple of his friends. The daylight highlights them ominously and casts misshapen shadows on the ceiling of the plane.

I look to Kevin, expecting him to say something, but Michael is the first to respond.

"Get 'em yourself."

"You need to understand who's in charge here, *boy*!"

I look at Michael. His jaw clenches hard at this for some reason. Does he feel the need to fill the antiauthority role for Kevin? He makes two fists and takes a step forward.

"The major is in charge, *Corporal.* Not your pudgy ass," Michael yells back.

The corporal puts his hand on the grip of his holstered pistol. He rambles down the ramp like some kind of cowboy. His mates follow him.

He reaches the tarmac and faces Michael. He is short and soft. I can tell that he thinks the threat of his gun should intimidate us, but Michael doesn't flinch, and Kevin is standing firm next to him. The corporal doesn't notice as Kevin slips his hand into his jacket. The corporal is staring Michael in the face and fiddling with his gun as if he's about ready to pull it.

"Allow me to interject," Kevin finally says.

"Fuck off," the corporal says.

"Here are your choices," Kevin continues. "You can disobey the major and leave your stuff on the plane. You can try to force us, which will also land you insubordination and an ass-whooping. You can try to pull your weapon, but I guarantee you'll be dead before you hit the ground."

Kevin flashes the corporal his gun. He looks shocked.

"Or you can piss off and carry your own bags. I suggest that option."

The corporal looks at Kevin and gives him a good, hard stare down. I can tell he is actually running the scenarios through his head and coming to the same conclusion.

"You faggots better watch your asses." He turns and walks back up the ramp.

"Interesting choice of words," Jaden says.

"Do we have to fight with every authority figure?" I ask Michael and Kevin.

"Nope. Just the ones that abuse it," Kevin says.

"It's better, in the long run, to stand up now," Michael adds.

After we clear our stuff and the smaller supplies, a couple of soldiers drive out forklifts to carry the pallets to the base. We follow them back and forth with the smaller items until the plane is clear. The walk is far—probably half a mile.

As we walk, many of the suburban kids mix with the National Guard. Altogether, there looks to be three to four hundred of them. The racist kids we tangled with at the airport give us sneers. Still, our group has grown too. Some Mexican kids from West and North High are walking with us. I see a group of Mormon kids from Utah, whiter than the suburbanites. They seem close knit and hardworking, but surprisingly, they walk with us too.

We have finally finished piling up all the gear in the hangar when the major comes back out on a golf cart; with her is a soldier carrying a machine gun.

"OK, children," she starts. "You will follow me to your sleeping quarters, and I will explain to you how things work."

She is walking backward while she yells to us through a bullhorn. We start to follow. Her voice is deep and loud. She is used to commanding attention.

"This is a Forward Advanced Civilian Colony. Due to the recent events in the United States, the government decided to construct multiple colonies around the globe for relocating people affected by the Yellowstone Caldera. Many of these colonies are in friendly areas;

most are not. The National Guard is here to help protect and run the colony. Other military personnel are here to project American power."

This is news to us. We knew that the eruption didn't release the wave of death and destruction that was originally feared. We knew our parents were still alive and dealing with the massive amounts of ash, but colonies for resettlement? Sounds crazy, but maybe our families can join us all one day.

"Your job is to help establish the colony," she continues. "You will be divided into different groups based on skill set and abilities and then given specific training as soldiers, nurses, cooks, carpenters, and so on. Once trained, you will work to secure and build the colonies so that someday your families may join you."

We have exited the hangar and are walking toward the other buildings, and everyone seems relieved to hear that our families may be reunited. I glance over at Kevin to see how he is taking this in. As he is never one for the stick or the carrot, I kind of half expect him to say something, but he looks unconcerned. I get the impression the major is not saying anything he doesn't know already.

"Once the division of labor occurs, you will meet at oh six hundred hours every morning to start your day of work and training. The expectation is to have this FACC fully functional and ready to take in larger amounts of civilians within one year. We need to do this while maintaining security and neutralizing threats outside our fence. Security is absolutely our number-one priority."

We arrive at the buildings, and she stops. "This is the female sleeping quarters. You can go set—"

"No." Kevin finally speaks.

"What's that?"

"No, ma'am. We are not separating."

The major shakes her head with a bothered look. I wonder if she received warnings about Kevin.

"With all due respect, ma'am, because of the prevalence of sexual assault in the military, we will not separate."

This seems to strike a chord with the major. She looks moved, almost even distraught, for a split second. She slightly shakes her head and returns to her stoic military face.

"Son, you cannot bunk together just so you can have sex anytime you want."

Annie jumps in. "I have sex with girls too. So separation by gender really wouldn't stop us."

There are a few snickers from the crowd, but the major gives Annie a considered look. It looks like she is actually thinking this over.

I decide to jump in too. Kevin is 100 percent right. I am not comfortable with Vivi and Lupina being far away from me at night.

"We are a tribe. We need to stick together," I say.

The major says, "Fair enough. There are four main barracks. Divide how you like. If you can't organize and divide up in an agreed fashion, I will do it for you."

CHAPTER 7

(–)

• • •

On the following Sunday morning, I woke up early. Actually, I got out of bed when the sun came up after tossing and turning all night. Since I couldn't sleep, I decided to retrace the same bike route Lupina and I had taken through the city the day before—down Sixteenth Avenue to Civic Center Park to Cherry Creek to Confluence Park to Little Man Ice Cream. It had been one of the best days of my life, but my heart was still heavy with the drama of our squad and Kevin's "appetite for destruction." Michael, Jaden, and I were going to discuss it at Maker later, but I wanted to clear my head first.

I felt a whirlwind of emotions stirring—a constant fear the police were just going to show up or Kevin would do something crazy, while at the same time I was totally, absolutely head over heels for Lupina. Her returning of my long-hidden feelings set my crush afire. I was up all night, staring at the ceiling, thinking of her while worrying about the consequences of our juvenile delinquencies. I finally felt I had something to lose at the same time I was at most risk of losing it.

I put on my headphones, blasted some heavy bass rap, and headed out of the garage on my bike. I was helmetless so that I could listen to the sound of music through my headphones while thinking things through.

I bounced my bike to the beat and hopped the curb onto the median of the Seventeenth Avenue Parkway. The parkway's large median was all lined with trees, branches arched over the split lanes. I had trained many hours for cross-country running up and down the dirt trails on the parkway medians of Park Hill. One of my favorite collections of memories was running up and down those medians as the arching trees changed across the different seasons.

On that day, however, I was putting my mountain bike to full use. I flew down the thin dirt trail. I jumped curbs at intersections and weaved around trees while I raced toward Colorado Boulevard. When I got close to the busy street, I noticed I could time the lights to avoid stopping. I was ahead of the cars on the lanes to my right, and I could trail behind the oncoming cars turning left in front of me. I stood up on my bike and sprinted toward the intersection. The light turned yellow as I got close, but I sprinted faster. When I reached the end of the median, I jumped off the large curb and landed in Colorado Boulevard. I sneaked behind a car turning left and shot diagonal toward City Park.

I could sense the stares of the idle drivers on Colorado Boulevard as I blasted into the park at full speed. It felt exhilarating to be reckless, especially as others watched. I started to see the danger appeal for Kevin. I wondered if he danced with destruction for other reasons—almost as if he wasn't trying to feel alive but was trying to feel death.

As I cruised into the safety of City Park, I decided to put the thoughts of Kevin and death behind me. I just wanted to think about Lupina and the kiss and her proposing legs. I pulled out my phone and started streaming Kishi Bashi's *Lighght* through my headphones. She had turned me on to him the week before. The music was quite different from the hip-hop or rap Jaden and I preferred or that depressing music Kevin and Michael liked, but the sound of looping violins and the singer's soft voice mixed well with thoughts of Lupina.

I took a slight detour up the path to the iconic viewpoint near the Museum of Nature and Science. I felt the rising sun on my back. The morning light cast an orange glow over the park, reflected in Farrell Lake, and lit up the skyscrapers and mountains in the distance. I felt a weird sadness similar to what had hit me when I had watched Kevin walk off into the distance the night before.

"Ugh, stop dwelling on Kevin," I thought. "Just focus on the beauty of the city, the view, and Lupina's music." I wished Lupina were with me to share the view and music. We had synced up music while chatting online a few times before—starting the same song at the same time. I realized that what I liked most about her was how she saw beauty everywhere, more like she bathed in the surrounding beauty. It was a corny thought, but I remember thinking that having someone by my side who shared the same sense of beauty in life—in music, in travels, in people, and in books—was probably the closest I could get to a soul mate.

I played this beauty fantasy in my head as I rode down the stairs and into the park and past the lake and the Martin Luther King Jr. peace statues toward East High.

I tried to imagine our long life together, a life filled with adventure and revelry but also quiet times of sharing a book or discovering new music together. I remember I played a future fantasy of us trekking through the mountains together, stopping to rest by a river, and just lying down to watch the clouds pass as we listened to music and the dancing sounds of the river.

As I cruised down Sixteenth Avenue, I thought about stopping by her house, serenading her with some cheesy eighties song, and asking her to ride off into the sunrise with me, but it was too early. I didn't want to come across as a stalker. And besides, I had to meet with Jaden and Michael and deal with Kevin.

I passed the spot on Sixteenth of *the proposal* and smiled. My heart actually started beating faster as I remembered it. I thought about the guy with the crazy Jewfro biking by and yelling at her to say yes. Maybe he was right. Maybe this was the best time to get married, before life wore us down, before time and failures turned us into loveless zombies like my parents or, worse, into broken, literally broken, people like Kevin's.

I finished the Lupina-Pax bike route and headed toward Colfax to meet Jaden and Michael at Maker. The music and the dreams of a future with Lupina were cathartic, but so was the exercise. I arrived at Maker, feeling clearheaded. I topped off the ride with a Lupina colada. I added some vanilla protein powder and took a sip as I headed back to the art garage.

"Damn," I thought, "this is really bland. Did Lupina just say she liked it to make me feel good?" I laughed at the thought of this.

I walked into the garage. Jaden and Michael were waiting for me. They were not smiling.

I thought, "Do I seem entitled for enjoying a smoothie after a nice bike ride through the city while Jaden and Michael were still freaked out about almost getting shot by the police?" They looked at me without saying anything.

"So," I said. An awkwardness hung in the air.

"So," Michael said. "You done with the fucking reindeer games?"

"Ah yeah, man, I was done before we started. Remember, I thought the other night was a bad idea. But the true question—is Kevin?"

Jaden looked at Michael and shook his head. "Michael? What did he tell you? What's this shit about getting revenge on the police?"

"Crap. What the hell does that mean?" I barked.

"He said something about a coup?" Michael said.

"A coup? A *coup*! What? He's planning on taking over the government? That doesn't make any sense, even for Kevin."

"No, I don't think he was talking about bringing down the government. I don't know what he meant. You know how he gets. He went on some rant, and I didn't understand half of it."

"Well, wait. Let's just ask this: do you think he is going to go all Columbine?" Jaden asked.

"Man, I can't see Kevin killing people, especially innocent people," I said.

"Does he think the cops or authorities are innocent? He told Michael something about a coup," Jaden countered.

"His dad has guns," Michael offered.

"Shit, I just don't see it. He's crazy, but he's not crazy in that way."

A loud noise rattled the art garage. We all jumped. I even heard a little squeal come from Jaden, but I was too scared to say anything. The large garage door started to move on rickety rails. Light poured in from underneath the raising door, divided by a large shadow. We all watched as the door opened. Kevin waited in the alley. He was holding a bike—an old one, not Bucephalus. The bike was laden with long PVC pipes, and he tried to balance it all.

"A little help, please?" he asked in a weirdly courteous voice.

I hesitated for a second and then went to help him with the pipes, all the time wondering what he was up to now.

I noticed a chariot connected to the back of his bike—the kind parents dragged their toddlers around in. Supplies spilled out of the chariot.

"I don't know what the hell you're planning now, but I'm done," Jaden said.

I carried the pipes over to the worktable, put them down, and looked back at Kevin. He had a goofy smile on his face.

"What are you talking about?" he asked as he wheeled the bike and chariot into the garage.

"The crap in the box. Whatever you're planning on building to cause destruction or whatever, I'm done. I was done when police stuck their guns in my face," Jaden snapped. An anger driven by fear boiled in him.

"First off, I am sorry about all that, and you're right. You're done. You're all done," Kevin said. "Second, I owe you a dragon. We're going to make a dragon. That's the 'crap' in the box."

Jaden, Michael, and I looked at each other, still skeptical.

"What about the coup? You still wanna bring down the government?" Jaden asked.

"What?" Kevin looked at Jaden. Then he smiled the biggest smile I had ever seen on his face. He looked at Michael and to me and shook his head.

"Counting coup?" he asked.

"Yeah, that's it. What the hell is that?" Michael said.

Kevin placed the bike and chariot against a table. He grabbed a stool and sat down. He looked at us with tired eyes, but a smile still spread across his face.

"You ever heard stories about Native American tribes, how they would sometimes best their enemies by sneaking up and tapping them with a stick, a coup stick, and then run away unharmed? It was considered a great act of bravery and prestige—more so than declaring war or going on a rampage. In many ways, they're right. It really isn't that brave to kill someone. I mean, they're dead; they can't come after you."

Kevin paused and looked at all three of us, one at a time—the big grin still on his face. "But to go after your enemy and embarrass him and give him the chance to come after you but not catch you—that is truly an act of bravery and skill. That is counting coup."

"So, you not gonna kill anybody?" Jaden asked.

"I'm not going to kill anybody," Kevin replied.

"Well, personally, I really didn't like cops pointing guns at me, but you do you then."

"Why?" Michael interjected.

"Why what?"

"Why you putting yourself at such risk? You're throwing away your future just to prove a point."

"Why aren't you doing more?" Kevin asked. "The criminal-justice system promotes eugenics, and you sit in your big house with a big smile on your face. But do you know what the biggest danger is to our society?"

I felt like rolling my eyes.

"It's not the systematic racism, it's not the surveillance state, it's not the militarization of the police, and it's not the rigged political system owned by the one percent. It's the fact that people are OK with it—especially young people. The biggest danger to our society is the overobedience of youth."

And then I rolled my eyes.

Kevin gave me a hard look. "In their youths, Pax, your father and grandfather wouldn't put up with this bullshit."

"Yeah, they also wouldn't be labeled terrorists and tried as adults."

"All the more reason to do it."

"Whatever, man."

I shook my head. I knew this wasn't right, but I was tired of arguing with Kevin and the paranoid logic he could twist to win a debate. Despite what he said, Kevin was still aiming for the kill. The smile and sophistry were just a facade.

"Can we just make a freaking dragon now and bring down the government later?" I asked.

CHAPTER 7

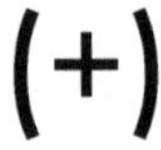

● ● ●

WE LOOK AROUND OUR BARRACKS and at each other. Three interesting groups decided to room together—the diverse kids from East, the Mexicans from North and West, and about twenty Mormons from Utah.

We stand in a rough semicircle, broken up across our divisions and the scattered bunk beds lining the walls of the barracks. We take each other in with slight smiles.

A nervous laughter breaks out across the group at the absurdity of the situation. A couple of weeks before, we were high school students, and now we are thrown together in dilapidated army barracks in some Central Asian country. The barracks, our new home. The tribe, our new family. At this point, the only thing we can do is laugh.

The major enters our barracks; with her are soldiers carrying supplies. She gives us a strange look, wondering what to make of the giggling, but she too starts to laugh or at least smile.

"OK, kids, I know it's been a crazy journey," she says, her voice softer than before. We keep laughing. She raises her hand to get us to stop. "Enough, enough. Look, there is a lot of work to do, but we decided to give you all a week to clean up and fix your barracks up before we start assigning roles. At that point, your work time will belong to the colony."

We stop laughing and watch her. She seems pretty cool, not your typical drill-sergeant type. And she did let us choose our barracks.

"We have only one bucket and mop for each barracks, and overall, our supplies are limited. You will have to make do. If you need anything, you can request it, but don't get your hopes up. The key here is improvisation and creativity. Think of it as a high school art project," she says with a fake flare of her arms.

I look around. The decor is best described as spartan filth. There are wooden bunks with old mattresses left over from the Tajiki army, and that's about it. At least soldiers are carrying in large bags of new sheets, blankets, and pillows. We have electricity, but there is no air conditioning and no running water, just outhouses and an outside spigot. I can see holes in the roof with pools of water damage below.

However, we have a good group for this—Kevin with his ingenuity and a bunch of stagecraft nerds, and I can assume the Mexicans and Mormons will work hard and work well together.

The major takes a final look around and nods; then she walks out the door. She turns around from the outside and yells back in, "Well, get to work."

Kevin instantly takes command but not by yelling out orders or plans. He introduces himself to the two other groups. He is not one to work a room or be social, so this is just calculated, a step in a process. He is somewhat revered around camp for his action at the Denver airport and the rumors about him standing down the suit. Everyone seems eager to shake his hand.

He goes to the Mexicans first and shakes hands. We all decide to follow and make introductions all around. There are about thirty teenagers in this group with a couple obvious leaders. They seem to command the respect of the others. Francisco, or Cisco, is their main guy. Clean cut and debonair with an intelligent and kind face, he goes back and forth between Spanish and English with an enunciation that is captivating in both languages. Hector is by his side. He is quiet with a mean, no-nonsense look on his round face. Hector is short in stature but built like a tree trunk. By his side is his girlfriend, Felicia, matching him in stature and stern looks. In contrast to Hector and Felicia, Paco is tall and lanky with poofy, unkempt hair—a Mexican version of me. A troublemaker's smile always adorns his face, a happy face with a smashed nose. He looks like a bundle of tight nerves wrapped around a wiry frame. At first glance, he seems affable, but there is something almost menacing in the bouncy and confident way he carries himself.

The Mormons come over and join in the introductions. They are a smaller group of mostly boys but led by another couple, Spencer and Ezra. He is of medium height with short-cropped blond hair, blue eyes, and a wide, welcoming smile. Ezra too is blond and blue eyed. She has a round, warm face and seems very social—almost too social, like the type of person you get tired of running into because it always results in a twenty-minute pleasant conversation. I am tempted to ask why they joined our tribe. It seems illogical, but this is a question best saved for another time.

As we make the introductions, Lupina takes hold of my hand. We are now an official couple, like Hector and Felicia and Spencer and Ezra. There seems to be a power in being together.

"So, one mop for one hundred people," Spencer says.

"Yeah, that's the government for you. One person working and ninety-nine watching," Paco adds, and everyone laughs.

"We should make a game of it. See who can mop a section the fastest," Spencer replies.

"I'll set a timer," I say and show him my running watch.

With that, Paco goes over to the bucket and opens a bottle of cleaning solution. He picks up a large container of water and tries to balance it while opening the valve. He struggles, and a Mormon kid helps him hold the container. Paco opens the valve and fills the bucket.

"So, who goes first? We'll set a timer on how fast you can mop a section," Spencer says.

"I'll go," Annie volunteers.

A collective "No!" comes over the East kids, and Annie looks pissed. I can see she is about ready to go off on some feminist tirade—fueled more by being told no in front of the new group. She doesn't get why we say no.

"You can't go first, Annie," I offer.

"And why the fuck not?"

"You will set the bar too high."

"Well then, you go. You've always excelled at mediocrity."

I give a nervous laugh. I walk up to the mop and bucket and look at it, making sure I understand how it works. I want to make a joke about Mexicans having an unfair advantage, but we don't know each other well enough to make racist jibes—like East kids do on the basketball court.

I grab the mop handle, dip the mop head in the bucket, and then squeeze out the surplus liquid. I put the mop on the ground. Spencer is holding up his watch, ready to start the timer. Everyone gathers around to watch me. I start to feel self-conscious. I look at Lupina. She has a proud smile on her face, and this relieves me. I see Kevin. He isn't smiling but busy hooking up his speaker box and phone. I put a free finger on my watch timer.

"Go!" Spencer yells.

I slap the mop onto the dirty floor and run it back and forth as fast as I can. I put my full body into it. I start shaking my ass. Everyone laughs. The Mexicans are yelling at me in Spanish with what I'm pretty sure are racist jibes. I dip the mop back into the bucket and squeeze out the dirt. The water blossoms clouds of dirt. The floor is filthy, but at least we have plenty of people to mop.

I start mopping again and decide to get more into the movements. I move my butt to the beat of Kevin's music—surprisingly a James Brown song and not some moody punk song. Everyone is laughing. I try to mimic the Godfather of Soul's dancing. A collective clap to the beat breaks out among the tribe. I keep up with the moves—spinning, pushing the mop handle away only to retrieve it right back with my foot. I then decide to go for it. I don't know if I can pull it off, but the crowd emboldens me. I do another spin and then stop and plop down into the splits. I pull it off. I am on the ground totally split, but I am stuck. I start laughing so hard that I fall over and can't get back up. Everyone else is laughing too. Tears are filling my eyes, but through them, I see Jaden run and slide across the floor toward me on his knees. He jumps up and then kicks up the mop handle and takes over. I watch from the floor still laughing. The view is surreal, like being backstage at a concert. The light floods around Jaden and breaks between the people in the distance, dancing and clapping to the beat. Unlike me, Jaden can sing the song to perfection.

Lupina comes over and joins me on the floor. I sit up, and we start clapping with rest of the tribe.

When the song finishes, a good section of the floor actually looks cleaner. However, we don't stop.

"Utah! Your turn!" Kevin yells out. He is sitting up on a bunk now and watching the revelry with a big smile. The speaker box rests on his legs. He fiddles with his phone and picks an old song from the fifties.

There is no hesitation from the group of LDS kids. Spencer steps forward and takes the mop from Jaden while his peers clap and shuffle in unison like backup singers. Spencer's dance moves are overacted with big arm movements and a pained face. He pours his heart and soul into the song. He twirls around the mop handle, steps up, and jumps off bunks. He ends the song on both knees singing to Ezra in a plea for love.

"Paaaaaco!" Kevin yells out. He puts on a song by The Smiths, "This Charming Man." Paco steps forward. He shimmies his hips and flicks his hair forward like a troubadour. Surprisingly, Paco knows the lyrics of the eighties song fairly well. He works the room—going up to all the pretty girls and serenading them. He seems to spend too much time in front of Lupina. She blushes and buries her face in my shoulder when he dips to a knee.

"Annie. Annie! You've been very patient, my dear," Kevin says at the end of the song.

Annie gives a bow. Paco stands up and goes back over to the bucket. He dips and drains the mop in the bucket and hands it to Annie.

Kevin starts "Girl Anachronism" for Annie. Annie plays well with the frantic piano, drums, and rapid-fire lyrics. Like some kind of crazy exercise, she manically bounces around the room, pole-vaulting up onto the top bunk and jumping to the other side and back through to catch the mop handle before it falls. She then weaves between people in a full sprint with the mop dragging behind her. People jump out of the way to avoid the whipping mop. For her finale, she sprints and then slides up to a bunk with four Mexicans sitting on it. She squats down and lifts up one side of the bunk very high. The Mexicans start to slide down to the other side, and they all yell out. The tribe erupts in hysterical laughter.

Kevin picks a song for Charlotte. When we first started the song and dance, she and couple others had cut up some rags and were wiping down the barracks. They too started watching when Lupina joined me on the floor. Charlotte, who seems so reserved, has no trouble dancing with the mop, which she does elegantly, waltz style to a Kishi Bashi song. The mop makes a very apt dancing partner as she glides around the barracks.

I watch Kevin. He is the true artist, selecting the right song for the right person and impromptu orchestrating the dance—in so many ways better team building than some empty competition. The dancing is a non-zero-sum game. How did he guess that Paco would know a Smiths song—an English band from the eighties? Or the right song to pull Charlotte out of her shell or Annie into her element?

Lupina interrupts my thoughts. She places her hand high up my thigh. I look at her, and she kisses me hard.

We start making out. With the laughter and Kishi Bashi in the background, the kissing becomes frantic and heated. Her hand moves up my leg, to my excitement. I start to caress Lupina all over and move my mouth to her neck and ears. She stands up and guides me back to our bunk.

We are kissing and stumbling as we walk between the beds to the bunk Lupina, Vivi, and I share—with me on the top bed and the girls on the bottom. Ours is in the corner, far away from the main area where everyone is dancing.

I remember that I didn't see Vivi in the dancing circle. She has been reserved and withdrawn since coming to Tajikistan. I think she really misses Mom and Dad.

I stop kissing Lupina and look at our bunk. Vivi is cuddled up in a little ball on the bottom bunk. She is gripping Elle, her tiny pink-and-green elephant blanket. She is lying on her side with Elle nestled in her arms between her knees and chest—a child within a child.

"Maybe now isn't a good time?" Lupina asks as I stare at Vivi.

I nod a yes and give Lupina a peck on the cheek. We hold each other soft and tight between the music and the dancing and the sleeping child.

CHAPTER 8

(−)

• • •

We unloaded and spread out all the dragon stuff—PVC pipe, bloodred fabric, wire mesh—tons of supplies across the worktables. We stared at it for a minute.

Nobody said anything. Kevin pulled out his phone and started streaming some of his depressing music to the speakers in the art garage.

"OK, Pax, how about you build the wings while Jaden and Michael build the body?" he said.

We gave a collective shrug.

"Pax, start by cutting the pipes into two four-piece sets, fifty-nine and thirty-four inches in length. Make sure you measure twice and mark it twice. There's a handsaw in the bin over there."

Kevin looked excited, almost happy. He went over to Jaden and Michael and put his hands on their shoulders.

"You guys ever make papier-mâché before?"

I went to work on the pipes while Kevin gave instructions on making papier-mâché. Then he started to build some kind of wire-mesh body cavity for applying the papier-mâché. After that, he attached the mesh and some connectors for the pipes to the bike.

Kevin didn't have any plans or drawings for the dragon. He drew it all out in his mind and spouted out directions as needed. I would have doubted the end product, but I remembered how he could do long division in his head in elementary school.

I have to admit; we were all enjoying the construction of the dragon. Like exercise, there was something cathartic about the creative process. We were smiling. It was almost like old times. Jaden especially took to the papier-mâché parts. I even started to dig the sound of the music Kevin curated. I guess there was a certain kind of beauty in darkness too.

"Pax, have you ever told Michael and Jaden the mannequin and M80 stories?" Kevin asked. His sly smile was back on his face.

I shook my head. "I know what you're up to," I thought.

Michael and Jaden threw me curious looks.

"Kevin, you're just trying to downplay our bad behavior."

"No, I'm not."

"What's the mannequin and M80 story?" Jaden asked.

"Stories. Kevin wants me to revel in the troublemaking of my forefathers to downplay the serious shit we're in. Isn't that right?"

Kevin shrugged. "They're good stories."

"Then you tell them."

"All right then. Have you met Pax's grandfather?"

Michael and Jaden shook out a no. They stopped applying the papier-mâché and watched Kevin intently.

"Well, just imagine an old Jewish hippie cowboy—where does he live again?"

"Cortez."

"Yeah, that's right. He lives in an old cabin in the desert southwest part of the state. He's been growing his own hydroponic weed since waaaay before it was legal and cool to do so.

"Well, once he was up visiting, and he told us this story of when he was a teenager, how he and his brother liberated a bunch of mannequins from a Dumpster by the old May D&F department store.

That whole summer, they dressed the mannequins up as pretty ladies and terrorized their neighborhood."

"And especially their mom," I added.

"Yeah, how?" Michael asked.

"They would have make-out sessions with them in the back seats of cars, legs hanging out the window; set it up half-naked, bending over in people's gardens. The final straw was when they snuck into their parents' bedroom and placed a dolled-up doll between their parents. They took a photo and then showed everyone in the neighborhood, claiming that their parents were swingers."

Michael and Jaden reared back, laughing at the thought of a Jewish hippy cowboy planting risqué mannequins around town and in his parents' bedroom in the sixties. I was surprised how well Kevin retained those stories. He had heard the tales a few years ago from my grandfather, stoned and halfway incoherent, around the dining room table.

"But the best part is when their mom demanded they get rid of the mannequins."

Michael and Jaden leaned forward.

"So, if you have to dispose of three mannequins, you don't just throw them in Dumpsters. No, you take those mannequins to Daniels Park. You drive to the cliffs above where everyone parks their cars to make out, and you line them up one, two, three; shoot them in the head; and throw them off the cliff in plain sight."

At this, we were all laughing, breaking the tension from earlier.

Finally, Michael asked through his laughter, "Wait. What about the M80s?"

"What's an M80?" Jaden asked.

"It's a firecracker. A big one. Totally illegal," I answered.

There was a pause, a silence as everyone looked at me to finish the story.

"M80s were my dad. One summer, his friend snuck a box of them back from Mexico. They also terrorized the neighborhood. They blew up newspaper boxes and school plumbing systems, blew school doors stuck shut. Oh, and tons of mailboxes met their demise that summer."

"And here we've been using baseball bats like a bunch of suckers," Jaden said.

"Yeah, like I said earlier, you do something like that now, you go to jail for a long time. Unless it's rape, the justice system doesn't mess around anymore."

"Especially if you're black," Michael said.

"Especially if you're black," I agreed and gave Kevin a look and a wink.

We went back to work. Kevin took the fresh-cut pipes from me and fastened them to clamps and then to the bike. The frame was complete, but Jaden and Michael were still slapping papier-mâché to the mesh.

Kevin grabbed the bloodred fabric and said to me, "Hey, Pax, you wanna learn how to sew?" A snarky look adorned his face. He knew I would want to impress Lupina by learning how to sew. He also knew I knew he knew this.

"Of course," I said.

At the worktables in the sewing area, Kevin spread out the fabric. "The first thing about sewing is you make everything inside-out to hide the seams, so you have to kind of think backward," he said.

"Cut the shit, Kevin," I said.

He stopped and looked at me. The smile was gone from his face.

"How did you know we were here?" I asked.

"Ah. We have tracking apps on all our phones, remember, in case shit happened at night. You can track my phone too. I'm not stalking."

I forgot about the tracking apps and already felt bested by him. That wasn't even the issue. The issue was the lie he had told Jaden and Michael.

"Whatever, man, not important. This plan of yours, this counting coup, it's bullshit. Jaden and Michael may not know you the way I do, but I know what's going on."

"Pax, who do you think I am? Do you really think I would kill people, especially people I don't know who have done me no wrong?" he said. He actually looked hurt, deflated.

I took a deep breath and stared out the window, out over Colfax. I wished Lupina were here. I could almost feel her presence at her favorite spot in the sewing area.

Kevin interrupted my thoughts of Lupina. "I just want to show the authorities, the police, that they don't have power over me. That they can't do whatever they want and walk around like they're kings of the world. I'm just going to hit them with paintballs. I swear to you, that's it. A couple of shots from my paintball marker, and I laugh as they try to catch me sporting away on Bucephalus. It's just counting coup. Honest."

I looked at Kevin for a long time and tried to think of an argument he wouldn't shoot down.

"It's not about that," I finally said. "It's not about the cops you are trying to show up. I mean, if you were so concerned about how the police treat black people—how they treated our friends—you would have come back to the van sooner to check on Michael and Jaden instead of messing around planting more acid tubs. And this whole appetite for destruction thing—that's bullshit too. It's not authority or society you're trying to destroy."

"Yeah, what's it about then? What am I trying to destroy?" he asked.

I looked him straight in the eyes and said, "Yourself."

He stared back at me for a long time. I swear I could see the pain. The pain of his mother's death. The guilt and shame for not liking her—for her not liking him since the day he was born. The pain seemed to pull down on his face.

"So you say," he said, but his words felt empty. "I guess that's my problem."

"Is it? Is it though? I actually think suicide by cop is pretty selfish. I mean, don't they have enough shit to worry about besides some punk kid with a death wish hitting them with paintballs? Do you think they want your blood on their hands? And what about your dad—hasn't he been through enough? Or Todd or, hell, even me?"

Kevin stared down at the table, at the red fabric spread across like a sea of blood. He looked tired and worn. "I just don't care anymore," he said.

He paused and looked at the floor with wide eyes and pursed lips.

"And all we can ever do is play counting coup with death. I mean, it's a zero-sum game we will never win," he said.

He turned to the front stairs and started walking away.

It reminded me of the night he walked toward the second set of traffic cameras—a dead man walking.

"Hey," I said and caught up to him. "You're just depressed, man. You never dealt with your mom in a healthy way—you know, like seeing a counselor."

Kevin stopped at the top of the stairs and turned to face me with a strange look. I could tell the wheels were turning in his head, like an astrophysicist trying to explain string theory to a toddler. He looked at me and said, "I appreciate your caring, Pax. I really do. But that shit doesn't work for me. Do you know what it's like for someone like me to sit down with the mediocre minds of psychoanalysts? I can explain things better than they can ever understand, and when I slice and dice and examine and explain my life, they think I am rational and healed, and I am anything but. And those drugs—those drugs make me into something less, something I am not."

"Keep trying. Find—" I started to say, but Kevin interrupted.

"Pax, I don't care. You're going to have to leave me alone on this." He turned and marched down the stairs.

I stood up at the top of the stairs and wondered what to do. I tried to think of what advice Lupina would give if she were with me. I knew the right thing was to not let my friend slip away. I rushed down the stairs and called after him.

"Kevin. Wait." I put my hand on his shoulder.

Kevin whipped around and punched me in the stomach—in front of all the customers, members, and employees we all knew. He hit me surprisingly hard and caught me unprepared. I doubled over and gasped. I felt a heave in my stomach and could taste the smoothie for the second time—even worse than the first.

I struggled to get up and look for Kevin, but he was already out the door, and I was too embarrassed and tired and hurt to care anymore.

Instead of chasing Kevin, I retreated up the stairs, still holding my stomach and shuffling my feet like a defeated old man. I reached the sewing worktables and sat on a stool. I folded my arms across the waves of bloodred fabric and buried my head. And then I cried. I sobbed like a child. The stress was all too much. I just couldn't take it anymore. I could feel my tears run onto my naked arms and down to the fabric. I stayed like that until the tears stopped, and then I sat up and took a deep breath.

I couldn't think about what to do next. Michael and Jaden were working in the garage and didn't know what had just happened. We couldn't finish the dragon without being able to sew the wings. And I was just sad and lonely.

I slipped my cell phone out of my pocket and called Lupina.

"Hey, honey," she answered with a cheerful voice, and I already started feeling better.

"Hey, you up?" I asked and realized it was a stupid question. "Um, I need your help."

"What's wrong, Pax?"

"Long story, but basically I am trying to make wings for a dragon, and I don't know how to sew. Can you come down to Maker?"

Lupina arrived five minutes later. Her long legs stretched out of short mom shorts and her oversized Kishi Bashi's *151a* album T-shirt—a picture of a girl riding a tiger while daydreaming—classic Lupina.

I smiled, but she only looked concerned. She put down her bag and gave me a big, long hug. She didn't say anything. She just rubbed my back and held me close. I melted into her warmth.

We stayed clasped together for a while until I pulled back and looked at her while still embracing. I just wanted to see her. I was amazed. I thought, "This girl I have known since childhood grew into a beautiful woman, and now she is holding me and staring into my eyes with love."

Getting punched in the stomach by a good friend seemed like a distant event. I wanted to kiss Lupina. I started to get aroused.

"OK then," Lupina said. "You said something about dragon wings?"

"Uh, yeah."

We pulled apart. I waved my hand at the fabric on the table.

"Kevin was teaching me how to sew, but I said he was depressed, and he punched me in the stomach."

"What?"

And just like that, Kevin was a looming cloud back over us.

I told Lupina about Kevin's weird, happy behavior when he arrived to make the dragon and then about his plan for counting coup with cops—how I realized it was just a suicide mission, and Kevin pretty much confirmed that.

"So what are you going to do?" she asked me at the end of the story.

I shook my head and shrugged. "What do you mean? I can't stop him."

Lupina gave me a hard stare. "Stop being so apathetic. If one of you were sick—and that's what this is—then Kevin would go all out to help you, and you know it. Think about how Kevin takes care of Todd, right? We need to find him. We need to make sure he doesn't get hurt."

I felt a bit chastised, but then Lupina stood up and offered me her hand.

"Are Jaden and Michael still in the garage?" she asked.

I nodded, and we walked to the back exit together.

We entered the garage, holding hands. Jaden looked up and smiled. He was still applying papier-mâché with Michael on the wire frame of the dragon.

"Hey, Lupina! Check out our dragon," Jaden said. "Michael and I decided to call it Rudolph."

"Where's Kevin?" Michael asked. He looked straight at me. "Have you been crying?"

I didn't know what to say. I felt embarrassed. Lupina gave my hand a gentle squeeze.

"About Kevin," I said. "You all know that his mom died while we were in middle school, before you two met him at East, right?"

Jaden stopped working on the dragon and looked at me. "Yeah, we knew that."

"Well, with his mom's death and then Todd's diagnosis, he kind of went crazy. He got heavy into drugs and went down a destructive path. He even tried to kill himself."

"What?" Jaden said.

"Yeah, his dad caught him right before he could hang himself, but soon after that, he was put into a hospital. He went through rehab and then wilderness therapy, but even with that, even with getting off drugs, well, he is still very depressed.

"So this counting coup, this going after cops, it's not about avenging the treatment of black people or showing up authority. It's just another suicide attempt."

Michael pushed a long breath through pursed lips. I could tell that I was confirming thoughts about Kevin that he'd had before.

"What should we do?" Michael asked.

"Find Kevin. Help him," I said.

CHAPTER 8

(+)

• • •

I STAND ON TOP OF the metal roof of our barracks with Kevin and Annie. The spring sun beats down on us. We are fixing the roof and waiting for the Mexicans to bring us more roofing material they are stripping from the outbuildings. We watch them and the LDS group at the outbuildings. We are not allowed to touch or even go inside one of the outbuildings, the one the LDS are working on. An officer is with them from the National Guard. I guess he is their leader or bishop. Even a couple of soldiers from another base near Afghanistan are up to help build and dedicate the building. They are creating a church or temple. I think they called it a mobile tabernacle or something. And non-LDS are strictly forbidden from going into it, even the soldiers.

We are taking turns carrying metal from unused buildings to patch and apply it to our roof. I went to check out the LDS building when Annie, Kevin, and I were gathering roofing materials earlier. Spencer, who is always nice and sincere, gave me a firm no. I cannot see inside. Ever. Well, unless I convert, I guess. My curiosity isn't that strong. Ha.

Paco, Cisco, and Hector are on carrying duty now. They pass by the Mormons and give a nod. Kevin, Annie, and I are on roof-patching duty. We alternate jobs to get rest from the heat of the roof.

Jaden and Michael are painting with others. Jaden has painted a triple MMM on the outside of the barrack. When asked what it meant, he replied, "Mixed Mexican Mormon," to reflect the makeup of our barracks—the mixed ethnicities of East High, the Mexicans from North and West High, and our odd little contingency of Mormons.

Another smaller group of Mormons are working on a garden around our barracks as well as their tabernacle. They are putting up a fence and even rain collectors that run off the gutters. I am impressed with how hard they work. They take few breaks despite the heat and work well together.

Lupina, Vivi, Fetien, and Charlotte are inside. They went to a local village with Kevin and Eva and traded for a bunch of cloth, and now they are decorating the inside with colorful curtains and dividers they are hand sewing together under Charlotte's direction.

The major gave us a week to fix up our barracks. Slowly they are turning from Spartan filth to something more hospitable and more… ours. We are nearing the end of the allotted week. Soon the military will divide us into our roles for training and work. We provided a couple of choices, but somehow, they will be making the final decision. I am worried about the division. It's not like I am making a career choice or anything, but I am leaning toward military, so I can learn to be a soldier and protect Vivi and Lupina. That choice comes with obvious risks.

I stand up tall and stretch my legs and arms. I am holding a water bottle and am tempted to pour it over myself to relieve the heat. But we are sharing the water, so I don't.

I stretch my neck and shoulders and look over at the suburbanite barracks. They seem to be competing with us. They started pilfering the unused outbuildings—except the tabernacle—after seeing us strip the roofs. They used garish colors to paint their barracks in what looks like school colors, as if we are still in high school. Around the outside, they put up CrossFit exercise stations. I don't see anyone working outside or even using the exercise stations. They are probably escaping the heat inside. The sun is brutal.

Another group of Mexicans are gathering and piling branches and sticks from a nearby pine forest. Cisco and Kevin came up with the plan to fix the metal roof and then cover it with pine branches to absorb the heat and provide insulation. A pile of branches already sits next to the barracks that we will have to apply, and they will be bringing more.

I sit back down on my heels, glad to have a quick break from working. We hammered in the latest patches and are waiting for Paco, Cisco, and Hector to bring over more pieces of roof.

Annie stands on the peak of the roof with her hands on her hips, looking off toward the mountains. She seems to take the heat pretty well. She is also used to running long distances in all weather conditions. Kevin and I are sitting on our heels, careful not to touch our hands or bodies to the hot roof.

"So, where's the ash?" I ask Kevin.

"What's that?" Kevin asks. He motions for the water bottle, and I pass it.

"The ash from Yosemite. It will make its way here, right? When is it going to come and start blocking the sun?"

Kevin takes a couple of gulps from the bottle. The roof shakes a bit as Annie walks down toward us. Like most, she wants to hear Kevin's insights.

"Oh, you mean the ash from Yellowstone," he says. "Not really something we should be wishing for, but it will probably start showing up in the next few days. It won't be as dark as the cloud we saw over the Rockies or even from New York, but yeah, it will cast a haze."

Cisco and his buds are walking toward us, slowly, carrying scavenged pieces of roof. Kevin looks toward them and back at me.

"You know, Pax, things will start to go pretty bad pretty quick," he says.

Annie is now standing on the other side of Kevin. She squats down, takes the bottle from Kevin, and downs a swig. We are a few feet from the edge, close to the ladder where they will pass up the roof pieces.

"Yeah," I reply with a nod.

"You're doing a great job with this construction. You have a natural knack for it."

This feels good to hear. Kevin is sparse with compliments, but then I get what he is trying to say. They are dividing us by roles soon. I told Kevin and others that I wanted to go the military route. Kevin is hinting that I should not choose military. He is concerned I cannot hack it. Funny, he's not telling Annie the same thing, and this bothers me more than it should.

"So, you're saying that because you don't think I should go the military route?" I ask.

"Yeah, I guess. Pax, we're in a Muslim country, and we basically declared war on Islam. And this ash you're asking about, next summer, there will be no summer. When the food starts to go away, everyone will be at each other's throats—here and at home. It's going to get really, really ugly."

"I know this," I say. I am angry. I stand up. "I can handle it. I need to handle it."

Kevin looks up at me through a squint and blocks the sun out of his eyes with his hand.

"That's not the point."

"It's not? You didn't tell Annie to go into nursing. You don't think I can handle it. I am sorry I was against the whole counting coup bullshit, but that was a joke, a fake danger. I have a reason to take risks now. I'm going military because I want to protect the ones I love. You can't persuade me otherwise."

"I know. I understand. But that's not the best way to protect." He stands up and looks at me, eye to eye. I glance between him and Annie, who is watching the exchange with interest.

"Actually, I think having guns and military training *is* the best way to learn to protect."

Kevin looks at me and then toward Cisco and his friends, who are walking our way. They are almost at the ladder. He breathes a heavy sigh.

"Not if you're dead," he says and takes a step toward the ladder.

I am in an office at headquarters, thinking about Kevin's advice. There's a weirdness to the headquarters, a strangeness that permeates all around. After sitting awhile, waiting for my name to be called so I can find out my role, I finally figure out what it is: the air. It is cooled, contained, and buzzing with heavy electronics. There are computers, air-cooling units, and other pieces of equipment all over the place—a lot more electrical output than our few spare lights in the barracks and no stifling heat.

The major comes into the office with an aide. I stand up, not sure if I should salute. They are assigning roles. We had to wait in a long line as they called on us to meet with the officers doling out the assignments. Once assigned a role, we exit out the back. I am one of the last ones called.

The major doesn't salute me. She just sits down and opens a laptop on the table. Her aide sits next to her.

"We have an interesting problem with you," the major says.

"Yeah, what's that?" I reply. "Um, what's the problem, ma'am?"

"The model has you selected for construction with military a short second."

"What model?"

She scrolls through her Toughbook laptop and then turns it toward me.

"Well, it's based on your grades, your cross-country times, your social profiles, and a bunch of other data—we calculated you are better served going into construction. But you did put your main preference as military, and since it was the secondary result, we wanted to give you the option."

I look at the screen, but it doesn't make much sense. I do pick out words like *Instagram* and *Snapchat* with scores next to them. It suddenly dawns on me that they were mining massive amounts of data to come up with those scores. I want to know more about this process, but before I can say anything, the major speaks.

"So, while we're not doing this with everyone, we want to give you the final choice."

At this point, the aide speaks up. He is a black man, older than the major. He wears a sergeant's rank and a kind face, but his eyes look hardened, worn, like many of the soldiers'. He leans forward. "Just to be clear, if you choose military, you may have to kill people."

"I understand, Sergeant." I am still thinking about what Kevin said. I am not bothered by the idea of killing people if it keeps Vivi and Lupina protected, but I am scared about their fate if I am no longer around. Who will protect them if I am killed in action?

"Can I ask you something? Who else is going military?"

The major flips the laptop back around and punches on the keys.

"It's not confidential information, so I have no problem telling you, but this should really be a decision you make on your own."

"I understand."

"OK, in your barracks, from your school…Annie, Michael, Eva, Danny." She names a few others, but I don't hear Kevin's or Jaden's name. I am surprised that Kevin didn't go military. I start to think that maybe he was right. The best way to protect our people is to stay alive and stay close. I just cannot believe Kevin didn't choose military.

"Kevin isn't going military?" I ask, wanting to double-check.

"Oh, he chose military," the sergeant answers.

"But the model said he shouldn't?" I ask.

"Well, it's a bit more complicated," the major responds. "The model picked him for military too, but we picked him for something else."

"Ah," I think, "they know that Kevin is too reckless, too antiauthoritarian to follow orders in an army."

"So, is he in construction?" I ask. Maybe it wouldn't be bad to be teamed up with Kevin, building the colony while staying close to Vivi and Lupina.

"Oh no, we chose him for leadership," the major says. "He and a few others will work closely with us and be trained in all areas."

I start to scoff at this but keep it to myself. It seems unbelievable. Kevin, who was on a crusade to bring down authority, is now going to be the authority. I balk at him and his pedantic advice.

"I'll go military," I say.

"You sure?" the sergeant asks.

"Dead sure."

CHAPTER 9

(–)

• • •

"WELL, CAN'T WE JUST CALL him? Tell him to chill out?" Jaden asked.

"He won't answer. But try. I'm going to see if I can track him," I said. I clicked the anarchy A and opened App-It-Tight 4 Destruction. The app Todd and Kevin had written could track all our phones.

"Straight to voice mail," Jaden said.

A map of Denver showed the three of us at Maker and Todd at his house. An icon pointed off the screen and got my hopes up that I could still track Kevin. I scrolled to the left. The map started taking me into the mountains.

"Huh. That's weird. He couldn't be in the mountains so quickly. And why?"

Lupina looked over my shoulder as I kept scrolling the screen into the mountains. It finally found the location icon, but it only said, "Dad."

"Kevin's phone is off. He's tracking his dad, Mark. He's probably on a bike trek or something. Hey, that reminds me. I still have a key to their house from when they biked the Colorado Trail together, and I looked after Mark's plants and stuff."

I started to get anxious. I was worried that my argument with Kevin had been too convincing. Telling him that suicide by cop was selfish could have caused Kevin to just go home and do it straightaway.

His dad wouldn't be there to save him this time, and we were probably too far away.

"We need to get to Kevin's house fast."

We left our bikes and the unfinished dragon at Maker and hopped into the Monte Carlo. Jaden floored the gas. We peeled out onto Colfax and past East High.

Lupina put her hands under her legs to protect them from the tattered seat.

"See, I told you the seats suck."

"Yeah, but if the seats didn't suck, you wouldn't have had duct tape," she replied.

"You talk too much, Pax," Michael said from the front seat without turning around.

"Eh, two-headed monster, I guess?" I replied.

Lupina gave me an apologetic look, but I just rolled my eyes at Michael and the whole destruction crusade. It was a stupid game, and I was done with it. Worse, the appetite for destruction had just provided a means for our depressive friend to end his life.

The Monte Carlo stuck a screeching halt in front of my house. I jumped out and ran in at a full sprint. I grabbed the key from my desk and started running back out before my parents knew I was home. I felt the adrenaline kick in and my heartbeat increase as I ran back to the waiting car.

"This is nuts," I thought. "Do we really want to find Kevin's body? Do I really want to expose Lupina to his death?"

I hopped back into the car and asked, "Do you think we should call the cops?"

Jaden violently shook his head no.

Michael turned around to look at me as if I were crazy. "What? If the cops are involved, they will find out about all the shit we've been doing, and we'll go to jail. Correction. Jaden and I will go to jail, and you guys will get off with a slap on the wrist."

Michael's words commanded silence, but after an awkward minute, Lupina broke it. "If Kevin kills himself, the cops will be involved anyway."

I reached over and put my hand on Lupina's knee.

"Well, let's make sure that doesn't happen," Michael finally said.

With that, Jaden pressed the gas down even further, and we barreled through the quiet residential streets of Park Hill, the lawns and sidewalks sprinkled with families doing yard work and playing in front of their homes. They all stopped to watch the Monte Carlo race by and threw cold looks our way.

"Careful, Jaden. Let's not make this situation any worse," I suggested.

To Jaden's credit, he slowed down, but we were close to Kevin's house.

We pulled up in front of the bungalow in North Park Hill. I took a deep breath and turned to Lupina. "You can stay in the car. You all can stay in the car. This is something I have to do alone."

Lupina shook her head. "No, Pax. We're all coming with you."

"I don't want you to see—"

"I can handle it." She looked a bit disappointed.

We all got out of the car and walked toward the front door. For a second, I thought that Kevin couldn't have beaten us to his house since he had biked to Maker, but he could have Ubered. Still, we were no longer rushing. It seemed like a somber procession to the front door.

I inserted the key into the door and paused for a second. I opened the door, and we entered.

Mark's house was devoid of any traditional feminine touches. I remember Kevin complaining a long time ago about how his mom really wanted a girl. They couldn't have kids after Kevin was born, and she resented him, resented his dad. He told me how his mom and dad once got into a fight about it when they thought Kevin was sleeping. She blamed Mark for producing a son. She was the glamorous girly-girl type, but even still—that seemed like a terrible thing to say. Honestly, though, I always thought she was a piece of shit. A year or so after her death, Mark sold the family home and downsized into something more affordable but still in the neighborhood. I never made the connection before, but the house was such a bachelor's pad, such a change from their previous home. The living room was filled with bikes and camping gear. A selection of topographical maps, tools, camping food, and laptops was always strewn across the dining room table. Dark woods, dark colors, and weird worldly souvenirs were the only decorations.

We stayed together in a close huddle as we went through each room of the house. Kevin's orderly room was a contrast to his dad's expedition storage style. Kevin wasn't there.

We moved into the kitchen. I felt chills shudder through me. I suddenly remembered that Mark had caught Kevin in the kitchen trying to hang himself. Then again, that was in their old house—a rope thrown over high, exposed beams. I slowly peeked around the corner into the kitchen and saw no suicidal shadows.

I looked at Lupina and exhaled. I started to think that Kevin wasn't in the house, that he hadn't gone through with it.

"We should check the garage," Michael said.

I looked at Jaden and Michael. I was starting to feel better, but their faces showed more worry.

"I can't see him doing it with exhaust. I know it's the easiest way, but it's not symbolic enough for him."

The garage sat detached from the house on an alley across the backyard. We stepped outside and onto the deck. Weather permitting,

Kevin and Mark ate most of their meals at the outside table on the shaded deck. Trees shadowed the deck and Mark's climbing wall. We crossed the backyard and opened the door to the garage. It was empty. We stepped inside and looked around.

We all breathed a sigh of relief.

Then Michael said, "Bucephalus is gone."

He went over to a large footlocker on the floor and opened it.

"And his paintball gun, mask, and cape."

"Great," I said. "So suicide by cop it is."

"I am going to call his dad." I pulled out my phone and called Mark. It went straight to voice mail. I hit the anarchy A app and checked to see if the Dad icon still showed in the mountains, but it was missing. I scrolled back to Denver and didn't see Kevin's icon either.

"His dad's phone is offline. He must be out of range now. Damn, we should have called him earlier."

"But what do we do now?" Jaden asked.

I looked from Michael to Lupina to Jaden.

"Rally the troops," I said.

I turned to Lupina. "Can you have Charlotte go over to Todd's house? Todd can track police scanners while Charlotte coordinates with us. Jaden and Michael can drive around by car, and you and I will stick to the Cherry Creek and South Platte bike paths, since Kevin is technically on a bike."

"Guys. It's Kevin." Charlotte's voice burst into my headphones. Lupina and I wore our headphones while biking on the Cherry Creek bike path. Michael was with Jaden in the Monte Carlo. We were all conferenced on our phones.

"Is he back on the app?" I asked into the microphone.

"Ah, yeah."

"That's great," I said. "We should be able to track him down."

"Yeah, but there's a reason why he has his phone back on."

"What?" Michael asked.

I shook my head, not ready for any bad news.

"He is livestreaming video," Charlotte replied.

"Oh shit," Michael said. "He's gonna get us all busted."

"Well, at least it'll make it easier to track him. Charlotte, where is he at now?"

"Looks like he just jumped northbound on the Sixteenth Street Mall."

"Crap," I thought. The mall was a long pedestrian shopping and dining strip with free bus service, lots of people, and lots of cops.

"And I'm not sure you can catch him. He's going really, really fast. He's dodging buses and pedestrians and oh! Shit!" She gasped.

I could hear Todd's faint voice in the background. "No, no, no."

"What? What happened?" Lupina yelled. Other bikers shot us weird looks, but I didn't care.

"He just shot a cop."

"*Fuck!*" Michael screamed into the call. Lupina and I both winced.

CHAPTER 9

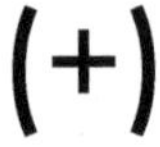

• • •

Two weeks into military training and we are bored children babysat by bored babysitters. We run and march and run some more. The National Guard just escort us along in their jeeps and look with resentment at us and at the professional soldiers who leave the base armed to the teeth in war parties of helicopters and caravans of Humvees. Sometimes the soldiers are gone for days and come back with wounds and war stories. The resentment of the National Guard as babysitters shows.

Even the training lacks intensity. Over the past two weeks, we have run and marched. Most struggle with this, but cross-country folk like Annie and me excel. I am impressed with her strength and grit. I feel bad about the comment I made to Kevin and her about nursing. She is a natural warrior and makes a point to beat everyone at everything.

Everyone else seems to be tired of the running, especially the National Guard, who don't even run with us. They just escort us along in their jeeps, watching out for the local armed militias, which we haven't seen in a while.

About a week into our training, we were jogging on the plains before it turns into the forest. We were all bored, and the lead jeep wouldn't let the faster runners run too far ahead. Annie, Paco, and

I and the two trail-running brothers from Utah were stopped and waiting with the lead jeep for others to catch up when we heard loud sounds crashing through the forest toward us. We were near a trail-head of an old, worn-out road. The National Guard, normally sleepy and bored, shot up to attention and manned their weapons. They thought it was an attack on us from the local militia. We'd had a few weak pokes at the fence in the first few days, but after the professionals beat the militia back, they considered our surroundings fairly safe.

However, when we heard the rolling thunder of trucks heading our way, we thought it was a surprise attack. The National Guard told us to get behind their jeep while they readied their weapons. Annie, though, took off for the forest. I went behind the jeep. I watched Annie disappear into the forest at the same time four or five Humvees came crashing out of the forest at full speed toward us. At first, I thought we were all dead. I should have followed Annie into the trees. But the National Guard relaxed their stance. The Humvees belonged to the professional soldiers out projecting "American power." As they flew by us, they fishtailed, kicked up a bunch of dirt, and called the National Guard babysitters. Our guards were pissed and sick of the babysitting as much as we were.

But today is supposed to be the first day of actual warfare training outside of the firing range. The ash has finally arrived and covered the sky with an eeriness even more sinister than the natural grayness that permeated New York. The ash silt slowly starts to cover everything with a thin layer. It even gets into our eyes and skin, but according to the military, it is low in radiation. Still, we take iodine as a precaution. I can't imagine what it is like for the people we left behind in the West—our parents and friends not *lucky* enough to be whisked away to a colony.

The major stands on the roof of the Hummer to address us. The sun sits behind her, veiled in the gray ash. A weak orange light blankets the sky all day like a giant lamp, as if we are inside some huge arena instead of outside.

"Soldiers," she starts, "we have decided to accelerate your training."

A hurrah comes over the crowd, but it seems weak coming from a bunch of teenagers. I take a closer look at the major's face. It shows no encouragement at the enthusiasm; she seems worried, stressed.

"Today we will conduct a war game."

Another weak "rah-rah" and she raises her hand in annoyance. Everyone shuts up.

"We will split into four groups based on your barracks. You will be led separately into the forest. Somewhere, in the middle of the forest, there is a red flag. The game is capture the flag. It's simple; the first team to capture the flag and take it back to their starting point wins.

"Now, the National Guard troops will escort you and will ref the game. They will be armed. You will be using your training rifles."

Someone starts to protest, and the major cuts him or her off immediately.

"Quiet!" she yells. "This isn't a game anymore."

I am tempted to say it technically is a game but keep silent. I have never seen her lose her cool.

"Now, when you come upon an enemy within range, you will yell, 'Surrender.' This exercise is about stealth and surprise, not blindly firing a gun. If you surprise your enemies, they are out. Period. The refs will judge the game. That's it."

With that, the major jumps down off the Hummer unceremoniously and then hops in and drives off. There is no "Good luck" or "Good hunting." She seems to carry the weight of other problems.

We huddle into our MMM barracks group and follow the soldiers to the edge of the forest. As we walk, we plan our strategy.

"Annie, Pax, set the timers on your watch," Eva commands.

"OK," I respond, but she doesn't say anything else. I start the timer and wonder what Eva is up to.

About one hundred teenagers went into military training. Our barracks is the smallest group. This is a bit worrisome. Many of the jocks from the suburban schools got selected for military. They greatly outnumber us.

Danny is still sitting out but gaining more mobility. Annie, Michael, Eva, and I are with Paco, Hector, and a few other Mexicans. I heard Cisco, Spencer, and Fetien are with Kevin in leadership training. There are also a couple Mormons in our group, the two tall and lanky brothers with longish sandy hair.

We decide to send out runners to flank or get to the flag. Annie and I volunteer to be the runners on the right flank. The Mormons will take the left flank. We will try to outflank the other groups by going far out of the way and then circling back around behind the enemy lines. Michael and Eva and the Mexicans will slowly and cautiously move forward while the Mormon brothers and Annie and I try to surprise the enemy from behind.

"Don't get killed, Pax," Paco jokes. "Lupina would be very lonely."

He says this with a smile, and I shake it off. They all seem to have a crush on her but have been respectful and even admiring of me. I feel proud.

And Paco doesn't seem like a warrior, with his ever-present smile and skinny frame, but someone said something about golden gloves, and his friends seem to pay him much respect.

"No worries, Paco. I would haunt her body as a ghost, Dia Del Muerta style."

"You ready?" Annie asks while shaking her head.

"Are you?" I respond. I instantly regret teasing her. I know she will set the pace and push me harder to keep up with her. We hear a gunshot in the distance. The game has begun.

We are ready to take off, but Eva shouts out at me. "Pax, how much time passed since we've been walking?"

I look at my watch. "Fourteen minutes. Why?"

Annie has already taken off, and I am eager to catch up.

"Annie!" Eva yells.

Annie turns around and starts running backward.

Eva points her arm in the direction Annie is running.

"Two!" She points left. "Three!" She points back the way we came. "Five! Go!"

I don't know what to make of Eva's weird cheer. But I nearly catch up to Annie. She has turned back around, and we are running parallel to the start of the forest. I look back over my shoulder, and the rest of our group has started to disappear into the forest.

We decided to skirt the edge of the forest for a bit. We will then head in and—we hope—come around the outside of the other groups.

I watch Annie run in front of me—like many of our past cross-country practices. Her impressive calves are hard not to notice. On her back is the training rifle. Charlotte and Lupina made us straps, which we attached to the guns so we could carry them on our backs and run unimpeded.

This helps, but I am still having trouble keeping up with Annie. The course is fairly clear, but her pace is just too fast. I reach deep down. I imagine that this is actually a war situation. Lupina is in danger and in need of help. "I need to save her," I think and dig deep.

I pick up my pace and catch up to Annie. When I am right behind her, she nods toward the forest and heads in without slowing down. The Mexicans who gathered branches for the roof explored the forest and told us the best route to get behind the enemy groups.

In the forest, I thought I would have more of an advantage with my long legs and trail-running background, but Annie blasts through the obstacles with ease and speed. Her short legs quickly jump the rocks and sticks in her way, and her shorter height makes it easier to duck the branches.

After about ten minutes of trail running, we are both battered and cut up. Annie keeps pushing on. I can see little streams of blood start to wrap around her massive calves. I look down at my own legs. They are scraped and bleeding too.

I am not sure what possesses Annie to push herself this way—through the pain and fatigue—but she is unrelenting. I wonder who it is she is trying to save. Herself? I think about her life—her need for attention, her playing with danger, and her appetite for destruction. She is a lot like Kevin. A darkness drives both of them.

She is farther ahead. She glances back. I expect her to stop and wait for me, but she picks up her pace. A few minutes later, she is gone. I am alone in the forest.

I start running faster up and over a small hillock and stop at the top. I am breathing heavily and trying not to double over so I can look for Annie, but I don't see her anywhere. I am on my own.

I check my watch. Only a couple of minutes have passed since we entered the forest, and Annie already ditched me. We are probably pacing at six-and-a-half-minute miles. Normally I run in the fives, but in the forest, we are slower. I take a final resting, big breath and start running again.

I am pissed at Annie for deserting me. She is like Kevin; they are both talented but too into themselves. Maybe that inner strength is part of what makes them great, but it is frustrating and honestly not good for the group in the end.

I reach what I think is a good spot to head left, toward the enemy groups. I turn toward the center. I slow my pace to more of a prance. I am trying to be quiet and efficient at the same time—avoiding branches and sticks and trying to step on rocks or hard dirt while at the same time keeping an eye out for enemies.

After a couple more minutes, I turn left again. My goal is to work my way back behind the other groups. I stop, hide behind a tree, and scan the scene. I do not see Annie or anyone else. I jog up a bit more to another tree, crouch, and look around again.

I continue this until I see a group of teenagers in the distance. They are slowly moving forward by having one person run up while the others keep cover and then join the advancing person. This is effective, but it will take time to move, and, more important, they are only looking ahead and not behind.

I quietly start to move forward on the unsuspecting group. My adrenaline pumps. My flanking strategy has worked. I am behind the enemy lines. My heart moves at a pace faster than when I was running. I feel like a hunter tracking prey. I sneak up to a large tree and stop, hidden behind it.

I undo the strap on the wooden rifle and slowly slide it off. I grip it in my hand and peek around the tree. They stagger movement ahead without covering much ground.

I look around for Annie. All of sudden, I don't want her to steal my thunder. I hope she will not pounce on the teenagers before me. I decide to go for it. I pick a line that looks easy and quiet. I take off in a fast run toward the teenagers. I am quiet stealth and fast fury. I feel like a Native American hunter and think back to Kevin's counting coup story. He is right; this is the grandest way to best your enemy. I close in on the group and watch intensely for them to move or notice me. They don't, and I get surprisingly close. I break out in a sprint.

"Surrender! Surrender! Surrender!" I yell.

They jump up and look back at me with scared looks on their faces.

"Surrender!" one of them shouts back. He is up ahead and ducked around to the other side of a tree.

"Nope. Nope." A ref dressed in camo comes up. He was watching the whole thing, but I didn't see him.

"He got all of you. You let someone sneak behind your lines, and you're all dead. Head back to your base."

The group gets up and starts jogging back toward their base. I recognize one of the taller racist kids from the airport. He is scowling at me. I just smile my shit-eating grin and wave. He looks back toward the ref and then puts two fingers into his mouth. I am wondering what he is up to, and then he whistles loud.

"The dead can't whistle," the ref says.

It's too late. The signal is out. His other group of friends will know I am behind their lines.

I look beyond the bested enemies. I see some rustling of branches way off in the distance. I hide behind a tree and keep a watch. I spot heads above the brush. There are too many of them. I lost the advantage of surprise. I decide that after wiping out their other squad, my best strategy is to stretch them out, make them chase me instead of going after the flag.

I turn around and take off in a run. I am following the squad I just wiped out. They started off jogging back to their base but are now walking with their heads hung low.

I go back into stealth mode again and sneak up behind the tall racist. He isn't expecting any danger. I break into a quick sprint and smack him on the ass with the flat part of my rifle.

He screams out in pain. "Ow, what the hell, man!"

I continue to run past him. "Counting coup, asshole!" I yell at him.

I head up further into the hills and hear him tell his friends where I am and that I am trying to circle back around them. My plan worked. I will just continue to stretch them out. If they are chasing me, they have no chance of getting the flag.

I am far enough away from them that I start to circle back a bit—in a wide arc to the left and back down again. I figure I am away from the action. There is no need to run very fast or keep quiet. I am moving at an easy jog when I hear the gun go off. The game is over. I know I helped contribute, but I am not sure if we won.

I start running faster, and with no concern about stealth, I make good time.

When I get to the edge of the forest, everyone is gathered. I can see by the smiles on our team's faces that we have won. I am elated. I look forward to bragging about my big move. When I get up to the team, they all yell for me. I smile but then see Annie. She is holding the flag. I guess she stole my thunder after all.

We are congratulating each other. I can't wait to tell my part of the story, about sneaking up on the group and then smacking the racist kid on the ass. I wonder if my moves allowed Annie to sneak through to capture the flag.

I walk up to Annie. She has her arm around Eva, and they are smiling. I feel happy for her too.

"Hey," I say.

"Hey," she says back.

Before I can say anything else, I notice everyone looking up at the sky behind me. The smile disappears from Annie's face. I turn around and see it.

A helicopter. One of ours, billowing smoke and trying to get back to base. It doesn't make it.

Despite all the previous running, Annie and I are the first to reach the crash scene. We look at each other with "Now what?" looks on our faces. The helicopter is fairly intact, but smoke and fire still emit from it. I take off my shirt and go up to a door that is slightly ajar. I wrap the shirt around my hands and try to pull open the door. I can feel the heat through my shirt. The door is heavy and stuck. Annie comes to help me. She too has her shirt wrapped around her hands. Together we grip the door and pull. It barely moves. I mimic Annie. I dig my heels into the ground and throw my back into it. The door flies open. I almost fall, but Annie catches me.

We take a couple of steps forward and look into the helicopter. Inside, human forms are present but disfigured and misshapen. We see blood and burned clothes but also hear moans for help.

I am wondering if we should go in and help, and if so, what we can do. I have no medical training. To my relief, the soldiers from the forest and other teenagers have joined us. The soldiers tell us to move out of the way. Annie and I step back from the helicopter, glad to be relieved of duty.

On the other side of the helicopter, jeeps from the base are closing in too. Medical staff jumps out of the jeeps and runs toward the helicopter. I see Lupina among them. I want to go to her. I am shivering and in shock, the sweat on my bare skin piqued by the wind. I cannot stop shaking. I want Lupina to embrace me, to warm me, but she is busy with the other medical staff, pulling bodies from the helicopter.

I start to get protective of her—wondering if handling the bodies of dead soldiers is something she should be doing. But I have seen Lupina be caring and strong at the same time. She is just built for this kind of thing.

I am still shaking when I feel warmth wrap around me. Michael and Eva have found Annie and me. They huddle us together and put their arms around us. It feels weird at first, but then I just surrender to the warmth, to their care. The Mexicans and Mormons from our group also encircle us.

We all watch together as the medical staff help two soldiers out of the helicopter. They are still alive. After carrying them out of the helicopter, they place them on stretchers. Lupina starts cutting away their clothes with big metal shears. Another nurse is preparing an IV bag while two doctors check for injuries.

Seeing nothing urgent, a doctor orders the two soldiers to be taken to the vehicles. Lupina runs with the staff as they load the soldiers onto ambulances, which then drive off back to the base.

She turns back around with a soldier and runs back toward us, carrying something. I can't make out what it is until she splits the black mass in half and throws one portion to a soldier. They are body bags.

I am thankful the teenagers on military duty are not required to help with the dead. A couple of refs from the forest tell us to march back toward the base. I put my shirt back on. It is torn and covered in black soot and grease. We break out into a slow jog back to the base. I look back over my shoulder at Lupina. She has disappeared into the helicopter.

No one says anything. There are no congratulations on winning the flag, winning the war game. I tell no one of my counting coup. I just focus my stare on the ground and try to get the images of the dead out of my head.

CHAPTER 10

(–)

● ● ●

A DEATHLY SILENCE OVERTOOK US. No music, no conversation, the noise of the outside world blocked by my high-tech headphones. I felt stateless. I glanced at Lupina to get my bearings. Her face was placid with equanimity. She gave me a slight smile.

Time seemed to freeze, but Charlotte finally broke the silence.

"Unless cops bleed white, I am pretty sure it was just paintballs."

"Thank heaven for small favors," I said.

"Oh! He just got two more. He is really flying. How fast does that bike go?" Charlotte asked.

"He put three electric motors on it. One on each wheel and one on the crank," Todd said. "He can get it over sixty."

"Holy shit. You guys should see this. He is punching gaps through cars at intersections without slowing down. Ah, he just hit cops four and five. He turned west. And just lit up a cop car."

"The police scanner is going crazy," Todd said.

"What street did he turn on?" I barked. "He's heading our direction."

"I'm not sure. He just passed the performing-arts complex and is heading the wrong way on a one-way street."

I turned to Lupina and said, "He's nearby. Let's head up."

We sprinted our bikes up the ramp to get to the street. When we reached street level, we saw a line of cop cars turn north on Speer Boulevard. They were chasing Kevin, but he split the traffic by driving between the backed-up cars. He took another right against a one-way street and headed back toward the mall.

"He's shedding the cops in the traffic and one-way streets," I said into the microphone.

"Nope, he just pulled a one-eighty. He's heading back to you two now," Charlotte said.

And just like that, Kevin shot back out from between the buildings and onto the sidewalk adjacent to Speer. He went against traffic and headed back toward where Lupina and I watched him from the other side of the street.

He had on his black cape and mask. The short cape flapped furiously in the wind. A red anarchy A flashed on the forehead of his black helmet. His paintball marker and hopper were fixed to the handlebars. He moved the marker to point right and started firing at the cop cars trying to get through traffic. He must have fired from a trigger on the handlebars, because both hands were on the grips.

Two cops jumped out of their cars and drew their weapons. Kevin turned around, looked at them, and then blended into the cars, covering himself with the civilians too close to him for them to shoot.

At our intersection, he turned right and flew by us. He lifted up his left arm and gave two fist pumps and then headed down the ramp to the Cherry Creek bike path. I gave Lupina a look that said, "Well, at least he didn't shoot us."

"He's heading down the Cherry Creek path," Charlotte said.

"Yeah, we can see him," Lupina answered.

"Where are Michael and Jaden?" I asked.

"We're stuck in traffic. I think there is something going on at the Pepsi Center, because we aren't moving."

"Great. That's where he's heading."

By the time Lupina and I headed back down the ramp onto the bike path, Kevin had disappeared from our sight, but we followed anyway. As we biked down the trail, cops ran to the edge of the street above. Their guns were drawn. They pointed them at Lupina and me. We slammed on our brakes. I lost control and almost spilled my bike but was able to stop. For a split second, I felt absolute terror more so for Lupina than myself.

The cops realized we were not the target and started to run north in a feeble attempt to follow Kevin. They busily talked into their radios.

"Holy crap. The cops just pointed their guns at us," I said.

I heard a scoff from Michael. "Now you know how it feels."

However, I was not pissed at the cops. I was pissed at Kevin. He had put us—put *Lupina*—in this danger.

I looked to Lupina. Her lungs drew a heavy breath, but she continued to stare down the path. She saddled up and headed forward. I had no choice but to follow her following Kevin.

Charlotte spoke up. "OK, he's back up to the street level, but he's not heading to the Pepsi Center. He turned east and is going back downtown. He's on Larimer now."

Lupina and I picked up our pace, but we were not very close to Larimer Street.

"I don't know how we can catch him. He's too fast," I said.

"You can't," Charlotte responded. "Oh no. He's going after civilians now."

"*What*?"

"Ouch, in the nuts. In the nuts! Wow, he is really lighting them up."

"This isn't funny."

"It's kind of funny. And besides, they look like a bunch of frat-boy douchebags."

"Where's he at now?"

"He just turned left. I think he is heading north. He's going even faster now. There aren't many people around. He's heading toward the South Platte Trail. OK. He's on it now. He's heading north. I think he's done. I think he's heading home."

Lupina and I headed toward Confluence Park, where Cherry Creek met the South Platte River. Our bike path coalesced into the South Platte River Trail. If Kevin headed north, he would leave downtown and the cops behind. Lupina gave me a hopeful look.

I felt good about the chances of Kevin surviving the night, but I started to worry about the fallout from his attack on downtown. Would the cops remember Lupina and me on the path? If they suspected Kevin, would they rope us in too, trace our phones? I could only imagine the cops throwing a ton of resources at catching the culprit who had embarrassed them.

My concerns were interrupted when Charlotte started yelling over the call. "Oh shit, he just went down! He just went down!"

I was about to ask where, but I knew he would be hard to place on the path via the video. I pulled out my phone and opened the anarchy A app. It showed Kevin's location less than a mile from Lupina and me.

"We're close," I said.

Lupina and I glanced at each other, and we both started to sprint down the South Platte.

"Michael, do you have his location?" I asked.

"Yeah, we're on it."

We arrived at Kevin around the same time. Michael and Jaden parked the Monte Carlo and ran down an embankment to the path. Kevin's bike and gear were strewn all over the place. At first, we couldn't see Kevin. I thought that he might have jumped up and run away, but in the bushes near the river, I saw something move.

The tall grass was shaking with a rustling noise. We ran to the noise and saw Kevin all dressed in black, shaking and all contorted on the ground. Kevin trembled, caught in the middle of a seizure.

I bent over, gently removed his helmet, and turned him onto his side. I wanted to make sure he wasn't choking, but I was worried that his back or neck could be injured. A fresh scrape slashed across his black helmet.

After he stopped shaking, Kevin rolled back onto his back and groaned. He lay there dazed. He stared up at us with a look of confusion and bewilderment. Kevin always seemed so present, so perceptive with his penetrative eyes. But he was just gone, oblivious.

He slowly started to come back. I've thought back to that moment and wondered what it was like from Kevin's perspective—waking up on the ground, body bruised and battered from the crash, and looking up the long grass to see Michael, Jaden, Lupina, and me staring down at him. The trees and branches above us swayed in the breeze.

Slowly, Kevin processed the events before the crash, the rampage through the city with cops in pursuit, the escape to the South Platte.

"Where's my bike? We need to move," he said with a voice still shaky and strained. He started to move but grimaced at the pain.

"Where are you hurt?" Lupina asked. She knelt down and took Kevin's hand.

Kevin lay there for a second. He moved his legs and arms and then said, "I'm fine." He got up, a pained look still on his face. "We need to go."

Michael and Jaden helped him up and started to walk him to the Monte Carlo. Kevin tried to go to Bucephalus, but they stopped him.

"No, buddy, you can't get back on that thing. You could have another seizure," Michael said.

"I'll take it," I said before realizing what this meant. "Let's get him in the car, and then Michael can take my bike, and Jaden will drive him to the hospital."

"I can't go to the hospital, man," Kevin said. "The cops will question anyone who comes into a hospital. Just take me home. There's medicine and a medical kit."

I wanted to argue but couldn't. It would be too suspicious if a kid came with road rash all over his body.

Michael and Jaden carried Kevin up the embankment to the car and laid him down in the back seat.

Lupina and I picked up the debris left from Kevin's crash. The bike seemed to be OK. I looked around for paintballs, but strangely, there were none. I checked the hopper. It was empty. "So he ran out of ammo," I thought and laughed.

"You know, if you get caught on that bike, they're going to think you did all this," Lupina said. She was holding Kevin's cracked phone and his mask.

"I know. I know. I didn't realize it when I opened my big mouth."

"And can you even drive that thing?" she asked, pointing at Bucephalus.

"It has pedals. I can ride it. I'll leave the electric motors alone."

Michael ran down the embankment and joined us. Above, we could see Jaden drive off, the lights of his car lighting up the branches overhead as he turned east.

"You sure you want to hop on that bike?" Michael asked.

I glanced at Lupina and saw a pleading look on her face. I could tell she wanted to ask Michael to ride the bike instead, but she didn't want to step on my pride.

"I'll be fine. I'm going to keep going north on the South Platte. I used to bike it a lot. It's dark and deserted, and the cops won't look there. You two should head to Kevin's fast and make sure he's OK."

"No, Pax. We will stay with you. You don't have to do this alone," Lupina said.

"Yes, I actually do. If I get caught on this bike and you two are with me, then you get busted too. I couldn't bear that."

Lupina started to protest, but Michael interjected, "He's right. And we need to get going. I don't know if Jaden can get Kevin out of the car by himself."

I saddled up on Bucephalus and then gave Lupina a smile.

"Be safe," she said.

"I will." I winked and started biking away. I stopped the bike and looked back. "Oh, and, Lupina, I love you."

"I love you too, Pax."

I faced forward and started biking down the dark path. Behind me, I heard Michael yell, "I love you too, man."

"Likewise, big guy, likewise."

Kevin and I called the northern stretch of the South Platte River Trail "World War Z." The path went by some of the ugliest parts of the city—a sewer treatment facility, a power plant, and an oil refinery. The smells were worse than the views. This ugliness kept the path bereft of spandex-clad cyclists and joggers, who stayed on the southern portion and the Cherry Creek path, but it also attracted a lot of homeless people who found a water supply and shelter under the overpasses. Growing up, Kevin and I liked to bike the path because it was so deserted, and there was something beautiful about its apocalyptic ugliness. We could even take our mountain bikes off the cemented trail and recklessly bike over a worn footpath that shadowed the river. It was a way for us to get some mountain biking in if we couldn't get a ride to the mountains or didn't want to bike the fifteen-mile trek from our houses to the foothills.

That night, World War Z was just dark and scary. I kept my headphones around my neck so I could listen for any sudden sounds. I felt at any moment the police would just pounce on me or someone would jump out from the bushes and take me down. For all the times we rode through World War Z, we never rode it at night.

I used this fear to power the pedals faster. But more than anything, I wanted to get to Lupina. She had just told me she loved me. I wanted to see her and hold her in my arms.

I was about three minutes into the ride when I decided to try out the electric motors. The bike was heavy, and I wasn't making good time pedaling. I slowly twisted the throttle on the right grip. The bike instantly surged forward. "This isn't so bad," I thought. I turned it more.

I started flying down the path, leaning into turns and curves. The bike was remarkably quiet. I could still hear the rush of the river and the breeze in the trees. It made sense why Kevin had gone with an e-bike instead of his loud, motorized dirt bike.

I could also understand what Kevin was feeling as he tore through the city. The power of being so nimble and silent and lethal at the same time was immensely gratifying. I found the trigger on the left handlebar and gave a couple of squeezes. Although empty of paintballs, the CO_2 still fired a crisp, empty blast of air into the night horizon.

I throttled the engines even more and felt my hair dance in the wind and the cool river air on my face. The smell of the city hit me—from the sewer plant and the refinery. I look back and think now how it smelled like burning corpses.

I reached the Sand Creek Trail in record time. The trail wrapped around the oil refinery between Denver and Commerce City. Always a weird scene, the views from the Sand Creek Trail took on a new light at night. The spires and intermittent lights in the oil refinery looked like alien architecture in the darkness. Behind the spires, the city sparkled and danced in the moonlight. At the top of a couple of spires, burning flames stretched out toward the moon, a slow, futile prayer for illumination.

I pulled the throttle and shot down Sand Creek and into the acrid burning smell.

I arrived at Kevin's house before Michael and Lupina. Kevin was sitting on the porch, going through his medical kit. Jaden opened the door and handed Kevin a glass of water. He took a long draw, emptied the glass, and then put it on the floor.

"Damn, Pax, you got here fast," Jaden said.

"Bucephalus, she's a thing of beauty."

Kevin smirked. He was opening a package of chocolate.

"After all that, and you just want some candy?" I asked.

"It's medicine. It has cannabis in it. It helps with the seizures. And the pain for that matter."

Jaden jumped forward. "You holdin' out on us, Kevin?"

"Kevin, I thought you were off of drugs?" I asked but felt like a nag.

"It's medicine," he snapped.

He broke off three pieces and popped them into his mouth. He chewed methodically and then swallowed. He looked up at Jaden, broke him off a piece, and then handed one to me.

"You took three!" Jaden exclaimed.

"It's really strong."

I popped the chocolate into my mouth and let it slowly melt. I figured I could use the stress relief.

Kevin was slowly peeling his clothes off when Lupina and Michael pulled up. Lupina jumped off her bike and ran up to me. She threw her arms around me and squeezed me tight.

She pulled back and looked at me. "Wait. You used the motors, didn't you?"

"Yeah. It was awesome."

Lupina just smiled and kissed my cheek. "I'm glad you're safe. I'm glad you're all safe."

We went up the porch steps to check on Kevin. He was still trying to strip off the multiple layers. He had on full downhill-racing gear, which had minimized the damage from the crash.

"Guys, you were just letting him do this by himself?" Lupina ran up and helped him.

Jaden and I looked at each other and shrugged. I watched Lupina help strip Kevin without a hint of jealousy. She was the nurturing type, and I felt confident in her love for me. She helped clean and dress Kevin's scrapes and cuts, and then we helped him get into bed.

Kevin and I didn't say anything to each other as he crawled into bed.

Back on the porch, Charlotte had showed up and was sitting with Jaden and Michael.

"Is he OK?" she asked.

"Yeah, he'll be fine. Honestly, I think the seizure wiped him out more than the crash or the escapade," I responded.

We sat on the porch for a while, enjoying the warm spring weather and recovering from the adrenaline-filled night. I was waiting for the chocolate to kick in, but I already felt more relaxed.

Lupina was sitting on my lap, resting on me when I felt her phone vibrate.

"I think you got a text," I said.

"Nope, my phone's in my purse. It's yours."

"My phone is in my back pocket."

"Oh." She sat up and pulled out Kevin's phone. We looked at it. The screen had a crack across the middle, but we could still read the message box: "Out of Storage. Video Recording Stopped."

"Oh no!" Lupina gasped. "I never shut off the recording. That means Kevin livestreamed us helping him."

"We're screwed," Michael exclaimed.

I ran the scenarios through my head, and they all ended with the cops figuring it out within hours after watching the public livestream.

"Should we bolt?" I asked.

"What do you mean bolt?" Jaden responded.

"The cops are going to figure this out quick, and then we all go to jail. I think we should make a run for it. Maybe head to the mountains or California or Mexico."

"What?" Michael said. "All we did was rescue our friend who crashed his bike."

"We conspired. We helped plan. We participated in nights of destruction. We knew and didn't alert the cops, and we aided and hid a criminal who assaulted multiple cops."

We were starting to get heated up when Charlotte stood up and said, "Dudes, calm the fuck down. Todd killed the livestream as soon as Kevin crashed."

Michael blurted out, "Well, why didn't you fucking say anything?"

"I just wanted to see how far you would go."

Jaden started to laugh. But Michael just shook his head. "Not funny. Not funny at all."

"Well, I could have let you take it all the way to Mexico."

We all started to laugh. Jaden and I broke out into a giggle fit. Everyone stared at us, trying to make sense of our unstoppable laughter.

"Oh yeah. Kevin has some pretty strong cannabis chocolate if you guys want a piece," I said through my hysterics. "What do you say we all get high and cast Kevin's counting coup on the big screen?"

Jaden went into the kitchen and grabbed a bunch of munchies while I sneaked a piece of chocolate to Michael, Charlotte, and Lupina. After I turned on the big-screen TV, I video-chatted Todd in. His mom, Sally, had put him to bed but fixed a tablet above him. He was lying down, looking up at the tablet so he could still communicate with us and watch the video.

Lupina put a couple of pillows on the floor in front of the couch, and we nestled in together. The stress dissolved out of me. Between the warmth of Lupina's body next to me and the body high from Kevin's medicinal marijuana, I felt better than I had any time since the night the smokestacks fell.

I pressed play on Kevin's phone and cast it to the television. I half expected Kevin to start by reading some manifesto or a suicide song, but the image that popped onto the screen was beautiful.

Kevin stood on the top steps of the capitol, opposite to where Lupina and I had been the day before. From the phone fixed onto the handlebars, we could see the barrel of the paintball marker point into the west. The sun had just slipped behind the mountains and cast a quintessential Colorado sunset into the broken clouds.

The barrel stayed fixed for a good five minutes as the orange and purple hues swam in the clouds and the final bright rays of sunlight faded into nothing. The sunset stuck with me—the final one I saw from Colorado. There was something about a sunset; it wasn't just the colors or the shades of light. We never look directly at the sun, and clouds hardly gain notice, but when the clouds shade the sun and dance the dance of darkness and light, the beauty comes out, and we pay attention. I watched the sunset reflect onto the screen, cast from Kevin's phone. I glanced around our group and saw the soft light of the sunset reflection bathe my friends' faces. I looked back to the TV and wall.

On the screen, Kevin pointed the bike down the steps. He started the descent. The big tires and shocks of his adapted downhill bike easily absorbed the bumps. When he got to the flat part before the final set of steps, Kevin gunned the electric motors and launched forward—clearing the final steps and landing on the sidewalk before the street.

A collective "whoa" came over our group. Kevin torqued the motors and flew down Lincoln Boulevard toward the Sixteenth Street Mall. He zipped past cars and then cut diagonally onto the bus and pedestrian mall.

"This is where we jumped onto the livestream," Todd offered over video chat.

Kevin darted onto the large median between lanes and passed a Mall Ride bus. He jumped back onto the lane and punched it. Charlotte was right; he was not slowing down as he crossed intersections. He would just aim the bike at openings between cars and shoot the gap. The speed and small length of the bike made it possible to squeeze through tight fits, but still, it was fucking crazy.

We all watched in fascination as Kevin flew down the mall. We could see on the edges of the screen the heads of pedestrians whip around to follow this ominous black shape on a strange-looking bike silently fly by them and then dart between the rows of speeding cars.

"Here it comes," Charlotte said.

Kevin slowed his bike a bit and careened back to the median. He pointed the bike at a cop standing by a kiosk and fired the paintball gun. We all flinched back as the cop absorbed the shots in a petrified spasm. Kevin cut across over the median and sped up. He punched through two rows of cars at the intersection, barely missing a collision, and then veered back toward the median, where he lit up two more police officers.

We watched the rest of the escapade that Charlotte had commentated earlier. Our group seemed to lean right and left with Kevin's moves and flinched back on the close calls. I even gave a little cheer when Lupina and I came on the screen for a split second, but then I realized in the video that we were watching Kevin with interest and hoped it wouldn't come back to bite us via the livestream.

Nevertheless, despite our cameo that might bring the whole police department down on us, I couldn't help but think Kevin had made a true work of art. It was terrible and stupid and a total pain in the ass to the police, but it was still a work of art. From constructing the bike to the plan to the ballet-like moves through traffic while hunting and being hunted—Kevin made a masterpiece, a swan song.

When Kevin reached the South Platte on the TV, we heard a strange noise from his bedroom. Michael was the first to jump up and go to the room.

"Oh shit. He's having another seizure."

I closed my eyes tight.

"What? He shouldn't. He took his meds, right?" Todd asked.

This was not good. As bad as Kevin had seizures, he would never have two in a row. Lupina and I got up and went into the room. He was shaking uncontrollably. Michael already had him on his side. At least he was in the safety of his bed.

I felt my head spin. I suddenly wished I hadn't taken the chocolate. It was so strong. I wished Mark hadn't disappeared on one of his trips. I wished, despite the masterpiece, that Kevin hadn't put us in a situation where we couldn't take him to the hospital. Finally, I thought, "Fuck it." That was his choice.

"Jaden, can you drive?" I asked.

"Yeah, man, I ain't no lightweight, Pax."

"Well, we need to take Kevin to the hospital."

"Crap," I thought, "another late night, and we have school tomorrow."

CHAPTER 10

(+)

• • •

We are back in the barracks when Lupina and the other nurses in training return from the main base, escorted by National Guard troops. The base is on lockdown. When the troops reach our barracks, they turn around and leave without saying anything.

I have waited by the door like a nervous parent for Lupina. When I see her, I want to run to her, but I don't. She looks tired, worn out. Still, she gives me a halfhearted smile when she sees me. I go up to her and reach out my arms to embrace her, but she stops.

"I don't want to get blood all over you," she says.

"I don't care," I respond and hug her. After a few seconds, she relaxes. We hold each other.

Charlotte joins us outside. She is carrying soap and a change of clothes.

"Let's get you cleaned up," she says.

I let go. Charlotte walks Lupina and the other nurses over to the outside spigot. Earlier, we rigged up an outside shower around the spigot. Kevin made the rods, and Charlotte stitched together curtains from old tent fabric. We also laid metal and rocks over a small trench to reduce mud, but the one spigot serves as our shower, drinking-water source, and clothes washer.

I leave Lupina to her privacy as she cleans up and changes clothes in the shower. The other nurses from our barracks wait for her to finish with Charlotte and me.

"She's too young to go through something like this," I say to Charlotte.

"Lupina will be fine. She is not easily upset."

"Good quality for a nurse, I guess."

"Good quality to be your girlfriend, I guess," Charlotte replies.

This takes me aback. Charlotte considers me a bad boyfriend? Does Lupina? I am not abusive. I am caring and totally in love with her. I give Charlotte a weak, pleading look.

She rolls her eyes. "Pax, if you want to be there for her, you need to let her be strong. Just because someone is nurturing doesn't mean they need to be nurtured; usually, it's the opposite. She is tougher than you think, and it's insulting to baby someone like, like, well, it's just mancaring."

"Mancaring?"

"It's like mansplaining but with emotions. You think a woman needs help when she doesn't."

"Did you just make that up?"

"It's from the Italian word *mancare*." She pronounces it *mahn-CAR-ay* but spells it out. "*M-A-N-C-A-R-E*, defined in Italian as 'to be lacking, to fail to keep.'"

"You're full of shit."

"Google it. Oh, never mind," she says and laughs.

Back inside, we pile spare blankets on the nurses and surround them in the common area. Lupina sits between Charlotte and me. I put my arm around her and rub her back, but she seems composed, strong. Everyone looks to her for news. I am distracted by what Charlotte told me outside. Am I mancaring for Lupina? It seems like a partnership.

When I am down, she is my rock, and I want to reciprocate. Should I stop rubbing her back? I wonder. I stop.

"Well, the two soldiers pulled out of the helicopter survived and will be OK," Lupina says with hesitancy.

I find Annie in the crowd. We give each other a shared look of relief.

"What's the bad news?" Kevin asks.

"Two other helicopters didn't make it back. All in all, twenty-four soldiers died."

A collective gasp breaks through the barracks. War has made its way to our base, our home. I look at Kevin. He is about to say something but shuts his mouth. Instead, he quietly gets up and leaves the group, leaves the barracks. I want to follow him, but I don't want to leave Lupina. Is this mancaring? Does she need me?

The group is quiet. Do they need me? It seems lacking without Kevin here, without his leadership and insights. In the circle, in the darkened barracks, I can hear a couple of kids crying from under their blankets—the only sound we can hear. The strung-out crying feels like a thread that once pulled would unravel us all.

I understand how they feel. This is scary as hell. We are in a foreign country far away from home. Outside the fence, there are people who want to kill us, and they just killed many of our soldiers—the toughest in our toughest machines.

The uncertainty and the lack of control are the worst part of it. We have no idea what's waiting outside the fence, what's going on in the rest of the world. We have no control over it. We don't even have guns. Maybe that is why I chose military, so I could have some semblance of control.

I decide to take control now. Charlotte's words are still in my head, but I don't care. The only known, the only thing we do have control over is our group, our tribe. I stand up.

"Look. No matter what happens out there, whatever happens to the soldiers, we have each other." This sounds weak, clichéd. I try again. "We are strong. We are a tribe." This is better, but I really suck at this.

"Pax is right," Cisco stands up and says to my relief. "We need to make a promise that no matter how crazy shit gets, we will be there for each other. It doesn't matter if we lose our protection; we will protect each other."

"From both those outside the fence and those within," Michael adds.

"We should make an oath," Paco says.

"A ceremony," I say.

"Like blood brothers and sisters," Felicia adds.

"I'm not cutting my palm," Charlotte says.

Lupina stands up. "On the plane, when we escaped Denver, we all drank water mixed with Kevin's iodine to help protect us from radiation. The military left us a big bottle of iodine in the medical supplies. That's what we have been doling out from."

She gets up and walks across the room to the office where we keep the medical supplies. On her back, a small smudge of blood stains her clean clothes. Even though she cleaned up and changed, I didn't. I look at my right hand, the one that rubbed her back. Smeared blood has stained the palm red. I wipe it on my pants.

Lupina comes back with the bottle of iodine and a gallon jug of water. She uncaps the water, pours a bit onto the floor, and replaces it with a healthy dose of iodine. The iodine goes into the jug with a dark-red swirl and then diffuses into the water. She gives another squirt. Before she takes a drink, she looks to the Mexicans. "Is this OK?"

They all nod their heads yes.

She looks at the Mormons. They seem a bit reluctant, but when Spencer says, "Go ahead," they all nod yes.

Everyone in the barracks stands up. We make a big circle.

Lupina takes a sip and then passes the bottle to me.

"To the Tribe of Iodine Wine," I say.

To my surprise, everyone repeats my words.

I take a sip and pass the bottle to my left, to Annie. I notice a smudge of blood on the outside, from my left hand. I forgot to wipe off my other hand. There is the blood of dead American soldiers on our vessel.

The vessel makes it around the circle to Charlotte. There is only a tiny amount left. I realize that Kevin wasn't part of the ceremony.

"Save some for Kevin," I say.

Charlotte nods and then takes the final sip.

We are done, wondering what to do next, when Kevin rushes into the barracks. He looks gone. He has that distant look on his face like when he is thinking through too many things at once.

"We need to leave," he says.

No one says anything. The comment is so crazy that there's no rational response. We all watch Kevin walk straight to his bunk.

"Leave what?" I finally say, wanting confirmation.

"Leave the base. Head to the forest. Tonight."

Everyone is in shock. As much as we are lacking control within the base, the unknown outside the fence is so much scarier.

As if to add an exclamation to his words, Kevin pulls out his backpack from underneath his bunk. It is still mostly packed, but he starts adding odds and ends.

"Kevin!" I shout. "What the fuck is going on?" I want to add "with you" but don't.

Kevin stops. He takes a deep breath and turns around. He is staring at the floor for a long time, and everyone is waiting for an explanation. He finally looks up at us.

"The helicopters were not shot down by Muslims," he finally says.

This sounds crazy, but then I think about it. Do terrorists have enough firepower to take out three helicopters?

"Then who shot down the helicopters? The Russians?" Michael asks.

Kevin just slowly shakes his head. It almost looks like tears are forming in his eyes.

"The Chinese?" Spencer asks. We are between both countries, so this seems plausible.

Kevin closes his eyes. I do see a tear escape and run down his cheek. He takes a deep, defeated breath. He opens his eyes.

"No. It was us. Americans. The civil war started."

There is a dead silence in the barracks. Finally, I can hear the LDS group whispering to each other. Spencer steps forward.

"What happened, Kevin?" he asks. His voice is trembling.

Kevin takes a few seconds to consider. He closes the opening of his filled backpack and then places it on the floor.

"There is a split back in the States between a war party—one that is establishing these colonies—and a peace party. The peace party was OK with colonies for resettlement of youth. However, some in the military started bombing Muslim countries in retribution, purposely killing civilians.

"The government tried to stop rogue military strikes, but then there was a coup, a real coup, and, well, civil war broke out."

We all take this in. It seems to make sense. Some people would seek revenge and take it out on innocents. Other Americans would balk against this and try to stop it.

"What side is our base on?" Lupina asks.

"Well, another base nearby was massacring local populations and wouldn't stand down. We sent our helicopters to take out their leadership and assert command over the smaller base, but they fought back.

They destroyed three of the helicopters. So, I guess you can say we are on the side of peace for now."

"So why should we leave?" I ask.

"Because it won't last. We are a target both internal and external. The war will spread here. Chaos will spread here. It's not safe."

Spencer and many of the Mormons have tears running down their faces. They cannot believe what they are hearing about the downfall of America.

"How do you know all this?" he asks.

With Cisco, Fetien, and Kevin, Spencer is also in a leadership role. However, this information obviously was not shared.

"I planted listening devices in the headquarters a week ago. They relay a signal via Bluetooth to some old phones we stopped using. The phones record everything. When Lupina came back and said three helicopters went down, I knew it wasn't from local populations. So I went and listened to some of the recordings. Hell is breaking out. Honestly, no one on the base knows what side others are on. They do not trust each other. That is why we need to leave."

I think about the Tribe. We just took an oath to protect one another. Will that oath be tested? Will we be able to survive outside the fence? How bad will things get on the base? Will we be attacked from the outside or torn apart from the inside?

The unknown outside the fence seems scarier. I have backcountry camped enough in the mountains of Colorado to know how much food and water is required to survive. Can we find enough for us all to survive? That's as big an issue as a civil war. It's even a bigger threat than pissed-off local militias looking for retribution.

And how can Vivi keep up outside the fence? She is just a child, and the hikes, the hunger, and the dangers outside may be too much for us let alone a small child. No, escape is a bad idea.

"Kevin, if the base is still on the side of peace, we should stay here and fight and not go run off into the wilderness to hide," I say. "Maybe escaping to the wilderness is a trait you inherited from your dad, but we are not safer there."

"If America falls, the world falls. What comes next—the brutality, oppression, savagery—that's the norm; that's the bulk of human history. We just kept it at bay. And when it comes, it will come for us with a vengeance."

I feel like the Tribe is watching us, as if locked into some kind of battle for our future, for our soul.

"Kevin's right," Spencer says. "Despite all the hate toward America, we are the ones who ended colonialism, fascism, communism. We kept the barbarians at the gate."

"This is ridiculous," I think. I am worried I am losing the battle. Kevin is being all pro-America, and the Mormons are eating it up. World War II has nothing to do with starving in the wilderness, and now they are siding with someone who terrorized cops.

"You're no patriot, Kevin. You destroyed traffic cameras and shot police with paintballs."

Many in the Tribe give a collective "Whoa."

I hear someone mutter, "That was him?"

This seems to have the opposite effect of driving people away from Kevin. They are impressed with his bravado.

"I did those things because I am a patriot, Pax." His voice is reserved, tired. "Look, you all have to make your own choice. I am leaving. Those who want to come can come." He hoists his backpack off the floor, spins it on, and then buckles the straps.

I decide to take a page from Kevin's book.

"The average person consumes three to four pounds of food a day. There's what, eighty of us? That's literally a ton of food a week. How many tons of food are you carrying in your backpack?"

I pause and then scan the Tribe, all watching us intently. More to them than him, I say, “Kevin, we aren’t all like you. We can’t survive outside that fence for long.”

Kevin looks at me. I can’t tell if he is disappointed or understanding.

“I understand,” he says. He walks to the door. Part of me thinks he is relieved we aren’t joining him. However, he turns around at the door and finds Michael and Annie in the crowd.

“I’ll keep in touch,” he says.

I don’t know what this means at first or why he’s looking at Michael and Annie, but then I realize he must have left phones for them. He is planning on keeping up communications with them using phones that will work with Bluetooth. Part of me is relieved that he will keep in contact, but then I wonder why he didn’t leave me a phone. They nod, and Kevin walks off.

And just like that, he is gone.

Second Story: False Flag

CHAPTER 1

Fetien

• • •

I AM A COLLECTOR OF secrets, often an easier task for someone quiet and reserved. People tell me things they normally would not tell others. They figure it is a one-way conversation. I am soft spoken and nice, so their secret is safe and barred from being used against them. In many ways, I am invisible, so their secret is not even a telling, is not even real. Being black, foreign, and female is a superpower. It can make you invisible and the center of attention at the same time. Invisible to people's concerns, to people's worries, to people's vision, but the center of attention to all their stupid little questions.

No, most Ethiopians are actually Christians (way before you Neanderthals converted). Yes, they are fine features (for a black person, you mean). No, I do not do anything to my skin to make it that wonderful color (my ancestors did all the work). Yes, you can touch my hair (can I touch yours?). No, I do not run marathons (yes, I do, and I would crush you).

Stereotypes are such a strange thing. They make you invisible and center stage at the same time, like being stateless. Americans see me as foreign, and Ethiopians see me as American, but to everyone, I am a curiosity or just nothing at all.

My mother was literally stateless, an Ethiopian born in Somalia before the chaos and disorder swapped countries, born in a true refugee camp, not this ordered, Americanized military base. She knows a level of hunger and want and secrets I could never imagine. But I have my stash of secrets.

For example, I know all of the Oreo Sisters have a huge crush on Kevin. I know Eva is attracted to his intelligence, his deep brooding, his need to be "saved." She followed his every move online and IRL with a whole crazy system in her head for tracking Kevin. To her, my superpower serves as a tracking beacon for Kevin's movements. She is always bouncing annoying questions off of me.

I know Annie is attracted to the challenge of Kevin, a notch on her belt. I was in the same room when Annie tried to hook up with Kevin at a party a few months ago. She failed miserably, and I felt ecstatic. I believed in my head that he shot her down because he was secretly in love with me. Unlike Annie, I keep my sexual desires well buried and hope Kevin recognizes this in his similar shyness. I suppressed a smile and sneaked away into another room when they broke out into an argument about sexuality.

My joy turned to confusion when Kevin blurted out, loud enough for me to hear from the other room: "You of all people shouldn't condemn someone for their sexuality."

What did that mean? Is Kevin gay? Was that part of his odd attention to the kid in the wheelchair? But I saw his sideways glances at me, his too-long gazes, like so many men drawn to my *exoticness*. I would have never guessed him to be gay in a million years.

I had to keep my feelings for him a secret. To press for an answer about his sexuality from Annie or Eva or, God forbid, Kevin would reveal my feelings, my wants, giving up my game of being the nice, quiet one who did not want or demand anything.

A week after the failed hookup, I overheard the truth. I was the usual spectator in a conversation between Annie and Eva. Annie said that Kevin is not gay or even bisexual like her. Kevin told Annie he was asexual. Asexual—I was not 100 percent sure what that meant. When I Googled it later, it seemed impossible, especially for a male. But in the end, it just made us want him even more.

So, for me, sneaking outside the fence is a way to train my run and to look for Kevin. Another secret: I can outrun Annie and Pax. Not even Annie knows my true pace. She knows that I am a marathoner and that my father was an accomplished marathoner. However, she does not know I took up the mantle because he wanted it passed on to his son, my brother. She does not know that what drives me is a fire fiercer than hers. And she does not know that even in a quick cross-country race, I would beat her.

When Kevin disappeared a week ago, I used my invisibility superpower to follow him outside unnoticed. As he jogged toward the fence, he turned back to see if he was being followed, to see me. He stopped, smiled, and gave a knowing wave. I froze. Part of me wanted to follow him into the woods, but it seemed so sudden a decision for a person so quiet and reserved like me. And I lacked all my stuff. But I should have actioned my want. I should have followed Kevin into the forest right then and there.

But I just watched him turn around and resume his jog toward the fence. I watched as he found the cut in the wire fence and pushed his backpack and then himself through. I marked the tear in the fence and the spot in the forest where he disappeared. Then I went back inside and joined the Tribe of Iodine Wine.

But now I follow his path early every morning. I am slashing my way through the forest at a slower, uneven pace, but it feels rebelliously fast with risk. My feet have taken on a new nimbleness since coming to Tajikistan. I was not used to running in the forest. I was not a trail runner like Annie, Pax, or those brothers from Utah, Sam and Seth. But I like it, a combination of playing chess and running at the same time. The trees and rocks and branches are enemies standing in my way, training me to quickly find a line and maneuver around. You really have to pay attention.

But I can still think through thoughts while I run. I can still work the heap of clay in my mind until it is soft and pliable and solvable. I think of my family back in Colorado as I run—a problem impossible for me to solve. We have heard no word since the helicopters went down over a week ago. No word really since the civil war started before that. My brother was attending the University of Colorado. I hope he made it back down from Boulder to be with our family, to be with our community. There is a large, tightly knit contingent of Ethiopians in Denver, but with the chaos, with many bigots wrongly assuming we are Muslims, they are a target. And I have no idea if they are safe.

I push this thought out of my mind and increase my pace to danger level, crashing through the small branches and bramble with no concern for my safety. I can feel slight slashes on my legs and arms but run through it. Problems either need to be solved or used to make you stronger.

My heart races even more. In the distance, I see the end of the forest, the start of the plain, and further on, the fence. On this run, I am no longer looking for Kevin, but I need this hope to hang on to, to dampen the embers of worry about my family's safety, about my safety.

In my fantasy brain, I am with Kevin. Even though I have seen no evidence of him, I pretend I found him in the forest, and we became partners, lovers. He is teaching me survival camping skills, and I teach him how to hunt. We are like a hunter and huntress on the African plain, oh my. As I rush toward the forest end, I am flushing out a deer into the open, toward a cliff trap where I will tire the deer and Kevin will come in for the kill. "That's more than three to four pounds of food per day, right, Pax?" I narrate in my own made-up story, still mad at that pompous turd for pushing Kevin away without a chance for me to join him.

I blast out into the open. With no barriers, I increase my pace to my fast marathon speed. I can run a sub-three. Not many people know that. I increase my pace even more, chasing my fantasy deer, being chased by my fantasy Kevin.

The sun is bright and in my eyes. As usual, I sneaked out of the base before sunrise, but I am exiting the forest to a hot sun despite the haze. The dry heat is similar to what I remember in my home country, similar to Colorado for that matter—a high-altitude, bright heat with an extra sharpness even after the volcano exploded and the ash shrouded us all.

Since the helicopters went down, we no longer have to train in our leadership roles with the officers. I kind of miss it. I was honored and completely surprised to be selected as a leader. They knew my marathon times; they knew my intelligence and my secrets. Being selected opened my eyes to a whole other possibility. Maybe I should never be the one who wants quietly, the one who is reserved and nice, relegated to a secondary position for women, like my father and uncles assume, relegated to an invisible curiosity by American peers who assume they should speak up first, assume they should be in charge. The American military, the most powerful force in the history of the world, revered and feared by all my relatives, said I was a leader, said I should be in charge. What a badge of honor. What a freedom. So I will speak louder. I will run even harder, faster, stronger. I will find Kevin.

But not today. After ten miles of forest running, I am back on the openness of the plain. Out of the trees, I open my gait and glide back toward the fence, back toward the barracks.

Most of the teenagers have reverted to sleeping in. My superpowers are not needed to sneak out now or even sneak back in. I just need to be quiet and avoid Annie or Pax, who still get up early and separately run their short, boring laps around the inside of the fence.

I see no sign of them at the fence near me, so I nimbly slip through the tear Kevin made and jog toward our barracks. Then I see them by the outbuildings, Annie and Pax, together for once and not bickering or competing. I stop and squat to watch them out of my secret-collecting habit. I do not know what they are doing, but then I understand and smile.

They are jogging awkwardly toward our barracks, each rolling a tire, bent over and struggling to keep it upright. I see a fairly good-sized pile of tires near our barracks. They must be collecting them from the junk pile near the outbuildings.

I watch them for a second more and then decide to join, to stop being an observer. I launch forward from my kneeling position and run toward them with a big smile on my face.

"Hey, Fetty," Annie says. She looks me over while surprise covers Pax's face. He probably does not even know Fetty is my nickname. But, of course, it is; I am money.

"What are you guys doing?" I ask, trying to deflect Annie's coming curiosity.

"Were you running?" she asks.

I ignore the question and just shrug.

"We didn't see you," Pax interjects.

"I used to do this as a kid," I say, pointing at the fallen tires.

"Dude, hold on. Were you running outside the fence?" Annie presses.

Oh, this is going terribly. I start to doubt my decision to step up from the shadows. Pax looks at my legs.

"You have scrapes all over your legs. You *were* outside the fence. Wow." Pax actually looks impressed. Then he looks dreamily toward the forest.

"Were you looking for Kevin?" Annie asks with a sly smile.

Pax's far-off gaze snaps to attention. He looks at me and steps forward. I feel like I am being interrogated.

I am unsure of what to do, what to say. Being out of the shadows is harder than I thought. I turn around and take off toward the outbuildings, toward the pile of tires.

"I know a trick. I will show you," I throw over my shoulder.

I disappear into one of the outbuildings and try to collect myself in the darkness. I wait a minute and let my eyes readjust and then look around. I find what I am looking for, an old mop handle.

I run back outside. Annie and Pax are still waiting for me, standing there with bemused looks on their faces while they watch me run toward them carrying the mop handle. I must look like some kind of African huntress to their eyes. "Spearchucker," I think. Ha! What many of the ghetto girls used to call me!

I run up to them and stop. I place one end of the mop handle on the ground, firmly hold the other end, and then stomp hard in the middle. Despite being slight, I have strong, wiry legs, and the handle breaks in half. Annie laughs, and Pax takes a step back.

I throw one part of the shaft to Annie and then bend over and pick up the other. I go up to Pax's tire and right it. I give it a push to get it rolling and then place one part of the handle into the hole. I use the stick to roll the tire without having to bend over. I can move the tire and run pretty fast at the same time.

"Right on, Fetty!" I hear Annie yell from behind.

I roll the tire to their little pile and then drop it off. I turn around and run back toward them. Annie is rolling a tire, clumsily using the stick method with the other half of the stick. But she starts to get the hang of it.

Pax is standing there, dumbfounded. I run past him and give a wink.

I head back down to the original pile and hear Pax's footsteps behind me, but when I grab another tire and start rolling it back, I cannot see him. I keep rolling. Annie is running down toward me fast. And I hear Pax in the outbuilding, probably looking for another old mop handle.

I get to the pile, drop off the tire, and turn around. Annie is right behind me; then she catches up to me. I think, "This is going to be another competition," and wonder if I want to show my speed and my strength to Annie just yet, but she just runs next to me.

Together, we run past the outbuilding, where Pax is still scrounging. We pick up another set of tires and head back. Pax is standing in the doorway, empty handed and all disgruntled like.

"What's the matter, Pax?" Annie says. "Can't get your stick in the hole? I guess you'll just have to use your hand."

"Funny," he responds.

Annie and I laugh and make our way back up to the new pile.

We finish making the tire pile to whatever size Annie and Pax had in mind. Annie and I are waiting for Pax to hand roll the last tire to us.

"So what are we doing?" I ask.

"Hah, yeah. This wasn't just some kind of exercise routine," Annie says with a laugh.

Pax joins us. He stops and picks up the last tire. Then he twirls it around a couple of times and launches it deep onto the pile. I expect him to beat his chest, but he doesn't. He just looks at us, breathing heavily with a dopey look on his face.

"Well, Pax came up with the idea to build a CrossFit gym. Oh, wait, CrossFit is for douchebags. It's an 'obstacle course,'" she finishes.

"Yeah," Pax says between large breaths. "A way to get everyone off their asses."

"Cool," I respond.

There is a long silence that Annie fills, and I regret stopping, not controlling the conversation.

"So why were you running outside the fence?"

I have had time to think about my answer and am ready to face the questioning McQuestioners.

"I like the challenge, the risk, I guess. Running in the forest is much more exciting than around the fence."

Annie and Pax nod in agreement, but for some reason, I just keep talking. "And you know, ever since the civil war started, I have been really worried about my family. You know, everyone thinks Ethiopians are Muslim, and I have no idea if they are being targeted or being attacked." Voicing this secret makes it scarier, makes it more real. I can feel tears start to well up. Annie comes over and puts her arms around me.

"I'm sure they're OK, sweetie."

But Pax just looks at me and says, "You know, if you want to get ahold of Kevin, just ask Annie. They've been communicating via Bluetooth."

This shocks me. How? Why her and not me?

It shocks Annie too, that Pax knew. With her arm around me, I can feel a bolt charge through her.

"Pax, don't be a dick!" she snaps. "She's concerned about her family."

"You were right, Annie. She's looking for Kevin. She could be concerned about her family from inside the fence, like everyone else."

What should I make of this? I am upset, really upset. Kevin trusted Annie with a phone but not me? Pax sensed I was trying to cover up my story about going outside the fence with worries about my family and then attacked me over it.

I think about how I should handle his attack. I think back to my leadership training, the small amount I had with the military, along with Kevin and eight others.

During the training, Kevin and I were sitting outside with the other student leaders, hiding from the heat in the shade of the big hangar. We were waiting to go on our solo treks, waiting for the trucks to pull up and take us up into the mountains. We were to be dropped off, each in separate locations with a compass, a map, a loaded pistol, and two days of supplies. Each leader had to make his or her way alone to the main waypoint over fifty miles away.

At this point in the training, I was very nervous about the trek and unsure I should even be in the leadership program. I was the only black female. Some of the white kids from the other barracks even called me AA which morphed into AA-ron. I thought it stood for African American, but Kevin later told me it stood for affirmative action.

I think Kevin picked up on my apprehension and was really sweet about it. Many people think he is so cold, so distant, but he is actually incredibly sensitive to other people. I guess his sensitivity attracted me most of all. He noticed me rocking back forth while seated on the ground.

Kevin came up to me and sat down. "You know…there's a score for everyone," he said.

"A score?" I stopped rocking and looked at him. He had such a sweet, kind look on his face.

"For *everyone*. When I say everyone, I mean everyone in the world, not just the United States, not just us teenagers encamped here. *Everyone*. It rates the value of each person, not a value like how much money they have or their connections or creed or color. It's a value of how useful they could be in a time of crisis, if civilization broke down. This value can be stack ranked and put into models to determine what people or aggregated for what groups to save during a catastrophe. This score, they actually created it before the volcano, but they used it in part to divide up the roles here.

"Anyway, my friend Todd, the one in the wheelchair, had a negative score. I understand why, their pragmatic, utilitarian view. There's no room for the weak or whatever. I can understand, but I can never forget or forgive them for writing off my friend. Todd is not an example of weakness or what goes wrong in life. He is the strongest and most decent, most humane person I know, and they wrote him off."

He stopped and gazed off into the distance. My heart was racing. I did not know what Kevin was getting at, but his look was so intense, so engaged, it mesmerized me.

"When shit goes bad, I will always remember that they wrote off my best friend. That they killed him. They chose me to lead, to be one of them, but they will never control me. They will never own me. And they will meet my darkness."

I placed my hand on Kevin's arm. It was hot to the touch. Despite my infatuation, we knew each other very little. I attributed his confession to my superpower, but he placed his other hand on my hand and looked deep into my eyes.

"Your score, Fetien, is higher than anyone else in this group," he said. "You deserve to be here. You deserve to lead. You will be great."

"Higher than yours?" I asked, dumbfounded.

"Ha, yeah, I may be a bit of a wildcard. I had a negative score too. I guess you can say I convinced the leadership on Ellis Island to let me join in on all the fun."

I deserve to be here. I deserve to lead. I will be great. I shed Annie's arm and step forward to put my face directly in front of Pax's, only inches away.

"OK. Let us build this douchebag obstacle course," I say.

He looks shocked.

"Time for you to meet my darkness," I declare.

Oh, and that fifty-mile solo trek—I ran it straight through—finished in ten hours. Seventeen hours before anyone else.

CHAPTER 2

Paco

• • •

I WAKE UP TO WHITE people doing hard labor. Imagine that shit.

"Wsst. Hey, Paco, check this out," Cisco says.

I slide off my top bunk, scratch my balls, and walk over to the window.

And outside, a bunch of people are working, digging in the dirt, hammering structures together, all kinds of work, that butch blond chick, the cocoa-butter black girl, and Pax, stacking a bunch of tires into a big pyramid.

Even the *güero* white boys from the other barracks, the ones who shit their pants when Kevin pulled a knife at the airport, even they are helping.

"What are they doing?" I ask Cisco.

"I think they are building a big obstacle course. You know, like those Spartan Races," Cisco says.

"Figures," I say. "We fix the roof, the Mormons build a temple and a garden, and they build a playground."

Cisco shrugs. "Might be fun. And besides, gives you a chance to show them your stuff."

"Verdad." I miss training. I miss working out. We got some of that in the soldier-boy shit the army had us doing, but I am used to training four to five hours a day—sparring, hitting the punching bags, and running, running, running. I smile at Cisco and give him a nod. "Let's go."

We throw on some clothes and walk outside. The tire pyramid is huge, as tall as the roof of the barracks. Pax and that hot African chick are climbing it together while holding a tire. They look like crabs, side-climbing up the pyramid while carrying the tire between them. When they get to the top, they slide the tire in place. It's the last tire to complete the pyramid.

"Way to go, Fetty!" Annie yells.

Her name is Fetty. Funny. Figures. She could be my trap queen. Lupina is cheering too, for Pax. I wouldn't mind hitting that too, but Pax seems cool.

There is a crowd watching Pax and Fetty climb to the top of the pyramid. After they put the tire in place, Fetty climbs to the top while Pax holds the tire steady. She turns around to face us, stands up tall, and then dabs. Everyone goes crazy. In the crowd, there are a few white kids from the other barracks, and even they cheer. It feels good, like maybe we can all just get along and shit.

"So, what, you all friends now?" I ask Annie, nodding toward the *güeros*.

She shrugs. "They brought us alcohol." She points to two big tubs sitting in the shade filled with a pinkish-gray liquid.

"At least they good for something."

I look around for Jaden and Michael and some of the other black kids from East and then remember seeing them inside our barracks, sulking, with the hot, nerdy seamstress girl. I guess we're not all totally healed.

Annie turns to me and Cisco. "You guys should go check the outbuildings, see if there is anything you can use to build an obstacle," she says in one of those ways that is and isn't an order.

"Sure," Cisco says with a smile.

We whistle and nod at Hector. He peels away from Felicia and jogs with us down to the outbuildings. Inside, we find a cable reel and a bunch of old railroad stakes. We go outside and look for a spot to set up an obstacle. The stuck-up hot chicks from the other barracks are making colorful signs with arrows to point out the direction the course runs. We follow the signs and find a wide-open space between obstacles toward the end of the race.

Cisco, Hector, and I stake a bunch of the cable about six inches off the ground in a crazy pattern. The game is to run through the obstacle, stepping over the cable without getting tripped up. I got crazy fast feet, so I'll kick ass at it. We finish building it in, like, twenty minutes, look at each other, and smile. Easiest work we've ever done, and now we can play and drink without getting sideways glances.

We head back to the beginning of the course where everyone is gathered. We can hear some yelling as we get closer. It looks pretty heated. They're probably arguing over the rules or use of the course. So no peace? That was quick.

We walk over there, but it seems to have calmed down. OK, good, peace.

Turns out they were just arguing over the race rules between barracks. They decided on five-"man" teams from each of the barracks. The main beef was between making teams coed or not. They settled on letting the barracks decide. So if you want to run girls, you can.

We split away from the other groups and go back near our barracks to decide who will run. Before anyone can even say anything, Annie jumps in.

"No fucking way I'm not running," she barks.

She looks around at each of the boys, staring us down, daring us to challenge her. I never pass up a mad-dog challenge, but what can I do? I can't fight her, and besides, like, no shit, you can run, *güera*.

I look forward to that bull-dyke making the lily-white boys look bad anyway.

"And me too!" Fetty says.

This surprises me. I don't think I have ever heard her talk. And she doesn't just say it; she steps forward like she's making a declaration. She isn't mad-dogging us like Annie, but still, this is too much. We want to beat those rich fucks, and they aren't running girls.

I am about to say something, but Cisco nudges my arm. He shakes his head. "She can run, bro. She's a motherfucking monster."

I throw him a look. I'm about to ask him if he is thinking with his dick again, typical Cisco. But then I remember they were in leadership training together, so he probably saw shit I didn't.

And cool, if getting beat by Annie doesn't piss the *güeros* off, then the skinny African will blow their tops off.

Cisco, as if he thinks I am mad at him, turns to the group and throws my name in. I don't like people speaking up for me, but they respect him and don't question it, so I am kind of glad I don't need to argue.

Pax also volunteers. So, we are at four of the five.

Annie looks at the two brothers from Utah. "Well, which one is it going to be?"

I remember Seth and Sam from the military training. They both are tall and strong. They have tans and sand-colored hair. Shit, they even look like the desert. They are fit as hell and can climb like spider monkeys.

"Don't you think they should both run?" says Ezra, the cute little Mormon blonde. She throws a not-so-hidden look toward Fetty.

"I don't need to run," one of the brothers, Seth, says. "Sam is stronger than me, and I would like to see Fetty run." He looks at Ezra.

"Wow, trouble in paradise," I think.

"Pretty feminitastic for a Mormon, and oh, Ezra dear, Fetty's pace is faster than mine," Annie says with a quick wink at Fetty.

"Not everyone from Utah is LDS," Sam speaks up. "Our moms are big rock climbers and moved there for the cliffs and canyons. And yes, Fetty should run."

Ha, liberal-hypocrite smite. The best.

"That's wonderful," Spencer adds sincerely. "And not every LDS is sexist," he says while throwing his girl a look. Damn. Now there is definitely trouble in paradise.

So, that settles it. Five runners: Pax, Sam, Fetty, me, and Annie. The barracks with the best average overall time wins. I'm not sure what the prize is, but I guess the hot chicks and Lupina are working on it, so that sounds sweet.

The first group is fun to watch. Everyone is cheering and following the racers. Pax is strong for a pretty boy with long hair. He doesn't have too much trouble with the first obstacles. One of the tall kids that Kevin scared at the airport is racing against Pax. I guess he is some all-star lacrosse player or something. Figures. It is neck and neck all the way toward the end. About one hundred yards from the finish, Pax sprints ahead and wins. You could tell the other racers were too tired toward the end, too much sitting on their asses, not enough training. Pax crosses the finish line and gets a big welcome from our group and even a big kiss from Lupina. Damn. Now I really want to win.

There is no contest with Sam, that non-Mormon Utah brother. He totally looks like a spider monkey on the obstacles and is fast on the runs. He probably is the fastest so far, and in a way, that's too bad. His brother, Seth, should probably be running instead of Fetty; I mean, she's hot and all, but those brothers can fly.

Well, now it's Fetty's chance. The third-round runners don't look very good, though, just big muscle heads and Fetty. They all line up, and it looks funny. These big football-player types with skinny Fetty all in a line. I street fought bros like that before. They're all talk but too slow and tire easily. With their gym bodies, they don't have the right muscles in the right places. This shows pretty quick with Fetty. She's got that eye-of-the-tiger look on her face and takes off in a sprint. Damn, she's fast. And she clears the obstacles with no trouble. Even the one where you have to flip a big truck tire, she does with no problem. Everyone is laughing, even some from the other barracks, when Fetty crosses the finish line at full speed with a big shit-eating grin on her face. It wasn't even close.

Some of the macho boys are starting to get pissed. We probably already won the contest by winning the first three races. The only way we can lose is if Annie or I post a really slow time. I line up, thinking that I should just run cautious, not get hurt or stumble so I can get a decent time, but then I think, "Fuck it. Let's sweep those crybabies."

Some other muscle heads are racing against me, and they are eyeing me with a pissed look. Everyone else before us showed that this is an endurance race and not a strength race. They are probably looking at me and thinking, "That skinny kid's not strong, but he's gonna beat me." They're only part right. I'm gonna beat them, but I'm also strong as fuck. So they shouldn't test me.

But they do. I take off in a nice solid run and start to separate from the herd. I clear the first obstacle, the tire pyramid, with ease. I am running up to the next obstacle when I hear one of those big, beefy types running at me full sprint. I know he can't keep up the pace, but he doesn't have to. We start the obstacle—four long horizontal poles that we have to jungle gym across.

He catches up to me. We are hanging from the pole when he launches toward me and kicks me in the ribs. I hear people in the crowd yell, but it doesn't faze me. I've been punched a lot harder. I finish the obstacle ahead of the meathead and run to the next one, a big wall to climb. I'm tall and springy and can jump it by grabbing the top of the wall and catapulting over. I drop to the other side of the wall and decide to wait. The crowd is on the other side and can't see me. The meathead struggles to clear the wall. His feet scratch on the other side until he can finally lumber over to my side. He drops to the ground and sees me waiting for him. He stands up, trying to look all tough like he just didn't kick me unguarded in the ribs. I knock him clean out with one punch and start the race again.

I finish way before anyone else. The meathead doesn't finish at all but gets helped off course by his gay meathead friends.

It's obvious we really have no chance of losing when Annie lines up to run, but we want the sweep, and Annie has that fire burning in her. She is running against the other tall lacrosse player—the one Jaden punched at the airport. They take off, and it's a mad sprint to the tire pyramid. Annie, with all her CrossFit training, bounds up the pyramid, but the tall kid is right on her heels. Annie lunges onto the top tire ahead of him, cutting him off. But the punk swipes her foot out, and down she tumbles down the other side. We can actually hear the thump when she hits the ground. We all run to the other side of the pyramid. I just ran my race, but I get there quick.

Annie is on the ground in a weird position, like she landed head-first and then jackknifed over. Her face has the start of a bruise, and there is blood coming out near her elbow, but she looks OK.

Lupina runs up and starts asking her questions about whether she can move her toes. Everyone from our barracks is in a half circle around Annie, waiting for her to move her toes. The tall punk has gone over to his friends and is watching with a smirk.

I know Annie is OK, because she is grimacing with pain while holding her elbow. If she was really hurt, she wouldn't be moving and squawking. She starts to get up with a face full of anger and looks to go after the punk kid, but it hurts too much.

"Fuck!" she yells.

She wants to go after him, but she can't move her arm. She has that look on her face. When you see it, you know you're about to get your ass kicked. She's a fighter. I respect that. And that's when I go fucking berserker. We made an oath. We're a fucking tribe, as Pax and Cisco said.

I bolt straight for the group of *güeros*. The meathead I took out earlier looks scared and backs away, but a couple of other punks step in front of the tall punk. And he is still smirking, thinking he's all safe and shit.

I cut through his line of defense like a weed-whacker. One-two, one-two combinations. My superfast left jab, followed by my hard right cross—to their chin or nose—whatever they're showing—and they drop like flies.

The rest of the line disappears, and now the punk who took out Annie isn't smirking. He looks scared. He puts his hands up like to surrender but then drops his shoulder and charges at me like this is some kind of MMA fight. No worries. I sting him with a hard uppercut and then grab his head and start smashing it into my knee. He goes to the ground pretty easy, and I'm on top of him, MMA-style and all. I can feel people move behind me, so I glance back between shots to his face. It's just my tribe—Pax, Cisco, and Hector, clearing the rubbish and protecting my back.

The tall punk is pretty unresponsive. I kind of want to stop but don't. I hear Lupina.

"Knock it off!" she yells. Damn. She's got some lungs.

I nod, get up, and leave the punk bleeding in the dust while I walk over to Annie and Lupina. Annie's bad arm is cradled in her good arm. Lupina has her arm around Annie.

I walk up to them ready to be scolded by Lupina. But Annie is looking at me with big fuck-me eyes.

"Paco, you're my hero," she says, and she's not being sarcastic.

We head back to our barracks. Annie is walking slowly between us but keeps staring at me like Bambi.

Shit, maybe I did win a prize after all.

"And don't forget the booze!" Annie yells back to Pax and Cisco.

Definitely.

CHAPTER 3

Lupina

● ● ●

ANNIE SITS SLOUCHED IN THE chair in the office, almost crumpled but trying to be brave and tough. The lightbulb is out, so Paco holds a large flashlight on her like a heat lamp trying to hatch an egg. The light illuminates the blood and sweat beading on her skin. Fresh drops of sweat collect on her forehead, dotting her reddened face like a pox victim in reverse. The sweat-marked face is colored more from pain than the short race interrupted. I take a cloth and wipe away Annie's sweat, half expecting to feel the texture of pox-like bumps highlighted and shadow-full in the spotlight.

I wanted Annie and Paco away from the commotion in the other room. I can hear Pax telling the story of the race, Annie's fall, and Paco's rampage to Charlotte, Eva, and the others who stayed inside in protest. Their jeers and cheers cascade into our room. I break it with a gentle close of the door.

"Annie, listen, I'm going to try to move your arm. I want you to tell me the pain on a scale of one to ten, OK?" I say. I fear a break but thankfully see no protrusion of bone.

Annie doesn't say anything but nods.

"You're brave, girl," Paco offers.

"OK. Ready?" I ask but proceed without waiting for an answer.

Annie's hurt arm is resting on a towel on the desk. I start by lightly pressing on the flesh of her forearm.

"Three. Four," she blurts.

I move my soft finger presses down toward her wrist. I take her fingers in my hand and slowly move them.

"Same," she says through a grimace.

"OK. I'm going to move your wrist now."

I lightly move her hand back and forth and then rotate her wrist. Her wrist is easy to move, but she yells in pain.

"Christ, six, seven, oh, that hurts!"

"Does it hurt in your wrist?" I ask.

She shakes her head no. "My elbow. It hurts in my elbow."

"Oh, sweetie, I'm sorry. Let me just check one more thing."

I gently place one hand under Annie's wrist as she takes a big breath.

"Good, good, breathe," I say and slowly lift her forearm up.

"Oh fuck!" She screams. "Infinity! Infinity being fucked by infinity and having a bunch of infinity babies!"

I lightly place her arm back on the towel. She probably broke her elbow. We need an x-ray, pain pills, and a cast—all these are available in the infirmary on the main base, but I do not trust the base.

Since the helicopters went down, we have received no guidance or lead, just the obligatory deliveries of food from scared and sullen soldiers. When I see them and the looks on their faces, I am reminded of my father and the other men who burned through my mother's life, all our lives. The tiring burden of supporting something you don't want to support. They all had that same guilty look in the weeks before disappearing forever. There is the same resentment in the eyes of the soldiers delivering food. They know what's going on; they know way more than we do. And they know at some point the food is going to run out.

I am getting such a bad vibe that I don't want to chance a night visit to the infirmary. I don't want to provide the men an excuse to desert us or beat us down. I've seen that happen too many times.

There is a knock on our door. Cisco slides in.

"I brought you something, Annie," Cisco says from the doorway. He is holding a Nalgene filled with the pinkish alcohol from the other barracks.

"We tested it. It's not poison," he says. He seems a little tipsy, giddy. He opens the lid and passes the bottle to her good hand.

"Oh, thank you, thank you, thank you, Cisco. You are a true gem," she says.

"And you're one tough cookie, Annie," he says and then nods to Paco and heads back out into the group.

"Cisco," I ask, "would you be a dear and send Charlotte in here?"

Annie takes a big swig of the booze, grimaces, and then downs another gulp. She hands the bottle to Paco as I go fetch the iodine and bottle of fresh water.

"Don't worry, Paco; you're still my hero. And I'm still going to drain you dry," I hear Annie not so quietly whisper.

Paco coughs as he hears this, even before putting the liquor to his lips.

I prepare the iodine.

"The Tribe of Iodine Wine," I think. To purify water, to lessen the effects of radiation, to disinfect and wash away our wounds. I gently pull the towel to flatten out Annie's arm. She rests her head on her good arm on the desk. To my surprise, Paco places the Nalgene on the desk, and then with his free hand, he lightly runs his fingers through Annie's hair. I notice his bruised knuckles gliding through her spiky hair, gentle and strong.

I pour the clean water over Annie's elbow to wash away the dirt and blood. I dab it with a sterile pad, and Annie tenses up. I pour more water.

"Annie, sweetie, you're doing great. This next part is going to sting a bit, but then we're almost done."

I position the iodine over her elbow. I am about ready to pour when Charlotte opens the door. Everyone jumps a bit. Annie groans in pain.

"Yeah?" Charlotte asks. Her voice is testy.

"Hold on one second," I say to her. The iodine drips out of the bottle. I move it over the cuts on Annie's elbow and lightly blow on it.

I apply another layer of iodine and another gentle blow and then pat it dry.

"Almost done." As gently as I can, I tape a sterile pad to her elbow. Without prompting, Charlotte comes over and helps me lift Annie's arm from below the armpit while I tape the pad to the other side.

"I need you to make a sling," I tell Charlotte.

"Got it," she responds.

"She broke her elbow, so it needs to avoid putting press—"

"I got it!" she barks. "I understand how slings and bandages work."

I gently put Annie's arm down and pat her head and Paco's hand.

I throw the medical kit over my shoulder and escort Charlotte out of the office, leaving Paco and Annie alone.

I shut the door and ask, "What is your problem?"

"What the hell were you thinking?" she attacks me.

"Excuse me?"

"Making friends with *them*!" Her voice is loud, and the chatter from the rest of the group ends. Pax gets up and stands near my side. He better not speak up for me.

To his credit, he doesn't. Unfortunately, Jaden speaks up for Charlotte. He pounces up and jostles between Charlotte and me.

"Did you forget what they called us!" he yells, waving his hand toward Michael, Eva, and Danny behind him.

I take a deep breath. I give Pax a loving look as he stands, silent and stoic, by my side.

"Jaden, please don't give me crap about reconciliation," I start. "You, Michael, and Pax went into white neighborhoods to destroy personal property."

I feel Pax tense up. I don't think this betrays a secret or Pax's past, but I continue, "They called you names, Kevin pulled a knife, and you punched one of them. And now, we are stuck here in hostile lands with military support that soon will evaporate, and you want to give me grief for not making enemies."

"They're racist bigots. We need no harbor for them," Charlotte adds.

"You don't think there's prejudice on our side? What, you think because there are black people in our neighborhood that makes us tolerant? Like you don't look down on people from the suburbs or people from the country. Like we're above everyone else just because we live in a cultured part of town.

"Char, do you know why we left Park Hill and moved to Capitol Hill? Because when the he left us, everyone gave my mother, now a single mom of three girls, the cold shoulder. We even had trouble finding a home to rent. Don't tell me about prejudice when you live in ivory towers."

"They called us niggers! They cheated and hurt one of us. A girl!" Jaden tags back in.

"I am not excusing their actions, nor am I excusing yours. They do something, and we escalate. They call you a name; you throw a punch. They hurt Annie; Paco goes on a rampage. Just curious, what do you think's going to happen next? I guarantee the next escalation won't be with fists."

The group is quiet, contemplating what this means.

I break the silence with something I shouldn't say. "And, and... you don't have Kevin here to protect you." I can feel Pax go completely cold, but it had to be said.

I don't like this confrontation, the anger and fear filling the barracks. This is not for me. I turn and walk toward the exit.

"Where are you going?" Charlotte yells out.

"I'm going to see if Brad is OK."

"Who the hell is that?"

"The kid Paco pummeled."

I walk out into the cold night air alone and head toward their barracks. Doubt creeps into my decision. Her icy vines make me tense and scared. I don't know if making peace is safe or prudent, but it is the right thing to do.

I hear footsteps run up next to me, and Pax appears by my side. He doesn't say anything. I am not sure if he is here for protection or support, but he takes my hand in his hand and remains silent. And I don't think I have ever loved him as much as I do for this quiet gesture.

We reach their barracks door and knock. It is cold and silent inside. Someone opens the door. We stand there like missionaries trying to sell a paradise not wanted.

"Yeah?" the girl says.

"We just wanted to see if Brad is OK," I say and lift up my medical bag in proof.

"He's fine. They took him and the others to the base," she says and slams the door in our face.

Chills go up my spine. We stand there, frozen, for too long. We finally turn around and head back toward our barracks. I don't want to go back inside, so beaten, so wrong.

Pax senses my defeat and says, "Hey, I think we can use some alone time." He escorts me over to one of the obstacles, a ladder high up, resting between two beams. He lets go of my hand, jumps up, and knocks the ladder down. He aptly catches its fall. He tries to balance the ladder above his head while it wobbles up and down.

"Here, let me help," I say.

He slides the ladder down to his side. I take one end, and he takes the other. We walk back toward the side of our barracks and carefully step through the LDS garden. He places the ladder between rows of budding vegetables and leads it up to our roof.

He scales the ladder first. When he gets to the top, he brushes away a fine layer of ash from the flat beam on the peak of the roof. He climbs onto it and then turns around and offers me his hand. I give him the medical bag and ascend onto to the roof.

We make our way to the middle, shuffling our feet to clear the ash. We sit in the middle and kick down the branches covering the roof near us. They dust up a layer of ash. The ash-covered branches remind me of snow on the pines in the Colorado mountains.

We sit down and then turn to kiss. The long, slow kiss melts away the stress. He runs his fingers through my hair and softly kisses my cheek and neck.

"This is the best privacy I could muster," he says.

"It's perfect."

We slide down and nestle our way in between the branches. We lie back and rest our heads on the medical bag straddling the beam. Cuddled among the ash and pines, we cradle each other and stare up into the night sky. The moon casts a weird light through the haze, but we can still see a plethora of shrouded stars, numerous in the absence of any light pollution. The ambient heat from the now-set sun radiates from the roof and branches, bathing us in warmth.

We lie like that for a long time before Pax finally asks, "Do you think we should have left with Kevin?" His voice trembles, unsure and boyish.

"Sometimes two choices have no right answer. I don't like the vibe on the base. I don't like the way the National Guard looks at us girls. I don't think it's safe here."

I can feel Pax tense up, tense at me questioning the big debate he had with Kevin on the night he disappeared.

"But," I continue, "you were right. We would all have trouble surviving in the forest. The medical supplies, food, and shelter are lacking for a group this size, for our tribe."

"So, what's the right answer?"

"Well, I think you and Cisco hit it on the head. The only right answer is for us to stick together whatever happens."

We stay silent after for a long time and then drift off to sleep between the fallen branches, beneath a fine layer of ash. We wake up shivering to the morning sun breaking a weak light on the horizon.

We sit up and look toward the base. In the distance, troops are moving the Hummers around. They pull away from the buildings and drive back to the motor pool. Despite the haze, the moon and weak horizon cast enough light so they can drive without turning on their headlights.

"Let's go to bed. I think it's time," I say to Pax.

We enter the barracks. Everyone is asleep. One of the tubs of booze lies drained in the corner. Loud, passed-out snoring billows out from many of the bunks. I lead Pax over to the office. We open the door and slowly go inside, waiting for our eyes to adjust to the darkness.

"This is the best privacy I could muster," I say to Pax.

We hear a shuffling on the cot and look to see the forms of Annie and Paco. In the dim light, I can tell they are intertwined in nakedness. Annie wears only the sling Charlotte must have made. One of her breasts lies exposed, pressed next to Paco's naked arm. Typical Annie—not even injury is going to keep her from getting hers.

I lead Pax back out into the main part of the barracks and to my bunk. He doesn't say anything but seems nervous.

"Don't worry; everyone's passed out."

We reach the bunk, and Pax feels withdrawn and frozen. But I can feel his pulse beat hard against my wrist.

I stand and face him in front of the bunk. "It's time," I say.

I can see in the darkness that something is wrong. A look of panic and confusion covers Pax's face.

Sounding like a scared child, he says, "But…but what about Vivi? She's right below us. She will hear us and wake up."

For the second time that night, deep, cold chills run through my spine.

"Are you OK?" I ask.

He shakes his head.

"Pax, what is going on with you? Vivi's in New York. They left her with your aunt and uncle."

CHAPTER 4

Ezra

• • •

We are woken up with a slam of the door and the boots of soldiers pounding through our barracks.

Spencer is above me, in the other bunk. We are separate and chaste. There is a bishop among us on the base, a captain, and we are to be married soon. Then we can share the marriage bed. Other couples have started sharing beds already like the bossy officer warned—Felicia and Hector, Annie and whomever. I don't see Lupina and Pax sharing a bed yet, which is surprising, because I don't even think he's Christian.

Spencer and I will wait until we are married, but we are to be married soon, in the mobile tabernacle that we dedicated recently. This is the right way to do things. We are young, but this is the way it is supposed to be, especially in times of struggle. Spencer and the bishop even expedited the endowment sessions with the goal to get us married. With all the strife and worry polluting the base, the bishop felt a marriage and children to soon follow would bring new life into our world, a union to consecrate the colony.

And I know Spencer is the right man for me. He is so wise and such a natural leader. I foresee great things for him. Or I did. Now I am not sure. Now there are soldiers running through our barracks.

I told Spencer not to throw lots with the odd group from Denver—a motley crew of weirdos and the hood rats. But he always sees the bigger picture, so he says. Sometimes, I think, we shouldn't think in big pictures. Yes, LDS have been persecuted. Yes, prejudice is bad. But just because the nice boys said the n-word doesn't mean it wasn't deserved. Those hoodlums shouldn't have cut in line. Spencer saw their defiance and sense of community as something to follow, something to be part of. So I followed him and joined this motley crew. And now look at us.

Of course, we are all sober and alert when the soldiers come in. Of course, not everyone else is. The drunkards are stunned and slow to get up. The LDS gather; the ones like Spencer who have completed endowment cover their temple garments in sheets and blankets. We line up against the wall as the soldiers go up and down the bunks and rattle everyone out of their drunkenness. See. They don't even pay attention to us.

"Where's Paco?" one of the soldiers yells. He is the one who almost fought the scary black guy after deplaning.

"Where's Paco? Is he with Kevin?"

So they know about Kevin disappearing. And they know about that punk Paco going psycho on all those boys. I wonder how they know, but then I see. In the doorway stand those pretty girls from the nice parts of Denver—Kelly, Becky, and Lily—and they are leading the soldiers. I can tell. They have that look of confidence that tells the world who's really in charge.

Oh, Spencer, poor, poor, Spencer. We should be on their side. We should be leading the soldiers, but instead we are half-naked, cowering against the wall.

"Here he is!" another soldier yells from the office. He is laughing.

Paco comes out, totally naked and unashamed, showing everything to the whole world. I gasp.

But everyone else thinks this is funny. Even the soldiers are laughing at the naked, smiling Mexican. But then the Mexican sucker-punches the guard by the door, and he falls to the floor. He's shifty.

The leader doesn't think the sucker punch is funny. He fires his pistol up into the roof. No one is laughing now. Ha. The sound is deafening and silencing. The leader marches up to Paco with the pistol pointed directly at him. I kind of get the impression he is showing off for the girls. See.

"On the ground! On the ground!" he yells.

Paco drops to the floor.

Annie, the boyish-looking girl, comes out of the office now too, wearing only panties and her sling. She is shocked but also unashamed by her showing breast slipped out of her sling. Floozy.

We are separated naturally—the LDS on one side of the barracks and the drunken Denver folk on the other. The two climbing brothers, somehow with the same lesbian mothers, also join the drunken crowd. You can tell they are hungover too.

"Corporal, may I?"

I am shocked to hear my Spencer speak. The leader with the pistol looks annoyed and angered, and I'm worried about my Spencer.

He lets go of my hand and approaches the leader. He gestures with his sheet and points his arms toward Paco, still naked on the floor. Spencer walks the long walk over to him and covers him with his sheet.

The soldiers look with smiling faces as Spencer walks back to us, wearing only his temple garment, "the Mormon underwear," now in full view. He should be embarrassed, but he walks with his ever-present confident walk. That little bounce in his step was always something I loved about him. Spencer's walk always made him seem important and affable at the same time. You could just tell he was going places—literally, ha—and figuratively. But now, Spencer walks back to us in his underwear, and laughter breaks out from the girls in the doorway and spreads to the soldiers.

Oh, Spencer, what have you done? This is why we are persecuted.

I look across to the other kids from our barracks, expecting to see their laughter and ridicule at the revealing of our sacred temple garment. But they only stare with hateful faces at the soldiers.

A couple more soldiers come into our barracks. They walk around the girls, checking out their butts with sly smiles on their faces.

"Kevin's not in the Mormon temple," they tell the leader.

A gasp comes over the LDS. The soldiers are not LDS and are forbidden from entering our mobile tabernacle. Wait until our bishop finds out!

I look to Spencer and start to worry. The same hateful face the other teenagers in our barracks have is now mirrored on my sweet Spencer's face. I hope he is not going to do anything else rash. I worry the hoodlums and freaks from our barracks are starting to influence my Spencer.

"Listen up!" the leader says. "You have twenty minutes to assemble outside for a mandatory meeting."

With that, he turns on his heels and marches to the door.

"Grab him!" he orders the soldiers while pointing at Paco with his gun. "And grab his stuff."

He turns back around and heads to the door. One of the girls smiles and, I assume, returns a wink as the leader leaves the barracks.

Two big soldiers bend down over Paco. They pull down the sheet and then lock Paco's arms behind his back. Paco winces in pain as they yank him up by his arms. The sheet falls, and he is naked before us again, but no one is laughing. Another soldier picks up the sheet, and they wrap him in it, holding his arms behind his back while they spin him around. The big soldier throws him over his shoulder as Paco spits and cusses. He tries to wriggle in the sheet, but he is wrapped too tight.

"Spicy little burrito!" the soldier yells to his friends, and they all laugh.

Another stampede of feet echoes through the barracks as Hector, Cisco, and a bunch of the Mexicans start charging at the soldiers. They turn around shocked at the sound. They raise their rifles but look scared even though the Mexicans have no weapons.

"Back off. Back the fuck off!"

I see Michael and Jaden sneaking up the sidewalls, but so do the soldiers, and there are yells and guns pointing them down too.

I want to hide, to collapse small and away from the pointed guns. But Spencer is standing tall next to me, so I grab his hand and stand tall next to him.

But my heart starts to break as he releases my hand and joins the Mexicans and their crazy harassment of the armed soldiers. I watch as he sneaks up in his underwear. Other LDS join him. Oh, this is the worst.

Luckily, nothing happens. The soldiers start to look worried at the large group massing against them, even though we are unarmed, and they retreat out the door.

Everyone keeps pressing toward the door when the leader pops his head back in. He has a crazy look on his face but doesn't say anything. He just points his pistol and starts firing.

Screams break out, and I wince, but I keep watching the leader. He is pointing the gun up high again. He fires three or four shots until he finally hits our lightbulb, which explodes and leaves a shower of glass on the floor.

"See you in all in fifteen minutes!" he yells with a laugh. In the darkened frame of the doorway, he does a little spinny cowboy thing to holster his pistol and then leaves into the vacant light.

We gather, fully dressed but still disheveled, in the wide-open space between the barracks and the base. I look around at our group, the Wine Tribe or whatever. Many are still drunk or hungover and look both sick and scared at the same time.

I look over at the other groups of teenagers. There are so many of them, and they are well dressed and prepared for this meeting. We must look like such riffraff. They look at us with contempt and something else. I guess pleasure or snobbishness or both.

I can't believe I am on the receiving end of their upturned noses. I look for the pretty girls in the large crowd, but they aren't there. Then I see them. They are standing by the Hummers, away from the crowd. They stand like queens, and here I am with the pirates.

The leader gets out of his Hummer and climbs up on the roof of the vehicle. Paco is dragged out in front of the Hummer by two huge soldiers. They are holding on to his arms very tightly, but Paco doesn't look scared or in pain. In fact, he looks happy. There is a smirk on his face like that of the pretty girls.

"There is a new order now!" the leader yells into the bullhorn like the bossy woman soldier did when we first arrived here. Wait. Where is she, and where is the bishop? What does he mean, new order?

"We are redividing the roles into new castes. Teenagers from the MMM barracks will now be part of the untouchables. Because of your disobedient behavior, you will be doing all the dirty work."

There is grumbling from our barracks. I am pissed too. Untouchable? We should not be on the bottom! I want to grab Spencer and tell him to say something, that we are good people, not like these jerks who are now getting us into trouble, but I am scared Spencer will tell me no and show me up in public. I stay with my mouth shut but boiling mad at those hoods who put us here.

"There is also a new set of rules. Because you are dependent on us for your food and protection, you will do what we say. If you don't, you will be exiled outside the fence forever. If you try to sneak back in, you will be executed. If you approach the fence or try to communicate or help anyone outside the fence, you will join them. Is that clear?" He is yelling into the bullhorn, but his words, his anger, are directed at us.

"Is that clear!" he yells again, staring us down. He places his free hand on his holstered gun.

The other groups give a hurrah, but our group just mumbles dirty words under their breath.

"Paco, you are hereby sentenced to exile."

The two soldiers try to manhandle Paco, but free from the burrito wrap, he breaks their grip. He acts like he is going to throw punches, and they shy back. He smirks. Other soldiers approach with guns pointed, but Paco ignores them. He bends over, picks up his packs, and starts to jog toward the fence on his own. The soldiers look up to their leader. He just shakes his head and waves his hand at the Mexican running toward the fence. We all watch as Paco throws his bag over the high fence and quickly scales it. He lands, scoops up his bags, and keeps running toward the forest.

"Untouchables! Report for your duties at oh five hundred hours tomorrow morning."

The leader jumps down off the Hummer and lands awkwardly. He starts to limp his way back to the Hummer, and our group breaks out in a collective laugh. He turns around with a fierce look on his face and his hand on his gun. Our group goes silent, but I can still hear stifled snickers.

And to my dismay, the leader climbs into the Hummer, and the three pretty girls follow him.

As soon as the Hummers drive off, Spencer, Annie, and others from our barracks take off in a full sprint back to the barracks. I was ready to lay into Spencer, to plead with him to approach the leader and ask for us to be moved to another group. But he is no longer by my side. He is running with the others back to the barracks.

I hastily follow and enter, but they are not to be seen. The office door is shut, and I can hear him in there. I want to approach the door, but it is guarded by the black kid who had crutches and the two climbing brothers.

After what seems like an eternity, Spencer and Annie exit the office. I start to boil with anger, and this doesn't go away when the scary black guy and the skinny African girl come out too.

Annie tells the good-looking Mexican kid—Cisco, I think—that everything is OK, that "he has him."

Cisco smiles and pats Annie on her good arm.

Spencer sees me and the other LDS and approaches. I am about to let him have it. I don't care who is around, but the look on Spencer's face is not happy like Cisco's. It is extremely troubled and sad. He staggers up to us with tears in his eyes.

We all gather around him, but he just stares at the ground. I forget my anger and go up to Spencer. I put my arm around him.

"They're gone. They're all gone," he mutters.

"Who?" someone pleads.

"The major, the captain—our bishop—all the professional soldiers are dead. They killed them during the night."

There is a long, eerie silence. Some of the LDS start to cry. Wait. Our bishop is dead? How does Spencer know this? Did that slut and those niggers tell him that in the office? This can't be true. I won't be able to finish the endowment. How can we get married if the bishop is dead? I can't believe this. I heard no gunshots last night.

"Spencer, Spencer," I finally say. I finally get the nerve to talk. "How do you know all this? It can't be true. It was probably the terrorists."

Spencer stops and gives me a long, hard look as if he knows why I am doubting this, that I am only concerned about whether we can get married.

He gives me a cold stare and says, "Kevin. Kevin told us."

The night is long and full of muted noises. No one can sleep, but no one is talking. We are all digesting the news. All the professional soldiers, the major, the captain—our bishop—are dead. The homicidal people in charge hate us and have it out for us.

I am all mixed up. I can feel the fear and hate swirl around in me, ready to lash out at anyone. I am mad at Spencer for putting us in the MMM barracks. If we grouped with our kind, we wouldn't be under the thumb of that crazy corporal. However, I do realize that being in this situation has nothing to do with our bishop being murdered. He was so kind. What kind of people would do such a thing? I am so scared.

As if sensing my feelings, Spencer stealthily slides from the top bunk. First his feet and legs come into view and slide down to my bunk. He quietly steps on my mattress and lies next to me. OMG. What is he doing? Does he think that now the bishop is gone, we no longer need to wait for marriage? I don't think I am ready for this, and definitely not tonight, after all.

"Hey," Spencer whispers. "I know this is really scary right now, but I just wanted to let you know that I love you, and I will protect you till my dying breath."

"OK," I say. I feel bad. Spencer isn't here for sex; he is here to comfort me. I think.

Still, I hate that we are in this situation, and he is at least partially to blame.

"Spence?" I ask. "What are we doing here?"

He doesn't say anything for a while. I am not sure if I was clear enough. I don't mean Tajikistan or in bed together, but with the Tribe of Iodine Wine. I am about to clarify, but he speaks. He knows.

"I don't know; I just saw the way they stood up for each other, the bravery of Kevin, and thought this was the safest bet. Also—I don't know how to say this—it is such a tremendous fear for me. I am always thinking about how to keep you safe. It is constantly on my mind. And…and I don't like the way the others look at you."

"What do you mean?"

"I mean, they look at you like you're a piece of meat. And the way they use those girls…Becky and Lily—"

"But those girls are in charge."

"Those girls are not in charge. They are being used. And they will look for other girls to use. And…and…I don't know if I can protect you by myself. I know I will die trying, but if you ask me why, why we are in this tribe, I would say because they would die trying too."

I nudge over a bit and pull the blankets back. I welcome Spencer into my bed, and I fall asleep in his warm arms.

CHAPTER 5

Michael

• • •

THE FIRST ORDER OF OUR new enslavement is to bury the dead.

We wake to the sound of the corporal's pistol report outside our door. No one jumps or screams at his cowboy confirmation. The corpulent corporal proclaimed a new order yesterday, and an expected early-morning wake-up followed. We assume no bugles to wake us for the pledge of allegiance. A pistol and *yeehaw* is enough.

Woke but dreary and cloudy eyed from the booze and the breakdown of social order, we dress and walk wordlessly to the door.

Under guard and guns, they march us up to the base. Our tribe is the only group of teenagers on the march to the dead, but I glimpse others watching from the safety of the other barracks as if watching a parade. The pistol shot signaled the start of a new race to see which one of us drops first or follows Paco over the fence. Our spectators are missing popcorn and balloons, more because of the early-morning hour than the fake concern on their smug little faces.

We skip the pledge and head straight to the dead. They herd us toward the main sleeping area of the professional soldiers, now permanent. It's plain to see how they executed their master plan, how they stole victory in the dead of the night while we were drunk in a booze bacchanalia of counting coup conquest. Tape and cardboard on the vents advertise a sign of not-so-sweet salvation. Garden hoses stretch out from the building like life veins that bleed death. The hoses, resting snakes satiated from their meal, lie in the dirt and tire treads of vehicles now gone.

So, their weapon of choice: Hummers.

Exhaust. What did Pax once say? That's not symbolic enough for Kevin. In this case, it's the perfect symbolism. Too spineless to take the soldiers head-on, the National Guard opted to steal victory while real soldiers slept—cowards.

Greenhouse gas, think globally, act locally!

And now, too cowardly to even bury their dead, they have high schoolers do it.

"Simple," the pudgy little corporal commands. "Take the bodies due east near the fence, dig a large hole six feet deep, throw the bodies in, and bury the bodies. Anyone who does not follow orders gets to stay in the hole you all dig."

We are entering the tomb of the unfair soldiers when Lupina halts us.

"Wait. Stop," she says to us, but the little corporal wears a smile on his face and his newfound power. He watches her with licked lips. He must think a plea is coming, a begging from a beautiful girl to be spared the indecency.

"Anyone who doesn't want to handle the bodies should go start digging the hole," she offers. And without further "pleading," she heads into the building. I remember from the downed helicopter, Lupina was part of the team filling body bags with charred bodies. At the time, I felt relief that I didn't have to touch the burned bodies, but guilt gnawed away at me for watching others do it. Now, it's my turn. Pax and I follow her into the building while others contemplate their choice.

We enter the main, large barracks of the enlisted soldiers, kept separate in life and death from where the gutless National Guard sleep. The dead soldiers are frozen in a life and death unfair. Some are collapsed in agonizing asphyxiation around doorways and windows blocked off. Some rest peacefully in their bunks, forever unknowing of the fate fallen.

"We don't even have body bags," Lupina says under her breath. "They care so little that they can't even provide body bags."

The weight and fate of this hits me hard, and now I know what we are up against.

"Let's just use the sheets from the bed," I say solemnly.

We lay out a chessboard of sheets against the walls. We perfect the playing board to delay the eventual touching of the dead, matching the corners up just right, smoothing down the wrinkles.

When the chessboard is perfected, we walk outside under armed supervision to check on the hole. The sun has risen and vomited its fire-orange inertia across the dark-gray clouds. In the distance, the hole diggers are making too much progress for us to delay the placing of the pieces on the chessboard.

We go back inside and stare at the bodies again. We start. This is the first but by far not the last time I will touch a dead body. Eerie coldness, so foreign, unnaturally stains their skin. The flesh seems infectious, releasing a toxic transmission that once touched will spread like a virulent meme. Will I be a carrier or one of the stricken?

I seriously wish for gloves but know not to ask, not to show fear or any weakness. Without talking, we place all the pieces. Here are the pawns, dead soldiers who died not fighting.

We make our way into the officers' quarters. Here is the queen in her own private room. The queen is dead. Eva and Ezra share a hug and then move the major's body off the bed. I go to help, but Lupina tells me, "We got this." I stand back and watch as Annie, Fetien, Eva, and Ezra carry, four cornered, the queen out of the room, down the officers' hallway, and toward the hole.

I walk down the hallway, following the procession, and poke into another room. The captain—bishop to the LDS kids—is laid on his sheet on the floor. He is surrounded by LDS boys. They gather around their bishop and say a long, sad prayer. They arrange his body in white garments lovingly with no care for the coldness of touch.

For a moment, I wish I had that kind of kinship, that kind of connection. I think of the sergeant, my knight—the gentle, hard soul who checked me in to the military role with fatherly pride. That day, we chatted about my father, the football player he remembered from when CU won the national championship. He paid me the nicest of compliments: "You are your father's son."

I always lived in my father's shadow, so these words hit hard. I inherited his physique, his prowess, but I was forbidden from following in my father's footsteps. "The cost is too high," he would tell me when I asked to play sports. "Strengthen your mind. You will have your mind your whole life." And that was the end of the discussion—until I brought it up again. When some of his old friends from his playing days started having CTE issues from too many concussions in their youth and their brains started to deteriorate, it hurt my dad to say, "You will have your mind your whole life."

And then, in middle school, kids ramped up teasing me about not playing sports. I had just won the geography bee. My mother, father, and grandmother were all there. He brimmed over with pride when I won. I'd never seen him so happy. And I was happy. But the next day when my black "friends" found out, they called me "snowflake." They yelled it over and over, "Snowflake! Snowflake! Your dad's a man, but you a bitch." And even though I stood up to them, started throwing some punches, the name still stuck, just behind my back.

I went home that day and begged my dad to let me play football, to let me prove myself the way he did. I figured he was so proud of my geography win, so proud that I showed prowess of mind, that I could now show my manhood on the playing field too.

But he just looked at me, eyes welled up with tears. "My best friend killed himself. We played together in college, and he went on to the pros. He was the strongest person I ever met, and now he's gone. You, Michael, will have your mind your whole life."

I never asked to play football again.

But, of course, I adored my father for all the levels of strength he carried—the strength to excel at a tough sport and the strength to change. And for the sergeant to say I am my father's son…

I leave the LDS and their bishop and go back down to the enlisted barracks. I walk along the chessboard and look for the sergeant.

My knight, of course, is with the fallen, laid out on one of the sheets, on the back wall, two spots from a covered window. I missed him earlier when I helped lay out the enlisted men and fretted about the coldness of touch.

I go to his sheet square on the chessboard. I stare at him and think of my father, of his strength, of his sense of friendship and duty, and of all the things he wanted for me.

I kneel over the sergeant, my knight in khaki armor. I fold his arms. I close his eyes. And I say my own prayer, not one of redemption or remembrance but one of revenge.

After the dead are buried, we make it back to our barracks, drained and dreary but eager to work. We contact Kevin. We have no need for secrecy, no need to hide away in the office, to hide our phone. If the Ceremony of Iodine Wine didn't seal it, the burying of the dead soldiers certainly laid it to rest—we are one.

I hold the phone Kevin gave me. I stand on a chair like a preacher, a mouthpiece for the holy, and transfer Kevin's written words.

"He's online," I say.

The tribe lines up, ready for words. Pax steps forward and lays witness.

"I'm sorry. I was wrong. We should have left. Kevin saw this coming," he confesses.

Forgiveness and acceptance is passed around Pax. We didn't know. We could have left too. It was our decision.

"Let's leave now," Fetien says. "I know where there is a hole in the fence. The hole Kevin left through."

The congregation murmurs a confirmation.

I punch into the phone: "We are ready to leave."

We wait for a response. Heaviness weighs in the air.

Kevin responds, "Paco says hi. He wants me to tell you he killed his first deer."

We all laugh at this, for the levity but more for the confirmation of a food source. Then it dawns on me—it's not just food they found but weapons. My mother is petrified of guns, wouldn't let them in the house, wouldn't let me play with toy guns, but I know enough to know Paco didn't bring down a deer with Kevin's pistol.

As if hearing our laughter, Kevin sends, "I'm not sure we can support everyone. It's hard outside. I need more time."

I relay this to the group. Despair and disappointment show on their faces. The burying of the dead opened a door into a bleak future. We know more hellish things are coming. We feel it in the air.

Kevin says, "There are other choices. You all must decide."

I relay and then respond, "What?"

"You can stay and placate."

An angry "No!" comes over the congregation.

"Or you can stay and fight."

"What does he mean, stay and fight?" Felicia asks while Hector, her beau, raises his fist in defiance.

I relay.

Kevin responds, "Kill the guards. Take over."

A quiet hush fills the room. We play this option over in our minds.

Pax finally breaks the silence in a defeated sort of defiance. "What does Kevin recommend?"

I relay, and the wait is the worst so far.

"Revolt. We have weapons. We will lead the attack. We just need one silent kill at one of the guard gates to let us in."

He has it all planned out. Of course. He is war ready, but are we?

I send, "We will take a vote."

We take a vote.

Very few people choose submission. Many, including Pax, Annie, and me, choose to fight. Most, like Lupina and Jaden, choose flight, to escape. The decision is made. We will leave in peace.

I send, "We choose to escape."

"Very well. I need a few more days to get more supplies. Gather and steal what you can."

The next day starts with more indignation, but we take it in stride. We are not victims. We have a plan. We are leaving.

To show their power, the guards order us to dig new latrines for the other barracks while the other teenagers watch. The hole diggers from the day before are blistered and beat from digging, so they construct the covers while we dig the holes. Compared to touching dead people, this is no problem, even under the laughs of the other barracks.

The boys Paco beat down show more bravery, maybe with the absence of Paco or the presence of guards with guns; I'm not sure. One of them, the fat kid who had trouble getting on the ferryboat in New York, takes a shit in the new latrine while we are still digging. He laughs his snorty piggy laugh while doing it. We think nothing of it. Just cover his emission with dirt and fantasize about life outside the fence.

Fetien, too, is preoccupied with life outside the fence. I see her sneak glances to the fence often.

"There it is, Michael," she says with a nod of her nose toward the fence. "There is the hole in the fence where we will find our freedom."

"And Kevin," I want to add. She thinks I don't know about her crush, but it's always been obvious. I smile and nod. "In due time, Fetty. In due time."

We are almost done with the latrines. Most of our tribe has gone back to clean themselves up. I am applying the finishing touches, watching over Fetty in the distance, drifting and drawn to the fence. It looks like she is going to sneak quietly away. I wonder if I should stop her but just watch her walk invisibly toward the fence. Then I hear words I will never forget.

"Why should they get all the pussy?" the voice from the other side of the latrine says. The question is answered with a cackle of laughter.

He continues, "All I'm saying is we should get some teenage trim; that's all. Look, what about the towelhead? No one will notice. No one will care."

"And she's Muslim. She fucking deserves it."

"Shit, yeah."

At first, I am confused by what they are saying, what they mean, but when they appear walking from the latrines and stalking toward Fetty, I know.

She is too preoccupied with the fence to notice them coming. She cannot make her escape. They grab her and throw her down.

I follow. There are five of them. They are not boys from the barracks but guards with guns. I am not sure what I can do, but two of them pin Fetty to the ground while their ringleader starts to undo his pants. Two other guards are closer to me, but they have guns. I could take a gun, but I honestly don't know how to use it, how to even cock it.

Fetty starts to scream as I slowly move forward. I hope the yelling will startle them to stop or beckon help. But the rapists cover her mouth to stifle the screaming. I look around, and only a few teenagers from the other barracks are watching, spectating. We are on the other side of their barracks, and no one from the MMM barracks can see us. There is no help coming, no stopping.

I know what I have to do. I am my father's son.

I charge at the smallest guard standing near me. Before he can turn around, I punch him as hard as I can in the back of the head and knock him out cold. He drops his gun. I leave it and pick him up instead. I throw him over my back with his feet up and held to my shoulders.

I use him as a shield as I run at the three rapists. If the other guard wants to shoot me, he has to shoot the guard on my back. When I get to Fetty, the rapists look at me and my sack-o-potatoes shield with confusion. I whip the potatoes at one of the rapists while I jump on the other.

I tackle the rapist and crush him to the ground. I can hear the strength and air wheeze out of him, but I do not stop. I start smashing my forehead into his face. Between close-quarter head butts to his face, I stop and yell, "Fetty, the fence!"

She gets up and takes off running toward the fence faster than I have ever seen anyone run before. Her long, fast stride stretches out toward the hole in the fence, and then she glides through it with ease. She is free.

She is the final person I see before everything goes black.

I wake to the chubby corporal standing over me.

"We should kill him," someone says to him.

"Yeah, nah, let's have fun with him first."

* * *

I am chained to the flagpole. Someone pulls a rope tied to the chains on my wrists, and this drags me up off the ground. I stand up on my own feet to relieve the pain.

I hear and feel a crowd behind me. Quiet complaints and whimpers roll out from behind me. I can hear the familiar voices of Lupina and Pax and Jaden. They are distraught. My tribe is too scared. But I fear no one is coming to help me. Kevin is in the forest. No one else is my father's son, my brother's keeper. He would be my only chance; I know this. Kevin and I shared a connection that's hard to explain. He never judged me on my size. He never asked if I played sports or acted intimidated, or worse, never thought it was funny when someone called me snowflake or the *definition of useless.* Kevin respected my intelligence. He is my brother's keeper, and he is not in the crowd.

I am looking for someone else in the crowd, not the crowd of terrified teenagers but the crowd of guards. Where is he? I saw him earlier, that round-faced black guardsman. My nigga. I find him and look at his face. I hold his shifty-eyed stare.

The sun is breaking bright in a brain bruised through eyes I cannot cover. It's hard to make out the detail of his face. The sun is directly overhead. It helps dull the sharp pain if I look straight down, but I decide to stand up proud, not to cower. I embrace the sharpness of the light. I move my gaze from the guardsman to directly stare at the sun. It is eclipsed by a wavering American flag, haloed in the light and dark. The stripes look like lashes; the stars look like bullet holes.

"This is what happens when you attack a guard!" the corporal yells to the crowd. And just like that, I am whipped. The corporal, like most dangerous men, has a penchant for historic symbolism.

The whips are weak. My grandmother spanked me harder. Racism, passed down through the decades, may be preserved, but at least they lost their ability to whip a nigger hard.

I stand up straighter and take the weak blows. I open my eyes wide to the sun and the fettering flag. The brightness numbs my concussed consciousness to a throb and pushes the weak whips into the periphery.

My eyes move back to the black guardsman, though I cannot see him from the scorched impression of the flag and sun. My eyes are wildly dilated but my vision clearer than ever.

I hold his stare, and I yell, "Never again! Never again!"

CHAPTER 6

Charlotte

• • •

My cold exterior came to haunt me. Usually a shield to keep people away, it became a portal for people to ask me the unaskable. Annie has a broken arm. Lupina has a bleeding heart. But Charlotte is cold, calculating. She is "our only hope."

David, the cute, nerdy boy from the other barracks, sneaked over to our barracks as soon as it happened. They tried to gang-rape Fetien. Michael saved her. They took Michael. Thankfully, Fetty escaped through a now-mended hole in the fence.

They paraded us all to the base, to the flagpole, to watch the public punishment of Michael. They made no mention of his heroic act, like we didn't know he saved Fetty. They only mentioned he attacked the guards.

They whipped him. He yelled defiantly. They whipped him harder. And now we can't leave. To leave means to abandon Michael to a sure and punitive death.

We had taken a vote before all this happened. Many, like Annie, voted to stay and fight. Most, like Lupina, voted to leave. I voted to stay and placate. Stay and be quiet and weather the storm. I know the dangers of action. To make the other choices would unravel the threads that hold us together and would certainly end in many deaths.

I remember in our AP economics class, the teacher talked about the velocity of money. The more it moves, the higher number of transactions, the better the benefit for the economy. He also said the same is true for action: the more you network, the more posts you have, the more connections you make, the more likely lucky things will happen to you. I always thought that was stupid.

Mainly because the inverse is true too. The velocity of connections is good when you are in an environment you want to participate in. To me, a wallflower watered in bitter disdain, the velocity of connections is just annoying as fuck. And now that civilization has collapsed, those connections and strings become very dangerous. They become the ties that bind you. They are the chains on the flagpole.

So I voted for inaction. I voted to stay and remain quiet and hidden. And despite my vote for peace (or maybe because of it), they asked me the unaskable. I must kill the guard at the gate.

Jaden pleads, as if I didn't already know, "They'll kill Michael."

Even Pax and Lupina are silently on his side as they gather around me "in support." The majority of the tribe is avoiding me, avoiding the debate. They are hiding on the other side of the barracks, taking apart the roof and bunkbeds, hammering sharp pieces of tin to the two-by-fours to make rough weapons.

Annie offered, "I was supposed to do it, but I can't with one arm."

Ezra is not trustworthy. Fetien is gone, safe now, with Kevin and Paco. These things are obvious and not said. But what isn't said as well is that she must be white. The killer. This saves Eva and the Mexican girls from being asked. She must be white, because in their plan, the seductress needs the appearance of a girl from the other barracks.

So not only are they asking me to kill someone, they are asking to make me into a pretty, vapid prostitute. The humor of this is not lost on me.

"Just think of it as a role in a play. You'll be in costume. You'll play a part," Jaden says.

I look to Lupina. She just lowers her gaze.

"You want me to look like a harlot? Me?" I ask.

"You can do it," Jaden says, but his look retracts what he just implied. "I mean, you are great with costumes and makeup. You can make anyone look like anything."

His flattery is weak, but so is my response. "I don't even have womanly hair," I say and bounce my boyish bob with my hand.

Still staring at the floor, Lupina offers in a quiet act of contrition, "You can have it. You can have my hair."

I am Xola. The female antihero from one of my favorite graphic novels, *Borderline*. Xola is a woman who kills men. Xola suffered a lifetime of abuse by men—from her abusive father to a rapist classmate to a long line of asshole boyfriends. Through all the abuse, Xola developed borderline personality disorder with a healthy mix of self-destruction and destruction. Both a sadist and a masochist, she puts herself in dangerous situations.

"She asks for it."

Provocative clothes, apparent chemical dependencies, and just being alone on dark corners in dark alleys or dark bars almost always lead to a man who tries to rape her. And when they come, sometimes she lets them complete the cycle of self-destruction, the recreation of trauma, part of her BPD. When they enter her, she drains them, not of semen but of blood. A quick slice to the jugular and they bleed all over her while she watches the life drain from their eyes and the power from their position on top.

Xola looks at herself in the mirror. The diminishing supply of lightbulbs in the barracks contributes to a weird symphony of light. Moonlight falls in through ash- and dust-covered windows to cast a murky, ugly glow. The feeble light is cut with a large flashlight Pax holds, bearing down on the back of Xola's head, now covered in Lupina's appropriated hair. The light casts strange shadows in the dark mirror.

The long dark wave of Lupina's hair curls and frames around Ezra's overdone makeup—big red lips; gaudy fuck-me eyes winged with eyeliner; her reddened, excited cheeks. Some tight-fitting clothes from the Mexican girls show her ample cleavage. She lets the girls out. Always big but hidden behind frumpy clothes, now they are out to play, out for everyone to stare at.

Xola stands up and does a model curtsy in the crusty mirror. Her butt sticks out, tight and curvy. Her legs are slick and shaved. Xola is sexy as fuck.

She turns around. The flashlight highlights her nascent curves, her transformation. Everyone takes her in. Even the guys making the weapons have stopped their work to check her out.

Jaden, standing next to Pax and the large flashlight, carries a salacious look priceless in its relation to his arguments. His mouth is literally open and slack jawed. Everyone stares at her with amazement.

Everyone except Lupina—with her head newly shorn, her doe-like eyes look even bigger, more childlike now, without her hair, and they shift their gaze downward.

"Oh my God!" Xola mimics at Lupina with a sickly fake voice. "You could be soooo pretty. You should totally let me do your makeup."

On her walk to the base, Xola can see the flagpole in the distance with the mass of Michael collapsed around the base. The sight of Michael chained makes Xola nervous for what she must do. Another chain to bind, a stitch to the hitch of heavy obligation.

She thinks of the Order of Lucretia from *Borderline*. The secret Order of Lucretia is a fraternity of men, of good men, who have taken an oath of protection and revenge for the women in their lives. If any one of their daughters, wives, sisters, or lovers is hurt by a bad man—a rapist, an abuser, a predator—the Order of Lucretia steps in and takes care of the bad man while the man with the relationship to the woman has an alibi, has nothing to do with the crime. The Order protects their own from the bad men of the world. Why? Because it happens all the fucking time.

I wish I had men from the Order of Lucretia in my life while growing up.

In the graphic novels, Xola is discovered and then covered for by the Order of Lucretia. Sometimes, she does their work for them before they get a chance. The order is made up of cops and jury members, men with means, and when Xola's self-destruction comes calling—lands her in a situation from which she cannot escape—the Order of Lucretia saves her.

Michael is from the Order of Lucretia. He saved Fetty from being brutally raped. Michael is a good man. He is worth saving. He is worth killing for.

Xola feels Kevin's cold knife tucked up her sleeve. The knife is fastened to a strap tied across her shoulders and to her other hand. With a strong bend of her left elbow and a flick of the thumb, the strap releases the knife down her other sleeve. If she is searched, arms out, the knife should remain hidden under her blazer, but with a flick of movement, the knife is unsheathed and available.

Xola's high heels click on the cement leading to the guardhouse like the click of an executioner's watch. The guard is one of the men who tried to rape Fetien, Xola tells herself. He deserves to die. Click, click, click.

"Halt!" the guard commands. Oh, how cute: he's playing soldier boy.

Xola stops. She duckfaces her lips. She sticks out her tits.

"Can I come forward?" Xola asks in a honeyed voice.

"What do you want?"

"What do I want? Oh, honey, I just want some company."

Silence. Is he not a bad man?

"Becky and Lily get to have all the fun. That's not fair," Xola says coyly, trying a new tactic. "And I'm hungry and need a warmer bed to sleep in."

"Ah, come on in." The door opens. The guard takes her in with his eyes. He stares at Xola's big tits and luscious lips. He touches himself as he watches Xola saunter by. She turns to him, starts to kiss him hard, and pushes him against the wall. She grabs the back of his head with her left hand. Her right hand comes up. And then she slits his throat clean through like a thin piece of thread.

Xola is covered in blood. Her eyes are closed. This time, she did not watch the life drain out of the eyes. Her hands are shaking. Kevin's knife slips from her hands but oscillates wildly at the end of the strap. It slices through the air and cuts her dress, cuts her hip.

She lowers her hands to look for the small flashlight she needs to send signal to the forest. She has trouble getting the flashlight out with shaking hands. The strapped and bound knife continues to dance around her legs, leaving little slices in its swing. The pain wakes her back to reality. The flashlight is finally found and lit, alerting Kevin, Fetien, and Paco waiting in the forest.

"Char, Char?" a soft, distant voice asks into the guardhouse. There is no response. Kevin's face, darkened with mud, peeks through the window. He sees me standing there, shaking. He reaches in and unlocks the gate. Paco and Fetty come in. They are dressed in dark clothes, and Paco is armed with a machine gun.

Kevin follows. He is carrying bolt cutters and a machine gun strapped to his back. He looks at the dead body on the ground. He takes the soldier's machine gun and hands it to Fetty.

"Can you lead us to Michael?" Fetty asks.

I nod. I start to walk toward the door like a zombie in heels. Kevin stops me. He puts a hand on my shoulder and then drops to a knee. I have no idea what he is up to. He places the bolt cutters on the ground and slowly takes off my high heels. He gets up, hands me the bolt cutters, and hands me the fettered knife.

Kevin takes up his machine gun. "OK, let's go," he says.

I follow them to the flagpole. We sneak along walls of the buildings. We wait a minute to watch for any movement, for anyone hidden from view in the darkness. Nothing happens.

We run toward Michael. He looks asleep. I wonder if he is still alive. Fetty kneels and touches his head, touches his face. He starts to stir.

"Michael, thank you, thank you. You saved me," she says.

He looks up at her with disbelieving eyes. Then he looks at all of us. His gaze stops and focuses on me. I must be quite a sight, unrecognizable, wearing my wig and gaudy costume and warm patina of blood.

Kevin puts his gun down and takes the bolt cutters from me.

"Hold up your arms," he whispers to Michael. "Spread your hands."

Michael complies. Kevin cuts the chains. The connection breaks, and each new end of chain swings downward.

"Can you run?" Kevin asks.

Michael nods and gets up, strong. We run back to the wall together and gather.

Kevin pulls a pistol out and hands it to me handle first. I shake my head no.

"No more killing for me tonight."

"It's not for you. It's for Annie. She is waiting by the tire pyramid. The other barracks are armed now. When we attack the base, they may attack our barracks. Others are hiding in the outbuildings, but Annie is going to spring a counterattack from the pyramid."

Kevin stops and looks me in the eyes.

Slowly, he commands, "I need you to take Michael and the gun to Annie. Understand?"

"Yes," I say. I take the gun with my left hand.

"I'm not going," Michael says. "I'm staying with you three. I'm fighting."

Michael's words are a declaration. They leave no questioning and no doubt.

"I don't have any more guns," Kevin says.

Michael reaches out and softly takes my right fist, still gripped around Kevin's knife. He releases my hands from the handle of the knife. He pulls on it and the strap. I turn around, spin, like a dancer in a musical. I feel the string release from me, unbound. The strap slides over my arms and out the other sleeve.

I stop spinning.

Michael cuts the strap in half and then wraps the strap around the broken chain Kevin cut down the middle. He binds the chain to his arms to keep it from thrashing around while he moves. I help him tie the strap tight. He looks like an armored superhero. When we are finished, he raises his chain-laden arm and places a hard, strong hand on my shoulder.

"Charlotte, thank you, thank you. You saved me," he says with the softest of voices. Then he looks toward the flagpole with the hardest of stares.

I walk alone and barefoot across the base to our barracks, wondering what to do if I am spotted, if I am stopped by other guards. Can I take another life? Do I have it in me to use the gun? Can Xola or some other heroine spark another possession to save me?

My heart starts to race when I see people, crouched but running from behind our barracks toward me. The gun feels heavy in my hand. I am not sure if I can use it. Then I realize there is no need. I recognize the people running toward me. I see Pax, Cisco, Jaden, Eva, Danny, and others. They are running up to join Fetty, Paco, Michael, and Kevin in the fight even though they are armed only with the bulky spears. We run past each other without saying anything. They look at me with both admiration and fear when they see the blood covering me, but they pass by silently.

I make it to the tire pyramid without detection by any enemies. Annie is stooped five tiers up. She is watching the other barracks and watching me at the same time.

"Oh, girl," she says, taking in my ensemble. "You done right."

I nod. I take a couple of steps up the pyramid. I hand her the gun.

"Are you OK?" she asks.

I don't respond but head toward our barracks.

"Char, Char, go to the outbuildings. It's not safe in there."

I ignore her and enter our deserted barracks. I head to my bunk. I strip off Lupina's hair and throw it to the floor. It lands like a sullied and frayed mop top.

I reach my bunk. I crawl under the covers and wait for the blood to dry and the bullets to come.

CHAPTER 7

Annie

• • •

I WAIT ON THE TIERS of the fucking pyramid because I am a stranger in a strange land and all that crap. I am all alone, waiting to take on the whole teenage suburbia of Denver, armed with nothing but Kevin's virgin pistol. That's cool, peeps. I can handle this shit. Why??? Because ima fucking badass.

That's why. Poor, poor Char, Char. The first to draw blood is collapsed all spent and done in the barracks, and I wonder, where will it end for all of us? In holes in the fields we dug two days ago or hiding from future nightmares? Where will it end? Where will it end!

Oh well. Charlotte's cool as shit and now has her own web to climb out of. Goal: just to keep the jackbooted thugs from stomping down on her and my other chill, chill friends in the outbuildings.

Now I just wait and make little mole holes in the pyramid by shifting tires with my nonbroke arm and full-swole legs. My short stature finally good for something. I have all these holes to hide in if the suburbanites overrun the barracks and want to play whack-a-mole. But I can't see them being so brave, to peek into a hole where I may be hiding, gun cocked and ready.

Truth be told, this is scary as hell, the waiting and anticipation. Any minute now and the base will scream with gunfire. Any fucking minute now.

The brave, gunless soldiers from our tribe ran up to join Paco, Kevin, and Fetty. Follow them around and wait to pick off and pick up the scraps of weapons.

Wait. Where is Michael? He didn't come back with Charlotte. He better not be dead. He better not be fucking dead! Now I want this shit to start. Bring it, motherfuckers, bring it.

Should I go ask Char about Michael? No, just wait and bring it. Later is the time for questions. Now is the time for bullets.

And so it begins. One, two, three. The volleys are fierce as fuck at first…I have happy, happy thoughts that these are the gotcha shots coming from Kevin and crew. No surrender called in this exercise. One shot and ur dead, dickhead.

Now, I can hear the firing die down, but it does not stop. I need to pay attention to the other barracks. I have one job! Lights are coming on. People are waking up to the cacophony of chaos from the base. God, I hope my crew is killing it.

OK, OK! They are gathering all sheepish outside their barracks, and the mofos have guns. Oh shit. Oh shit. They seem to be arguing about an attack. Kevin told me they were instructed to attack us if any fighting broke out, but do they have the balls? Will they shoot from their barracks, or will they come up for a sneaky peek?

And here they fucking come!

Only a handful of them sneak their sneaky sneak my way, just the ones with guns. They lack the bravery of my tribe, willing to run into a firestorm with no firearms. These wimps sneak up to our empty barracks fully armed. Oh Christ, I can feel my heart bumping all the way up to my throat like a rapid frog croak. I hope they cannot hear me, see me. I am mud faced, a dirty warpaint to blend me into the black pyramid and the dark night. A black cap covers my bright-boy hair. I feel safe in my mole hole with my disguise, and those stupid fuckers are watching the barracks and not the pyramid anyway.

Here they come. They tiptoe past me and to the barracks. What should I do? Who should I hit? It is hard to see, but I make out my mofo foe, the one who knocked me down this pyramid and broke my elbow. How do I know? He has big white stripes of bandages on his face where the lovely Paco broke his fucking nose. He wears no mud face, no warpaint. He lacks proper war planning.

Come a little closer. Come into our web. They approach the door. Are they planning on coming in and firing? I am tempted to wait and see if they would actually do it, but Char Char is in there. No, time to start the dance.

I take aim at mofo foe. I pull the trigger, twice. He drops. Without thinking, I fire at the others. One more falls, and another follows his friends with a hopping limp back to their barracks. I suppress a nervous laugh as they skedaddle their way back to the other barracks and the safety of their cowardly lion friends.

My enemies have returned to their barracks but started a barrage toward us from afar. My job now is to wait, to hide in a mole hole of the tire pyramid and wait for the battle on the base to end and for whoever wins to come calling. Oh shit, how many bullets did I use? I have no resupply, but I just need one more bullet.

I slip down into a mole hole and open the revolver with my bum hand. The pain is excruciating, but I have to know. I am forever grateful that my dad taught my brothers and me about guns, how to clean them, fire them, respect them. I check the chambers and see only one bullet shining deep and desperate in the moonlight. That's enough. I snap the cylinder shut.

I can feel bullets coming into the pyramid to die. They know I fired from here and return the bullets tenfold, but I am glad because if they shoot at the pyramid then charlotte is safe, and the layers of tires should protect me. Hopefully.

The wait is seven layers of hell, full of demons and fire and Bridgestone. I stay crouched and cocooned in my mole hole and listen to the gunfire and explosions ring out from the base. The gunfire from the base keeps on keeping on. At least the other barracks have finally quieted, saving energy and bullets. But I am scared too, so scared that we are losing the battle of the base.

The not-so-worse part is the battle won't die, and neither will one of the mofos I shot. He is still moaning on the ground. The sound sickening and amplified in my own little speaker box pyramid. I am tempted to crawl out, to expose myself and put him out of his misery. But I just wait. I am a coward and not sure for which: not wanting to expose myself or not wanting to put the final, merciful bullet in him.

My ringed view of the sky is starting to lighten around the edges when the gunshots begin to fade. I look up and see the full moon through the haze of ash and gunsmoke. The moon is centered in the circle of my tire, a circle within a circle. I say a prayer to the moon goddess or whatever, a prayer that my friends are safe and we are wringing victory out of the battle and my final bullet will be used in celebration and not suicide.

But then I hear a truck coming toward our barracks fast. This is it. The moment of truth. If they roll men or fire into our barracks, into Charlotte, then I will know we lost. I will know what to do with my final, merciful bullet.

But the truck runs past the pyramid, past Charlotte's web, heading toward the outbuildings! God no. Please let it not be the enemy.

I decide a different outcome for my final bullet. I launch out of my silo and bounce down the pyramid. I chase after the truck in a mad rush, my arm pointed like an arrow flying through the night with my gimpy arm clinched in half prayer to my side, sling bound, but bouncy with pain in the fury of my final run.

The truck stops well ahead of me, and people jump out and run into the outbuildings where everyone is hiding. Am I too late? If shots ring out, I will lose my bowels and probably my life.

I clutch the gun in my hand and tighten my grip, ready for my final stand. A boy comes out of the building in a hurry and approaches the truck. Others follow.

Hands up! I yell.

They notice me running at them. I am waiting for the grand decision. Will they raise rifles or hands? But the butch boy raises his hands in surrender. I realize we are safe. We have won. The boy is not a boy, but Lupina shaved and fetched to help with the wounded lying in the back of the truck.

She climbs in. I put my gun away and watch from outside the truck. Others exit the buildings and crowd around.

Hector, Felicia, and Jaden are inside. Hector is calm but holding his stomach with hands drenched in blood. It's oozy, and I get woozy. Felicia is covered in blood too and tending to Hector lovingly and full of worry. Strong girl that Felicia. Jaden is on the floor rolling in pain. His clothes look charred and painted in darkened blood. He is crying and whimpering and reminding me that we are only kids thrown into the world of fucked-up adulting.

Lupina looks at Hector and shakes her head. Felicia looks up at her with pleading eyes.

"Please, please, help him," she says.

Lupina kneels and holds one of Felicia's hands. "Give him peace. Give him comfort," Lupina says. "There is nothing anyone can do, but it may take a while for him to pass."

With that she turns to help Jaden, and I turn to get the fuck out. Too much reality for me tonight, but then I think about the suffering I doled out. I think about the kid I shot who didn't die, who was moaning in the dirt. I get the strongest urge to go save him, to help him, to balance out all the killing tonight, to balance out my killing.

I jog back toward the pyramid with my half prayer and flaccid arms.

I see Pax walking toward me. He is carrying a weapon but looks like a really tall little boy playing war. He sees the boys I shot and shakes his head violently as if seeing ghosts. He gives them a wide berth.

He sees me and stops. He blinks his eyes like he is trying to figure out who I am, and I remember I have warpaint mud on my face and a black hat on my head.

"Pax, Pax, it's me, Annie," I say.

He doesn't say anything but just stares at me. He is holding his rifle, and for a moment I am scared he doesn't recognize me, that I might fall in the fog of war.

"It's Annie, your friend." I take off my hat. He seems to wake from his stupor. "Pax, are you OK?"

"Lupina? Where's Lupina?" He asks like a boy asking for his mom.

Oh, poor Pax. We all had it rough, but I don't know what he saw or didn't see. I don't know what happened on the base while I was poking in and out of my mole hole.

Pax looks lost, and his rock is tending to others.

I go up to him and take his rifle. I put it on the ground and wrap my good arm around him and hold him tight. I close my eyes. I put the side of my face to his chest and can feel his heartbeat pounding like a drum. I take long, big breaths, which he starts to mimic.

I need this too. I clench my eyes tight to keep from crying into Pax's chest.

"They were alive," he says. "I am sure they were alive." His voice is frightened and confused.

"I know, buddy. I know."

And then I remember what I did, what I saw. The one I dropped who I am not sure is alive.

I open my eyes and look at the boys on the ground. The one moaning before is stiff and still next to his dead compatriot. And they are gone. All of them.

"I don't know what's true anymore," Pax says.

I start to cry. I water a pool of tears on Pax's quivering chest as the morning sun and the ash fold their arms around us.

CHAPTER 8

Felicia

• • •

When I was young, we buried my *abuela*. After the funeral, we returned to her small house for the funeral party. Growing up, my cousins, brothers, and I had spent many fun times at her house, playing games, making tamales, and just celebrating family. I think we held the funeral party there to hang on to her spirit. We wanted to hang on to that feeling of family she created. The love of our matriarch kept the family all together, made us whole and important and cherished. No one was willing to give that up too soon.

Her funeral was my first funeral. I didn't know what to expect. Didn't really know how to act, so I watched and copied my aunts, uncles, and older cousins.

I kept my face firm. I talked in a quiet voice. And I wouldn't cry. Even when I saw my beloved *abuelita* in her casket at the church, I wouldn't dare cry.

But what I remember most about that day is the smell of her house. It was typically filled with such wonderful smells, like carnitas and fresh handmade tortillas. I carry many good memories of growing up with those smells. But that day, my mom and aunts cooked at their homes and brought the food to her little casa in Commerce City.

No, the smells weren't food; they were something else. *Muerta y mierda*.

The smells in Commerce City were typically bad, but I don't know if an evil wind ran that day, because all I can remember is it smelled like shit. It smelled like burnt shit. I was young and stupid at the time, and I kept wondering if that was the smell of death, if the terrible smell of my dead abuela haunted the house even though we had already lowered her casket into the ground hours before. I didn't know it was just the smells being kicked up into my abuela's poor neighborhood from the nearby sewer plant and oil refinery. At the time, I thought the death smell could haunt your house like a ghost even if the body was in the ground.

Now at my latest funeral, we bury Hector in the garden near our barracks. And I am haunted by the death smell. Kevin had us round up all the dead soldiers. We piled them in front of the flag where they whipped Michael. He said we didn't have time to dig graves, so we made a funeral pyre, poured gas on top of them, and lit it up. It smells like burnt shit. It smells like death.

I couldn't move the dead. I couldn't help make the pyre. A bullet hit my arm when Hector made his stand. A soldier surprised us in the halls of the base, and Hector charged him, unarmed. He took two bullets in the gut but still disarmed the *pendejo.*

Saved us. My Hector, the hero. Not like those soldiers who killed the other soldiers in their sleep with exhaust. We fought them like men. But now we bury Hector while they burn.

With my hidden wound, I couldn't help pile the dead. But I lit the pyre. I put the lighter to the gas-soaked flesh. Then I stood back and watched as the killer of Hector burned. Watched as the fire quickly spread to his fellow traitors. Watched as they all turned into a blackened heap of burnt shit. *Muerta y mierda.*

Cisco leads us in prayer, but the smoke from the base still fills the air. The evil wind is changing and blowing the smoke our way. God, the smell is awful.

Cisco coughs and then continues, "Hector, you were the strongest among us. The most loyal. Our rock. You showed loyalty and strength in your life and in your death. The only gift we can take from this tragedy is an example of how to live our lives, how to protect our loved ones, our tribe."

"Amen," everyone says.

Everyone is gathered around. Kevin, the girls who didn't fight, and even Charlotte, the one who dressed up slutty and slit that guy's throat all cold blooded, is here. Jaden too, patched up and done with his crying.

The only one off to the side is Michael, the big black man they whipped under the flag. He is standing on one of the trucks, watching us and watching the other barracks. He has a big machine gun pointed at their buildings. His face is angry and unforgiving. I understand that look. Sacrifice isn't the only gift Hector left us.

The boys start to throw shovels of dirt on Hector's body with ease. The dirt makes a sad drumming sound as it lands. The sound is constant and building like war drums. It's appalling how skilled we've become at burying bodies.

I try to be strong against the sickening sound of dirt drums and the smell of scorched death. I need to be strong like Hector. I take a step forward, and with my good arm out, I bend down and grab a handful of dirt. I kneel and throw it on my Hector. Then I fucking lose it. I can't stop crying. I am grown-ass woman now, not a small child, but I can't help it. This isn't like losing an old abuela. I just lost my love.

My girls put their arms around me, crying too, holding me close, hurting my arm, but I take the pain. I need the pain. I chew on it to mash away the crying and weakness. The pain makes me stronger.

We stay there at the foot of his grave. I've stopped crying, but my girls still moan while the boys fully cover Hector and bury him deep in the ground. Finally, they lift me up. The pain shoots through me from their hands on my arm, on my bullet wound. We are walking as a mass back to the barracks when Yesenia pulls her hand away and looks at the fresh blood.

"Felicia, you're bleeding?" she asks.

I ignore her, but she stops me. She puts her hand on my wound, and I flinch away in pain. She pulls her hand back and looks at the new blood.

"We need to get you fixed, girl."

But I don't want to get fixed. I don't want to be helped. I want to be strong like Hector. No one could fix him.

Lupina is called over. She didn't even try to fix Hector. Now that too-good half breed wants to help me. She starts cutting at my sleeve with a pair of big scissors.

"Were you shot?" she asks, surprised and too loud. Now everyone gathers around me instead of paying respect to Hector.

I don't say anything.

"If we don't take care of this, you will get infected, and then you'll lose your arm and probably your life. Very painfully."

For a softy, she knows how to cut to the point. I let her take me into the office.

I am cleaned up and stitched and wearing a new sling like Annie. Lupina doused me with iodine and gave me a small bottle as well as some antibiotic pills.

"Luckily, the bullet didn't hit bone and went straight through, but if any infection breaks out, you could be in a world of trouble," she says.

I'm about to thank her when Cisco knocks on the door and sticks his head in.

"Meeting time," he says.

Kevin called a meeting. Everyone is in the barracks. Michael joined us too, but he parked the truck by the door and keeps staring out the window at the other barracks, ready to pounce in a heartbeat.

We walk by, and I say to him, "Light 'em up."

He looks at me and then looks back at the other barracks without a smile or nod.

Yesenia punches me playfully in my good arm, but it still hurts all over.

"This shit is crazy," she says with a shake of her head.

I look out the window, following Michael's forever stare. A pool of blood has collected by the truck from where Annie dropped those two chickens sneaking up on our barracks. Way past the pools of blood sit the other barracks, quiet and cooped and under Michael's angry watch.

"What? I think we should waste them all," I say.

We join the rest of the group and turn to look to the chair where Michael preached from the other night.

"You ever see that movie?" Yesenia says. "The one with the white schoolboys that crash on the island. All the adults die, and then the kids go all tribal and start fighting each other. That's what this feels like."

I nod, but that know-it-all Eva butts in with her too-loud voice.

"You mean *Lord of the Flies*?"

"Yeah, that's it, crazy fucking movie. I keep hoping them soldiers roll up and save us and take us back home."

"You know, it was a book before it was a movie," Eva says.

I give Eva a shut-the-fuck-up look. I read the book too, but no need to make Yesenia look stupid. Eva purses her mouth shut and goes back to minding her own business.

Kevin walks past us. He is getting ready to start the meeting, to go to the preaching chair, but he stops and turns to us.

"Yesenia, friend, those soldiers, they are coming," he says.

He climbs up on the chair and looks at us all, a cold, hard look like the look a parent gives before breaking the bad news.

"They're coming. That much I guarantee. They just aren't coming to save us."

Now everyone shuts the fuck up.

Kevin starts. He warms over the cold he just unleashed on the room.

"Our hearts are with Hector," he says. "As Cisco said, we lost one of the strongest and bravest who died saving others. We all sacrificed a lot. Our innocence, our health, our Hector. Maybe even our safety. But we kept our freedom and our honor. We will continue to fight for that as long as we can. We will live the way Hector lived. With pride and honor. And here is what we are going to do."

Kevin looked right at me when he mentioned Hector by name; now he returns to his gangster stare.

"Felicia, you and Spencer are going to make peace with the other barracks."

"Peace!" I snap. "Hector is dead!"

"They didn't kill him," he dictates. "Eva, Michael, and I are going to leave soon for a day or two, and I want this peace to be quick and permanent. Or would you rather have the blood of hundreds of teenagers on your hands?"

He looks at Spencer and then looks back at me. We both nod.

"Here are the terms. Our group, our tribe, will leave the base within three days. We will leave enough food and light weapons for the other barracks to defend themselves, but we will be carrying and driving out what we can."

I want to yell out again, but at least I don't have to. Everyone else is standing up and yelling at Kevin.

Kevin watches us patiently. He lets the yelling run its course. Then he raises his hand, and everyone goes quiet.

"This isn't a negotiation. This isn't up for vote."

No matter. Lupina steps forward and speaks.

"Kevin, if we were just going to leave the base anyway, why did we have to kill all those soldiers? Why did Hector have to die?"

Lupina's all right.

"We needed the weapons and the supplies. We needed to neutralize the corporal. And there are other reasons you will just have to trust me on. It's not safe here. It's not very safe outside the fence either, but with the weapons and each other, we should be able to survive."

"Ha, should be able to survive?" I think. Not the best sales pitch.

"Where are we going?" Pax asks, but Lupina throws him a sad, weak look.

Damn, dude, you should stand up for your girl.

"We are heading to the mountains. To a region called Badakhshan. It's fairly ungoverned and full of mountains and valleys where we can hide."

I want to ask, "Hide from what?"

But Yesenia blurts out, "Badassastan? Well, that fucking fits."

Everyone laughs at her comment—everyone but Kevin. He just looks to the floor and recites, "Let this grisly beginning be none other to you than is to wayfarers a rugged and steep mountain."

With that, he steps down off the chair. He waves me and Spencer over. I am not sure why the white boy and me were chosen to make peace. I think to check each other, to make sure I don't go too hard and Spencer doesn't go too soft.

"Listen, Spencer, Felicia: part of the terms is they need to stay in their barracks until we leave; understood?"

We nod.

"OK. Good. You better get going then. I recommend carrying a white flag, but trust me; they're more scared than you. Oh, and one more thing," he says with a soft, quiet voice, pulling us closer. "You can let them know that unfortunately their girls who were staying with the soldiers were killed in the firefight."

We take the long walk over to the other barracks. Spencer has a pillowcase taped to a broken mop handle. He waves it in the air, both defiant and friendly at the same time. It seems like a surrender, but it's not. Still, I feel better knowing Michael is back up on the truck behind us with that big machine gun. You never know when a scared sucker is just going to pop off a few rounds, and he has the bigger gun if that happens.

We reach their door, and it opens. They were watching us the whole time. We enter. I am ready to do battle, ready to lay down the law, but when we enter, they just look like a bunch of scared kids. The barracks is packed full of kids, and I realize all three buildings are hiding in here. The body heat and fear hang in the air like a stifling blanket. Despite the scared kids, there are still a few off to the side with hard faces and machine guns.

"We've come to make peace," Spencer says.

"Damn," I think, "way to start all soft." Maybe he fears the ones with guns.

"Peace?" an armed teenager snaps, taking advantage of the soft spot. "Brad and Tony are dead! And where are Becky, Lily, and Kelly?"

Spencer looks flustered, all red in the face. He starts to talk but doesn't know how to break the bad news.

"They're dead," I jump in. "And if you don't shut the fuck up and do what you're told, you all are going to be dead too." I wonder if this is too harsh, but they're not the only ones who lost people.

"Listen," Spencer says. "The terms aren't bad. We are leaving. We'll be out of your hair in three days. We'll leave enough food and some weapons for you to survive for a long time."

There is some grumbling and debating between their leaders when Spencer follows up. "This isn't a negotiation."

They stop and stare at him, surprised by his firmness. I'm surprised too. And then he takes it up a notch.

"You need to stay in your barracks for three days. You can't leave to use the latrines you watched us build. You can't leave to say the pledge of allegiance at the flag where you watched Michael get whipped. You can't leave, period. If you do leave, then Michael, the one you watched get whipped, the one who saved Fetien from being raped while you watched, is going to unload a fifty-caliber machine gun on all of you. Understood?"

We turn to leave. I stop at the door and turn around. They are looking at me like a bunch of beaten dogs. They look even more scared than when we entered.

"We'll fetch you some buckets of water," I say and turn to follow Spencer back to our tribe.

CHAPTER 9

Eva

• • •

I DRIVE THE TRUCK OVER a battered jeep road with Kevin running shotgun. Michael is on top of the truck with his big machine gun scanning the forest. To be honest, I feel honored to be chosen by Kevin for this mission. I love being with him, being his confidante, spending time together, but we are not alone in the truck.

In the seats behind us are the girls—Becky, Kelly, and Lily. Their hands are tied in their laps. I sneak looks back in the rearview mirror. They look like petrified dolls, their porcelain faces reddened with terror and streaked with ruined mascara. They are scared and unsure of their fate. They probably think they are being driven out to be dropped off in exile like Paco or, worse, to be killed and dumped in a hole like the soldiers smothered by exhaust in the dead of night. But I have a pretty good idea what Kevin has in store for them. I mean, he didn't get those three machine guns for free, right? Fetty, Paco, and Kevin couldn't attack the base with a pistol and a knife. So he made a trade. Three girls for three guns sounds fair.

I don't feel bad about their fate, not bad at all. Maybe that's why Kevin chose me for this mission, because we are both the same, both skilled at playing the long game and making the hard decisions—when you get the bow and arrows, you hunt your enemies down;

when the rival vampires are at your feet, you wipe them out. The benefits outweigh the costs. The ends justify the means and all that.

Kevin and I are the only ones who know the true reason why we are here. We were to be the Hitler Youth. We were to be the Child Soldiers of the Sudan. They didn't evacuate us to save us; they evacuated us to train us into the future soldiers of tomorrow. They just didn't realize that Kevin and I couldn't be trained, couldn't be owned. And now their soldiers are burning in a pile, and their lackeys are under our thumb…or in the back seat with hands tied.

At the very least, those girls whored themselves to the soldiers to receive a privileged position. At the worst, they directed the soldiers to kill the other soldiers and make us slaves. They went up to the base after Paco's beatdown on the night of the killings. I saw them oversee the soldiers as they searched our barracks and then exiled Paco over the fence. I saw them watch with suppressed smiles as Michael was whipped. So no love lost on my part, not one bit. They deserve what's coming.

At first, I was a bit jealous. Kevin told us to "save the girls." When we attacked the base, we divided into three groups. Paco led the Mexicans into the barracks where the enlisted men slept. Fetien led East High School and Utah to take out the guards around the motor pool so we could use the trucks and heavy machine guns. Michael, Kevin, and I went into the officers' quarters.

We separated from the others and sneaked toward the guard in front of the officers' door. Kevin told Michael to sneak around the sidewall and then to the wall where the guard was stationed.

He then pulled me close and whispered, "OK, when Michael is in position, I need you to run out and wave your arms and act like you are crying. When the guard runs out, Michael will jump him."

I felt scared but wanted to be brave for Kevin, wanted to help our cause.

"Don't worry; if things go south," Kevin said, "I will shoot the guard. But then we will have to charge the quarters."

Things went as planned. I ran toward guard with my hands up and boobs bouncing. He ran out with his rifle up, but Michael pounced on him from behind and drove the knife into this throat. Kevin and I ran over to the body. Kevin picked up the gun, cocked it, and then handed it to me.

With confidence, he told me, "Don't put your finger on the trigger until you're ready to fire. But make sure you don't shoot the girls. Understood?"

We made our way into the building. The whole time, Kevin kept reminding us, "Keep the girls safe. Don't hurt the girls."

I thought that Kevin wanted to keep the whores for himself. I was jealous and mad. But he's just a man, right? No matter what Annie claimed about his asexuality. That's why he wanted to "save" them, the spoils of war. But it turned out he just wanted to save them for a later date, for a trade.

We sneaked into the building undetected. We followed Kevin upstairs to the hall for the officers' apartments. At the end of the hall was the major's room. I knew it was her room, because I had helped carry her body out.

We made it to her door and then stopped. Kevin quietly tried to turn the handle, but it was locked. He signaled to Michael to knock down the door. Kevin crouched down with his back against the wall and aimed his machine gun the other way down the hall. I followed his lead on the other side of the door.

Michael lined up a few feet away from the door. His big body and anger were framed in the doorway. On either side were Kevin and I, crouched, guns up, like two tigers ready to pounce. Michael clenched his fists. The veins of his arms protruded and interlaced with the chains strapped to his wrist. Michael took a couple of deep breaths and charged the door. He jumped forward and then grunted loud and kicked the door open.

It seemed like a long time, but in a couple of seconds after charging into the room, we heard a woman's scream and then gunshots. Kevin was surprised by the shots and looked into the room. I watched his face for signs. He smiled his dark smile and then returned his gaze to follow his rifle sight down the hall.

The screams kept coming from the major's room as the corporal's henchmen ran out into the hall. Kevin waited for what I thought was way too long, and then we fired our guns. Kevin fired first, and then I pulled the trigger. The gun kicked and spurted, but I held it steady and fired down the hall as their bodies fell.

After the movement and killing ceased, Kevin jumped up and ran down the hall to check all the rooms. Michael soon followed, with a pistol in one hand and the bloody knife in the other.

In two rooms, they pulled out the other girls and sent them toward me. I collected them and pushed them toward the major's room. As I walked down the hall, I could hear firefights breaking out all over the base, gunshots from where Paco's and Fetien's teams had waited for the signal from our team, the first shots. Then I heard louder and closer shots as Michael and Kevin cleared the last room.

Kevin came back down the hallway, jogging and jumping over the fallen bodies with a serious smile on his face. He came up to me and looked deep into my eyes.

"Eva, you need to keep them hidden in this room. Don't leave. Don't make a sound until Michael or I come back for you. Understood?"

I was to be left alone with the crying whores. I wanted to gripe, to have Michael stay with them while I joined Kevin in the fight, but he put his hand on my shoulder. "It may be a long wait, but I have faith in you. This is important. Michael and I will collect the bodies in the hall when all this is over, so we'll be back fairly soon."

Then he kissed me, quick and on the cheek, but with love.

He left, closing the door as he ran out. I turned to the girls, who were still wailing and crying. The girl who was with the corporal was crying the loudest. He lay in a pool of blood on the bed, and she was in the corner, pushing with her legs as if to escape up the wall and away from what she had witnessed.

I went up to her and punched her in the stomach. I told her to keep quiet. I pushed her with my knee to the floor, where she lay with a whimper.

I stepped back and went back to the door. The other girls timidly ran around me, trying to stay far away from the dead corporal and me. They went to their friend and stayed huddled in the corner together.

I looked at them with disgust and then noticed on the wall above the bed, a bloodstained portrait painted around a gouge in the plaster. I looked down at the dead corporal. He was bleeding out his back and front. Michael had punched him so hard with the knife in the heart that it went all the way through him and into the wall.

I smile again, thinking of the blood spot and Michael's monster punch with decades of force behind it. I keep smiling and look over at Kevin riding next to me. I think of his kiss and his trust in me. What a great night.

But Kevin is not smiling. He is watching the road ahead with a concerned, worried look.

"Slow down," he says.

Up ahead is a large group of people, armed with machine guns and surrounded by sheep. What a funny, crazy scene, an army of sheep and men. From a distance, they almost look like mythological creatures mixed together in a bastardization of parts, lower torsos of sheep with tall human bodies carrying weapons. The humans have long beards, and their heads are wrapped in local cloth, similar in pattern and color to what we traded for earlier to make the curtains and dividers in our barracks.

"Stay here," Kevin says to me. "If things go bad, drive straight at them and run them down. It's fairly bulletproof and can run over them. Understood?"

"Sure. Fairly bulletproof," I say with a smile.

He turns to the girls. "Get out."

"No, no, please—we don't deserve this," one of them says.

I think they have finally figured out what is happening.

"Just take us back to the base. We'll do whatever you say."

"If you don't come with me, they're going to kill us all, so you can't convince me of another path," Kevin says.

They try to come up with a way around his logic but just start to cry and plead instead. They look at me as if in some weak search for female solidarity. "Please. Help us," they say to me.

"Think of it this way," I step in. "All you've ever aspired to, all you've ever wanted, was to be an object of male desire. Your fake looks, your sexy posts online, your behavior on the base. You didn't want to be a scholar, an athlete, an artist; you just wanted to be something a man wants to fuck. That's your highest achievement. Pfft. So in many ways, you're getting what you wanted. Mission accomplished. Now get out before we drag you out."

Kevin snorts at my speech. But I've had enough. The soldiers with guns have taken their weapons off their shoulders. They are walking our way. I get out of the truck and open the back door. I pull the first girl out and throw her to the ground, where she lies crying. I start to go after the next one, but she gets out on her own.

Kevin escorts the third girl out and starts to lead all of them toward the small army. I follow. He turns to me with a shocked look on his face.

"No. Go back," he commands.

I want to protest, but he looks scared.

"They'll try to take you too," he says.

I turn around and head back to the pretty bulletproof truck. I look up at Michael. He is crouched down, trying to stay covered but still pointing the big gun down the road. I hop in the truck and watch Kevin hand over the girls to the men with guns.

They seem to be having an argument. Kevin keeps holding up his hand and showing three fingers. He shakes his head no, points back toward us, and shows three fingers again. Are they trying to bargain for me too? Why the hell did I get out of the truck?

I start to get scared. They are still arguing about the trade but have absorbed the girls into their herd. A big, scruffy guy who looks like their leader pushes Kevin, and another soldier points his gun at him. Kevin doesn't look scared. He just turns his head and nods at Michael.

I hear loud bangs as Michael fires warning shots over their heads. I see a small tree nearly split in two.

Everyone crouches down, shocked, but Kevin stands tall. I start to rev the engine. Now they look scared. Kevin holds up the three fingers again. The leader nods.

With that, the soldiers disappear back into the forest. The leader turns around and gives Kevin the three fingers.

The soldiers take the girls but leave the sheep and a couple of shepherds. Under Kevin's direction, the whole herd walks toward us and slowly passes. Kevin walks up to my window. I roll it down.

"After we pass, turn around, and then follow us back to the base," he says over the sheep noises.

I nod yes.

"Hmmm," I think. "I guess they were worth more than a few guns after all."

CHAPTER 10

Pax

• • •

We are stacking food outside one of the supply stores when I hear a commotion from above. People stop working. We all look up at Fetien yelling down at us.

She is up in a guard tower. The tower is pockmarked and tattered from one of the .50 calibers we stole out of the motor pool. On the night of the Battle of the Base, after we took over the motor pool, we went around and easily took out the guard towers with the powerful guns. At the base of the tower lies a bloodstain puddle from where the dead guardsman was thrown out and discarded after the firefight. His body was moved to the funeral pyre, but the bloodstain remains.

"Look! Look!" Fetien yells. She is waving at us and then points down toward the main gate. We can't see the gate because of the buildings in our view, but there is a smile on her face, so we know danger isn't coming our way. She looks into the scope on her rifle, but still, the smile is wide on her face.

She pops back up. "It's Kevin, Michael, and Eva! And they brought some friends!" she yells with a hearty laugh.

We all start heading toward the main gate. They left three days ago, and even though Kevin said the mission could take a couple of days, the wait was a long one.

We stop working and go around the obstruction of the buildings to view the main gate. When Fetien mentioned friends, I thought Kevin had befriended a local militia or humanitarian group, but no, not quite.

In the distance, we see the Humvee and Michael still at the .50 caliber. Spread out in front of the vehicle is a huge herd of sheep, roughly as many sheep as there are people in the Tribe of Iodine Wine. Kevin is mixed in with the sheep to herd them along. I see a couple of unarmed shepherds with him from the local population. They look harmless but skirt the edge of the herd and casually walk with the sheep.

We walk toward the herd. More tribe members leave buildings and duties to join the happy parade moving toward the sheep.

"Hey, Pax, there's your four pounds of food!" Paco yells at me, and everyone laughs.

I take it in stride. I deserve it, I guess. If I didn't tell everyone we couldn't survive outside the fence, then Michael wouldn't have been whipped, and Hector wouldn't have died. Kevin was right; I was wrong, and I have to live with that.

Still, I have had an uneasy feeling bothering me since the Battle of the Base. I was caught up in the heat of the battle. We just took out the guard towers with the machine guns. And the fighting seemed over. We fanned out to look for stragglers. I was armed finally, with a gun taken from the hands of a dead guard. I went into the officers' quarters to make sure the corporal and his closest allies were *neutralized* and not hiding like cowards.

Alone, I went upstairs. I stopped in the hallway to see more bodies on the floor. It was like a scene from some horror movie: bodies strewn awkwardly on a floor coated in blood. I stood there for a long time, not wanting to move forward and cross the threshold of the dead.

But I saw the major's door at the end of the hallway. It seemed to be calling me forward. The door was closed, but all the other rooms were open. I walked down the hall. My steps were careful and chosen between the bodies and slick blood. I reached the door and knocked. One, one-two. No answer, but I swear I heard someone inside the room. I don't know. I just don't trust myself. I also thought I saw Vivi sleeping and cuddled with Lupina after we arrived in Tajikistan. The stress, the weight of all that happened since the smokestacks fell, lay heavy on me, and I don't know what to believe anymore, including myself.

I knocked a couple more times. One, one-two. One, one-two. I noticed the doorjamb was broken. I pushed the door open and dragged myself in. I only took one step inside. I saw the corporal dead on a bed full of blood. A blood spot hung on the wall behind him. He must have been shot, because his heart was bleeding from both sides. Two pools of blood gathered in front and behind his body. So with absolute certainty, I knew he was dead.

That was all I wanted to see. I wanted to make sure he was gone. I stepped back and left the room. I turned around and took a couple more steps into the blood-ridden hall when an alarm went off in the corner of my mind—maybe, the part of my mind that knew Vivi was in New York when the other part thought I needed to join the military to protect her. That part thought I saw three girls huddled in the corner, shaking and scared but alive in the room I had just left.

I stopped, ready to turn around and check again. But I swear I heard the door close behind me, so I left without looking. I just ran down the hallway, skipping limbs and sliding on blood. I ran back toward the barracks, back toward Lupina, until I saw more bodies and Annie, who held me against what I didn't know was true or not.

That uneasy feeling—of not knowing if those girls were alive, of not knowing where they have been since the battle ended when I ran from the slammed door—that feeling stands up. I didn't see the girls on the funeral pyre or anywhere else on the base. I didn't know if they were alive. And that uneasy feeling screams at me when I see the sheep.

Everyone is cheering, happy, giving me crap about the daily four pounds of food, walking toward us with Kevin shepherding and Michael guarding. The tribe parades and dances their way to Kevin and his sheep, but I feel like death. I feel like we just lost our souls.

The euphoria of the tribe starts to drain with the creation of a new parade. My uneasy feeling has only grown, taken on a life of its own, but now, instead of everyone being happy about the return of Kevin and his gift of sheep, they are worried about the new journey into the mountains. We are leaving the base.

Many people treated the new sheep like pets when they entered the base with Kevin. They especially took to the little, happy lambs bouncing around. They ran up and petted and played with the reluctant animals like they were a new litter of puppies and not a food source.

I watch Charlotte, always quiet; she has been absolutely silent since she sliced the guard's throat to start the frenzy of killings. She picks up a scared little lamb. The lamb has a bad leg. It tries to keep up with its bouncing mates but stumbles and struggles. Charlotte wraps the lamb in a shawl like a mother with her infant. She holds the lamb close to her body. They stare at each other for a moment. The lamb licks the salt off of Charlotte's face, and she breaks out in a rare, sweet smile. "Well, there's forty pounds of food we won't be eating," I think.

But not only do the sheep and lambs carry the burden of a slaughter; they also carry the burden of a long, slow walk into the mountains. Our journey will not be by truck; it will be by foot, and Kevin is anxious to get us out of the base.

* * *

We started leaving soon after they showed up. The caravan is made up of five supply trucks, one small gasoline truck, and two armed Humvees—one in the front and one in the back. Everyone else, like the sheep, is hoofing it out.

We leave on a small road into the forest and up toward the mountains. I note where Lupina walks, that she is OK and safe, and she sends me kind smiles. But we haven't been the same since the night of the exhaust, since I thought I saw Vivi in her bed. She is loving and caring and wants to help me; however, I feel she no longer views me as a boyfriend but as a patient. It's pitiful. I'm pitiful.

I'm being tortured in my mind by not knowing what is real and what is true. I know the opaque image of the girls cowering in the corner under the blood-spot portrait will haunt me, not just for the gruesomeness of it or for the implications of me ignoring them and not saving them, but also for the uncertainty of it, not knowing if what I thought I saw was true or not.

I decide to act, for the sake of Lupina, for how she sees me and how she wants a strong man in her life, not a pitiful, scared boy who doesn't believe what he sees or believes what he doesn't see. I decide to end the internal debate in my head right then and there.

I see Kevin walking alone, still basking in his shepherding, his victory, his control. I walk straight up to him.

"Is this what we have been reduced to? Selling girls into sexual slavery for sheep?" I bluntly ask with the aim of shocking a reaction out of him, jarring some kind of sign that those girls were alive and he was behind their exploitation.

But he looks cool and calm, like he is expecting this from me. He doesn't know I am asking for the sake of my own sanity. He just thinks I'm being an argumentative dick.

"We did it to survive, Pax. If you all had escaped out of the base without a fight, Paco and I would have had to kill a bunch of locals for needed supplies. There was no easy way out."

His straight answer washes me in both relief and dismay. I am relieved that I am not crazy, that I did see those girls alive. But I am drowning in the answer and the truth. We exchanged girls for sheep. I could have stopped it, but I didn't. Is he right? Should I have stopped it? Maybe I didn't see them because I didn't want to see them. Maybe my instinct for survival was overriding my moral compass and pointing me down a darkened path.

"Fine. That's where humanity is headed," I say. "A massive battle of survival. Does that somehow excuse us to participate in the slave trade? For fuck's sake. We fought the National Guard and killed many people because Michael stopped Fetty from being raped, and then you sell girls into sexual slavery. I mean, are we no better than them?"

Kevin looks at me. We have drifted to the other side of the road, putting sheep between us and the people following Kevin.

He responds, "We fought the base because it was them or us. A zero-sum game. We did it for the Tribe of Iodine Wine. Didn't you take an oath? And yes, we are better than them. We're alive."

"Well, I don't know if this is a world I want to be alive in. I mean, you sure have taken to it, ironically, but I-I am—"

"What does that mean?" Kevin cuts me off, insulted.

"The world has gone to shit, and you are thriving in it."

"The world has gone back to what it always was, and that's not necessarily a bad thing."

"You're fucking crazy." I finally say it.

We stop walking. Kevin turns to me as the sheep make their way around us with their bleating and their ignorance of the eventual slaughter.

"No, not really. Pax, honestly, we only had decades left. Between global warming, AI, and genetic engineering, something was going to end us in the next fifty years. Maybe this was just a reset button to extend the long game."

"Reset by who?"

"I don't know—the great programmer in the sky or maybe us. Funny thing is, I heard chatter from the base before the civil war. Rumors, conspiracies that it wasn't even the Yellowstone Caldera that blew. It was the Valles Caldera in New Mexico near Los Alamos. And it wasn't terrorists that kicked it off with a bomb; it was people in our government."

"What? Why?"

Kevin starts walking again now that a conspiracy theory has distracted me from the accusations of his craziness. I follow at his heels.

"I don't know. To remake the world in their image. To recolonize the troubled areas. To go all authoritarian. Hell, the ash is even a way to slow global warming without admitting global warming exists.

"If you want to know who is behind a crime, you need to look at who benefited the most. The Muslims aren't benefiting. We're colonizing their lands, not the other way around."

At this, I stop, but Kevin keeps walking. Something in his words gnaws at me. Kevin admitted to a horrific crime. He sold teenage girls into sexual slavery to save us. But he admitted it too easily, without debate, without any proof except my clouded memory. He confessed like he didn't think it was the greater crime.

Kevin turns and takes me in—stunned and standing still. He looks at me with his penetrating gaze.

"Oh, don't you fret, little boy; the world may only have had decades left, but I only have months." He reaches into his pocket, takes out his epilepsy medicine, and shakes it over his shoulder as he walks away. The pills dance in the half-empty bottle.

"Release control in three, two, one..." he says to the sheep and me.

The sun is starting to set. I feel like I am going to float away. The binds that hold me to earth, that hold me to reality, will sever, and I will float off into nothingness. The government is behind the catastrophe. We sold girls into sexual slavery to survive. We are alone with a shaky leader on the run in the wilds of Central Asia. I don't know what to believe anymore, and I've lost the will to care.

We are settling down for the night. Everyone is worn and tired from the long walk away from the base. Supplies are unloaded from the trucks. Meals are handed out. There is no slaughter tonight. The sheep are safe. We eat MREs—bland, stale, prepped meals—TV dinners for the post-postmodern world. I go through the motions of eating the flavorless single-serving dinner. I eat in silence, alone, staring at the ground, looking for the strings that are holding me down, holding me steady. I see nothing.

My meal is finished. Someone removed the package from my hands on my lap, and I have no recollection of its removal. I was just staring at the empty ground the whole time. The package was there, and then it was gone.

I feel a soft rub on my back. "What are you looking for?"

I look up, dazed. Sitting next to me is Lupina. She rubs my back and looks at me with her prescient eyes, even bigger in the absence of her wavy hair.

"Huh? Ah, nothing. Strings, I guess," I mumble.

"Strings?" she asks. Her voice is soft and kind. She is not prying or accusing me, but I don't know how to reply.

Craziness is like a string that once pulled can unravel everything. I want to say this but don't.

"Did you know that the forest is connected together by strings?" Lupina asks.

"Huh?"

"Yeah, it's true. I heard it on NPR with my mom and sisters one afternoon. We were driving back from a hike in the mountains, through the forest, so it left an impression.

"See, there are strings connected to all the roots. These strings are actually fungi, a completely different species from the trees, but they have a…what do you call it…a symbol—"

"Symbiotic?"

"Yes! That's it. A symbiotic relationship with the trees. They give the trees vitamins and minerals that they mine from the rocks and soil. Then the trees give them sugar in return."

"Hmmm. That's cool. I can't see them. I guess I wasn't staring hard enough."

"They're deep underground. But do you know what the crazy thing is?"

I shake my head. I know lots of crazy things but not strings in the ground.

"The crazy thing is the strings create a huge network that connects the whole forest. If one tree gets sick, the others know about it. They can share nutrients with the sick tree. And if that tree starts to die, its nutrients are fed to other trees via the network of strings, even across different species of trees."

Lupina stops and leans close into me. I feel her lips kiss my cheek. I am reminded of when she whispered, "Yes," into my ear ages ago on a bike ride through a safe and sane city.

"We are all connected, Pax. If one of us is sick, we will all take care of that person. We are a tribe," she whispers.

I feel tears come to my eyes. I want to tell her everything. I want to tell her about the girls and Kevin's confession and the rumors regarding the false flag operation that made the world go mad, but I am worried she will not believe me. She will think the girls and conversation were hallucinations, like seeing Vivi sleeping in her bed. And the conspiracy theory to follow is just a frayed end of a crazy thread.

I pull away from Lupina and look into her eyes. They are so open in their earthy-green warmth. I feel I can lose myself in those eyes, crazy or not, and still be happy, content.

I am ready to tell her everything, but I feel I don't have the whole story. Something about what Kevin confessed is still eating away at me, and I want to be right. I want to be worthy of Lupina's love.

But I have no chance to confess anyway. Orders for camp are handed out. They are setting up a big tent, and we are in the way.

We brought a large roll of tent fabric to create a huge tarp-like tent with no walls, just a cover for the rain. It's all hands on deck as we set up the tent. Seth and Sam erect three large poles like a wide tepee, leaning in on each other. One of them climbs the poles somehow and ties the top together. He is then passed the start of the huge fabric, which he fastens to the tied poles. They spiral the fabric out and create a tent that looks like a circus top erected in a small clearing between some trees.

People start to build nests underneath the tent. There are about eighty to ninety of us. With some mild relief, I do see a few new faces from the other barracks, but it is mainly the Tribe of Iodine Wine and a bunch of sheep—all teenagers now, no adults, like in the book Eva mentioned earlier. Even the local shepherds have disappeared back into the forest.

The sheep are placed around our big tent, a big, furry, mutable wall in the absence of a wall. Most of us are armed now, and we place guards around the sheep to keep them from straying, to keep them safe, us safe.

Once the tent is finished and the nests are made, Felicia and Yesenia stand up on a large supply box in the center of the circle. We gather around them. Without saying anything, Yesenia lights a candle that Felicia is holding.

"Hector's spirit will warm us tonight," Felicia says. And that's it. They step down and place the candle in a pan on the ground beneath the big tent. She and Yesenia build their nests around the pan. With Hector's candle, we still have the same amount of heat insulating us through the night as if he were here.

Everyone looks exhausted from the march and the chaos and violence that preceded it. I am exhausted too, mentally and physically. I want to build my nest with Lupina and lose myself in her warmth and green eyes, but I have to man the first night watch.

"Pax, you and Paco are on first watch, away from the camp. Michael and Danny are up and down the road in the Humvees. You two need to watch approaches through the forest. Annie and Jaden will relieve you," Kevin orders, and there is no chance to counter.

I am stationed farther out from the camp, watching approaches instead of sleeping sheep. I sit on a rock and look down on the valley from which we crossed. The night air is cold. I keep stomping my feet to stop them from going numb.

I just stare down at the valley and replay the events of the last ten days in my head, from the building of the obstacle course to our bloody battle and the exodus from the base to Kevin's crazy statements.

I want to get my eventual confession to Lupina clear. I want to present the facts objectively, but I start to question everything Kevin told us, everything I thought I saw or didn't see, and this only leads me to more questions and to the nagging feeling that didn't go away when Kevin admitted the horrific crime. A monster lies under the bed to jump out and devour us at any moment.

I am startled when Annie comes up to replace me on watch.

"Hey, Pax," she says, and I jump up. "Fuck, it's cold out here. So much warmer in the circle of sheep at camp."

"Yeah, that's a lot of bodies," I comment.

We stand there on the rock for a long time, not talking. Her bad arm is hidden under a coat, stuck still in a sling. Her good arm is holding on to Kevin's pistol buried in the coat's pocket. We don't say anything else. It seems awkward, but I feel that Annie doesn't want me to leave her alone either.

Finally, I make a decision. There is a sickness in our forest that needs to be removed.

"Hey, Annie, I need to go away for a couple of days."

"What the…why?" she objects.

"Just something that I need to do."

"Um, sure?"

"Please tell Lupina that I love her. I should be able to track the sheep to make my way back, but if I don't, also tell Lupina I'm sorry for letting her down."

"Pax, are you OK? We all saw, and did, some crazy shit."

"I am not OK. But I want to be."

And then I leave. I jump off the rock and head back down to the valley.

I make good time retracing our steps. Even at night, it is easy to see the path we followed with the destruction the sheep left in their stead. I can travel fast only carrying a rifle and minor supplies. At least I received this training from the military.

In a couple of hours, I make it back to the forest outside the base. The setting seems weirdly quiet and dark, but something is up. I see lights in the barracks of the teenagers and no movement on the base. But I can feel movement around me, in the forest and on the road.

I look toward the main road and see pickup trucks, without lights on, heading toward the base. At the same time, people stealthily emerge from the forest and creep toward the base. They are far enough from me that I can remain hidden, but I can make out local clothing and turbans. They are soldiers from the local militia.

Now I know why Kevin was in such a hurry to get out of the base. He didn't just exchange the girls for the sheep; they were only the down payment. Kevin gave away the base and all the teenagers just to get control.

And now our peers, our countrymen, if we still have a country, are just sitting ducks in their barracks, too scared to come out, too ignorant to know what is coming their way.

I feel a need to do something. I have a gun, but I can't fight off the whole militia. Still, I pull my rifle down but stay hidden. I aim it at the roof of the barracks. I fire three shots. I can hear slight dings from bullets hitting the roof. Some of the militia peel off and come toward me, but the teenagers are aware. Many have exited the barracks in panic. They see the militia coming. Some take off in a run, while others ready their guns.

I did my duty, and now I must make my own escape before the militia catches me. I sling my gun onto my back and take off running back through the forest.

Behind me, I can hear a firefight break out on the base. I start to doubt if I should have fired those warning shots. Did I just get people killed unnecessarily? Would it be better for the teenagers to just get captured and to then be controlled by the militia? If they bought Lily, Becky, and Kelly for sexual slavery, then the fate left to the others would not be kind. At least now they have a fighting or fleeing chance.

I stop near the top of the first mountain about two miles away. The peak is the final point where I can still see the base. I doubt anyone would be able to keep up with me. Still, I take my gun down and steady it. I wait, just in case anyone is close behind. I take a final look at the base. The fighting has stopped. I see trucks, now with their lights on, circling the barracks, probably looking for stragglers. The militia has won. The teenagers never stood a chance, but at least I gave them an opportunity to escape. Maybe some survived.

I comfort myself with that small hope and turn back to the jeep road, back to the tracks of the sheep. I still have my gun in my hands when I hear more gunshots coming from the base and louder explosions with an intensity greater than even our battle. I turn back around and look. There are multiple Humvees coming in from the other side of the base and soldiers, American soldiers, attacking the base, attacking the militia. The battle is fierce and deadly for both sides, but finally, I can see some militia retreating to the forest. Most don't make it.

I feel elated. I want to go back down to the base and claim part of the victory. Then I realize what Kevin said before he gave his big speech about the grisly beginning and the mountain and the journey to Badakhshan. He said the soldiers were coming; they just weren't coming to save us. He meant that literally. The helicopters were shot down by another American base, shot down in the middle of the civil war. The base is not too far from us, south near the border of Afghanistan. When Kevin and the tribe took out the leadership on our base and ran a killing coup that removed the National Guard, the other base must have heard about it. Then they sent a large force to remove us, but Kevin conned the local militia to take over the base at the same time and meet their demise at the hands of the other base.

I know I cannot go back down to the base. Chances are some teenagers will have survived, and they will remember me and what I did. There is no safety on the base. I head back toward our camp.

I think about Kevin and the long game he played as I start jogging up and over the mountain, following the path of the sheep.

Kevin played a masterful game of cutthroat. He pitted two stronger enemies against each other and came out stronger and on top. But still, hundreds of people died or, worse, like the three girls sold into slavery. So many of the casualties were innocent, especially our fellow youth from the other barracks. And all his maneuvering was just so he could be in control. If Kevin could do that with no remorse, what else is he capable of? How safe are any of us—Lupina, Charlotte, Jaden, Annie, all the people I love and swore to protect? Are we safer now? I do not know. But with absolute certainty, I am aware of one fact, one truth. Kevin must die; his string must be severed. I pick up my running pace and hurry to rejoin the Tribe of Iodine Wine.

Third Story: Buck Breaking

CHAPTER I

Isolation

• • •

(Lupina)

In the middle of the night, I reach out for Pax in a slow, unconscious search for warmth. My hands slide out of my sleeping bag across the ground cover to his bag. They stretch farther from the warmth of my bag and body in search of Pax.

The nests we made under the tarp are surprisingly warm. All the people, ringed by sheep and capped by a huge tarp, encircle us in warmth. But I want to feel him close to me finally. I want to absorb his heat and comfort against the chaos and destruction of the past few days. I sluggishly start to wake as I feel his absence.

A coldness comes over me. I fully wake and pat the empty sleeping bag. Pax is gone. I am left alone. Again. I am deserted. The one thing he should have never, ever done.

I am unaware of the time. I start to hope that he is still on night watch, but I just know his watch has ended. Even though the night still surrounds us, I suspect Pax's watch ended a while ago. Pax is gone. I can feel the chill of his absence in my bones.

Still, I wait under the tent, chorused by snores and weird sheep noises. At first, the surrounding sounds were soothing, helped me fall asleep while Pax went out on first watch. Now, they are tormenting. I wait in the dark, alone, deserted, focused on his departure only to be mocked by the content sleeping sounds.

I wait and wait for him to come back, but he doesn't appear. Another sleepless night waiting for a man who left to come back. Waiting and wondering if it was something I did or something I was that led them to desert us. My father and now Pax.

Before deserting me, Pax seemed distracted but fine. He told me something weird about strings, and I told him the tribe takes care of their own, that I would take care of him. The drama from the last couple of days wrecked our nerves. We didn't show much affection. I didn't think much of it.

But we were going to finally share a bed together, a little nest as he called it, under the big tarp. But once again he never made it to our shared bed. I never thought it was a struggle with homosexuality or anything like that. I just thought he was shy, immature, or overly sensitive to doing the "wrong thing"—pushing me into a sexual relationship. Then I thought it was part of his PTSD, like seeing Vivi when she wasn't there. Now, I don't really know. Now, I don't really care. Now, he is just another deserter.

But I start to worry he is hurt or lost. Or maybe he is with someone else. Maybe he found an attraction I couldn't match. Annie maybe? I saw their long embrace by the pyramid when I was helping Jaden. I didn't think much of it. They had just fought a battle. Maybe they needed comfort in the chaos.

Or maybe I'm not tough enough for him. Maybe I'm not white enough. Maybe I'm not sexual enough for Pax. Maybe he viewed me more like a sister since we grew up together. Maybe.

But maybe desertion isn't my fault and never was.

I sit up and look around from my nest. The tarp blocks the moonlight, but in the center of our circle is a candle Felicia lit for Hector. The candle flickers its weak light. She lies near it with her friends.

The candle sits in a small pan. Felicia almost looks like she is spooning with it. The candlelight softens Felicia's sleeping face, usually so stern, so serious. She looks happy and content. When they set up the candle in remembrance of Hector, the first of us to fall, Kevin said the light of a candle produces the same amount of heat as a human body. So having the light under the tarp with all of us would be like Hector was still there, still emanating his heat in the cold of the night when we needed it most.

I don't see Pax in the light of Hector's candle. By the crack of dawn, I crawl out of the nest and investigate. I make my way past the sleeping people to the ring of sheep. They are still bleating and making noise.

The early-morning air creeps up the back of my neck. I feel weakened, naked without my long hair—cut and given to Charlotte so she could dress in disguise and kill the guard at the gate. I pet my head in a feeble attempt to feel my hair but only find my buzz cut, prickly and foreign. I run my hand down to my exposed neck and then cross my arms.

I find Eva on watch outside the circle of sheep. She and Fetty are guarding the sheep. Fetty is on the opposite side of the circles of people and sheep. They keep the sheep in a close-knit ring around our nests while watching the forest.

They are armed and look hardened beyond their years, like the professional soldiers whose toughened gazes were immortalized and embalmed by the exhaust. The dead soldiers' thousand-mile stares indelibly marked us as we moved their bodies to the sheets and out to the hole.

"Hey, Lupina, are you on watch?" she asks me with a doubtful look as I approach.

"No. I'm just looking for Pax. He never came to bed last night."

She puffs her cheeks out and starts to blow out a small stream of ghostly air into the cold morning sky.

"Let's see. What was the watch schedule Kevin handed out last night? I am pretty sure he was on first watch. He was going to be watching approaches, so he was away from the camp, but I'm sure everything is fine."

She says all this like it's a boring fact, not knowing or maybe not interested about the thousand shards of caring and scaring I have going through me right now.

"Who relieved him?" I ask.

"Um, that would be Annie; then Sam relieved Annie; yeah, so maybe check with her, I guess."

I work my way through the ring of sheep and start walking between the sheep and the sleeping people. I circle between the two rings looking for Annie's bright shock of blond hair poking out from bags and blankets. I am nervous that I will see Pax's long hair next to hers. But I can't blame him. I can't blame Annie. This is wartime, I guess.

I reach the other side of the ring, and Fetien waves to me. Her bright smile breaks her battle-stare face. I wave back, distracted, and then go back to my search for Pax.

Finally, I see Annie's bleach-blond hair, about three layers of people deep in the ring. I try to tiptoe to her, watching out for sleepers while looking to see if Pax is next to her at the same time.

I am relieved but even more scared when I reach her and realize Pax isn't there. Then where is he? Why can't I find him?

I am standing there, staring into the distance outside our rings, making one last scan for Pax in the surrounding forest when Annie wakes up.

"Dude, I am so sorry, but I didn't want to wake you last night, and also, I couldn't find you."

"Annie, what's going on?" I plead.

She pops up, nimble and steady for a waking person with an arm in a sling. Her sleeping bag slips to the ground like a shed cocoon.

"Pax left," she says.

"What?" This is the worst news. He *is* a deserter. People around us start to stir, but I don't care.

"Annie, what the fuck is going on?"

"Oh, Lupina, I honestly don't know. He seemed troubled. I asked if he was OK, and he said no, but he wanted to be OK. Then he took off. He did ask me to tell you he loved you and that he is sorry he let you down."

"Where did he go?"

"Lupina, sweetie, I'm so sorry. He didn't tell me where he was going, but he did say he was coming back."

Everyone seems to be up and asking their own questions, wondering what is going on. I want more answers too.

But then we hear gunfire, distant but heavy. Loud gunfire from the big machine guns, rapid and rupturing through the forest. My heartbeat joins the destructive symphony at the thought of Pax mixed up in that gunfire.

Michael and others are down the road in the big truck, guarding our backs. From the truck is where we hear the loud gunfire. Crashing like a wave over us, it wakes those still sleeping and startles the sheep. Kevin is up and moving, yelling orders at us. But still no Pax, anywhere.

I look toward Fetien and see her running very fast with the hardened look on her face. She runs toward the gunfire.

Annie is trying to put on her shoes but struggling and cussing at her one arm. I focus on her, trying not to be scared of the gunfire, which is increasing in intensity.

I bend down to help her put her shoes on.

"Oh, thank you, Lupina."

"Annie?" I start to say, trying to hide the concern in my voice—worried that if I start to crack, I will break. "Which way did Pax go?

Did he go that way?" I feel tears start to build up. I point toward the road from which we came, toward the gunfire. I lower my face and hide my crying eyes in my pointing arm.

"Yeah, he headed back down the valley. Lupina, he'll be fine. Pax knows how to take care of himself, and, well, if not, he can take off into the forest fast."

Then she reaches into the sleeping bag and pulls out Kevin's pistol. The one she used to kill Brad and Tony on that horrible night in the Battle of the Base. She hops back up and looks up at me.

"Lupina, he'll be OK. Got to go."

And she too takes off toward the gunfire, while I am left behind with the scared sheep.

I can't mull over the gunfire or over Pax's disappearance. I need to work. I need to help. There about twenty to thirty people still left, unarmed with the sheep. We need to keep the sheep together and move away from the gunfire. But what about our supplies? We have no time to break camp.

I see Charlotte, Jaden, and Felicia and others still gathered in the middle of the circle by the candle. With Eva and Fetien heading to the battle and the sounds of the gunfire, the sheep are starting to panic and dissipate into the woods. We can come back for the supplies. But we could lose the sheep if they wander off.

Charlotte slept the night between the lamb and its mother, and she has already swept the lamb up into her Babybjörn. She placates the worried mother and some of the other sheep while she leads them down the road away from the gunfire. But other sheep are still disappearing into the forest.

"Hey! The sheep are escaping. We have to keep them together," I say. "Jaden, you take a group and gather the sheep. Felicia, Yesenia, and I will gather the ones going that way."

I point to two different directions.

"Let's herd them down the road past the other Humvee." I point down the road away from the gunfire. We posted a Humvee in front as well as behind. If Michael and the rear guard fail, our best chance is to be on the other side of the forward truck.

"Fuck the sheep. We should just take off into the forest," Jaden says. He looks scared and skittish. He was hurt pretty bad in the Battle of the Base by an explosion but nothing physically permanent.

"We need to save the sheep."

"We need to stay alive."

"Jaden, we can either die by gunfire or die by starvation. Have faith in Michael and everyone else."

Jaden doesn't say anything but starts jogging to where I pointed. I watch him for a second to see if he'll just sprint off into the woods, but he starts pushing and heckling the sheep to the road. Others join him.

I look at Felicia. She bends down and picks up Hector's candle. She raises it to her face. She puckers her lips to blow, but instead she kisses the flame out with wet lips. We turn and go after the strayed sheep.

(Pax)

I am jogging back, up and down the mountains and valleys, to the tribe. It took me three hours to get to the base. With the climb and fatigue, I should make it back in about three and a half, and I am well over halfway there. Overall, the Tribe traveled for about ten hours to get to the first camp. I am nearly tripling their speed, but I am running and not shepherding a bunch of sheep and carrying supplies. If I hurry, I can arrive before sunrise and sneak into the nest and join Lupina without her ever noticing my absence.

In all the drama and shadowplay that I've been replaying over and over in my mind, from the girls being traded for sheep to the second battle fought at the base, I lost my focus on Lupina. The center of my world. I honestly felt ashamed. Weak. Unworthy of her tremendous love. I was ashamed that I thought I saw Vivi in Tajikistan, an admission of insanity. I felt humiliated that I was wrong about the eventual decay and destruction of the base that Kevin predicted. I walked around like a reprimanded dog with tail tucked between legs.

And now that I have recanted my wrongs about Kevin's prediction to the tribe, and I've admitted insanity to Lupina, I have to somehow find a way to *neutralize* Kevin without destroying the tribe and without showing Lupina that I am crazy *and* dangerous. I have to stand up and be my strongest when I look my weakest.

Part of me wants to just see how things play out with Kevin leading us. He said his epilepsy medicine will run out, and then he will lose control of himself, something he cannot bear. In many ways, when Kevin loses control of himself, he is at his most dangerous, his most self-destructive. Waiting for Kevin's medicine to run out is not a safe play. And how can I live with what I know, the exploitation of the teenage girls from the other barracks that he traded for sheep? Not to mention the cutthroat game he played that resulted in the possible deaths of hundreds of people, mostly Americans, when he directed the local militia into base at the same time the other American base attacked. To just sit back and let Kevin lead us while I know of his crimes makes me complicit in those crimes and any future harm he facilitates by or upon us.

These thoughts, these dilemmas are running through my head while I try to concentrate on the dark, moonlit road falling beneath my running feet. My mind is elsewhere. I'm jogging on autopilot while wrapped in Kevin's web of deceit and destruction. I am so distracted that I almost miss hearing the vehicles behind me before it is too late.

I stop when I finally hear the sound, dangerously too close. The vehicles are revved up and battering over the bumpy road at a pace much faster than we took the day before.

I run into the forest several feet in and hide when the Humvees start to pass me. There are four total, and they are full of American soldiers. The surviving teenagers back at the base must have told the soldiers in the Humvees what happened and where we went. So they took off after us. They are coming to collect on Kevin's sin and treachery, but they are coming for all of us.

As soon as they pass, I take off in a full sprint, chasing them down the road. I run as fast as I can, but I figure I am a mile or two away from camp. They will make it well before me, and I have no way of warning the tribe.

Our only hope is for Michael and the rear guard to see them and stop them until I can help. Hopefully, if our defenses don't hold, Lupina will be able to escape. I have a weird déjà-vu feeling of running to save Lupina. And it hits me that I played a fantasy in my head during our military training before the civil war broke out. The fantasy of me running fast to save Lupina and Vivi. I used the fantasy as motivation to run faster. Now, however, we aren't playing war games with fake guns; there is no counting coup, no flag to capture. There are soldiers bent on revenge, heading to kill my friends.

I run faster.

I pull my rifle down, which slows me a bit, but I have to warn Michael and the others on watch. I almost trip when I aim the rifle and fire it into the air.

I hope the sound will reach and warn our tribe, like I warned the other teenagers before they met their demise at the hands of the local militia that Kevin let into our base. I hope the results will differ.

I recover from my stumble. I start sprinting again as fast as I can while holding my gun ready in case the soldiers stop and investigate the gunshot they heard from behind. I am nearly ready to collapse when the early-morning sky is riddled with a deluge of gunshots, big heavy ones from the .50 calibers. The sound and the destruction following taps my adrenaline and gives me needed energy.

I run around a curve and slow to a jog while moving closer to the trees on the side of the road. The machine-gun fire is very close. I can hear bullets, most likely shot by Michael, rip through the trees nearby.

I stop running and shield myself behind a large tree and peek up the road. The soldiers are yelling out commands. They are collecting behind three of the Humvees, suppressed by the tribe's firestorm. Up far ahead, around a slight bend, one of their Humvees is smoking. In the gun turret, I see a dead soldier hunched over. I hope my warning shot tipped Michael off, but I get an uneasy feeling that I am culpable in the soldier's death now.

I watch the soldiers shielded behind the Humvees. I remind myself that they are going to kill my friends, right or wrong, no matter what guilt I feel or truth I know about what brought them to this point.

I start to aim my rifle, but they sprint for the trees, splitting into two groups going in opposite directions. I wonder if they knew I was behind them and ducked into the trees, but they don't look my way and only head deeper into the forest.

They are not running at or from me. I am aware of what they are doing. They are trying to outflank our rear guard. I must stop them. I can only go one direction, so I slip into the forest on my side of the road. I move into a faster trail-running pace like when I outflanked the other barracks in our war games. I feel the adrenaline shoot through me as I fly past branches and skip over obstacles. The training and my desire to save Lupina and help the tribe push me forward fast while heightening my senses.

I catch up to a group of the enemy soldiers and start to slow down, making sure not to make any noise. They are about fifty yards ahead of me and moving forward at a careful pace.

The sun is above the horizon and colors the forest with a surreal pink light. I can make out more details about the soldiers. They are in camouflage but not the typical military issue. It looks more like the camouflage hunters wear with the southern leafy foliage and brown colors.

I move forward and try to track each soldier. I am pretty sure six or more ran into the forest, but I only see four. Am I being tracked too? Did they double back to outflank me and take me out?

I start to get terrified and frozen with fear. I focus on the fact that Lupina needs me. My tribe needs me. I push forward. The four hunters have stopped moving and are setting up to fire on Michael. Through the trees, I can see our Humvee in the distance. The large .50 caliber has quieted down, but small arms fire occasionally spurts out from others nearby. I see my tribe members head into the forest to outflank the enemy Humvees. They are unaware that snipers are setting up. I must act fast.

I never fired the gun during the Battle of the Base. Despite all the death and destruction, despite seeing such horrors, I picked up the gun too late and never needed to fire it. I am not sure if I can make my first kill. I am not built like Michael or Kevin or the others who so easily took up arms.

But I can't think about this now. My tribe is running into a trap. I kneel on one knee and aim the rifle from behind a tree. I think about just sending warning shots to alert our flankers, but I need to do more. I need to join the game. I need to be a man.

I take aim and fire away. I am close enough that I can easily hit two or three of the enemy before they can react. I hear the bullets hit their flesh and their desperate gasps of pain. A sickening thud sinks in my gut as they fall to the ground heavy and dead. I keep firing until I see no more movement, and then I just freeze there, trying to comprehend what I just did.

Michael hears my gunshots and starts firing into the forest. Trees and branches are bursting all around me. Michael thinks I am the enemy. I fall to the ground. I try to melt into the leafy ground cover to make myself disappear into the earth, safe from Michael's bullets and from the horror I just joined.

The machine gun stops firing, but I stay frozen. Up ahead I see three more soldiers dressed in hunter camouflage running toward their fallen friends. They see one of the dead soldiers awkwardly pressed against the tree with wounds on his back. Their leader looks my direction, knowing the shots came from behind. He doesn't see me but motions for his friends to follow him toward where I am hiding.

From my prone position, I ready my rifle again and aim to fire. I need to fire soon but hesitate. The soldiers are closer, and I can make out their faces. I freeze.

They are not soldiers. They are teenagers, like me, sent to a colony in a far-off land. They look to be from rural areas and are probably wearing their own hunting clothes. I don't want to kill any more kids. I just want to go home and be back where it is safe. I can feel tears well up inside me, but then one of them jumps back in shock when he spots me in the underbrush. He readies his gun, but I fire again, instinctively, just a reaction of self-preservation. He falls to the ground. He is dead. I am a conscientious killer of kids.

My gunshots bring another firestorm from Michael, and the other teenagers take off in sprint back toward their Humvees. They are caught in a crossfire and decide to retreat. I watch their leader run past me. I slightly turn my head to make sure they are going away, to make sure I don't have to fire anymore.

He is about twenty yards away, but he sees me move out of the corner of his eye. He looks young but mature, hardened like he has seen too much. He ducks his head and takes off in a full sprint, crashing through the branches. He thinks I will hunt him down like I did his friends. He is probably as scared as me, but I have no desire to shoot someone running away.

Michael's firestorm stops, and it is eerily quiet. The teenagers are gone, either dead in front of me or retreated behind me. I start to think about how I can approach my tribe without getting shot. How I can remove myself from the ground cover? I lie there not wanting to move, cemented to the safety of the ground.

Suddenly, I hear a horrendous sound from behind me, from back where the soldiers retreated. A banshee's cry fills the forest. A loud, remorseful scream for the dead. I know the voice. It is from the leader of the teenagers whose friends I killed, whose friends he had to abandon to flee the crossfire. He is safe now, but the tragedy of his loss has hit him. He lost people of his tribe. The screams change from sorrow to anger. I can now make out words.

"I will kill you!" he screams. "I will kill you! As long as I live, I will hunt you down!"

CHAPTER II

Cold Hands / Warm Heart

• • •

(Pax)

I stay still, facedown on the ground, taking small and quick breaths to not be seen or heard. My muscles are tense and push against the ground as if trying to dig myself down, underground.

The screaming has stopped. The gunshots have stopped. But the quiet seems more threatening.

At any minute, the teenager from the other colony who yelled a death curse at me may sneak up behind me. Or worse, the members of my tribe may continue their flanking maneuver right to me and shoot at my prone, threatening position. I don't know what to do. I just want to bury myself deep in the ground and wake up when the world no longer has lost its fucking mind.

After what seems like an eternity, I hear a loud symphony of gunfire from the other colony near the road. It seems more futile in its intensity. Through the gunshots I can hear yelling and the revving of the Humvees. They are retreating. The barrage covers their flight.

I am safe. The battle is over. I start to formulate a plan to reveal myself to the tribe without getting shot. But instead they come to me.

At full speed, Fetien, Paco, and Seth crash through the forest, guns raised with hate on their faces. Especially Seth, he is in front, face reddened, enraged, and whip marked from crashing through the forest. He starts to scream as he fires his gun. He breaks out onto the road, crosses, and then gets behind another tree. He loads another clip and then turns around and unleashes it on the retreating Humvees.

They fire back, and the trees around Seth spit out woodchips and bark. He fires until his gun empties; then he stops and puts his back against the tree, taking deep breaths with eyes clenched closed.

Fetty and Paco join him from the other side of the forest. I want to join, but I hear Fetty call out.

"Seth! Seth! They are coming back!"

She backs into the forest while firing quick spurts.

"Run, Seth!" she yells; then she turns around and sprints back down the road toward Michael.

I wait and watch Seth, who shakes his head and then takes off in a sprint and follows Fetty and Paco back to the Humvee. I decide this is my only chance to avoid being shot by my friends. I jump up and head toward the road and merge with Seth, Fetty, and Paco in retreat.

Seth throws me a quick side glance but doesn't say anything. We can hear the Humvees revved and gaining on us. We sprint around the curve toward the disabled Humvee splayed across the road. I want to head back into the trees, but I am worried about splitting off the path and tripping on something. If I stumble, I will surely get caught or killed.

All four of us run full speed down the road. We are all very fast runners, and this must look like the end of some relay race, but I can feel large rounds whipping through the air past us or splitting into the trees on our side. This is no game. They are firing through the curve in the forest at us.

We sprint the final step and rush behind the abandoned Humvee. Cisco has driven our Humvee closer to us, and there is a line of our tribe waiting in defensive positions. The enemy Humvees approach the turn in the road but stop. I jump as Michael lets loose on the .50 caliber. I turn around and stay hidden with my back to the Humvee and try to catch my breath. However, Seth, Fetty, and Paco jump back up. I watch as they run while crouched down. They go behind Michael's Humvee and then back into the forest. They loop back around and head back through the forest toward the enemy in another attempt to flank.

I sit still, emotionally and physically exhausted. I feel the energy and my will to fight drain out of me. I can't do this anymore. I don't know what is driving them with such intensity, such ferocity. I am completely drained. Last night, I ran to our old base and saw two different firefights; then I ran back to the camp only to be overtaken and thrown into a firestorm where I just killed four teenage boys. I can't fight anymore.

I stare in the distance back down the road toward our camp. I see a body strewn on the road, awkward and still. I get up and start jogging toward it, keeping my head down and the Humvees between me and the enemy fire.

As I approach, my eyes confirm what I already know. Sam, Seth's brother, is dead. Ripped apart by rounds from the enemy .50 caliber. That's what drives Seth and the others after the soldiers, another casualty of Kevin's war, another lost Tribesman.

I stare at Sam's body lying on the tire tread marks of the Humvee. The scene is surreal. I can't stop staring, ignoring the gunfire behind me. He lies on the ground in an unnatural pose, like Annie when Brad tripped her on the tire pyramid and she broke her elbow in the fall.

Sam looks like a dancer in a contortionist pose jumping into the night sky. Streams of blood flare out from his body like ribbons. All around, shell casings dot the ground like stars. The scene looks like a bizarre painting, part beauty of motion and part gore and death—a fallen dancer jumping into a sky of star shells.

"That's way too much gunfire."

I look up confused and see Kevin standing next to me.

"What?"

"All those shells. We wasted way too much ammunition," he says, waving the barrel of his gun at the constellation of shells on the ground.

"Oh. I'd be more worried about our supply of candles than our supply of bullets," I respond, thinking about the candles we will be lighting for both Sam and Hector now.

"Yeah, well, those two things are directly related," he says and then gives me a wink. "Welcome back. See anything cool?"

He turns back to the Humvees, not waiting for a response. He whistles and waves his arm to call everyone back. He jogs against traffic toward the disabled Humvee.

I am not sure how long I stood there staring at Sam's ribbons of blood. I'm not sure when the gunfire ended. But I glance down the road and don't see the enemy guns. Our tribe is cautiously making their way back to us. Cisco and Michael stay with the Humvee. It is parked, shielded, and blocked on this side of the disabled enemy Humvee. A bunch of our warriors materialize out of the forest. The enemy, outgunned and outflanked, has retreated for now.

Everyone gathers around Sam and stares at his dancer pose. I turn back to watch Kevin. He has climbed up on the enemy Humvee. He jumps into the gun turret and throws the soldier's body over the side like he is discarding trash. He starts stacking rocket boxes of ammunition on the roof. He whistles to Paco, Fetien, and Seth, who have emerged from the forest. Fetien and Paco start taking the ammunition off from the enemy Humvee to Michael's. They open a door and stack the boxes of bullets. Seth ignores Kevin and slowly walks toward us, toward his fallen brother.

I don't want to see Seth with his dead brother. I can't take any more stress and mourning. I tell myself I need to check on Lupina and do the cowardly thing. I run away. I jog back toward our camp.

After going about twenty yards, I can't help it—I stop. I turn back and look at the scene. I have to see. Seth is on the ground, kneeling in front of his brother, while all our warriors are standing around watching. I think that Seth needs Lupina more than I do. No one is comforting him or saying anything.

Again, I decide I need to stop being a coward. I need to be stronger. Not stronger like our warriors who ran through the trees toward the enemy; I've made too many kills today. I need to be stronger like Lupina. I walk back to Seth. I put my weapon on the ground and then put my arm around Seth. He is crying into his hands. His body shakes violently with sobs and drained adrenaline.

Cisco pulls the Humvee up behind us. We are blocking the road. Cisco doesn't honk, and no one says anything. The emptiness of the scene is filled by the growl of the vehicle, waiting behind us.

"Let's bring him back. We'll bury him away from here," I say.

Seth nods but doesn't move. I pat his back and slowly get up. I motion to Eva and Spencer. We carefully straighten Sam from his awkward dancing fall. I grab his hands and notice they are still warm but sticky with blood. Spencer lifts his feet while Eva supports the body. She gets the worst of the blood as the red ribbons stream over her. We lift the body onto the hood of our Humvee. I move to the right front tire.

In the distance, I see Kevin. He is deflating the tires of the enemy Humvee with his knife, the one Charlotte used to kill the guard. The Humvee sits diagonally across the road. He is effectively blocking the road so enemy vehicles can't follow us. But this won't stop the hunters from tracking our trail of sheep. I can feel them, especially the one who screamed at me, silently coming through the forest after us. I know he will never stop stalking us, never stop hunting me.

I suppress this dread and jump up on the Humvee and sit in front of the passenger window. Spencer sits on the front with his feet on the bumper. Seth is escorted into the shotgun seat. I hold Sam's hand to keep the body from sliding around as the Humvee slowly moves forward. Spencer has his back turned to Sam. He uses his backside to keep the body from moving.

Sam stays splayed across the hood like some kind of morbid hunting trophy of loss. On the way back to camp, on the way back to Lupina, I hold on to Sam's hand to keep him from sliding off the truck. I hold it tight as his hand turns from warm to cold.

(Lupina)

The sound of the gunfire ebbs and wanes behind us like the hot breath of a killer stalking prey, close, forbidding, imminent. I run my hands into the wool of a sheep to hold on to something real and alive. The wool is coarse but warm. I guide the sheep back toward the road and move my hands to another sheep like a blind person reading braille. I fumble around in the chaos of the crowd and try to make order. I try to put us on the right path. Danny is waiting in the forward-guard Humvee down the road, and we need to reach him before the wave of gunfire crashes over our line of defense and sweeps us away.

Jaden, Felicia, and others are running back and forth, gathering the sheep and herding them back to the road. Another of section of sheep are up ahead, following Charlotte and her lamb. There are about twenty of us. We are all unarmed and mixed in with the sheep. Everyone else has joined the battle. The gunfire picks up into a chaotic climax. I want to cover my ears with my hands. I want to bury my eyes in the heavy wool of the sheep. I try to avoid thoughts about Pax being mixed into the gunfire whirling around us. I try avoid thoughts about what happens if our defense fails.

I see Danny and our Humvee in the distance. I gaze around into the forest on both sides of the road. I don't see any white cloud bushes moving deep into the forest. We have gathered our sheep, and they are safe. For now. We need to hurry toward Danny.

"Jaden, Felicia, down the road! We need to hurry!" I call out. The looks on their faces are tough and resilient, but I can see fear in their eyes too. We start to hurry down the road.

It seems we are making better time as Danny and the Humvee are closer to us, but I realize they are driving our way, in reverse, slowly down the road toward the battle. Danny is tense and crouched over the machine gun. The gun is pointed our way but above our heads into the distance. Danny and his gun may be our final chance.

We start parting our way around Danny without saying anything. The only communication is a hard bleating from the sheep that mixes with the rumble of the truck's engine. Danny's face looks hard and determined, like Fetien, Eva, and Annie when they ran toward gunfire. This gives me a bit of relief, as he is our last line of protection.

"Hey, Lupina. I'm stayin'." Jaden climbs up onto the Humvee and leaves us.

"What about the sheep?" I say but know this is not my battle to choose for Jaden.

"No, I'm gonna stay. I'm gonna fight."

Felicia, too, turns around and starts marching with the Humvee against the flow of sheep. Her face looks hateful. She removes a homemade shiv from her pocket and grips it hard in her good hand. Her other arm is bandaged and sling-bound from her gunshot wound in the Battle of the Base. The arm lies limp across her belly, but gripped hard in her other hand is Hector's candle. White veins from the strong grip crisscross her hands and seem to blend into the white wax of the candle in a pattern of lace.

The rest of us, Ezra, Yesenia, and the others, hurry to catch up to Charlotte and her lamb leading us down the road. Now that the gunfire seems to have stopped, and we are more used to shepherding the calmer sheep, we make good time. Still, I want create as much separation from the death and destruction as possible.

The sheep rebel against the jogging pace we created. Now that they sense we are safe, they slow back down into their meandering walk. I double back and keep pushing the stragglers up ahead. I place my hand on their rumps and give a soft push. They bleat and respond with a weak protest.

I glance back down the road and see no one. Danny's Humvee, Jaden, and Felicia are gone. This is both scary and reassuring at the same time.

The path is slightly ascending, climbing up the side of a small mountain. My legs start to tire from the pushing and constant badgering of the sheep. We continue up the path. I see Charlotte stopped at the peak. She and her lamb are looking down the other side.

I move my way through the sheep to her in a hurry, curious and scared at what has stopped her momentum. I reach her, and she points down the valley toward a river in the distance and a large wooden bridge that crosses it.

"We need to make the bridge," she says flatly. These are the first words she has said to me since she mimicked Kelly and told me I would be so pretty with makeup on. Soon after, she killed the guard. I hope someday she will forgive me for not taking her place.

She starts walking forward again, and the sheep follow her toward the river. We reach the river, and the sheep are nervous again—probably at the running water and rickety bridge we are funneling them across. I am nervous too, more so for what is behind us than ahead. I keep sneaking glances back toward the road and the mountain as I push the sheep forward.

When I finally hear the rumble of a vehicle behind me, I don't want to glance back. I fear the answer. If we failed, then the enemy will close in on us. What then? Should we jump into the river to float away or run into the forest on the other side and hope the sheep will block the road long enough for us to escape?

There is no easy answer. There is no safety unless the vehicle belongs to us. I turn around to face the truth and see Michael at the gun. There are people on the hood of the Humvee. They look injured. I can make out Pax; his crazy hair is hard to miss. He is alive! But is he hurt?

I leave the sheep and the crossing and run to Pax. My nighttime angst evaporated on seeing Pax on the hood of the Humvee. I am glad he is safe and glad I am carrying my medical bag.

I run to him, but he doesn't leave the Humvee. A rifle rests across his lap. He sees me and quickly waves; then he places his free hand back on the rifle. I know he is not hurt, but he looks to be holding on to the person lying across the hood with his other hand. Spencer slides off the Humvee and runs past me toward Ezra. The person lying on the vehicle looks like Sam or Seth. I reach for my medical bag, but when I see all the blood streamed over the vehicle, I know it is not needed. I am too late.

I look up at Pax. We are close now. Cisco has stopped the Humvee. The look on Pax's face is swirling confusion. He looks happy to see me but scared and sad at the same time. Worse, there is something in his eyes, distant, hard to describe. I realize what it is when he slides off the stopped Humvee and walks toward me. He doesn't embrace me like he usually does—the embrace of a scared boy in a lost world. He seeks no comfort. He just looks in my eyes. His eyes, I realize now, are like those of the soldiers embalmed in exhaust, like Eva and Annie who ran toward the gunfire. His eyes look dead.

"I'm sorry I left," he says flatly, in the same tone Charlotte took earlier. "I thought I could make it back in time." He shoulders his rifle and then turns back around to pull Sam off the Humvee with Eva and Jaden's help. I see Seth in the passenger seat. He stares off straight ahead into the nothingness.

We have all crossed the bridge—sheep, people, and supplies—everyone but Pax. He waits on the other side of the bridge, watching the road and forest with an unwavering stare. He is sitting, nestled next to the guardrail with his rifle pointed at the forest like he expects a monster to come crashing through at any moment.

"Hurry up!" Kevin yells. He is standing on one of the supply trucks. I am part of the detail gathering fresh water from the river into our large water tubs. In only two days, we went through a substantial amount of water. Eva and Paco are filling the tubs while I administer the iodine to purify it. At this rate, we will run out of iodine in a few weeks, and I need to save some for injuries and if anyone shows signs of radiation sickness. Kevin seems to think there isn't enough radiation in the ash to get us very sick. At any rate, using iodine to purify water and help stave off radiation sickness may be the least of our worries. "We should save it for injuries," I think cynically.

Up further on the bank at the edge of the forest, another detail is digging a grave for Sam. I look for Seth. He is still in the parked Humvee looking over his brother's body. Above him, Michael sits perched at his spot at the big gun scanning the other side.

"Let's go!" Kevin yells again. He jumps off the supply truck with a small gas can. He is not yelling at us or the gravediggers. He is yelling at the large group of people gathering loose wood from the forest. They are running back and forth piling it on the bridge. I watch them and look at Pax. He totally ignores the commotion behind him and keeps his ever-present watch on the other side of the river. What is he looking for? What is he scared of? I feel guilty when I start to question if what Pax is looking for really exists.

We start to carry the water tubs back up to the trucks. They are a lot heavier now and awkward to carry. I want to ask for help but don't want to take away from the other details. Eva and I stumble and slide back down the bank toward the river. My foot sinks into the muddy water. The cold, snowmelt river glides over it. My idea of jumping into the river to escape was a stupid one.

Eva helps me out of the river, and we look at the full tub, perplexed. I am tempted to ask Pax for help but don't.

"Here. I've got an idea." Eva takes off her belt and ties it through a handle. "I'll pull; you push."

This works. I get my legs low and push the tank up the bank while she digs her heels in and pulls. We drag it to the supply truck and go back for another. We see Paco pulling up another tank on his own. He copies Eva's belt strategy, but he is a lot stronger than he looks.

We finish pulling up the water. I stop to rest and catch my breath. I look back to Pax sitting on the other side of the branch-filled bridge. He is looking up the mountain, scanning the road we walked. All of a sudden, someone materializes out of the forest at a fast sprint running toward us. Pax is startled, but luckily his gun and view were pointed up the mountain road and not at the edge of the forest.

Fetty runs out of the forest, carrying her rifle and hard stare. She runs past Pax without saying anything. I watch her as she glides past the pile of branches. She runs up to Kevin, stops, and says, "We're all clear."

Kevin nods and walks to the bridge with the gas can. He starts pouring the gas all over the branches. I start to worry he will light the bridge with Pax on the other side, but he says something to Pax that I cannot hear over the rushing water.

Pax turns around and stares at Kevin without saying anything. Kevin says something else and goes back to dousing the branches with gas. Pax seems to have a look of hatred on his face. The rifle starts to twitch in his arms. I am scared he will do something irrational. A desperate look covers his face like a man ready to jump off a bridge.

"Pax!" I yell. I wave and give my best warm smile. "Come on!"

This seems to knock Pax out of his hate stare. He looks up to me. He doesn't smile, but a small look of contentment comes over his face. Kevin is finished with the gas and starts to walk back our way. Pax follows. His brief contentment is gone. He burrows his scornful stare into Kevin's back.

Now I am scared. I walk toward the two of them before Pax can do anything crazy, but Kevin stops and turns around.

I reach them when I hear Kevin say, "You wanna do the honors?" He holds a lighter up to Pax.

Pax just shakes his head while staring Kevin down. Kevin bends down and pours a couple of drops of gas on a pinecone. He stands up and lights the cone. The fire spreads quickly and nearly burns his hands. He casts it quick to the bridge and shakes his fingers off. The branches go up in a loud gush. Kevin walks off, and I hear Pax mumble over the fire and cold, rushing water, "The bridge is already burned."

We don't even say words for Sam. Seth stays in the truck as Sam is quickly buried. Then everyone hurries down the road while the bridge goes up in flames.

I stare at the new grave as everyone starts walking away. Pax lingers at the end of the caravan. He is watching the bridge and watching the other side of the river more than checking on me or paying final respects to Sam. I feel we need to do something, say something, about Sam and his passing.

I look to Seth. He is still in Michael and Cisco's rear-guard Humvee. Cisco is hanging back, waiting for everyone to move forward. Michael, like Pax, is watching the other side of the river, scanning the trees with his gun.

Seth seems catatonic and lifeless in the Humvee. I look at Cisco in the driver's seat next to Seth. He just lost his good friend, Hector, during the Battle of the Base a few days before. He is talking to Seth, giving him comfort. This makes me feel better. If anyone can console Seth, it's Cisco.

Still, I feel bad that nothing was said at the funeral. I reach into my medical bag, and for the second time today, I remove the bottle of iodine. I uncap it and pour a few drops on the loose dirt covering Sam's body.

I look up to see if the caravan is gone. The Humvee's engine purrs, but Seth and Cisco are just watching me. I see what looks like a faint smile on Seth's face in response to the sacrifice of iodine. Then Cisco starts to drive the Humvee off. I am concerned I will be left behind with no care, even by Pax, who is still just watching the other side of the river.

"Hop in," Cisco calls out to me as he turns the Humvee up the road. He stops. I feel drained, and a ride sounds nice. Heaven knows Kevin will push the pace to get us far away from the bridge and the soldiers who attacked us.

If I'm exhausted, then Pax must be absolutely beat. He didn't sleep last night after he ran off. He didn't sleep much before that with the Battle of the Base and then the rushed exodus. Maybe that is why he looks so shaky and unstable.

"Sure, hold on," I respond to Cisco and then jog over to Pax.

His eyes are bloodshot and heavily ringed. "If he had shorter hair, he would look a bit like Kevin," I think. I put my hand on his shoulder. I see a slight glimmer of who he used to be, back in Denver, back before all this craziness. He smiles a tired smile.

"Hey," he says.

"Let's hitch a ride," I say.

"No." He shakes his head. "No, I need to watch the road. They're coming."

"Pax, Michael will watch the road. He has our back."

"No, he's hunting us. The burned bridge won't stop him. I need to protect us. I need to protect you."

"Pax, you can't protect anyone if you're dead tired." His face looks shocked at this. Then his eyes seem to focus off in the distance.

"You need some sleep," I continue. "When was the last time you slept?"

I don't wait for a response. I just wrap my arm around his shoulder and guide him to the Humvee. He walks with me. I open the door to the Humvee. He slides his gun along the floorboard and turns around to say to me, "If they attack, I need to be able to jump up fast. You go in first."

I climb into the Humvee. I take off my backpack, and Pax hands me his. I place the backpacks between the seats to make a bridge. I lie across the make-do couch on my side. I use my leather medical bag as a pillow. Pax joins me. He lies on his back, and I start to run my fingers through his long hair. He lets go of an audible, drawn-out exhale. Then he closes his eyes and takes in a long inhale through his nose.

I want to whisper that this is the best privacy I could find, but there is a solemn silence in the truck that I don't want to break. As Pax drifts off to sleep, he breaks it. "I can still smell them," he says.

"Who?" I ask quietly. I expect him to say something about the burning bodies on the base; maybe burying Sam and the burning of the bridge reminded him of the funeral-pyre death smell that will haunt us all for the rest of our lives. But no, it's not death that Pax smells.

"Their perfume." He laughs a sleep-deprived laugh and follows up from his slumber: "I can still smell the girls' perfume."

I try to sleep, but Pax's instability keeps me awake for a long time. I just run my fingers through his hair and watch his face twitch and turn as he fights the nightmares of his mind.

CHAPTER 3

Rennet

• • •

(Lupina)

"Lupina, Lupina," I hear a soft voice say. I think the voice belongs to Pax. I feel him next to me. I wake up and open my eyes. The trees are moving forward. The branches seem to swim through the twilight-colored clouds. Wait, no, we are moving backward. I look at Cisco. He is watching the road in the rearview mirrors.

"Lupina," he repeats. "We are at camp."

"How long?" I ask. "How long were we sleeping?"

"About six hours. You both needed it."

I hear two muffled bangs on the roof of the Humvee, most likely from Michael, and Cisco stops reversing. He parks the Humvee in a way that blocks the road.

"Seth, buddy, let's get you some food and rest," Cisco says. Seth nods.

I softly shake Pax out of his sleep. I run my fingers down his cheek. He looks so tranquil, so sane. I don't want to wake him from his much-needed sleep, but he needs food too.

"Pax, honey, let's get going."

He wakes up and looks up at me. He smiles. His eyes are those of a child again—the pretty, gray, long-lashed eyes I remember from his childhood. They are not sick with worry or guilt. They are happy eyes.

"I love you," he says.

"I love you too."

"I will keep you safe." Pax sits up. The worry is back. He looks down at his rifle and picks it up.

"We will all keep each other safe," I respond.

"Hey, can you two take Seth to the camp, look after him?" Cisco asks.

"Of course," I say.

We exit the Humvee with our packs, my medical bag, and Pax's rifle. I help Seth climb down. He reaches out his hand, and I guide him to solid ground. He still seems to be in a daze. "This is the boy who quickly scaled the obstacles in that stupid race," I think, "and now he needs help climbing out of a truck. Oh, wait, that was his brother." I feel bad I can't tell them apart even in life or death.

We start to walk forward to the camp. I am holding Seth's arm. Pax is walking next to us but keeps turning around to look over his shoulder.

"Hey, Lupina!" Cisco yells. "Can you please bring us some food?"

I nod. "First thing," I call back.

We walk the road to the camp. I see in the distance that they are having trouble with the big tent. We don't have Seth and Sam to help scale the poles, but it looks like Paco is trying his best.

Before we reach the camp, Eva jogs our way. She has her rifle shouldered and is carrying two MREs. She jogs to us, giving a quick, guilty look at Seth.

"I'll relieve Cisco for a little while," she says and runs past us.

When Eva runs past, Seth breaks my grip, and I start to worry as he runs toward the camp. I hope he is not going to lose his mind.

But he runs toward the poles and quickly scales them. He says something to Paco, who is barely hanging on. Seth helps right Paco and then shows him how to fasten the tent.

Cisco jogs up to us. He has a big, warm smile on his face watching Seth work.

I smile too.

"Eva said they are going to roast a sheep. I've had enough of those TV dinners for a lifetime," he says and then runs toward the poles.

"Way to go, Seth! Way to go, Paco!" he shouts.

Nice, we can finally have some rest and relief, and we are building, sustaining. I don't want to jinx it, but I feel this is the best time to address Pax's behavior. We are alone. Cisco is running toward the fire pit. Everyone is busy setting up the tent or prepping a big fire. Kevin is constructing a spit to roast a sheep.

Charlotte is watching her lamb and the other lambs as they drink their milk from the ewes. Finally, I speak to Pax.

"What is going on with you?"

He lets out a long breath. I get the sense he wants to talk, to tell me what's going on.

"We're not safe. He…he is very dangerous."

"I know, Pax; this is a dangerous world, but we will protect each other," I say. I wonder who this *he* is that Pax keeps mentioning: "He's hunting us. The bridge won't stop him." Where did Pax go last night? What did he see?

"Pax, there are seventy to eighty people here who swore an oath to keep us safe. You don't have to carry everything on your shoulders."

Pax just shakes his head and scoffs. "He didn't. He didn't take the oath."

Wait. Who is Pax talking about? OK, enough of the riddles. Does he mean who I think he means?

"Pax, who didn't take the oath?" I say, scared of the pending answer.

"Kevin," he whispers. "He never participated in the Ceremony. He's very dangerous. He is going to get us all killed. The girls, the battles—he is behind it all."

"Wait, what are you saying?"

"It's all been orchestrated by him."

This sounds crazy. I respond, "Kevin wanted us to attack the base, yes, even over my objections and our vote, but he didn't attack Fetty and Michael."

Then I start to wonder if Kevin even needed to orchestrate Fetty being attacked and Michael striking back, or if he just had to wait for guards to show their true behavior. Still, it doesn't mean Kevin is malicious even if he is reckless and cunning.

"No, that's not the really the issue; it's what happened to the base, the girls."

Right when Pax says "the girls," we hear a woman scream. It's not a loud, in-danger scream. It is a scream of anger, and it's coming from Charlotte.

"No! Don't do it!" she yells.

We run to her and the sheep. The two shepherds are back. Somehow, I missed them before, since we left the base. They have one of the lambs. Charlotte's lame lamb sits cradled in one of the shepherd's arms. He has a long knife to the lamb's throat. But Charlotte is armed too. She has her large sewing shears out. They are open and menacingly protruding from her fist. She aims them at the shepherd.

"Let her go!" she yells.

He looks scared and confused. He is yelling something over and over at Charlotte.

"*Panir! Panir!*" he yells.

"Give me back my lamb!"

Oh, no, this is our first slaughter, and it's already going wrong. And why do the shepherds want to kill a lamb? Shouldn't we let them grow first?

Kevin runs over from the fire pit. The flames are rising. The spit is ready for its slaughter.

"*Orom. Orom*," he tells the shepherd with his hands up.

"*Me'da. Panir. Me'da. Panir*," he says to Kevin. He seems relieved that Kevin is there. He is pointing to the ewes and then pointing to the lamb's stomach.

"*Panir?*" Kevin says. The shepherd nods.

Kevin turns to us. Everyone except Charlotte is watching him. She still has her gaze and shears fixed on the shepherd holding her lamb.

"Ah. Rennet," he says. "They want to make rennet."

No one knows what this means. We all look at each other to see if anyone knows what he is talking about. I look for Pax, but he is not nearby.

"What the fuck is that?" Charlotte asks.

"After a young ruminant drinks its mother's milk, you slaughter it and take out the stomachs, the *me'da*. The enzymes it uses to digest the milk can be saved and treated and then added to milk in small doses to make cheese, *panir*.

"They want to slaughter your lame lamb so we can have cheese," he says to Charlotte.

"No. Not my lamb." There is no compromise in her voice. She turns to face Kevin down. "Not now. Not ever."

Kevin looks tired. "Fine," he says. He picks up another lamb and pulls it off its mother's teat to loud bleats and a weak struggle. He walks to the shepherd and pushes the lamb to the shepherd.

The shepherd throws Charlotte's lame lamb to the ground.

"Hey!" Charlotte yells out, but she puts her shears away and quickly picks up the lamb. She swirls the lamb into her shawl and holds it close to her body. She gives the shepherd a scowl, and then she squints and looks away in disgust.

I look at the shepherd. He has slit the other lamb's throat. The blood spills out and colors the dry, yellow grass red. He slams the dead lamb to the ground and starts to butcher it in front of us while spewing out what I assume are a string of Tajiki cusswords. He cuts out the stomachs and hands it to the other shepherd.

I think we have finally reached a calm. We can go now back to setting up camp and getting some food. But the calm is broken, permanently.

"They were just kids!" I hear Pax yell at the top of his lungs. "They were just kids!"

Everyone freezes. Even the shepherd stops his butchering of the lamb and looks at Pax. He is standing with his rifle white-knuckle clenched in his hands. He draws deep breaths in and out. He is staring Kevin down with that hateful look again.

Kevin turns to face Pax with a look of measured concern.

"The girls. The boys on the road I killed. They were all just kids!"

"No one is a kid anymore, Pax," Kevin says with remarkable calm.

"They *were* kids, and I killed them because of you, because of your treachery!"

Everyone has stopped working and gathered around the two, battling it out again. However, Fetty has run up out of nowhere, quickly and stealthily. She is near Kevin. Her rifle is technically pointed at the ground, but she looks ready to pounce on Pax and his anger at any moment. Terror starts to fill my veins. This isn't just an argument. They are facing each other like a showdown in some old western movie. I am not sure which one is the sheriff and which one is the bad guy. It seems to be Pax versus the tribe, so does that automatically make him the bad guy? I start to edge cautiously toward Pax so he doesn't stand alone.

"Who did you kill?" Kevin asks.

"Four boys, when their convoy caught up, when Sam died."

"Boys didn't attack us. They were soldiers, rebelling American soldiers from another base who were on the same side of the coup that put the corporal in charge," Fetty says.

"They were teenagers, like us, but not..." Pax starts to trail off. "And why did they attack us? Kevin, tell everyone why we are being hunted!"

Kevin steps forward. He is unarmed but looks menacing as he approaches Pax and me. He looks straight at me and then back to Pax. Why?

"Are you sure you saw what you think you saw? How's your sister doing?"

Oh no! I never said a word to anyone about Pax imagining Vivi in Tajikistan. Pax looks at me, hurt, deflated, defeated. The gun twitches in his arms.

"Pax—" I start to say.

"Prove it," Kevin interrupts.

Pax looks back and forth between Kevin and me. He looks around the tribe at all the scornful faces. He looks so isolated. So alone.

"Show me. Show me these *boys* you killed," Kevin declares.

Pax stops looking around the tribe. He stands up straight and strong and returns Kevin's hard stare. The light from the fire dances on his face. In the dancing light, the shadows make his face bounce back and forth between a child's face and an adult's.

He takes a step closer to Kevin, closer to the fire. Now, it truly looks like a gunfight, a final showdown, except one that will play out offscreen.

"Fine. Let's go," Pax says.

"Fetty, you have a map? You can lead them to the valley, right?" Kevin throws over his shoulder to Fetien.

"No problem," she replies.

"Good. Meet you there."

And with that Kevin grabs his pack and rifle and joins Pax on the long walk back into the dark.

(PAX)

Growing up, Mark used to take us backcountry camping. I think Mark wanted to have more kids, so he liked the idea of taking Kevin and me. He always treated me like a second son. And after Todd's diagnosis, he especially took Todd under his wing, helping out Todd's mom, Sally. So after Todd's health started to deteriorate, one weekend would be Wilderness on Wheels and a movie; another weekend would be backcountry camping with Kevin and me.

On our treks, Kevin and I would follow Mark as we hiked up the trails. I would watch Mark, wishing I had a dad so virile, so involved with fatherhood in such a manly way. All my dad ever showed me was how to be away at work.

Honestly, these trips were how I learned about the great outdoors. I learned how to camp and fish and even learned fun survival tips. The closest my East Coast–born parents would go were ski trips and sending me away to summer camp, which wasn't even camping, not true backcountry camping.

While hiking, Kevin would usually be flipping and clicking a pen in his hand, a weird habit he had to help conjure some fantasy in his mind. As we hiked, he played far-off adventures that would decorate our hikes with sound effects of space battles or world wars and the clicking pen. While Kevin daydreamed, I would watch his dad and make believe about having a strong role model in my life. That was my fantasy.

I remember on one of those camping treks, we hiked for a couple of hours to a lake near timberline. The glass lake was crystal clear and beautiful. It perfectly reflected the clouds and trees and the mountain peaks well beyond where the trees ended—replicating them in some upside-down universe. The vista was gorgeous and popular considering the long hike. We followed the trail down to a stream leaving the lake. A bunch of college students were setting up camp while snapping pictures near the mouth the of the stream. They were beautiful people, so happy in their gear and scenery, so proud of their selfies.

"Throw me your bottles. We'll get water now, before setting up camp," Mark told us. Kevin and I threw him our Nalgenes. He deftly scooped up water, threw in some iodine pills, and wiped the lips with a rubbing alcohol–soaked cloth. He tossed the bottles back to me.

I was watching the coeds and nearly dropped my bottle. The campers had their hammocks set up and spread out among the trees around the lake in a way that was close but not too close to each other. The city of hammock tents seemed so cool, almost otherworldly. But Mark didn't think so.

"That's stupid," he said. He saw me staring in wonder at the coeds and their comfy hammocks. We didn't even carry a tent. We camped on the ground, close to one another with a tarp stretched above us.

"What's that?"

"Hammocks are stupid. They're going to freeze tonight. We are just below timberline, near a glacier-fed lake, and they are sleeping in thin, air-cooled bags."

"Hmmm."

"You see, you create warmth, Pax—tents don't; hammocks don't; you do. And when you don't insulate that warmth, you lose it. You don't want to be hanging in the air; you want to be nestled into the ground with a good bag. The ground is insulation. Put your bag on the ground, surround yourself with pine needles and debris, and make yourself a nice little nest. That's how you stay warm, not by hanging in the breeze."

* * *

I am in the ground. I buried myself to hide, to rest, to wait, to stay warm.

Kevin is dead. The forest is burning. And I'm being hunted.

I hid in a small gully in a rolling meadow. I dug a nook out of the gully. I buried Kevin's backpack and covered myself in my sleeping bag and a couple feet of dirt. I lay buried, with my water and a piss bottle, and waited for two days.

Slowly, cautiously, I move out of my hole in the gully. The dirt parts and falls away as I exit up and out of my sleeping bag. I crawl along burned ground to the top of the gully and peek around. The meadow is black in the morning light. The forest fire that we tried to avoid, the forest fire that most likely spread from the burning bridge to the side of the river from which we came, this fire must have swept through the meadow in a blazing grassfire while I slept. The ground is blackened and simmering smoke from the burn.

I feel brief relief that I hid in the meadow instead of the forest. If the fire had spread to a hiding spot within the trees, I would have been roasted. The quick grass fire didn't even wake me from my sleep as it flash-burned around me.

In the distance, I can see trees still burning in some intermittent pattern—some burn while others don't. I can feel the heat from the fire in the breeze. I need to make my way back to the tribe while navigating through a forest fire and avoiding the hunters from the other base. I slide back down to my hole and get out Kevin's binoculars and his map. I grab my rifle and work my way back up the gully on my stomach. I scan the countryside again with the binoculars. I am looking for any sign of movement, any flash of metal, or really any sign of life in the burning wilderness.

I see nothing. I figure the forest fire has scared away any of the hunters and soldiers. I think about where they would be setting up if they were waiting for us to emerge. The burned bridge. The metal frame of the bridge can still be crossed on foot. On the other side where there is no fire, where we would have to cross to get back to our people, that's where I would set up.

I study Kevin's map and try to match it up to the countryside. This is so much harder without an app. Mark showed us some basic navigation stuff. I need to find a waypoint I recognize. I look for the base where we all started from. I open the map all the way on the blackened ground. Ash and embers float down to the map. I brush them away.

I find our base. The gate is on one side, and the road we left is on the other. I trace the road over the mountain from where I watched the soldiers defeat the militia. I trace it to them chasing us down and to the spot where I made my first kills—where I was going to show Kevin the bodies of the dead teenagers.

I find the river where we finally caught up to Lupina. I think of her and grit my teeth with resolve. I need to find her. I need her.

In the far corner of the map is the valley where Kevin told Fetien to take the tribe. The valley where we will meet. Kevin marked it with a small plus sign. I trace my finger back to the river—the crucible I must cross while not being killed by the hunters from the other base.

I trace my fingers up and down the river, looking for another bridge, but I don't see one. I look for parts where the river widens, thinking this is the calmest place to cross. The best part for me to cross is down from the bridge. If I take the gully and follow the dry stream toward the river, it will put me close to where I need to ford.

I decide not to wait any longer. With any luck, I will be able to avoid the hunters and catch up to the tribe. I slide back down to my hole and gather the gear.

I am geared up. The backpack is packed. I carry my rifle with the map, binoculars, and water easily accessible. I follow the dry gulch all the way to the river. I constantly stop and survey all the viewpoints that could see me in the gulley. I look for hunters but see no signs of life.

As I quietly approach the river, I see movement and crouch down while bringing up my rifle. It's not the hunters but the hunted. I see a few deer feeding on lush grass on the other side of the river, the side untouched by fire. I look at the river. It does widen and seem to calm. It looks crossable.

I think about the food situation. I have enough snacks for a couple of days. On the map, the valley looks about five to six days away. I need the energy to get there, especially if I am being chased by the hunters.

The hunters are a problem. Do I really want to lead them back to the tribe, to the valley where we are looking at setting up base camp? They are hunting me, but maybe that's not so bad; now that I am rested, I can average twenty miles a day. They shouldn't be able to catch me. Maybe I should distract them far away from the tribe. But I still need food to maintain the chase.

I aim my rifle. The deer still don't see me. They are too preoccupied with the green grass and the river. There are seven deer and three fawns. I aim at one of the fawns, at Bambi, I think to myself with a slight laugh. And then I shoot it in the heart. Man is in the forest. Ha.

I need to move fast. I need to cross the river before the other hunters find me. I can't take off my shoes and socks. I lift the backpack over my head, hanging it off my rifle gripped tight in my hands, and head into the river.

The water is colder than I expected and instantly fills my shoes and drenches my pants. I take slow, steady steps on the river rocks, trying to maintain my grip before each step.

The current is stronger than I thought it would be. It's deeper too. I reach the middle of the river, and the water is near my belly button. I lean against the current to keep from falling over. My footing and balance are better in the deeper water. I take faster steps but am careful not to fall. If I fall and drench my sleeping bag in the water, I will have miserable nights ahead. I finally reach the other side of the river and climb the muddy banks.

I right my rifle and scan up the river. I see the hunters coming my way. They are making their way down from the bridge upstream like I assumed. I fire two shots their way. I am too far to hit, but I want to slow them down. I want them to think about what it will take, what it will cost to come after me.

I put my rifle down and lift the baby deer by its hooves. I sling it over my shoulder. I can feel the warm blood from the fawn run down my neck and chest. I bend over slightly and shake some of the blood to the ground. I want to give the hunters a trail to follow. I want to take them far away from the bridge and the road to Lupina.

I take up my rifle again and start running. I am about to cross over a small hillock when I hear something breeze past me, and then I hear a shot. Although I shouldn't, I fully turn around to see what I know is true. The teenager whose friends I killed is running full speed after me. He is still too far away to take proper aim, but he is firing while sprinting.

I keep running. The water and mud slog and slush in my shoes. I wish I had time to take them off during the cross, but I needed to kill the deer from the burned side of the river. I couldn't cross without scaring them away. The pack and deer feel heavy, but I am in good shape. I pick up my pace. I concentrate on the steps in front of me and tell myself a lie that the fawn and backpack will protect me if one of the shots actually connects.

I follow the river for exactly two more hours at a steady running pace. I know even with my heavy load, the hunters will not be able to keep up with me. Still, I need to lighten the load some. My legs are beginning to feel the fatigue from carrying the extra weight. I slip the fawn to the ground and get out Kevin's knife. I try to remember how the shepherds slaughtered the lamb, but I wasn't paying attention. I have cleaned and gutted enough fish, so I figure it can't be much different.

I put the fawn on his back and pin open the legs. I stick the knife into the anus and cut up, hard and deep, all the way to the sternum. On a fish, I could go all the way to the throat, but I can't get past the heart with Kevin's knife. Regardless, I spread open the carcass and just start cutting the organs away from the body. I strip out anything I don't want eat. I throw it into the grass. I leave it for the hunters to find and keep up their trailing of me.

I try to pull out the heart and lungs, but I am worried about the time. I wipe my hands and the knife on the grass and sling the carcass back onto my shoulders between the pack and my neck.

I put away the knife and pick up the rifle. I start running again.

I jogged for five hours along the river. I am starving—ready to eat and sleep—but I want to make sure there is enough space between the hunters and me, so I keep pounding ahead. Throughout the run, I was thinking back about Kevin and me growing up together. About when we learned about Todd's diagnosis, about him going through his mom's death. About the chaos of his life and the deafening silence and staleness of mine.

Somehow, we went from childhood friends who experienced so much together to members of the same tribe to mortal enemies. What caused this? Was it just the chaos we were thrown into, or was it choices I made or choices Kevin made? While we had hiked toward the burning forest, Kevin rambled some shit about an experiment. He had already known about those teenagers from the other bases—from the rural areas—the teenage boys I killed. He knew that other bases had teenagers from rural areas all gung-ho about the new world order. He had said something about the Hitler Youth and child soldiers. He also had said he wasn't even supposed to be here. That he was to be a fly in the ointment, a joker in the deck. His epilepsy should have held him back, but the bald, scarred man against the wall placed him as an unstable variable into an experiment. What the fuck was that? Is this just a game of kids for adults to manipulate. But Kevin played by adult rules. Didn't they know that?

My heart started to feel heavy. I wished I could take it out too. I had to stop thinking about him.

Instead of calculating our trajectories, I just started calculating the distance I was running. I ran for two hours and then jogged for another five. I am exhausted, but I figure, with all the weight, that my pace was at ten-minute miles. That means I have traveled around forty miles.

There is no way the hunters, even lightly loaded, would be able to travel that far. If they are running twelve-minute miles, they are seven miles behind me. If. If they could sustain that for seven hours, which I doubt, but saying they could, they are seven miles behind me—a bit more than an hour. That's too close.

I run again, faster now for another hour. When I am about ready to collapse, I throw the carcass down and take off Kevin's pack. I quickly gather rocks and make a circle. I want to avoid dodging another forest fire, so I make a fire ring of rocks. I fill the ring with dead branches and dried grass. I light it up with Kevin's lighter and add more wood. If the hunters are still following me, they will soon smell the fire.

I quickly start hacking away pieces of meat from the fawn. It is ungraceful and crude, but I strip the meat off and place in on a rock in the middle of the fire. I add more and more meat, enough to carry and sustain me for a few days.

I wait for the meat to cook. I take off my shoes and socks and look at my battered feet. Running on wet shoes created a lot of blisters. My feet are red and bleeding and look like the meat I just placed in the fire. I put my socks on the edge of the fire ring. I want to stop for the night. I want to just give up, but I can't.

I take out the map. If I traveled forty miles down the river, I am about ten miles off the map. Now is a good time to head back toward the tribe. I will move directly away from the river and take a right turn in about another twenty-five miles. Then if I head back up the direction I came for another fifty miles, I should reach the valley. I dig around for Kevin's compass and find it. I didn't need a sense of direction while I followed the river, but I will when I head back into the forest.

If I break away from my fire and lose the hunters, I should be able to travel at a slower pace. I should be able to rest. The thought of this gives me energy.

I pick up what is left of the fawn—the skin, heart and lungs, and head. I walk with bare feet toward the river. The fawn is still dripping blood as I drag it through the grass. I drop the carcass on a log by the river where it is easily visible. It looks like a cartoonish ghost, dead—really dead—and lifeless.

I am near another wide, calm part of the river. I look down at the river and decide to give myself one little reprieve. I dip my battered feet into the cold water. Quick stings blend into relief as the cold water massages my blisters and washes the blood away. I stay like that for a minute or two and then go back to the fire.

I pull the meat from the fire and let it cool on the rocks. I put my socks and shoes back on. My feet start to scream in pain, but I ignore it.

I rip off a couple of bits of meat off the rock and chew while I pack the rest of the meat in the small bag on Kevin's backpack. I right the pack on my back. I piss into the fire and then grab my rifle and step on a small patch of rocks leading back into the forest, careful to not leave footprints.

CHAPTER 4

The Queen of Badassastan

• • •

(Lupina)

THE TREK AFTER PAX AND Kevin left was somber and routine. We hiked and fulfilled our roles without much conversation. Paco, Fetien, and other runners would scout the forest. Michael and Danny manned the big guns. Every couple of days, we would slaughter a sheep. At night, Seth would fix the big tarp to the poles. Felicia would light two candles. After about five days, a cynical thought creeped into my mind: "At what point do we light two more candles?"

This question is still on my mind on the seventh day when Fetty, Annie, and Eva call a meeting. They want everyone involved, so we keep the Humvees together. We stop at the top of a pass so we can see the road stretch behind us. We all gather. No one should be able to sneak up on us with our view of the road. It's been quiet since Pax and Kevin left, so we feel relatively safe, but Michael stays at his gun and watches the road behind.

We can feel the coldness and harsh wind at the higher altitude on the pass. Annie climbs on top of the truck to join Eva and Fetty. She leaps up with nimbleness, despite her hobbled arm. Her hair swirls and shakes in the wind. Her black roots are about half the length of her hair. We have been here so long that she is two toned. I habitually run my hand under my hood and feel my own hair. I wonder how long it will take to grow back. I also wonder if it will reach my previous length again while I am alive or after I die.

I shake my head and close my eyes at the dark thought. I take a deep breath. I just hope the ladies have good news. I hope it isn't news of death or some stupid battle plan.

Fetty finally speaks. "We are near the valley."

A muffled hurrah comes over the tribe. We should be more excited. This means we can finally stop trekking. But everyone feels the same fear. If we stop, will we be caught? Will we have to fight a last stand?

But Eva, it seems, has a plan. "We are going to split up," she says. "The valley is over that mountain, away from the road. Most of us are going to take the sheep over the mountain." She points to a rocky crest in the distance.

"The trucks are going to keep going down the road in case anyone follows," she continues. "They will circle around the other side in a couple of days—"

A grumble comes over the crowd. The big machine guns have proved to be our best protectors.

"Dudes, chill," Annie says. "We need to switch from strength to stealth. If we aren't found, we don't have to fight. So were going to hike along the rocks over the mountain. We can't let the sheep graze. If they shit, we have to pick it up. Leave. No. Trace."

You would think teenagers would rebel at the thought of picking up sheep shit, but nobody cares. We just want to be safe.

"I know we are all scared. I know this has been a long, horrible journey, but I feel we are close to home," Fetty says.

I wonder about this home, this valley. Why was it chosen? What do Kevin and Fetty know that we don't?

I want to ask. I want more control over the next part of our life. We have been led around since the evacuation. But there is no chance to ask. The groups are already splitting. I am with the sheep.

* * *

I watch the climb over the crest from the periphery. I bounce back and forth, trying to keep the sheep on the rocks and away from the grass. A sheep poops a pile of round scat. I pick it up and carry it over to a collection sitting on a cloth on a flat rock. Someone will scatter the scat down the road following the trucks when we leave.

I drop the droppings and look up at the crest of rocks. The rocks and boulders reach high. One large boulder juts up, stretching toward the gray ash and clouds like a shipwreck. There is a narrow path underneath the shade of the shipwreck rock where we are leading the sheep. Some sheep are too scared or reluctant to climb these smaller boulders. Seth and Paco have constructed a rope system to carry over the recalcitrant ones.

I look back toward the shipwreck rock. I wonder if I can climb to the top. I look for a line that I could ascend. I wonder if I make it to the top and jump, is the height high enough?

A heavy sigh escapes me and my dark ideation. What is wrong with me? These dark thoughts are nothing new, but are they valid now? Is suicide actually a good idea now? It's not even all we have been through: the death of Hector and Seth, the disappearance—no, the abandonment—by Pax and Kevin, or even the terrible battles. Our recent troubles are not what fixes my gaze on the high shipwreck rock; no, this is just the grisly beginning. There is more to come. Do I really want to stick around for what the world will turn in to? I feel helpless. I have lost control.

"What a big pile of shit." I hear voice say next to me. I turn and look at Jaden. He releases the sheep scat on top of the collecting mound and then wipes his soiled hands off on his pants.

I wince at the thought of him getting dirt and fecal matter into his shrapnel wounds. I mentally add that to the list of other horrors coming our way—the day we run out of iodine and antibiotics.

"Oh, hey, Jaden, let's look at those wounds. Let me disinfect my hands, and we'll redo the dressings."

"I'm fit as a fiddle. No swelling, no itching," he says.

"You sure?"

"Lupina, I'm fine." He pauses and gives me a deep, concerned look. "Are you?"

I try to say something, but nothing comes out. I just give a weak smile.

"They're going to make it back," he says, but his voice sounds unsure. I am too unsure to agree or contradict, and he doesn't press the case. The silence grows between us.

Instead of saying anything else, Jaden just puts his arms around me and holds me. I start to cry into his shoulders. I feel needy at first, but then I just let myself go. I let all the stress that built up in me release as I cry.

I sit on a rock on the other side of the mountain. I stare at my hands, palms up. They are worn—scraped and blistered. I see dark markings, and I am not sure if it's dirt or sheep shit.

The journey over the mountain was more arduous than expected. Everyone is taking a break, taking in the view of the valley.

In the distance, we can see a large orchard, rows and rows of different types of trees, orderly and towering. Fresh fruit and nuts sounds heavenly. It looks idyllic. However, it is occupied. There are small huts mixed within the trees. Stoves from within the huts release strings of smoke into the air. A small stream leads down from the opposite mountains and meanders through the village.

I sit and watch the village with everyone else. While we were scaling the rocks, Fetty ran ahead and scoped it out. She is back giving a report to Annie, Eva, Spencer, and Paco. And I've had enough.

I am so tired of being led around. The government pulled us away from our families and left us in chaos. Kevin led us into a horrific battle, and now we are on the run. Even Pax deserted me, twice, controlling our relationship without input from what I wanted, what I needed. He's so lost in his mind that he is blind to what matters.

I look over to Charlotte. I wonder if she is a deserter too, but I have no right. In many ways, we were both led into a world we do not want. I feel a strong need to go to her for camaraderie, complain about the situation and terrible leadership. She is sitting near her lamb. The lamb is released from Charlotte's sling. It is trying to play with the other lambs. It bounces around in a clumsy way, tripping on its lame front legs. But it looks oblivious to its handicap. It looks happy.

I watch another sheep. I think it is a ram. It looks and acts differently than the lambs and ewes. It is aggressive; it even fought Seth and the harness, nearly knocking him off a boulder when they lifted him over the rocky crest. The ram is stomping through the herd of sheep and people, looking for someone to fight. The ewes cower from him, while the humans push him away with the butts of their rifles.

Fetty leads the group over to us. She stands up on a rock and starts speaking.

"Listen, we are all going to head down into the village as a group," she says. "Eva will lead us. She knows a few Tajiki words and has Kevin's dictionary. She will explain the situation to the locals."

"And what's the situation?" I ask. I work my way up through the ewes. I push them out of my path until I am in front of Fetty, Annie, and Eva. "What exactly are we going to explain in broken Tajiki?"

Fetty looks at Eva and back at me. She is ready to say something when Eva jumps in. "We don't really need a dictionary," she admits. Then she lifts up her rifle. "We have the numbers. We have the guns."

"No," I say.

"No?"

"We are not taking. We are done with the violence."

Eva looks irked. She starts walking toward me in an aggressive manner. Fetty jumps down off the rock and cuts in front of Eva.

"Did you forget where we are? All the hell we've been through?" Eva says.

"That's exactly what I am remembering. Things keep escalating like we're playing some stupid game that no one will quit. Sure, we walk into the valley with our guns. We dictate our way. Then one of the locals sneaks off and gets members from their tribe, and then we have another battle to fight. Or is your plan to eliminate all the locals and bury them in a big hole or burn them in another pyre?"

"You fucking pussy," Eva says. She steps around Fetty and then pushes me with her rifle. "You couldn't kill the guard. You had your best friend do it because you were too scared and too weak, and now you're going to dictate strategy."

"Exactly," I respond. "We shouldn't have even killed the guard. We should've just taken Michael and escaped."

Both of her hands are gripped hard on her gun. I grab the butt of the rifle and jerk her to the side. Then I pull the dictionary out of her big pocket and walk past her. I keep walking past all of them and head down toward the valley alone, armed only with my medical bag and a dictionary. I am expecting someone to run up from behind and hit me with a rifle or grab me. I hear heavy footsteps behind me, and I close my eyes and brace for impact.

Nothing happens. I open my eyes and see someone next to me, walking with me. Charlotte. She is carrying her lamb, and Jaden is by her side. I glance over my shoulder. I see Eva, Annie, and Fetty watching us with perplexed looks. Spencer and Paco sit perched on some boulders armed with rifles and big smirks on their face. They are watching Charlotte, Jaden, and me walking toward the orchard and village, followed by a long line of sheep.

* * *

We kneel in a circle pounding the fleece. Spencer, Ezra, Yesenia, and I hit the matted wool over and over with sticks while two old ladies dribble water on it and point to spots that need a good whacking. It feels nice to hit something with a stick. My heavy breaths play rhythm with the thumps.

Behind me, under the shade of a cherry tree, Jaden and Charlotte are turning the pressed and rolled felt into walls for our yurts. Charlotte sews the dense pieces of felt together with thick sheepskin thread. Seth helps hang the felt, while Jaden paints a design. Winter will be here soon. We are rushing to build more yurts to fight against the cold.

Cisco and Eva are on horseback pulling large rolls of beaten fleece behind them while herding half the sheep through the trees. The sheep are delighting in a meal of leaves and ground-fallen fruit. Beyond Cisco and Eva, I see the sign that Jaden and Seth made. It hangs over the small road leading out—the road that Cisco and Michael led the trucks in through. The sign says *CAXM.*

The trucks are hidden under leafy coverage. Most of the supplies have been unloaded and distributed or stored. The big machine guns sit dormant on the Humvees, but we haven't needed to use them. Still, Michael spends nights in his Humvee—and many of his days for that matter.

We renamed the village *CAXM.* I looked up one word in the dictionary as we made our way down to the village, Charlotte, her lamb, Jaden and I, followed by a bunch of sheep. The word I translated was *CAXM.* Pronounced, it sounds like "Sam," but in Tajiki it means *share.*

It turns out, the villagers did not have enough young people to work all the trees. They welcomed an exchange of bounty from the orchard for some *panir, gusfand*, and medicine.

We are building, sustaining. There are people working new fields, washing clothes, and hauling wood. *CAXM* buzzes as people work with purpose and fulfillment. Well, most people.

I glance over at the Humvee sitting under an arch of branches for cover. Michael is in the back seat, staring at us but not. Fetien is gone on one of her multiple-day excursions. She is out there, looking, but she never returns with news, only small animals for the soup.

We had to split the herd in two because of the rams. We all laugh as we watch the older ram, Butthead, chase around the ewes. Butthead is busy. He no longer tries to butt us. He is the only male in this split herd of females, and it is breeding season.

Charlotte's lamb is no longer a lamb. He too, it turns out, is a ram. Of course, we named him Beavis. Charlotte and I made stints for Beavis to make his front legs stronger. He is grown up and can walk on his own. He is with Paco and Annie's herd in the hills. Beavis and Butthead will fight each other if nearby during mating season.

"Boys," one of the old ladies says. She looks proud of her use of English. She has a leathered face framed with a beautiful hijab. She nods her hooked nose toward Butthead, who has mounted another sheep.

"Boys," Charlotte agrees. We all laugh and then go back to work. I laugh a hearty laugh and start to feel wetness.

I turn around and whisper to Charlotte. "Char, do you have any more tampons?" Jaden ignores me and keeps painting a design on the yurts. This design is a replication of doors all around. The doors are painted with grayish charcoal of ash from our campfires and dark-red clay the color of iodine. The doors may be a bit of a joke since yurts don't have doors, just a flap you pull back and open.

"Ha, tampons. Seriously?" Charlotte says.

"Yeah, seriously."

Charlotte digs in her bag. She pulls out a small, fluffy washcloth and tosses it to me. I catch it.

"No! We're all out?"

With my back turned to the pounding, I fold and slip the washcloth between my underwear and my body and then turn back around.

"They're all gone," Yesenia says. "And Felicia doesn't even need them."

Felicia is sitting nearby, facing the road with the sun on her back while she cleans her gun. She looks up from her disassembled rifle and gives a wink. Her belly is finally starting to show.

"Me either," Ezra says with a sly smile.

"What?" I exclaim.

"You little trollop," Charlotte says.

"Char!"

"We are married," Ezra says while making eyes at a smiling Spencer. "In God's eyes…"

Our group breaks out in riotous laughter. The Tajiki women want in on the joke. I try to think of the Tajiki word for *pregnant*. But instead, I stand up straight and give the universal big-belly sign for pregnant. I move my hands over an imaginary globe-like belly. The old ladies holler with excitement. They make their way over to me. I quickly point to Ezra.

"No. Ezra, Ezra," I say while pointing.

They wobble over to Ezra and start petting her hair. One of the old ladies sneaks Ezra a sweet nougat candy from her pocket.

"I miss tampons. I miss tampons most of all," Yesenia says.

I kneel back down. I stare at the pounded fleece. My arms fold still in my lap. I don't want to say what I miss most of all.

"Books. I *really* miss books," Charlotte says.

I look back at her. Tears start to well in my eyes. I blink them away.

"Well, maybe we should make our own books," I say.

"We don't have paper either."

"Stories. We can tell stories. We should add that to the campfire."

"Stories are good," adds Yesenia.

"Stories are good." We all agree.

EPILOGUE

• • •

(Pax)

I skip on a river of rocks until I reach a clearing past the trees. A verdant meadow rolls out in front of me and blends into the green trees and mountains in the distance. The sun breaks through and bathes the waving grass in bright light. The tall grass seems to sway and dance in the sunlight and soft breeze. I stop and look at the scene for too long.

I think about all that brought me to this point and what I need to move forward back to the tribe and Lupina. Of all the ties that bind, of all the strings that weigh us down, guilt is the heaviest. I am complicit; I didn't see them; I didn't stop it.

I turn around and head back toward the smoldering fire. I pass it and spit into the fire ring. It hisses at me. I slip off the pack and place it and the gun near the felled deer. I sit on the log, heavy and tired, next to the dead fawn. Flies gather on the carcass and buzz around us, annoyed by my presence. I take off my shoes and socks. I take off my pants. I tie my shoelaces together, stuff my socks into my shoes, and throw my shoes and pants over my neck, across my shoulders. I wrap the straps of the pack around my rifle.

I step into the cold, hard river. I hold my rifle and pack up in the air for balance. I make my way back across the river, back to a forest decayed and burning down, to a forest where I left the girls behind a closed door.

ABOUT THE AUTHOR

• • •

BRIAN PACINI USES SOME OF his own youthful indiscretions as background for his young-adult adventure novel, The Tribe of Iodine Wine.

Pacini lives with his family in Denver, Colorado. He loves seeking out new adventures and enjoys long bikepacking trips through mountains and deserts.

Website: iodinewine.com
Instagram: paxpacini
Email: paxpacini@gmail.com

Sex trafficking is neither a fiction nor a relic of history. Please consider researching and supporting organizations that fight human trafficking and sexual abuse.

National Organizations
RAINN:
https://www.rainn.org/

Hope for Justice:
http://hopeforjustice.org/

Local to Colorado
Laboratory to Combat Human Trafficking:
http://combathumantrafficking.org/

More information on organizations that fight sexual assault and human trafficking on a global and local level:
https://en.wikipedia.org/wiki/List_of_organizations_that_combat_human_trafficking

Twenty-five cents from all new-book purchases will be donated to causes that aim to prevent rape and sex trafficking.